THE

Sleeping Warrior

THE
Sleeping Warrior

SARA BAIN

urbanepublications.com

First published in Great Britain in 2015
by Urbane Publications Ltd
Suite 3, Brown Europe House, 33/34 Gleamingwood Drive,
Chatham, Kent ME5 8RZ
Copyright © Sara Bain, 2015

A CIP catalogue record for this book is available
from the British Library.

ISBN 978-1-910692-36-3

This book is a work of fiction. Names, characters, places, organisations
and incidents either are products of the author's imagination or are used
fictitiously. Apart from historical fact, any resemblance to actual events,
organisations, or persons living or dead, is entirely coincidental.

Design and Typeset by Julie Martin

Cover by The Invisible Man

Printed and bound by CPI Group (UK) Ltd, Croydon, CR0 4YY

URBANE
Publications

urbanepublications.com

FSC

The publisher supports the Forest Stewardship Council® (FSC®), the leading international forest-certification organisation.
This book is made from acid-free paper from an FSC®-certified provider. FSC is the only forest-certification scheme
supported by the leading environmental organisations, including Greenpeace.

To my mum, my brother and my three gorgeous sisters who
believe in fantasy and have always believed in me.

ACKNOWLEDGEMENTS

To my trusty computer that has never crashed in the middle of an unsaved document and to the clicky gamers' keyboard that makes typing a noisy joy. To all those books, works of art, landscapes, poems and songs that have provided my inspiration over the years. To Matthew of Urbane Publications, a hard-working editor who sees his authors as assets and not cash generators. And to the TV, for providing a poor, lonely husband some company while I am writing.

Prologue

HE HAULED ON HIS MASK.

The leather felt like a thick glove clapped to his face: hard, pungent and stifling the shameful scream from deep inside his chest.

He breathed away the ensuing panic and took a sudden comfort in his anonymity. He would soon hear the footfall of his quarry. The clicking heels in the darkness shifting swiftly towards him, and then it would begin.

A quick glance around and he tiptoed for cover between the dark trunks of the trees, dissolving into their soft shadows to become as one with the earth.

The movement against the dim light took him by surprise and he tried to contain his gasp by pursing his lips and letting his breath out slowly, his body shuddering with the effort. He could hear his own heart thudding in his temples beneath the unyielding leather; at his wrists and in his chest, the blood seeking to burst from his head. But he breathed it away, calling on his powers of control and allowing the tension to escape with each juddering exhale.

Straining to see into the gloom, he could just make out the silhouettes of a man and woman standing close to each other, speaking softly in a language the secret listener couldn't understand. The woman made to run, but the man caught her arm and kissed her outstretched neck. It was a lover's embrace and she fell to the ground in a swoon.

The man stood over the fallen woman. There was power in that stance. It was a tangible power. One that demanded respect and commanded awe.

Click, click, click.

She was coming. He could see her. The urgency in her stride marked her misgivings for having taken a shortcut home alone through the lonely park after midnight. He squinted into the shadowy car park but the man had gone, melting into the black shades of evening like a phantom.

She passed him. Her perfume wafted towards him in the still night air. He held his breath as her footsteps faltered. Could she sense him there? Could her instinct, her fears, disclose the danger? She moved on, a little cautiously now, and disappeared into the night.

He stepped quietly out of his hiding place and began the chase, his footfall matching hers in perfect synchronicity.

But she knew he was there. She was alone. Alone in the dark. She could sense him and the excitement welled in his chest as her fear drove her forward.

They picked up speed together and he could hear her whimpering like a frightened puppy as the echoing tap of heels fell back on her ears to mock her. He grasped the cold handle of the knife and couldn't remember how it got in his hand.

'What the hell... are you all right?'

He halted behind her as she spoke to the woman lying on the ground. His quarry was panicked to near madness but that instinct again, that urge to help another in trouble, would be stabbing at her conscience. He could feel her confusion; the dilemma piercing tiny holes in her will to run and save herself.

He stepped towards her and reached his hand out to touch her, forcing her to make the choice.

She made it involuntarily as his hand swiped mid-air. Her

will to survive put paid to all efforts of playing good Samaritan and she ran, screaming at full pitch.

He gave chase. Their footfall drumming on the tarmac, his bloodless fingers curled around the handle of the blade.

She was still screaming and the excitement moved from his stomach to his groin. She feared for her life. He would hear her scream and then watch her die.

He heard a thud and he was suddenly on his hands and knees, the breath wheezing from his lungs. It was a few seconds before he realised that thump was the sound of his own ribs cracking and he'd flown some distance backwards from where he stood.

He heard someone calling his name but the sound was coming from inside his head.

'Get lost!' he hissed, coughing away his confusion. 'It's too late to stop me.'

The sound of sirens screamed in the distance and his own instinct told him to flee.

He rose as quickly as his pain would allow and brushed out the tiny stone chippings embedded in the flesh of his shins.

She'd escaped him, embraced by the safe lights of a busy road, and he wanted to howl and let his anger out into the moonlight. Months of planning, months of waiting and months of anticipation had come to nothing on his first night of the hunt, frustrated by a ghostly shadow in the dark that knew his name as well as his game.

Retreating to the car, he remembered the woman on the ground and the longing returned with full fury. He would ease his pain tonight.

Adrenaline possessed him with unnatural strength and he hauled the body into the back of the car and left the car park, his hands shaking wildly against the steering wheel.

Some way down the road, in a quiet spot between the street lights, he stopped the car and sat for a while to allow his heart-rate to return to normal.

Calm now, he drove in silence for just under an hour to the deserted house in Surrey where he would always be safe.

'What was that, love?' He lowered the warm body into the kitchen chair and propped it up with rope from the cupboard. 'You want to know about it? Well, pain's the body's reaction to damaging stimuli,' he began with his hands clasped together in front of his chest as if performing a sermon.

'It's not pleasant but it's natural to feel it.' He moved across to the sink. 'Tea?'

'It's not so bad if it's self-inflicted or even accidental, but it hurts the most when someone else causes it. Someone just like you.'

He filled the kettle and adjusted the kitchen mirror to see her sitting in silence behind the image of himself. 'Sorry, love, but I'm going to ask you to strip. I know, I know, it's embarrassing and humiliating being naked in front of a stranger, but there's much worse things than embarrassment in this world and I promise not to look. It's the stains you know. They tell tales.'

It was then he noticed the dirty mark on the front of his own white shirt, clean on this morning. He pulled the mirror down to see what had made it and his eyes widened in shock. Sitting square in the middle of his chest was a large boot print.

He felt the shakes returning with the agony in his chest. He remembered when the mark was made but had no idea how it got there. 'I saw no one, nothing, just shadows.'

That voice again, calling his name. He pressed his gloved hands against his temples and roared. 'Monsters. All of you, monsters. It hurts, it hurts, it hurts!'

He slumped to the tiles, panting, his breath exhaling in jolting spasms. 'Need to cure it. Need to ease the pain.'

He remembered the knife on the table between the bone china teapot and the chipped cup of cold tea. The sharp tip, just jutting from the edge, winked at him in conspiracy.

'Need to feel again.'

He rose and picked up the knife, moving slowly towards the body tied to the chair, the ends of her fingers twitching slightly; the blue eyes staring in horror out of a slackened face.

'And you. You're going to be the first one to help me make it go away.'

'**HELLO, THIS IS LIBBY BUTLER** and it's the middle of the night so this had better be good.'

'Miss Butler, this is Sergeant Jonathan Fry. I understand you're the duty solicitor tonight ...'

'Wait a minute,' Libby sat up in the bed, her mood suddenly indignant, 'I was on last week.'

'Your colleague gave me your number, miss,' the sergeant's tone remained matter-of-fact. 'He said you could speak a few languages.'

'Bloody Maurice!' Libby hissed. Tony lay beside her, blinking in incomprehension. 'Can this not wait until the morning?'

'Sorry, miss.' The officer sounded genuinely apologetic. 'We've got a foreign man in custody and he needs a legal brief.'

'I suppose that'll be me.'

'Can you come down to the station right now?'

'Ask him if he's beaten a confession out of the poor bastard yet.' Tony added his thoughts to the conversation as he stretched his eyes. 'That's what coppers do, isn't it?'

She hissed at him to be quiet. 'Which station did you say you were at?'

'East Dulwich, miss. Just down the road from you.'

'Give me half an hour.' She jabbed the red button and threw the phone on the bed. 'At least it's not Camberwell this time.'

'Yet one more sorry criminal requires the earthly wisdom

and experience of Miss Libby Butler!' Tony yawned and threw his arm across his eyes.

'Maurice can speak seven languages, including Mandarin and Afrikaans, the bastard. He's stitched me up. No doubt there's another crisis in his chaotic love life. He's not going to get away with this.'

'I'll get dressed.' Tony threw the bed clothes off and made to get up.

'It's OK,' she began, taking a long look at him. She noticed the dishevelled brown hair, the glazed eyes and, moreover, the look of pained resignation on his face as he would give up one more good night's sleep in order to pamper her foolish insecurities: Libby didn't like the dark. She pushed him back onto the comfortable pillows. 'There's no need, really. I'm only going round the corner.' She snatched up the blue pinstripe skirt and white blouse from the carpet and heaved them on.

'You can't wear that, it's filthy!' Tony laughed.

'It's just chocolate. I'll give it a rub down.' She spat on the worst spot at her chest and scrubbed it with her fingers, turning it into a dirty brown smear. She sighed as she noticed the dark perspiration marks in the cloth. 'I've only got the green one, which doesn't go with blue.' She dived into the wardrobe. 'What does the Met expect when they wake a woman up in the middle of the night to explain the legalities of being a drunken bum on the streets of London?' She checked herself in the mirror and groaned. 'If I wear loads of make-up, do you think the lovely boys in blue will notice I'm not wearing a bra?'

'You'll have to wear a jacket.'

Libby turned from the mirror only to smile at the sudden display of concern for her struggling dignity. Sometimes she felt she didn't deserve her partner's adoration and this moment was one of them. The rest of the time, she knew she didn't. She swallowed the guilt and buried her thoughts in making herself look presentable with eye-liner, blusher and lipstick, before attacking her tangled brown hair with the brush.

'Will you see me to the car?' She didn't have to ask as Tony was already dressed for the event in his grey tracksuit bottoms with baggy knees.

'I'm awake and dressed. I may as well drive you.'

'You're a darling,' she squeezed his hand as her lips brushed his cheek in a light declaration of gratitude.

The drive took less than three minutes. The white clock on the station wall registered two thirty-three a.m. when Libby came through the doors and was greeted by an empty counter. She followed the typed instructions sellotaped to the desk, urging visitors to 'press the bell', and waited in the foyer. She cast a vague glance over the information posters for Crimestoppers; what to do when your kids are on drugs; and cash for heating the elderly in winter.

Her gaze caught the darkness behind the glass door and she threw her arms about herself, taking comfort that Tony was waiting in the car, in the shadows just outside, but beyond the catchment of the street light. While she waited, and the turning hands of time on the wall clicked in the background, Libby's thoughts trailed to why a professional woman, with a history of a happy childhood and a reasonably successful career, would have developed such an irrational fear after a simple walk in the park.

Granted, it had been dark at the time but she remembered the surging panic; her heart pounding in her ears; her breath slowly leaving her to choke on her own terror; and couldn't remember getting home that night at all or how she got the strange hairline cuts on the palms of her hands and fingers.

Thank God for those revellers. She must've given them a

real fright when she screamed at them, hysterical, that someone was following her. It didn't help matters that the headless body of a woman had been found by a schoolgirl in the park a few days later.

Libby's psychiatrist, Nicole, a friend of the family, had spent many months attempting to eke out a plausible rationale but had, so far, come up with little to fill her file with, save for some kind of post-traumatic reaction. Libby, of course, was perfectly capable of giving an accurate self-diagnosis and knew her apparent phobias were just a symptom of her life and the way in which she was failing to cope with its confounding complexities.

She almost jumped when a figure appeared behind the counter. 'A big Mac and extra fries, please,' she immediately regretted her words when she saw the destitution of humour in those raised, unplucked eyebrows.

'Hi, I'm Libby Butler. Your custody sergeant called.' She decided to keep it formal. 'I'm the duty solicitor tonight. I understand you're holding a foreigner in the custody suite who needs a brief right now. I don't actually understand the urgency,' she casually picked at her fingernails, 'or why this can't wait until office hours. It's not as if he's going anywhere is it?' She scanned her eyes around the foyer. 'This place could do with a lick of paint.'

The woman in uniform with the endless belt of hardware curled her thin lip into some semblance of a smile – any reasonable man would have called it a snarl – and threw the internal door open with a loud, resonating bang.

'It's got concrete cancer.'

'Oh dear. Is that terminal?'

'Very, especially since it also costs two hundred and seventy-five grand a year to run it. The Met's shutting it down and moving us all to Peckham and Camberwell.

'That should save them at least five pounds a year. Are you happy about the move?'

'Not really. I've got a bit of a soft spot for this place and so've the residents. They've organised a petition. Seems they want more contact with the police, not less. Just goes to show, you can't believe everything you hear in the news about the public's mistrust of law enforcers.'

'Really?'

'I'm Constable Suzanne Glover. It's going to be a long night for you, Libby Butler, duty solicitor.' The grey eyes scanned her body from fringe to toe and back again. Libby felt violated.

She stepped through the door, trying her best to keep her back as straight as possible. It was only then she noticed her left shoe, although the same style, was a different colour from her right. One was navy, the other black. She hoped the shady tungsten lights in the station would hide her embarrassing secret from the raptorial eyes of Constable Glover. Somehow she doubted it.

She was led into a room where messy desks lay all but empty and a few sleepy uniformed men waited out their tiresome shifts by listening to unintelligible banter on crackling radios. Constable Glover spoke to a small, stocky man in hushed tones. They looked as though they were arguing.

'I'm Sergeant Fry,' he began in a gruff voice, offering his hand as if it was a baton in a relay race, before marching past her.

'What's the rap then Sarge?'

He failed to acknowledge her stab at humour and idly poked his fingers at a wad of reports on one of the desks. At least he hadn't noticed the shoes. Not yet, anyway.

'At twelve forty-six hours yesterday, on the north side of the Rye, duty constables Willis and Gates arrested your man.'

'On what charge?'

'A warrant was issued six days ago when he escaped City of London police custody at Snow Hill.'

'Escaped?'

'From the custody suite.'

Libby's look was one of unreserved scepticism. 'You're telling me this man escaped from Snow Hill's impenetrable, heavily guarded, barred and locked detention quarters? Come on, Sarge, even you can't possibly believe that. They allowed him to walk and now they've changed their minds.'

Fry looked less assured of himself. 'That's what I've been told.'

'Were any warning markers issued?'

He chose to ignore the question. 'Last week the same suspect was arrested on suspicion of carrying an offensive weapon… You don't remember me do you Miss Butler?'

'Suspect and suspicion?' she rudely interjected. 'First, what was he suspected of and, second, either he was carrying an offensive weapon or he was not.' This was becoming tiresome already. 'All coppers look the same to me, I'm afraid, Sergeant Fry.'

'…Resisting police arrest and now he's wanted for escaping from police custody,' the sergeant continued, a bit more agitated now.

'You forgot to mention attempting to pervert the course of justice and …'

'I was getting to that bit.'

She sucked in her smile as the officious sergeant's indignation surged forth and his fingers curled into his fists.

'Just give me a copy of the particulars. I'll hear what your detainee has to say first. I take it you're holding this man?'

'The CID should be here after nine.'

'The big boys? Do they suspect him of being a terrorist?'

He shrugged the question off with a haughty sniff. 'My officers found him close to the crime scene.'

'Being in the proximity of a recent crime scene doesn't make him a suspect, Sarge.'

'He was re-visiting the scene to fantasise about his handiwork.'

'Your conjecture is hardly hard evidence. Do I detect a hint of prejudice here?' She noticed the sudden fervour in the sergeant's eyes and knew immediately that something was amiss. 'Sergeant Fry, try speaking to me as if you weren't a policeman.' She knew this was an impossible task.

To Libby's surprise, it was the female constable who spoke. 'Sorry, Miss Butler, it's been a long day for us. The electricity's playing up and we need to get the suspect to speak to us.'

'The detainee?'

'Your client's never spoken a word, but we know he understands English. He hasn't been near a phone.'

'He's not my client yet. So he hasn't asked to make a phone call? Let's see if he wants to phone a friend.'

'Or an accomplice.'

A long pause ensued, the heavy atmosphere fed by unspoken words. It was the sergeant who eventually broke the deadlock.

'The suspect was lifted ten days ago around the Ludgate Hill area.'

He continued cautiously. 'He was wearing fancy dress, in some old fashioned warrior's outfit, but the weapon he carried was allegedly razor sharp. It cut three fingers clean off one of the arresting officers when he seized him. Your man put up a bit of a fight before he quietened down and allowed himself to be taken into custody. He carried no ID, no money, no credit cards, no driver's licence…'

'You said a bit of a fight?' Libby couldn't help but be professionally defensive. 'Explain what that means. Was he responsible for the officer losing his fingers?' She sat on the edge of a desk and, fumbling in her bag for her tatty notebook and pen, tucked her right shoe behind her left calf.

Sergeant Fry shrugged.

'You used the words 'allegedly' and 'suspect', either he had a weapon or he didn't.'

'You ask a lot of questions.'

'I am a lawyer,' she breathed her words out, over-exaggerating the obvious. 'It's my job'.

He stood up to his full height, which wasn't much taller than her five feet nine inches in four-inch heels, and puffed his chest out. 'No weapon was recovered from the scene.'

'So he didn't have a weapon after all.'

'He must've thrown it away or something.'

'You said the officer cut his fingers off during its confiscation.'

Sergeant Fry set his jaw. 'You'll have to speak to the detectives.'

'I will, at length. Does he have a record?'

'We have no idea who he is, his name, address, or his country of origin. The Home Office has come up with nothing as yet and we can't consult the PNC, 'cos we can't ID him. Interpol are working on it and the EDT are coming in tomorrow morning to assess his mental health. I also believe the UKBA have taken a keen interest in him.'

'Careful, Sarge, or the CPS may want to question you for using an acronym without due care and attention.' The silence threatened to kill her.

'Do you suspect him of insanity or terrorism?' she asked again.

'We don't know. He's as silent as the grave!'

'Did he struggle with your arresting officers?' Libby glanced at the window and realised Tony's clock was ticking.

'He came along quietly.'

'And so at least we can assume he speaks English. I suppose I'd better talk to him and find out if he understands the charges at least. Come lead me, officers, to the block of shame!'

She stuffed the notebook and pen back inside the folds of her bag and waited for a suitable learned response, but none came.

She shrugged her shoulders and allowed herself to be led to the cells where another poor, irreverent spirit waited for the mercy of British justice.

The prison was as black as sin. Like a scene from a bargain shelf horror movie, the glowing strip lights along the corridor hissed and winked as she passed beneath them, leading to the shadowy caverns that contained the city's lost souls. There was a smell of burning electrics in the stale air.

'He's in there. The lights are playing up. Sorry. We can't get an electrician till after nine.'

'This is going to be a busy place in the morning!' Libby peered through the narrow window and couldn't repress the chill that swept up her spine. She vaguely saw the swipe of the key and the metal barrier clicking open. She felt the familiar pounding in her temple and the sweat beading on her breastbone and under her arms.

'This is stupid!' With one blue shoe trailing a black one, she stepped into the gloom with courageous effort. 'Hello, I'm Libby Butler, the duty solicitor tonight...' Her words trailed as she adjusted her eyes to the gloom.

'It's about fuckin' time,' someone from an adjacent cell yelled out.

'Watch your mouth, Davy, she's not here for you,' the police woman bellowed. 'You can go in the morning, after you've slept off some of that bad temper of yours.' She raised her eyes to the ceiling. 'He's got lodgings here!'

Someone sat on the bed in the corner of the sparse room, his legs tucked tightly against his chest. Libby was hit by an immediate assault of strange smells pervading the tiny space: oiled leather, earth, dust, rust, decay and blood. Long calves and forearms were swathed in thick leather embossed with strange symbols and peppered with metal studs. His face was concealed in dark shadow where the light failed to reach it. Libby felt the darkness closing in and all the terrors of the night swooping down. Her feet faltered and she clasped her hands to her breast. She'd forgotten how to breathe.

'There is nothing in the darkness that cannot be seen in the light.'

She snapped her eyes towards the black corner where the man sat, his presence powerful and menacing. His silken voice calmed her shattered nerves and she took a long, deep breath.

'I am ...'

'I know who you are Libby Butler.'

'Do you now?'

'Do what?' The female officer answered from behind her.

'At least he speaks English.'

'And how do you fathom that then?'

Libby turned to Constable Glover and was gripped by a sudden dizziness as the questioning look on the police woman's face was evidence she hadn't heard the voice. 'Did you give him my name?'

Constable Glover shook her head. 'I started this shift earlier this afternoon but had two RTAs, a poisoned cat, three cases of antisocial behaviour; six assaults; a couple of drunks and a lout with an indelible pen to deal with before I got here. I only got to the station about an hour ago and I'm about to get off home. I haven't had the privilege of meeting this one.'

'Do you understand why you're here?' Her words dissipated into the darkness.

She was answered only by soft breathing.

'Look, mister … whoever you are … I come in peace,' that inappropriate humour again, 'and I'm here to ensure these nice police people don't stampede over your rights with their hobnail boots. It's my duty, as your appointed legal representative for the evening, to make sure you understand what's going on, what can possibly happen to you and give you advice on how to perhaps avoid getting yourself into further trouble.' It was an awkward and unprecedented start, but this was turning out to be no ordinary case.

No response.

'You can, of course, accept or refuse my advice. If you already have a solicitor, you may wish to ….'

'You're wasting your breath, Miss Butler. This one doesn't need a lawyer, he needs a shrink!' Constable Glover had been reading his scant profile. 'He's either very foreign or very clever. For all we know, he could be a murderer – even Dracula himself.'

Libby shuddered in revulsion. Dracula was what the tabloids called the serial killer menacing the south London streets.

In five months, the same number of women had vanished from Clapham, Balham, Brixton, Forest Hill and Camberwell, all to be found in different stages of disembodiment, disembowelment, decapitation and decomposition in wheelie bins, back yards and rubbish dumps in Tooting, Streatham, Tulse Hill, Denmark Hill and Nunhead.

He was named after the famous Transylvanian count because all the bodies, or parts of them, had been completely drained of blood before dismemberment: the calling card of this particular beast.

Although eye witnesses had seen the murder victims close to the time of death, they all failed to come up with a description of the mysterious killer who appeared to shift in and out of the day and night like a shadow.

The women jumped at the sudden hiss from the corner of the room, a loud creaking of thick leather, and a face slowly emerged into the light. Libby gasped at the strong, angular features and the jet black hair that moved against his shoulders like a soft silk scarf in a whispering breeze.

Before them sat a young man with a face that would cause an angel to weep with envy, but housed in its exquisite beauty the black, mesmeric eyes of a demon.

'Wow!' Libby breathed out loud to no one in particular and felt her knees dissolving into her calves. 'Now I know what an angel looks like.'

Constable Glover had lost the power of speech.

The face dissipated once more into the gloom. Libby pulled her good senses together and turned to the police woman. 'Constable Glover, if you want to secure a prompt and effective investigation, I request a few moments alone with my client,' she heard her own voice stammering. 'Constable Glover?' the woman had seemingly turned to stone. 'Suzanne?'

Constable Glover awoke suddenly from her apparent coma and awkwardly sorted her short blond hair. 'What?'

'I need to speak with my client alone.'

'Your client?' Constable Glover had made a full recovery. 'Don't we all?' Her sharp eyes snapped towards the small camera affixed to the wall. 'You've got ten minutes to bring Angel Gabriel here to his senses. The Sarge wants to interview him before the Yard gets here.'

'I'll take as long as is necessary,' Libby snapped in defiance. She suddenly remembered poor Tony sitting patiently in the car.

He was probably asleep, but that was not the point. 'Would you do me a favour, Suzanne?'

The constable sighed in pained resignation.

'There's a bloke outside sitting in a dark blue Alfa Brera. Would you kindly tell him this is going to take all morning and he should go home?'

'You've got your own personal chauffeur?'

Libby sighed. 'He's my boyfriend and he doesn't like me running around south London by myself.'

'Wait a minute,' a sudden light went on in Officer Glover's eyes. 'Weren't you the woman who escaped the attack by the Vampire Killer a few weeks ago?'

Libby visibly paled. 'Yes, that was me, but they don't know it was the Vampire Killer. God, I really hope it wasn't.' There was a tremor in her voice. 'It's left me all a bit shaken.'

'I'll bet it has.' There was no sentiment in the officer's tone. 'OK, Miss Butler, wouldn't want to keep your man waiting.' The door slammed shut with a boom.

Alone with the stranger, the dust settling, Libby sat down on the cell's only wooden chair and averted her gaze to the small sink thrust into the wall to her right. 'You do know that, although you have every right to remain silent, some magistrates will draw an adverse inference from this. Coppers certainly don't like it because the less you say, the less evidence they have to condemn you.' She suddenly remembered what she was wearing and crossed her arms over her chest. Her feet, reflexively, curled beneath the chair.

'You are both frightened and embarrassed. Why?'

She was more surprised by his personal observation than by the fact he was speaking at all. 'I... I ... am just tired. I haven't slept very well lately.' She shook her head as if to rid her brain of the strange confusion she was feeling. She wanted to pour her heart out to the stranger, for she believed he understood her needs, her fears and her aspirations, and didn't condemn her for any of them. 'This is ridiculous! Would you come out of that dark corner so I can at least see who I'm speaking to?' She wanted to prove to herself, if no one else, that this was no more than an ordinary man. 'Please,' she added as an afterthought.

After a few strained moments, the couched figure in the darkness rose from the bed with a shriek of leather and stepped into the fizzing orange light.

He was a tall man, well over six feet, she guessed, with pale skin and a face that would sink those thousand ships if sheer astonishment was a tactical manoeuvre in warfare.

'You are familiar with naval battle strategies?' It was his turn to look surprised as he locked his dead gaze on hers.

No one could read thought alone.

She chose to ignore his response. 'What's your name?'

'Gabriel'

'Very funny! As in the angel I suppose?'

He shrugged. 'What other Gabriel do you know?'

From his accent, he had obviously enjoyed a privileged British education. 'Do you have an address?'

'I have no fixed abode,' his response was disappointingly rehearsed.

'What can you tell me about your first arrest?' She couldn't look at his eyes for fear of falling into them.

'Where am I?'

'East Dulwich police station.'

'What is that?'

She turned her head to the direction of his finger that pointed to the camera on the wall. 'It's a camera.'

'Its eye is soulless.'

She was forced to laugh. 'Yes, and there are plenty soulless coppers watching you behind it.' Her brow furrowed along with the reassuring smile. 'Tell me about the officer who lost his fingers.'

He turned his attention once more towards her and she wished she hadn't asked the question. Against his infernal gaze, she felt naked and strangely vulnerable. His silence told her to drop the subject quickly.

'Date of birth?' Lost for suitable words, she resorted to a less challenging question. She'd broken his silence and didn't want to lose the advantage.

He shrugged his broad shoulders once more and it was only then she noticed the strangeness of his dress. Clad in what could only be described as thick leather armour, this man was either a member of an historical re-enactment group; on his way to a fancy dress party; or some kind of religious fanatic.

She checked herself for fantasising the best possible scenario for herself.

'What's with the fancy dress?'

'Do you mean fancy as in capricious opinion?'

'No, I mean fancy as in satirical statement.'

'Irony and fantasy are not the same.'

'Tell that to the idiot who sold you those clothes. You smell as if you've just been dug up.'

To her astonishment, the fatally handsome stranger who had stumbled upon the name of an archangel tossed his head back and laughed out loud.

She couldn't help but share his humour in what she believed was an inane response.

'I like you, Libby Butler. You are blessed with a sharp wit and a resolute spirit, but I seriously doubt your honesty.'

'You know nothing about me, Gabriel, or whatever your name is.' She felt her defences rising.

'That is true and I also can rest assured that you know nothing about me, save that we share the same taste in strange attire.' He had noticed her shoes. He laughed again. 'Forgive me, I had no idea your dress objective expressly excluded a fashion statement.'

'Where were you on the night of Tuesday, the fifth of August, at two a.m.?'

He lowered his black eyes to the concrete ground. 'I do not understand your question.'

There was an honesty in his answer that unnerved her. 'I'm giving you a date and a time and I'm asking you where you were and what you were doing just then.'

'And I am telling you that, owing to a failure in communication between us, I cannot give an informed answer.'

'What failure? We are speaking aren't we? What bit of time and place don't you understand? Or can't you tell the time?' She glanced up at the small clock face on the wall behind him. 'What time is it now?'

He sat back on the bed and rested his spine against the wall, crossing his arms over his knees. At first his demeanour appeared casual. 'Thirty two minutes past three. It is the twenty fifth day in the month of June. Dawn has not yet broken; it is warm for this time of year and the rain falls softly.'

There was an air of challenge in his reply. 'You utilise an artificial instrument to measure a breath in space, but there is no accuracy in it.'

'Like it or not, Gabriel, time is something that we can't avoid. My wrinkles would agree with that.'

'Do you not understand that time is a concept devised by man and therefore can only be measured by mortal constraints?'

'Gabriel,' she breathed her words out in half-exasperated challenge, 'the clock will always tick. Seconds turn to minutes, that turn to hours, that turn to days. Get it? Eventually a whole lifetime passes and ...'

'The vain triviality of your minutes, hours and days has little impact on the natural order of the universe, for such is too vast for an ordinary mortal to understand. Yet, in your quest for theory over practicality, you believe infinity to be a measurable reality. You set out to quantify the distance between the present and the untold future by basing your findings on simple conjecture and calculable reason forms the basis of the study of science. This is, Miss Butler, a most terrifying world beset with insanity.'

'Hey, hold the lecture, Gabriel, it wasn't me who invented the bloody clock.'

'It was not a personal assault, I was speaking of your race in general.'

'My race?' She didn't know what to make of him. The clock sat behind him and he hadn't once turned his head around to glance at it. Neither of them was wearing a watch and it would be a good few days before Libby Butler would understand the rationale behind this strange man's words. 'Daddy's money for your expensive education has obviously not gone to waste!'

'Now you are being rude.' His smile told her he was not offended.

'If you are a foreigner, where did you learn English?'

'Is that what you call this tongue?'

'You understand it perfectly.'

'It is as you have said. You have no idea what I already know, or what I have been forced to learn. This place is heavily brushed with the taint of chaos and I neither understand nor like it.'

He brought his hands up to his face and clenched them tightly. She saw the strength in those hands: the long slender fingers, the thick sinews and the heavy calluses on his palms. She also saw the expression behind them and knew instinctively that, despite his outward confidence, he was confused and even lost.

'Look, Gabriel. You're in trouble and, at the moment, I'm the only friend you have. Of course, you've every right to choose another lawyer approved by the Criminal Defence Service, but I'm here now and I'd like to help you. The only way I can do this is to have your full co-operation. That means no more mind games, a bit of trust between us and no more sulking over the concept of time.'

He nodded with a tiny smile.

She straightened her shoulders. 'Now, from what I understand of this case, I think I can get you out of here very quickly, but you must speak to me and that means not in riddles. Do you think you can do that?'

His nod was barely perceptible and she let out an audible sigh.

'Right', she placed the sheet of scant particulars on her lap and fumbled in her bag for a while. She eventually pulled the small notebook and pen from it. 'Let's start at the beginning. What's your name?'

'Gabriel.'

She looked up at him, pen poised on the page, an indignant expression on her face, 'Gabriel what?'

'Radley.'

'Radley with an 'e'?'

He nodded again, not once taking his eyes off hers.

She wrote the name down. 'So the officer made a lucky guess with your Christian name?' She shook her head and sighed again, annoyed at his blatant lack of co-operation. 'The police will run a check on your name, Gabriel, and will be able to tell immediately if you're lying. The more you lie, the longer your stay at the Met's pleasure.'

He shrugged his squealing shoulders.

Realising this was probably all the identity she would get out of him, she continued. 'Date of birth?'

He squirmed for the first time and she took strength from obvious unease.

'You do know how old you are?'

'Years ....' he let his words trail. 'How old do I look?'

'Early twenties.'

'Then that is how old I am.'

'Twenty-two? Twenty-five?'

'Yes.'

She hissed her annoyance from between her teeth and resisted the urge to raise her eyes to the ceiling. 'And you say you've no fixed abode, so how long have you been in London?'

'Longer than I would care to be.'

'What were you doing on Peckham Rye?'

'Walking. Are all these questions necessary?'

It was her turn to lead the conversation. 'It's like I said, if you're lying, the police have the right to detain you, either here or in an approved detention centre, until they uncover the reasons why. Why would you want to lie to the police Gabriel?'

He sat forwards, his black irises clouding with irritation. He began slowly, his words spitting from the darkness. 'Questions are only useful if the questioner understands the answer. There is nothing I can say about myself that you would ever begin to understand. I cannot tell you how I got here or even where I came from, because I do not know myself. Once I do, however, I may decide to tell you, but only if I am certain you will understand and fully appreciate the truth of that information. Now consider the next question carefully before you ask it, Miss Butler, for we are fast losing confidence in one another.'

It was only when Libby felt the back of the chair pressing into her spine that she realised she was cowering away from him. The intensity of his stare caused her throat to constrict. She wondered if the man was suffering from a form of amnesia.

'I think I am the victim of amnesia.'

She opened her mouth to speak but the shock caused her to snap it shut.

'Two men sprang upon me from the dark and of course I struggled with them. I believed I was being attacked. I did not realise they were officers of the law until I ...' he hesitated, forming his words with care, '... noticed the badges of their office. It was then I ceased my struggle and allowed them to search my body and then throw me into a police car.'

'That's exactly what I thought. They sprung on you, you say? Did they ask any questions first or even speak to you first?'

He shook his head.

'Did they use excessive force? Did they tell you what they were looking for?'

'The answer to all of your questions is no.' His shoulders shuddered as he remembered the experience. 'They then stripped me naked, locked me behind bars, hurled ridiculous questions at me, blinded me with light, stuck something in my mouth and left me in a room for days.'

'Days? Did they tell you why you were being arrested?'

'They were adamant that I was not under arrest.'

Libby felt the excitement rising and was already preparing her case for wrongful arrest and unlawful detainment. 'Detained then?'

'No.' He paused to smile and that tiny instance of pleasant memory melted the severity from his features: a soft, radiant magnificence emanated from that smile and Libby could only stare at him. 'I had a shower. The water was warm and cleansing; the soap had a heady scent.'

She bit her lolling tongue. 'Hmmm, Eau du Carbolic is also one of my favourites.'

Getting over the fact he was once more leading the conversation and she was staring shamelessly at him, Libby believed she was making a connection with him at last. 'They took a DNA swab and your photograph, neither of which they were allowed to take without your permission. You were obviously strip-searched for weapons and the boys probably didn't like the way you smelled.' She noticed his stern defences rising once more. 'You probably smell better now and I have to remind you that you're not in prison yet. Did you tell them anything at all?'

'I remained silent throughout.'

'Did anyone tell you why you were being held?'

'Suspicion.'

'Suspicion of what?'

He shrugged again. 'They did not say.'

'Were you charged?'

He raised one smooth eyebrow. 'Charged as in 'accused' or charged as in 'attacked'?'

She was forced to laugh. 'Very funny. You know what I mean.'

'Do I?'

Not for the first time during her conversation with him, she lost her confidence. 'How did one of the officers lose his fingers?'

'Why do you not ask him?'

She searched his face for artifice, but could not read the expression. 'Were you carrying any sort of weapon at the time?'

'At what time?'

'Are you intimating that you did have a weapon at some stage during your arrest?'

'You may draw whatever inference you wish.'

Their eyes locked in challenge for long seconds, until Libby finally tore hers away. 'The police say you escaped custody. Did you escape or did they let you go?'

'I walked out.'

'That's enough for me.' Libby rose to her feet and scrunched the copy of the particulars in her hand. 'Gabriel Radley, or whatever your real name is, you are getting out of here now. Give me a few moments to make a phone call and speak with the nice officers upstairs and I'll be back quicker than Arnie.'

She rapped on the cell door before turning around to face him once more. She'd forgotten something important. 'You'll need to give me an address in London so the police can contact you if they subsequently get anything else on you. Can you give me an address?'

'I do not know this place.'

'Then this is going to be difficult if the police suspect you of giving false information. I may only get you out on police bail. I'll have to test all my powers of persuasion on that idiot of a sergeant. Would you be happy for me to give them the address of my law firm?' She reached into her handbag and fumbled through the sticky concoction of broken lipsticks, spilled ink and till receipts before pulling out one of her tattered business cards. 'Sorry it's a bit of a mess.' She leaned over in her chair to hand it to him.

The man stretched his arm out, the leather that clad him complaining bitterly, and their fingers touched by accident. Libby felt the shock surge up her arm and searing fire ripped through her body, shaking her to near madness, from that one simple touch. She gasped out loud and instinctively clutched his hand.

'You must do what you have to. I am, after all, your client.' He pulled his fingers away from hers, robbing her of the powerful sensations, leaving only a trace of him inside her breastbone that rendered her breathless and hungry for more.

She jumped up with a squeal as a tall young male constable opened the door. 'This way miss.' Libby followed him down the corridor as the long strip lights spat and blinked erratically above her head and she wondered what indeed she had learned about him and whether she was right in following her instincts.

'Instincts,' she thought out loud, 'for all I know, he could be a ruthless murderer.' Yet somehow Libby didn't believe this man was capable of murder. Of sin, yes, but murder …

The lights went out with a loud bang and the stench of dirt, then burning electricity and the faintest scent of oiled leather, was the first sense to grip her before the fear set in.

She felt the young officer's reassuring hand on her arm and allowed herself to be led swiftly up the stairs towards salvation and the light of the room above.

'Bloody electrics!' the policeman rasped.

Gathering her good sense together and clutching her handbag to her chest like a shield, Libby braced herself for the heated argument to come and strode towards the waiting duty sergeant, wielding the ruined sheet of particulars in her hand like a sword.

CHAPTER  Two

'SO WHAT'S YOUR DAY BEEN LIKE?'

The hot tea babbled from the spout of the fine bone china teapot. It was a comforting sound with distant chimes of family and home. He set the cup down carefully by the woman's hand and poured himself one before sitting at the wooden table and adding the milk in the same way he had done for decades of mornings and afternoons.

'White?'

He shrugged and emptied a small amount from the chipped milk jug into her cup, stirring it around with a tarnished silver spoon – five times, clockwise.

'This was my grandmother's tea set.' His eyes clouded in far-off recognition. 'The only thing I ever wanted from her paltry estate after she died.' He took a tiny sip, careful not to burn his lips. 'It's lasted well, don't you think?'

He smiled, an indulgent nostalgic gesture, and creaked his back into the wooden backrest of his kitchen chair. 'I do love a good cup of tea. Can't be doing with coffee. Coffee's for people who work too hard and need to stay awake.'

He set the cup back into its tiny china saucer and placed it on the table. 'I've got some cake if you want.'

He rose and ambled across the tile-style lino, slippery with water and detergent, to the well-preserved pride of home that had been in his family for years. He remembered when his mother first bought it and recalled her marvelling over a cupboard with glass doors.

'This was all the rage in those days and is probably worth something now,' he threw his thoughts out to his guest. 'You know, if you keep something for long enough it'll come back into fashion?' He laughed to himself and brought out a partly rusted tin from the shelf. 'Will fruit cake do? I haven't got anything chocolate. Chocolate's for kids and I don't have kids any more.

He grunted something inaudible and paused at the cupboard to reflect for a moment.

He walked over to the sink and grasped the handle of a broad knife from the bowl. He grimaced at the darkening stains on the blade and waved it beneath the hot running water for a few moments before drying it on the leg of his trousers. 'Sorry to appear so crude, all the tea towels are in the wash.' He sliced the cake thinly and set it on the fragile plate with intricately woven flowers around its rim. He placed it by the woman's cup and sat down again next to her.

'Now, where were we? Oh, yes, we were talking about our day. I can tell you, I didn't have a good one yesterday. I was really pleased when my shift was over. What's that?' he craned his neck to listen to the quiet question. 'It's not that I don't like my job, I just wish people would let me get on with things I should be doing and leave the paperwork to someone else. Bloody forms, I hate them.' The tea cup quivered against the saucer as his thumb and fingers tightened against the delicate handle. 'There's so much paperwork in the job these days; procedures to follow; forms to fill out, forms to fill in, forms to file.' His fingers drummed against the table, rattling the tea set on its surface. 'And everything needs to be authorised these days. You can't move without someone breathing down your bloody neck and telling you what to do, what not to do and how you should be doing it.'

Her quietness began to irritate him. It was not that he was unaccustomed to a woman's silence, he just felt it inappropriate when he was in need of some reassuring words. 'Why don't you have some cake?' He leaned forwards to push the plate closer to her but clipped the edge of the teapot with his cuff. It teetered for a moment on the wooden surface and crashed to the lino before he could grab it.

'You stupid bitch!' he wailed at the puddle of tea and the sight of his precious but devastated family heirloom lying in small bits on the floor. 'Mess! Mess! And pain! That's all women cause. Look what you've done!'

The chair slid across the lino as he stood up abruptly and lunged at her. He held his blood-stained fingernails up to the wide eyes. 'It's going to take me ages to scrub these clean before work tomorrow morning! Clumsy cow!' He grabbed her cup and threw the hot tea over her face.

The woman sat on the chair and did not flinch at his angry remonstrations. Complaisant in her nakedness, her dull grey eyes stared in the vague direction of the kitchen window at the cold sky beyond, seemingly dreaming of freedom.

The long rent in her neck from the edge of a jagged blade had silenced her terrified screams and her face, contorted in horror, the strips of flesh flapping from deep wounds to her mouth, were evidence of the brutality of her final ordeal. The tea, cold now, dripped lightly down her ruined face, staining her cheeks like bitter tears.

'There now, love, don't cry. People like us aren't allowed to cry.' His anger spent, the man gently blotted the moisture from the icy cheek with his cuff and patted the stiff shoulder, before rearranging the corpse on the chair. 'Doesn't matter about the pot. It was a stupid old thing anyway. I'll make you a fresh cup.'

—

'You're late!' Maurice breezed past her, staggering under the weight of case notes in his arms.

'And you're an arsehole!' Libby snorted.

'Charming!' she heard him sniff as he wedged his foot in the closing lift door.

She hurried through the aisles of shuffling papers and clattering keyboards, while phones sang, secretaries twittered and doors whined open and shut. She followed the heady aroma of fresh coffee and almost fell over the post boy's trolley as she made her way to the office she shared with three junior solicitors.

'You're late!' The new boy peered up from his desk. 'Carl's been looking for you all morning and he doesn't have his happy Monday face on.'

She noted the serious undertones of his statement. 'He'll have to wait until I get some coffee. I've had a long night and can barely keep my eyes open. I've just spent the entire weekend working on the Singh case – there's such a lot of case law to get through and I can't find any relevant precedents.'

'Carl wants you in his office now.' Selina wafted into the room, bringing with her a powerful stench of vanilla ice cream with a whispering sigh of freesia. And it wasn't only her perfume that made Libby feel sick.

Bored with a career in fashion modelling, Selina Fotheringham-Taylor had grabbed the best parts of life with her perfumed fists. Nobility, brains, charm, elegance, wit, body and beauty in no particular order were only some of her greatest assets.

THE SLEEPING WARRIOR

She was also possessed with ambition and would stop at nothing to achieve her ultimate goal of partnership status in the busy city practice – the same goal that Ms Butler had been working on for years now. Above all, she was younger and slimmer than her and that gave Selina nil points in Libby's personal popularity contest.

'How's the Bellingham case coming on?' Libby's sweet smile didn't conceal the little dig at her rival. She knew Selina had handled the libel case particularly badly and that she was still smarting from the terrible dressing down Carl had given her in front of her own client.

Selina refused to flinch as she sat at her tidy desk and pretended to study a letter in her in-tray. 'The newspaper settled out of court. The ending was a happy one for everyone.' She ran a manicured hand down the side of her long, blonde hair. 'I hear that Carl isn't pleased with the way you've handled the Weller case. He's seriously considering taking you off it.'

'No, he's not,' the protest in her tone was a little too loud. 'I'll ask to be taken off it. The man is a gangland thug and my conscience ...'

Selina placed her letter down on the table and crossed one hand over the other as if she was just about to perform a sermon. 'The golden thread of criminal law ...'

'Haven't you got an eyebrow to pluck or something?' Libby was not about to be preached the rudiments of criminal law by a mere junior. 'A bikini line to shear, perhaps?'

'I wax.' Selina was a hot-headed woman who always rose to a challenge. 'Unlike you, Libby, I keep well trimmed. I don't need a combine harvester to rid myself of unsightly fur.'

'And I don't need a muck spreader to put my foundation on in the mornings.'

Their teeth bared into a semblance of a smile, the two

adversaries circled each other around the office space, each taking in the other's respective imperfections.

'At least my hair colour's natural,' her enemy purred, eyeing the dark roots on Libby's scalp.

'Yeah, natural peroxide!'

'Ladies! Please! Can't we all just get on?' As the two pairs of hooded eyes turned suddenly on him, Brian the new boy realised he was treading on dangerous ground and was in imminent peril of becoming caught in the crossfire of deadly flying insults.

'Oh, we're just kidding, Brian.' Selina laughed at last. 'We've a kind of love-hate relationship. We respect each other really, don't we my little chubby friend?' She sat on the corner of her desk and crossed her long, skinny legs in front of her.

Sharp hairs bristled against Libby's spine. She hated that word. 'Let's say Selina and I have a don't-like-very-much-hate relationship that can be cordial at times when she's not exercising her cavernous jaw.'

'Having one of those menopausal days again, are we Libby?'

'You're just jealous that you haven't reached intellectual maturity yet. Like puberty, Selina, it'll come, if you stop dwelling on it.'

Brian had no idea what to make of either of them. 'Libby, some detectives from Scotland Yard are here and they want to speak to you. Carl's been entertaining them for over forty five minutes. I don't think he's enjoying their company very much and he's not in a good mood either.'

'What does the CID want with me? Why didn't you tell me?'

Libby remained calm, not wishing to reveal her panic at becoming the brunt of the senior partner's anger for a change. She made for the door with an elegant stride.

'It was totally obvious that you would mess up one day.'

Libby breathed the irritation out as her biggest rival spoke loud enough for the whole office to hear. She didn't believe she imagined the keyboards quietening for her response.

When Libby Butler was cornered, however, her retort was always devastating.

'I suppose it's something really important that only I can deal with, since I have more experience than the rest of you and I'm not the one in Carl's bad books. Bring me a cup of coffee would you? I'll be in the senior partner's office.' She slowed down her walk. 'Milk, semi-skimmed, just a splash!' she smoothed down her blouse and left Selina not knowing what to do with her open mouth.

—

Carl Bottomley, senior partner of Gore, Matthews and Bottomley, sat at his polished mahogany desk, his attempts to mask his annoyance obvious to his plain clothed visitors. Just like Carl, his office was well groomed and polished to a shine. There were no drifts of case notes and tatty folders littering the floors and surfaces and no dust on the shelves of his extensive case law and statutes collection.

'At last, Libby, come in and sit down.'The clip to his tone was audible. 'This is Detective Chief Inspector Andrew Prendergast,' he nodded towards a stout man, probably in his fifties. What was left of his hair was neatly trimmed into the shape of a skull cap with large parts of the corners missing. He had a bulbous, pitted nose and flushed cheeks – both tell-tale signs that the man enjoyed a drink or two, 'and Detective Inspector Lloyd Byron.'

Libby took a chair next to the detectives. 'A DCI, it must be something important.' Sitting on her hands and leaning forward, she turned all her attention to the younger detective. 'Are you mad, bad and dangerous to know?' She liked the look of DI Byron.

'It depends on who wants to know.' the younger detective laughed and his blue eyes twinkled with mischief.

'They want to ask you a few questions about the man you saw last Thursday,' Carl continued, trying his best to ignore the roguish interaction between the policeman and a member of his staff.

'Ask away.' Libby crossed her legs and placed her hands on the bag on her lap.

DCI Prendergast began the conversation. 'We understand that you interviewed a suspect at East Dulwich police station early Thursday morning.'

'Detainee.' She rudely corrected him.

'Very well,' he conceded the point, 'detainee then.'

Libby, grinning flirtatiously at one officer, turned her head to smile at the other. 'That is correct.'

'What was so urgent that couldn't have waited until morning?'

She shrugged and twiddled with a tail of the red silk scarf around her neck. 'Sergeant Fry told me to come along there and then. I didn't really think much about the time. I'm duty bound to provide free legal advice and representation twenty four hours a day, three hundred and sixty five days a year.'

The two officers ignored the sarcasm. 'We understand that you spoke to the detainee.'

Libby pursed her lips and gazed around Carl's commodious office, taking in the gleaming wooden shelving, thickly clad in law reports, and the long velvet curtains that concealed the city of London's panoramic rooftop vista. 'I didn't get much out of him, save that you coppers could be in a lot of trouble if he decides to file a complaint against you.'

'Oh, yes, and why's that Miss Butler?'

'The Snow Hill boys had nothing on him. Two officers attacked him; searched him; detained him; didn't tell him what for; failed to place him under arrest; and didn't even charge him. They took his photo and DNA samples without his consent; and then imprisoned him. To add insult to injury, he was picked up again in south east London and had to go through the same sorry ordeal all over again. Now DCI and DI, I'm a criminal lawyer and there are lots of issues here that need addressed. Should my client wish to take this further, I'll be helping him with his case against you.'

'You're in contact with the man?'

'No, but I've given him my card, just in case he wants to make a complaint.'

'Were you present during his release from East Dulwich?' The officers appeared too absorbed with their own line of questioning to acknowledge the gravity of Libby's accusations.

She shook her head and, from the look the two detectives gave each other, knew there was a lot they weren't saying.

'I must've left before him.'

'So you didn't see him leave?'

'Where's all this going?'

'Did you get a name for him Miss Butler?' DI Byron asked, his eyes still shining, while the other's pencil was poised against a fresh page of his notebook.

'Gabriel Radley.'

'How do you spell that?'

'With an 'e', as in my gorgeous handbag.' She thrust her bag in front of the policemen's faces to show them the embossed letters in the soft leather. She froze for a moment and closed her eyes against her own stupidity. She only hoped the pair of detectives hadn't spotted her mistake. 'He said he was of no fixed abode, but I kind've got the feeling he couldn't remember.'

'So, he speaks English?'

'With a public school accent.'

'How did you find him? I mean, generally?'

Libby shrugged. 'He's obviously very intelligent, he's also confused and I don't think he can remember much.'

'Are you saying he's suffering from some kind of memory loss?'

'I'm not a psychiatrist DCI Prendergast, but I think it's highly possible that he's suffering from amnesia and he intimated as much to me. He'd no idea where he was in relation to the world, let alone where East Dulwich was on a London street atlas, although he spoke English like a member of our fine British aristocracy. Did you test him for drugs or alcohol?'

The look the two officers gave each other unnerved her slightly and, for reasons she couldn't explain, she became steadily irritated by the questioning.

'Did he tell you about his first contact with the police?'

'You mean the criminal assault upon him and subsequent false arrest?' She waited for a suitable expression of guilt or outrage from either copper, but none came. 'He said enough for me to judge that he was stopped, searched and roughed up for little reason other than suspicion. For what, only you boys can say. It's possible that his memory loss was caused by trauma during his ordeal. I know you lot can be a little over zealous with suspects now and again.'

'Be nice to the officers Libby. They have a job to do, just like us,' Carl sniggered from his comfortable executive chair. She could tell he was enjoying watching her squirm.

'Forgive me gentlemen, but I really need to know where

all this is going before I can help you and why Scotland Yard's interested in the case. I'm sorry that the due process of law has helped him to escape your clutches, but my client has done nothing wrong. You've nothing on him and, dare I say, you wrongly arrested him and were holding him under false imprisonment. I took the precaution of asking Sergeant Fry to make a call to the CPS and they agreed with me there had been some alleged serious breaches of the code and even of his human rights. In the end, very reluctantly, so did Sergeant Fry.'

She looked down at her hands and, to her horror, noticed that two buttons in her blouse had popped open, revealing a grey lace bra that had once been white. She hastily buttoned them up and dared Carl to laugh with one of her filthiest looks.

'Do you know if the suspect came into any personal contact with Constable Suzanne Glover?'

Libby was taken aback by the question. 'I ... I .... don't understand ...'

'I believe that you met Constable Glover briefly that night.' Byron's eyes no longer twinkled, they'd become hard and cold.

'Yes, she escorted me to the custody suite. Her shift was over by the time I'd finished the interview. Why don't you ask her or Sergeant Fry these questions?'

DCI Prendergast shot a quick glance to his colleague before turning in his chair to face her. The gravity in his expression alarmed her.

'Suzanne Glover didn't return home to her husband and two children on Thursday morning, Ms Butler.'

—

The hall was deserted, save for an abandoned upright piano in the far corner and the sharp rays of morning criss-crossing the filthy oak boards. Only the dust stirred and it whirled and eddied in the bright shards of daylight, like miniscule angels trapped inside brilliant linear prisons, spilling across the lofty room.

A shadow entered from a door on the right. The dull thuds of cardboard blocks against wood stirred the silence. She lifted one black satin toe and then another, grinding the pointes into the rosin box: her stance haughty and strong, her hands and fingers soft as if pulling through warm water. She breathed in and then out and, with each breath, her arms moved obediently to the silent rhythm. She waited for the moment, her eyes closed in concentration, her lithe body yielding to the discipline of years.

As if an orchestra had struck the first notes of a rowdy overture, the arabesque came swiftly and with the power of an earthquake. Her leg reached out behind her and her heel kissed the back of her head, while her left foot formed a perfect arch, balancing her weight on the tip of one pointe. She unfurled her arms to either side, the softness of her fingers betraying the masculine tautness of her muscles as she flapped them lightly. There was no bend in her chest to suggest unnatural exertion – her legs formed a smooth, straight line behind her – a linear sculpture. It was a perfect, motionless pose: a faultless snap-shot of gravity and balance and a celebration of one of the most beautiful art forms known to man.

Her audience of one could have been an audience of thousands. This would always be her very best performance. She kept her movements purposeful and controlled as she opened to the rhythm of her memories.

The fluttering in her heart as the curtains came up. Her dance began with soft adagio in the shadows of the hall. A series of unfolding movements of smoothness and serenity, each arabesque and attitude was a still-life study in monochrome. Her dark pony-tail trailed submissively behind her every move in faultless synchronicity, like a shimmering shadow on a hot summer's eve.

The hot glare of the lights and the vibrant colours of the stage. Pas de bourée into a bright shard of sunlight, her feet barely seemed to move, and she paused in bras bas, her feet in first position, her head turned down towards the floor. Like an alabaster carving, swathed in black silk, the light tumbling around her, she stood motionless under the spotlight in calm neutrality.

The orchestra of blasting brass, rumbling drums and weeping strings. A series of complex turns struck like lightning, spinning her diagonally across the hall. Running, now, she thundered into an enormous leap, her legs parting in mid air with near-impossible elevation; into another – sissonne ouverte at 90 degrees straight into a grand jeté en avant. Chaîné up, chaîné down and an almighty bound in open second. Her ghostly blur shattered the shards of daylight as she soared above the boards, flickering from shadow to light, the dust crackling in the turbulent air.

The spell-bound faces shining from the dark amphitheatre. Her audience could barely contain his awe as he gasped and sighed at the powerful performance before him.

Standing with his back against the far wall beneath a dilapidated balcony, he could hear the music as if he sat directly above the orchestra pit and could see the colourful splendour of the stage; he could feel the silk of the swirling costumes and sense the vibrant life-force in this divine prima ballerina. He put his hands together in rapturous applause.

The hailstorm of flowers and the thunderous ovation at the end of the performance. Her expression remained inscrutable as she halted in mid-turn, her arms and legs splayed out in opposite directions to leave her body wide open. She had seen him. A perfect double pirouette en dehors, then another, then another en dedan. Fouetté, fouetté, fouetté, fouetté, fouetté, over and over again – a hazy silhouette of vigorous perpetual motion. Her dark form was a smudge as she spun on her toe, faster and faster towards him... flicker ...flicker ...flicker ... flick ... flick ... flick.

'Beautiful, truly beautiful!' her appreciative audience shouted his delight and clapped his hands together until his palms stung. He couldn't hide the star-struck admiration in his expression as she stood before him and narrowed her pale green eyes. She was a good head shorter than him and so slim that she looked almost fragile. 'How do you do that with your legs? You'd make a great pole dancer.'

The assault came suddenly and he was pinned against the wall by his neck, her knee bent at her right ear, the black pointe pressing the air from his windpipe, crushing the sensitive cartilage into his spine.

Slowly choking to death, he was powerless to defend himself and couldn't even muster up the energy to grab the foot from his throat. His eyes began to bulge, his face was on fire, but the pain slowly began to recede as unconsciousness beckoned. As quickly as it had attacked, the pointe withdrew and he slumped to the ground gargling.

'Lars has sent you?'

He could only nod as he held one hand to his throat and the other in the air, his fingers splayed in a gesture of supplication. Her Russian accent didn't surprise him as his senses slowly returned.

'Do you have a pen?'

It was an odd question in the circumstances but, having lost the ability to speak, he nodded again and fumbled inside his jacket. Still sprawled on the ground on his hands and knees, he drew out a black ballpoint and thrust it towards her.

'If Lars has sent you, then that means money.' The nod of assent was all she needed. She grabbed him by the thinning clumps of hair scattered across the top of his head and scribbled something on the bald patch, digging the point into the skin. 'Tell him to call me.' Her kick sent him spinning onto his back.

She took five wide backward steps into the middle of the floor and saluted him with a graceful, elegant curtsy to mark the dramatic finale of her best performance. She spun on her heels and marched across the room, leaving the hall empty save for an upright piano in the far corner; an injured man choking on the ground; and the faintest sniff of rosin in the settling dust.

—

Libby felt her spine tingle with ice. 'Missing? What? Where'd she go?'

It was probably the most stupid question she'd asked in her life and she would've kicked herself had her legs not been frozen in shock. She tried to bring some semblance of intelligence back to the conversation – 'I mean… oh, I don't know what I mean … sorry!' – but failed quite exceptionally.

'We didn't say she was missing, Ms Butler.'

She didn't like DI Byron's accusatory tone. 'Well, I didn't assume you meant she'd been abducted by aliens!'

'Now, why would you say that?'

She felt her cold spine pressing against the back of the chair for the second time in a few days. The two detectives leaned closely towards her now, searching her face with ravenous expressions.

'It's called sarcasm. It's a form of humour that expresses scorn or contempt,' she attempted to defuse a potentially explosive situation. The dull blinks reminded her that the recipients, by their very nature, were insensible to her wit. 'Constable Glover was out on duty for most of her shift and told me she hadn't met Mr ...' she couldn't bring herself to say his name as she clutched her bag tightly to her stomach, unconsciously trying to hide the tell-tale lettering ' ... the detainee. She did come into the cell with me and took a quick look at him and then she left. That's all the contact she had with him that I know of. Do you believe he has something to do with her disappearance?'

'We didn't say that Constable Glover had disappeared, Ms Butler. We are merely conducting investigations at this moment in time.'

Libby resisted the urge to roll her eyes to the ceiling again. Coppers were always so careful with information: probably, she believed, because they didn't know enough words. 'Can I get some coffee please?' She turned to Carl in appeal.

He uncrossed his arms, nodded and hit the buzzer to his secretary.

'Look officers, I'm sorry one of your people has gone missing and you'll agree that, since she's been gone for over three days now, she's a missing person, but I really don't see how I can help you.' Libby tried her best to be polite while fighting back a surging tide of personal misgivings. Her voice, however, betrayed her concern and she swallowed her words with deep intakes of breath.

Five women from different parts of south London had disappeared before being found dead in as many months. There was plenty of similar fact evidence to point an accusatory finger at one killer but he had eluded detection so far, despite a frantic police investigation, a step-up of law enforcement presence on the streets and hysterical media coverage.

'The man you tell us is called Gabriel Radley escaped from the custody suite on Thursday morning.'

Brief relief came with a sharp knock on the door and Carl's long-suffering secretary marched in with the drink and, the coffee sloshing into the saucer, almost threw it over Libby. 'Your coffee ma'am!' She thrust the saucer in her hand, splashing the white blouse.

'Thank you, Sarah, you're an angel,' Libby smiled sweetly and rubbed at the stains with her free hand. 'I see you have a long way to go before you attain that elusive Silver Service.'

Unable to defend herself with equal verbal competence, Sarah slammed the door behind her.

Libby turned once more to the detectives. 'You say escaped. You just told me he'd been released. There's a bit of inconsistency in these statements of yours, DCI Prendergast, perhaps we should tape this conversation.'

DCI Prendergast's inscrutable expression didn't change. 'The only explanation we have is that the door to his cell was either left open or the locking mechanism failed in some way as did the backup generator. It's possible that ... er,' he looked down at his notepad, 'Mr Radley took advantage of the power cut to make his exit. We have an officer missing and a suspect on the loose.'

'You believe that Gabriel Radley had something to do with Suzanne Glover's disappearance?' She put her hand up to stay the expected response. 'I say disappearance for want of a better word.'

'We just want to eliminate him from our investigations.'

'Or incriminate him.' She sighed after the long silence. 'Sergeant Fry released him. He was expecting a couple of Yardies that morning and was quite nervous about letting his detainee go. In the end, I persuaded him to make the correct choice.'

Carl chuckled in the background.

One detective looked bemused, the other insulted. 'Sergeant Fry is an experienced officer with an exceptional record and those 'Yardies', as you call them, were myself and Detective Inspector Byron.'

Libby gave a small embarrassed shrug. 'It's just a term of affection in this office. Of course, the Met could never be compared to a violent, gun-toting, gang of thugs. How is Operation Trident coming on?' Her attempts to wriggle out of her predicament were defeated by a pair of angry glares.

'So what exactly are you investigating here?' Carl, who'd been silent throughout the interview, decided it was time to step in. Time was money and he was wasting both this morning. 'Do you believe Ms Butler to be in some way, consciously or unwittingly, responsible for the disappearance of your constable?'

He continued speaking over the top of the protesting officers. 'It seems to me that Ms Butler was doing her job that morning and did it very well. I don't have to remind you that police rules are not only there to help you catch criminals, but also to safeguard the rights of innocent members of the British public who are misfortunate enough to stumble into one of your custody suites.

'Now, I don't know where this is all going and I don't really care. Ms Butler has now furnished you with the extent of her knowledge on this subject and so your inquiries, insofar as they concern her, are now complete.

'I suggest you return when you have more evidence and I really must ask you to leave.'

'Thank you for your time, we'll be in touch.' DCI Prendergast slammed his notebook shut and stood up, DI Byron mimicking his actions a second later. The former stopped for a brief moment to address her. 'Of course, should you see Mr Radley, you will call us?' To Libby, his question was more of a command as he slipped his card into her hand. 'I'll be speaking to your partner, Mr Ridout. I believe he was outside the police station on the night in question and could've been the last person that we know of to have seen Suzanne Glover that evening.'

After the door closed, Carl and Libby sat in silence for a short while on opposite sides of his desk.

'Thanks Carl.'

Another long silence.

'This could be awful for us, you know.'

'It'll be fine. They're not interested in illicit affairs between work colleagues.'

Carl smiled, that sympathetic, patronising smirk he normally wore when they spoke together about their brittle future.

It was at times like this that Libby really didn't understand what she saw in him. He had had numerous affairs with his staff during his fifteen and three-quarter years of marriage, the first possibly being Sarah, who'd never forgiven herself for exchanging her youthful beauty for cellulite and wrinkles. Libby wondered when it would be her turn to join the ranks of discarded mistresses.

'It'll be fine,' he breathed his words out in reassurance and edged around the desk towards her.

Carl, though in his mid-fifties, had maintained his lithe figure through gorging himself on a healthy lifestyle that included regular exercise and the GI diet. He did his best to make his face keep up with his body by colouring his hair and clipping the bristles from his nostrils, but he was getting older and had come to that stage in everyone's life where age becomes a chronic, disfiguring skin condition for which there is no cure.

He leaned over to caress her knee with his hand. 'I liked the way you dealt with Tweedledum and Tweedledummer. You were funny. You are always funny, my lovely Libby.' The hand moved up the inside of her thigh to come to a natural stop beneath her skirt. 'Why don't we do something together on Friday night?'

'Why not tonight?' She snapped her knees together, trapping his fingers in her legs, her mood playful.

'Have to take Oliver to rugby tonight; dinner party tomorrow; meeting with Weller on Wednesday evening at La Lanterna; and Emma's got Brownies on Thursday.' He leaned closer, pursing his lips and grinding his hips, reeling off his busy week-day activities as if they were a Motown playlist.

'Sorry, Carl. I'm busy on Friday night.' She picked his hand up by the white starched cuff as if it was a snapping crab. 'Let me know when you have time between your demanding family schedule for a quick shag with your socks on.'

Her obvious bitterness had the desired effect. Carl stood up abruptly and paced the room, slapping his fist against his forehead again and again. 'It's easy for you Libby, you don't have kids.'

She stood up now, exhausted with his excuses. 'It's easier for you, Carl, because you don't have a conscience.' She slammed the door behind her.

—

'Well?' Maurice Blais was waiting for her outside Carl's room, his arms tightly crossed against his Armani silk shirt. Libby had known Maurice for as long as she could remember, he had once been married to her father's younger sister. He grabbed her by the arm and shuffled her into the stationery cupboard.

'Well, nothing.' She shrugged, disheartened by her conversation with Carl. 'I couldn't do it. I did try, but I just don't want things to end right now. I'm not ready. I think I must still love him,' she breathed in despair.

'You should've finished it a long time ago, my dear Libby. Carl is a vulture who pecks at the bones of the living until there's no flesh left to satiate his lustful appetite. It's not right,' Maurice placed his hands on her shoulders, his French accent barely perceptible.

'You can talk! How's the delectable Jason?'

Maurice spun away from her in a characteristic fit of melodrama and slammed his fists on his hips. 'I caught him on Saturday night in the clutches of what can only be described as a baby!'

'No! Oh, Maurice, how awful.'

'It gets worse,' he pouted his full red lips and traced a plump finger against the reams of paper stacked on the ladder of shelves. 'I phoned the police and told them a pervert was molesting a child in my house. When they came, the bastard produced a passport proving the boy to be over twenty-one.'

'I suppose Jason, King of Counterfeit, has his uses.'

'The kid was no older than sixteen. He had the teenage acne to prove it!'

Libby patted the wobbling cheek. 'He's an arsehole, Maurice.'

'You're bandying that word around a lot today. Does your grim mood have something to do with the CID?'

The question woke her up to the present with a loud snort. She stepped out the door, keeping her voice down. 'Did the police phone you on Thursday night Maurice? You were, after all, on duty on Thursday night.'

'No, I don't believe they did. Why?'

'I'm just wondering why the duty sergeant chose me to brief a man in police custody.'

'And did you?'

Stopping at the coffee machine, Libby nodded distractedly. 'He was really strange.' She pressed the button for black coffee with sugar and watched the plastic cup as it filled.

'What, like psycho strange?' Maurice was slightly puzzled why Libby had changed her taste in coffee. 'Are you on another one of your stupid diets?'

'I'm sure those detectives believe he has something to do with the murders.' She grasped the cup from its metal claws, her head buried in confusion. 'They're too interested in him.'

'They think he's Dracula?' Maurice was suddenly stricken with horror. 'What do you think?' His hand shot protectively up to his four chins.

Libby shook her head. 'He's not a murderer, he's just lost.' She'd spent a large part of her weekend pondering the many unanswered questions dancing around in her mind since Thursday morning.

There was something about the stranger and she was simply unable to erase him from her thoughts ... she wondered where he was now.

'DI Byron looked like a nice chap!'

She shook herself back to her senses and managed to laugh. 'He has dancing eyes, but I don't think he shares your particular taste in music!'

'Mr Weller's in reception to see you Libby,' her tiny well-groomed secretary smiled.

'Oh no, I am not prepared for him!' she spat. 'Tell him I've taken ill suddenly and have gone to hospital for immediate treatment for, uhm, rapid, chaotic ventricular arrhythmia.'

'Do what?'

'That's what he'll say.'

'Sorry Libby, but he already knows you're here. I've put you in meeting room three.' The small, plump woman, with the bouncing curls of gold and the frilly blouse, pointed across to the reception desk where long glass panels failed to conceal the frowning faces within the company's walls. Gary Weller frowned back at her.

'OK, get him some coffee, a newspaper to read, a social conscience and an appointment with anger management and tell him I'll be out in a minute.' She turned to Maurice. 'Let's have a drink after work and we'll catch up on everything.'

'Sorry, my love, D'Artagnan has already asked me.'

'Is that his real name?' She curled her lip in suspicion.

'If you must know, it's Trevor, but I daresay he's good with a sword!'

She turned her attention to the important client who sat as still as stone behind the transparent screen and she pondered on the possibilities of turning negative thought into a positive, deadly weapon. Waggling her fingers at the evil that was Gary Weller, she fantasised about his horrible demise at her hands. A single hit by someone who was brave enough to run the gauntlet of his henchmen's bullets and get close to him, was all that was necessary to rid the streets of London of this loathsome creature.

The Weller fortune was born out of corruption, misery and death. He was the leader of one of the most notorious gangs of south London who dealt in drugs, human trafficking and pain with a corruption so pure and a criminal record so empty that they called him the Saint. Unfortunately for Libby, he was also a good friend of Carl's.

Carl. Libby's thoughts became entrapped once again by her fragile relationship with her own conscience. She needed to feel adored at this moment and she had to focus on her future. Perhaps the unhappily married Carl was not such a bad option after all. She turned around and marched towards his office.

'Weller's in reception, are you coming?'

The scene before her should not have come as a particular surprise, but Libby couldn't help her shock. Selina and Carl stood behind his desk in a passionate embrace, his hands massaging the flesh beneath her blouse.

'Lost something?'

The pair leaped in fright: Carl, as if suggestion was a command, attempted in vain to pretend that he had indeed lost something, while Selina stood preening her pristine paws like a cat in front of a warm fire.

'Mr Weller's in reception, Mr Bottomley, sir.' She bit back the traitorous tears. 'I dare say that you wouldn't have found much up there apart from a pair of silicon bags. You have to be careful, her nipples might come off in your hands.' The door slammed behind her with a loud thud.

FOUR DAYS HAD PASSED SINCE Libby last spoke to Carl with a civil tongue: those days had been the most uncomfortable and miserable of her life. Of course, he'd attempted to call her on her mobile at times when he knew Tony wouldn't be around, but she'd simply pressed the red button and robbed him of further excuse.

For the past two years, Carl had been the sole object of Libby Butler's clandestine desires; the place where all her ambitions had come to reside in comfort. She targeted him as the golden goal of her forthcoming future success in both love and career and now her dreams had been torn apart by a woman who was younger, more beautiful and much slimmer than she.

Feeling like a jaded Hollywood has-been, Libby had been delivered a slap of hopelessness and drowned her sorrows in her second bottle of Pinot Grigio rosè – not her first choice, but all that she had left in the wine rack. She glanced at the clock on the kitchen wall that said half past eight in the evening and thought about staggering to bed.

Tony was on late shift and had only left for the centre an hour ago. She thanked his odd working times for not having to face him for any length of time. While he was not there, she cried. While he was there, she fought back the tears by pretending she was in a bad mood, blaming the stress of her job for her desolation.

It was an impossible situation to bear and being forced to hide her emotions was taking its toll on her physical appearance.

Dragging herself from the soft sofa, she stumbled through to the bedroom, the wine bottle clutched tightly in her hand. She slumped down on the stool at the vanity and objectively observed its crowded surface. She saw herself in the mirror and dared to look deeper.

Staring back at Libby Butler was a worn out, twenty eight-year-old woman whose prime had already peaked and the dip on the eligibility chart was plummeting towards 'not a chance'.

Her hair was too long, too unruly and in desperate need of a freshen-up of colour. Her brown eyes, normally flecked with vibrant green, were dulled with the exhaustion of simply trying to exist. Her skin was pale, almost grey, and her lips pursed in indignation – for what cause, she could no longer remember. What was far worse, she was busting out of her size fourteen blouse. She rubbed at her eyes and forehead, as if to massage some enthusiasm back into her worn-out expression.

Libby had always been one of those fortunate individuals who could honestly attest that she was unfamiliar with depression. She believed that to fill her life with enthusiasm and positive thinking would keep the demons of negativity at bay.

The reflection before her, however, was lifeless with despair. If the eyes were truly windows to the soul, then Libby's were showing large cracks that let the rain in.

She took another glug from the bottle and believed that the night had few terrors in comparison to the heartless light of day.

'Hello, this is Libby Butler. Make it quick please, 'cos I'm busy,' her own voice squealed at her from the answer phone.

'Libby,' Carl whimpered from the flashing lump of plastic and wires, 'the two inspectors from the CID have just left. We must talk. Damn!' there was a long silence. 'I believe that we may've had a bit of a misunderstanding on Monday, but that can wait. You must phone me. Please, it's really important.'

She hauled herself across the room to the side of the bed. Her fingers itched above the receiver. Carl was always so cautious. Not wishing to arouse Tony's suspicion, he kept his intentions broad in the hope of getting a response from her.

She was sick with hurt, however, and needed to wallow for a while in her own misery.

She collapsed on the soft mattress and fell asleep instantly.

—

She didn't know what had awoken her. Her eyes snapped open and the dark surrounded her as it always did in the clutches of night. She felt the familiar chill creep up her spine as she realised the light had gone out. She fumbled for the switch.

With frantic fingers, she slapped the surface of her bedside table and found the clock, then the outline of the phone. Panic rose and she snatched her hand beneath the covers as she realised she lay in complete darkness. Being born and brought up in rural Scotland, the pitch black of evening shadows was no stranger to Libby, only this was London and orange glow from the streetlights should've been flooding her room. Libby pulled her hand up to her face, the back of it touched her nose, but she couldn't see it.

She recalled the newspaper headlines and the TV news bulletins that some of Dracula's victims had been taken from their own homes. That menacing shape of a shadowed figure standing over her bed returned from her fevered nightmares. She could make out the contours of its head and torso while demons cavorted around it. Libby felt her chest constricting as she made another attempt to reach for the light switch.

'There is nothing in the darkness that cannot be seen in the light,' the black shadow spoke to her and she opened her mouth and screamed.

—

Libby leaped from the bed as if shot from a gun and, falling over a stack of books, scrambled back to her feet and hurtled towards the door, whimpering all the way. She threw the door open and punched the hall light on. The bulb glowed for less than a second before it exploded over her head, showering her with tiny pieces of glass. Libby screamed again and felt her heart thrashing in her throat.

Weeping in terror and desperate to get away from what, she didn't even know, she sped towards the front door, squealing against the sharp pain of the glass as it pierced her feet.

Fumbling at the lock, her laughter turned to mania as the metal bolt clicked open. Tony had forgotten to lock it again. She threw the door open, the light in the corridor flooded her flat and she made a bolt for freedom.

A strong arm grabbed her tightly around the body and the hand placed over her mouth stifled her terrified screams. The door was kicked shut and Libby was hauled backwards into the darkness, her legs thrashing in the air.

'I will not hurt you.' She knew that voice and that smell. 'I cannot remove my hand from your mouth if you insist on screaming.' She felt his body pressed tightly against her back and hot breath teasing her hair. His velvet voice cooed at her to be still. 'Forgive me for this intrusion, Libby Butler, but I require your aid once more. Am I still your client?' She nodded her head vigorously, her eyes wild. 'I am going to release you now. Can I trust you not to scream?' She nodded again, her heart rate slowing by the second, and the hand and arm released her gently.

Leaping for the light switch, Libby howled like a tortured animal. She spun around and screamed again as the tall figure sat down on the sofa and crossed his arms against his chest. She carried on screaming until her throat constricted and she realised he was laughing at her.

'What the hell are you doing in my house?' Strange as it seemed, she didn't feel in any danger from him, despite her horrid ordeal only moments ago when she truly believed she was going to die.

She spied her handbag on the low coffee table and snatched it up. Fumbling inside it with a few choice swear words, she pulled out a packet of cigarettes and lit one up with a quaking hand.

'What are you doing?'

'Smoking, what does it look like? You scared the crap out of me.' She took a long draw and glared at him.

'What are you smoking?'

'Tobacco leaves: picked, dried and then rolled in paper. Some people perform such acts for ritual or pleasure but I do it purely to feed an addiction and calm my shattered nerves.'

'Have you any idea what smoking is doing to you?'

'Yeah, it'll kill me like you nearly did tonight. Only it will kill me slower. I prefer to choose the way I die, thank you.'

'It is like I have said, you are in no danger from me Libby Butler. It was your own irrational fear that caused you to panic.'

'And nothing to do with a strange man in my house who I didn't invite in?' She eyed him critically, seeing him in proper light, and decided that he looked a lot more menacing than she'd first believed.

He still wore the ceremonial battle dress that stank. He had the blackest eyes. It was impossible to tell where the pupils ended and the irises began. It was as if to look into them would be to tumble into a dark and bottomless well and never recover from the fall. He was an outrageously good looking man with finely sculpted bone structure, silky black hair and pale, unblemished skin. Long minutes passed before she realised she was staring at him, the ash from her cigarette flaking away to land silently on the carpet. It was then she became aware he was also scrutinising her. Libby stood before a complete stranger in a short t-shirt and knickers. She thanked God that she was wearing both. She refused to feel uncomfortable and bit back her humiliation. 'I gave you my business address. This is my home.'

'I followed you.'

She should have felt fear. 'Why?'

'I require your services. You are, after all, my only friend.'

'Come to the office on Monday morning and we'll talk about being new best buddies, but you really have to leave.' She managed to find an ashtray beneath a stack of magazines on the table between them and sat down behind it, concealing some of her immodesty. Understanding that he wasn't about to move, she decided to at least find out why he was here. 'Are you in trouble?'

'Not yet.'

'Then can you afford a lawyer?' She took another drag from the stump of her cigarette before the stub joined another thirty or so squashed into the makeshift ashtray that had been a fine porcelain saucer in a former incarnation.

He shrugged, watching her antics with an inscrutable expression. 'I do not need a lawyer. I need a friend.' There was a childlike honesty in his response that compelled her. Yet her cynical side warned her that this man was playing her like a favourite toy.

'Sorry, Mr Handbag, or whatever your name is. I enjoy the privilege of choosing my own friends and we've only just met.' He raised one smooth eyebrow and she could've slapped the sardonic curl from his lips. 'What do you want from me?'

'I need you to help me find this man.'

He picked up some colour print-outs from the pile of magazines on the table. Libby hadn't noticed them there.

He leaned forward with a squeal of leather and handed them to her.

Her eyes widened in horror as she studied them and noticed the stamp of the Metropolitan Police force and a case number on the back. 'Where did you get these?'

'I borrowed them from the police station,' he relaxed back on the comfortable sofa and let out a heavy breath.

'Is this some kind of sick joke?' She began to feel uneasy in his presence. The pictures showed the sterile remains of a corpse. One photo in particular was a severed head: its eyes closed, its mouth downturned in the saddest of expressions. The pallid features and angular cheek bones suggested it had once been female and its matted tussle of hair was evidence that she'd been a blonde. 'This is a woman. You said you were looking for a man.' She could hardly believe what she was looking at.

'I knew her. It is the man who mutilated her body I must find.' He shifted his position and leaned against the thick arm of the sofa.

Libby looked from pictures to man and back again. 'So, you're looking for her killer. I'm really sorry for your loss, was she a girlfriend of yours?'

He hesitated before answering, his eyes blazing with intensity. 'She was an acquaintance.' He hauled himself up from the sofa and, moving cautiously around the table, knelt down beside her.

The smell of earth, leather and sweat invaded her space and she flinched away from him.

'Are you some kind of minder?' Libby felt a sudden pang of sympathy for the stranger who crouched so close to her.

'Not a very good one.'

'Was this the murdered woman found on the Rye?' She studied the mutilated remains in the photos once more and curled her lip in disgust. 'Who did this and what do you want with her murderer? Are you looking for retribution?' His now customary silence annoyed her. 'Am I going to have to trust you on this one also?' She turned her head towards his, their cheeks almost touched.

His nod was grave.

'You're asking for a lot of trust from me,' her elbow nudged his stomach, hitting brittle leather.

Obviously taking his cue that he'd come too close for comfort, he took up his former position on the sofa and relaxed into it.

'First, Mr Radley, I'm not privy to this kind of information and even looking at these photographs may make me an accessory to a crime. I don't know how you came by these photos and really don't want to. What I do know is that you've taken a lot of risks over the past couple of days and now our criminal investigations department has taken an unhealthy interest in you. That means they'll hound you until they can come up with something to put you out of the way of their inconvenience. There's a serial killer on the loose and a strange man turns up a few days later at the crime scene.'

She lit another cigarette and ignored his disdainful sniff. She also noticed that he no longer watched her with a passionate concentration. The forensic intensity for every word, expression and gesture slowly began to ease and his black lashes began to flutter. 'An officer loses his fingers for reasons even he can't explain and this taciturn stranger has a tendency to disappear from custody suites. Now I'm certain there's a perfectly logical explanation for all of this, but you'll really have to start trusting *me* before I can gain any confidence in you. That means you'll have to start ....'

She couldn't believe he was sleeping. Libby was in full flight whilst delivering her lecture and he was comatose.

'What on earth am I going to do with you?' she had to laugh to herself and wondered why she hadn't phoned the police. Somehow she just knew that backup from the boys in blue was unnecessary and would be more trouble than the price of an emergency phone call to the tax-paying public

It was obvious the sleeping stranger was exhausted. He was probably starving and in severe need of a change of clothes: by the smell of him, he certainly could do with a bath. She dared to move around the table and prodded his shoulder.

His black eyes snapped open, causing her to stumble backwards in shock. His hand struck like a snake and grasped her arm, preventing a painful fall.

'God, you're fast!' Her laugh was nervous. 'Look, why don't you get out of those bits of prehistoric cow, have a shower and I'll get you some less attention-seeking clothing from my partner's former slim-line collection and something nice to eat. We've got a spare room at the end of the corridor that you can take for the night.'

His smile lit up the night sky. 'I need to sleep, but thank you for your kindness.' He stretched out on the cushions and the flame of consciousness snuffed out in an instant.

She cursed the ringing doorbell and, marching across the room, she remembered to place the security chain on the door before opening it just slightly. 'Yes?'

A portly woman stood outside the door in her floral patterned dressing gown and fluffy slippers; an equally proportioned man stood behind her in his paisley pyjamas, trying his best to peer into the flat. 'Sorry, Miss Butler isn't it? We're from upstairs. Is everything all right? We heard screaming.' There was an element of concern inside that harsh Midlands accent. 'We thought a murder was taking place.'

It took Libby a few seconds to gather her senses together. 'Oh, the screaming. Yes, well, it was a huge, fat, hairy spider. I really hate them and they are so prolific at this time of year. Sorry to have woken you.' She smiled as sweetly as she could in apology.

'All that screaming for one little spider?' the woman's tone turned to anger. 'You ought to get a bloody grip on yourself girl. You woke us up for a spider?'

'It took you long enough to answer my call, Mr and Mrs Whatever-your-names-are. It's a good thing I wasn't being murdered. My killer would've had enough time to clean up his tracks, make himself dinner, have a little nap and leave with all the family silverware by the time it took you to get here.' She slammed the door in the outraged faces.

Libby watched her new guest sleeping for more than half an hour before she finally rose from the side of the sofa and found him a soft blanket. During that time she'd pondered on why she felt compelled to help or even trust this enigmatic man who now slept like a baby in her living room. She came to the conclusion that, if he had been a killer, he would have had ample opportunity to chop her up and place her bits into bin bags to distribute around south London by now.

After all careful deliberations with herself, Libby decided that, for reasons best known to him, he was lost, alone, in trouble and was in dire need of some basic necessities in life. He had chosen her because she offered him a hand: something that no one else had done for a while. She was accustomed to waking up in the morning and finding a few waifs and strays in her spare room. Tony was a social worker and often took on voluntary work for a charity that helped kids to rehabilitate from drugs and abuse. Most of them posed no problem: a few of them had been shown the door, one in particular for attempting to cut Tony's thumb off in the middle of the night with a grapefruit knife. Tony was a really good man and Libby was his only sin.

She collapsed on her bed and hauled the duvet over her. The street lights winked at her from beyond the window and the flashing time on the face of the digital clock gently hypnotised her into a deep and restful sleep.

—

She awoke slowly to a familiar face.

'Tea?'

Tony placed the cup down on the bedside table and kissed her forehead.

'What's the time?' The response was automated, she had no idea where she was.

'Half eleven. You really needed that sleep,' he laughed, picking a few books up off the floor.

Libby's eyes snapped open. 'Is he still here?'

Tony laughed again, his grey eyes shining. 'Who?'

'Gabriel'

'Is he the detainee you told me about from the station?'

'He's the one.' She sipped at her mug of tea, watching Tony's reactions. 'Is he still on the sofa?'

Tony shook his head with a curious expression.

'Then he's either in the spare room or he's left.'

She sat up and whimpered from the pain in her feet. 'It's a long story, but the hall light exploded last night and I cut my feet on the glass.' She sat on the end of the bed and examined the cuts.

'Yeah, the carpet was covered in blood this morning when I got in. It creeped me out, but I traced your footsteps back to where you were sleeping and pulled a few pieces of glass out of your soles. Nothing went very deep, so I don't think you'll scar.'

She nodded, silently puzzled by his haunted expression. 'He's a bit of an enigma and hasn't learned to trust me yet, but he seems like a nice enough guy.' She took a sip of her tea before tumbling out of bed.

'Are you all right? I mean really all right?' It was an odd question.

She reached into the bottom of the wardrobe to pick up her jeans. They hadn't been washed in three days, but they were the cleanest piece of clothing she had. She answered his question with a distracted nod. Her thoughts turned to the failure in the electricity supply at the police station and then in her own flat last night. The only common factor being the man who was present at both premises at the material times.

'Some people are sensitive to things like radio waves, tiny amounts of radiation or even certain frequencies. I think Gabriel is one of those people. I think you'll like him. You love lost causes.' Libby pretended to busy herself with a brush in front of the mirror, masking her interest by concealing her reflection with a cascade of light, brown hair.

Tony sat down on the end of the bed and took a quick look around the room, as if silent listeners hid in the corners. 'Nicole's coming over by the way.'

'What?' Libby's voice rose an octave.

'It's just a social visit.'

'She only comes here when she wants something.'

'She's just coming for coffee. Anyway, she'll be able to tell if your Gabriel's a psycho or not.'

'I can answer that question and I don't even have an O-Level in Biology.'

He moved behind her and, placing his reassuring hands on her shoulders, forced her to look at their reflections in the mirror. 'How do you know he's not dangerous?'

'Instinct,' she shrugged his hands away and snapped up the bottle of mascara. 'Gut feelings and dealing with murderers and rapists all day.'

'Libby, sweetheart, I'm sure I'll like him too, but you can't judge a person you barely know on natural impulse alone.'

'I slept with you on the first date, didn't I? You were a stranger that I'd just picked up in a bar.'

'That was different,' his voice softened in sweet remembrance.

'And so's this,' hers hardened in obstinacy. 'In any case, he was in police custody the night Rachael Leverne's body turned up. He's not Dracula and the police know this. They want him for something else, but they're not saying what and I won't let them have him with no good reason. He needs a friend, not a shrink.'

'If he's still here, Nicole could speak to him.'

'He'll see through her and take off. I really don't want him to do that. I want to help him and so should you.'

Tony moved to the window and pulled the blinds back with his fingers. The red Ferrari swerved into a wide parking slot, taking half the kerb with it. 'I'm trying to help. You obviously haven't read the papers today.'

Libby hauled a huge blob of black mascara from her eyelash and wiped it on her jeans. 'And?'

Tony watched as the long legs rolled out of the Ferrari. 'The body of that police woman was found last night. Well, parts of it anyway. Wasn't she on duty when you were called out to the station?'

—

'New car? I like it.' The woman opened the door and sat in the passenger seat. Her smile would've made the Mona Lisa's appear hysterical in comparison.

'You have exquisite taste then.' There was a hint of nervousness in his voice.

'Does it work?'

'She has a twelve-cylinder, six-litre twin-turbocharged engine. She does nought to sixty in just four point eight seconds with a top speed of a hundred and ninety-five miles per hour. Of course she works.'

'I'm bored already. Are they for me?' She indicated with a slight nod of her head to the large bouquet of flowers sitting on the back seat, their heady summer scent invading the car's luxurious interior.

Lars Andersson chuckled to himself and offered her a cigarette. She shook her head and watched the people enjoying their Sunday afternoon on Hampstead Heath while he patted the steering wheel and opened the window wide.

'I thought you liked cars. What do you ride these days, a bike?'

He lit up a cigarette, aware of the danger he was in but assured that the woman who was affectionately named after a popular horror story would not try anything in a public place – in any case, he'd met her on a number of occasions and found her nothing less than cordial.

'You can't get away fast enough on a bicycle.'

Not for the first time, Lars couldn't quite believe that this lean woman with the pronounced Russian accent; the beautiful green eyes; the scruffy clothes; and the tumbling mahogany curls was the infamous Rose Red. If he hadn't borne witness to the aftermath of her particular 'skills' on a few occasions, he would've taken her for a student or nurse. 'What do you drive these days?'

'A red car.'

'Is that all?'

'It has a sixteen-cylinder, one thousand and one horse power, eight-litre V8 engine. It does nought to sixty-two in two point five seconds and has a top speed of two hundred and two miles an hour.'

'You're paid too much.'

'I'm worth it.'

'Why did you attack Myers?'

'He was rude.'

He reached over to the back passenger seat and handed her the flowers. 'Mr Weller sends his regards. There's an MK23 newly out of its box in there for you – a present from the boss. You have the address?'

'Your flowers are as cliché as your boss.' She laughed at his shrug. 'If I wanted a toy, I would've asked for a doll.' She pulled the gun out of the flowers and dropped it into the footwell. 'I've been staking the place out for three days now.'

'How many guns?'

'Six, sometimes eight, the place isn't exactly a fortress but it's reasonably well-guarded and nothing I can't handle. Why are we having this meeting?'

She finally got to the point and Lars rather suspected all the pleasantries that just passed between them were for her benefit: she was staking him out also.

'He's due to be moved to another safe house so you'll have to go in soon or not at all.'

She sat for a while, silently pondering his words.

'The price has gone up.'

Lars' grin split his face in two. 'We knew you'd say that. That's why we're offering double for the manuscript as well.'

'That wasn't the deal.'

The peril in those green eyes would've killed him in an instant had it been fired through a barrel and Lars wished he wasn't sitting so close to her. His colleague was still undergoing treatment for his smashed larynx and it was unlikely he would ever speak normally again. He received thirteen stitches to his head. Rose Red was not the kind of woman who tolerated weakness, however: 'Do you want the job or not?'

She turned her head slowly to face him, her eyes sparking with danger. 'Tell your boss that the price has just doubled again, to be paid in full when I deliver the goods. I'll bring him to you alive. That way, you can negotiate the whereabouts of the manuscript. You'll be surprised how quickly a man will squeal when his testicles are dangling from the edge of a blade.'

Lars pressed his knees together unconsciously. 'He's no good to us alive.'

'This is a quick in-and-out job. I won't have the time or inclination to search the house for his stupid book. Let him bargain for his life with it.'

His arms snatched protectively across his large torso when her hand shot off her lap.

'Deal?' She looked amused as she held her hand out to seal the bargain formally. He hesitated for a brief second before snatching her fingers and wagging them. 'I'll bring your package as arranged in exchange for the cash. Don't let me down.'

—

Rose Red slammed the door behind her and watched the gleaming Bentley power away.

'идиот!'

She walked towards her blue Vauxhall Corsa. Carefully placing the heavy spray of flowers in the boot, she flipped the keys in her hand and decided not to drive away yet. The day was warm, the park painted with the vibrant hues of summer. In her over-sized hand-knitted jumper, black jeans and knee-length leather boots, she strolled around the grounds for a while, joining the small groups of insignificant souls milling in the early morning sunshine, enjoying the city's great outdoors in blissful domesticity.

Rose Red liked times like this: times when she could merge into the normality of life and watch the world from the ground. Yet, today she felt there was something different in the air. Change was coming. She felt it tickling her spine and she shivered, despite the early warmth of summer. It was a long time before she returned to her top floor flat in Pimlico where her anonymity was shadowed only by the emptiness of her existence.

'OH, MY GOD! OFFICER GLOVER'S DEAD?'

'Worse than that. They think Dracula got her.'

Libby could only stare at his back as Tony nonchalantly stared out the window. 'That's terrible.'

'She seemed like a nice woman,' he hesitated remembering Libby's irrational irreverence for members of the force, 'for a copper'.

'We may've been the last people to see her alive.'

Tony turned from the window. 'Anyone who was at the station that night could've. Even Gabriel.'

'Oh, come on Tony, you don't believe Gabriel had anything to do with her murder.' She slammed her make-up brush down on the dressing table and, with a less confident expression, spun around to face him but the door buzzer ended the conversation. 'Did you phone the police?'

'I told you, I phoned Nicole.'

She snatched up her mobile that sat discarded on the bedside table.

They left the room together, Libby walking into the kitchen, while Tony answered the door.

Nicole Blais was Maurice's only daughter – his love child from a Martinique waitress – who inherited her father's love for all things expensive as well as his insatiable taste for men.

Built like a tigress with a vicious bite to match, Nicole had just left her third husband, together with his bank balance, mauled and bleeding red.

The imposing figure stood in the doorway, her shadow blotting the light from the window, her manicured fingers barely touching her hips, in a pink Versace dress with a pair of black Sergio Rossi shoes with velvet bows: hardly what anyone would expect from a psychiatric specialist.

'How are you, Libby?' Nicole demanded in her husky French accent.

'Can I get you a coffee?' Libby lit a cigarette and took a long haul on it.

'Are you still indulging in that filthy habit?' Nicole waved her hand in front of her face, a purely scornful gesture.

'It's a lot cleaner than some of your habits I hear. Now do you want a coffee or not?'

Nicole shook her head and turned up her nose. 'I don't take artificial stimulants any more. Do you have any rooibos?'

'Sorry, I'm fresh out of pretentious alternative herbal infusions. What about a glass of tap water?'

'Is it filtered?'

'Of course, I strained it through my knickers earlier this morning.'

'How are you Libby?' Nicole lowered herself into the seat of the sofa, crossed her legs and placed her hands on her knees. This was a bad sign. Libby knew her well enough to realise her responses were now being psycho-analysed by a professional.

'We're not in your surgery now.' She didn't like being the object of the psychiatrist's scrutiny, certainly not in her own front room. In fact, although she loved Maurice like a father, Libby didn't trust his daughter much and resented her weekly sessions with her: the empty condescending words that badly concealed her disdain; and that burlesque mask of pity and understanding she wore to hide her mockery.

'Are you still having problems sleeping?'

'Not at all. It's the getting to sleep bit that I'm having problems with.'

Libby heard a door open behind her. 'Did you sleep OK?'

Nicole's expression changed from one of feigned concern to genuine shock.

Libby bit the humour from her lip. Gabriel padded softly towards the sofa. She never knew a person could look so good in a pair of faded 501s and simple black t-shirt. He moved across the floor like a cautious wolf eyeing its prey in order to assess its vulnerabilities.

'Hi Gabriel, this is Nicole.'

Libby squealed in outrage as he silently snatched the cigarette from her fingers and stubbed it out in the ashtray before sitting down on the arm of her chair, watching Nicole with predatory eyes. Libby sat up straighter and decided to forgive him for his presumptuousness.

Nicole, taken aback by his obvious hostility, squirmed deeper into the sofa cushions.

'Hello Gabriel. Pleased to meet you.' It was a polite beginning.

He acknowledged her cordiality with a courteous nod. 'Enchanté, madmoiselle.'

'Tu parles français?' Libby tugged at his t-shirt.

'Obviously.'

'My name is Nicole Blais. I am a friend of the family.'

He hesitated for a moment, as if concentrating on his next response. 'And whose state of mental health are you here to determine, Miss Blais?'

Tony almost dropped the tray of coffee and biscuits as he walked into the room. 'She's here on a social visit. Be nice.'

Gabriel locked his dead-eyed gaze on Tony. 'You are not telling the truth.'

Averting all eye contact, Tony shifted the magazines across the coffee table with his foot and placed the tray down in the space. 'We've never even met and you're telling me I'm a liar?'

Gabriel suddenly put his hands over his ears as if to fend off a loud noise. He glared at the offending mobile phone in Libby's hand as her thumbs moved across the keypad with frantic speed. Noticing his obvious discomfort, she slapped it into his hand. He slipped it into his back pocket.

'All right,' Nicole broke the mental siege and, to Libby's utter surprise, turned to her. 'We're worried about you, Libby. Is this a good time to talk?'

Libby, taking a perverse comfort from the apparent protection of a complete stranger, felt powerful in comparison to her squirming partner. 'You can talk now.'

'Sweetheart, don't take this the wrong way. I asked Nicole to come here because I'm worried about you.' Tony knelt down on the other side of the chair and took her hand. 'You've been crying a lot lately. You can't sleep; you've been smoking more and your alcohol intake has quadrupled over the past few months. Now, Nicole ... no, we ... know you're suffering from some sort of stress disorder and we want to help you through it, if you'll let us.'

Tony's speech was delivered with such caring emotion that Libby felt her bottom lip trembling in self pity. It took but a few seconds to get over it before the anger kicked in. 'Is this a bloody psychological ambush? How dare ...'

'The woman is not suffering from insanity, she is riddled with guilt. Her fears are not conceived through mental trauma but through a series of self-indulgent deceptions that have returned to bite her.'

Libby's eyes widened to plates. Although it was impossible to believe, she realised the stranger whom she'd given shelter to for only one night, was about to blurt out her most hidden secrets. Either he was clairvoyant or he was an exceptionally astute man. She had to think quickly. 'I'm not going to sit here and let you deconstruct my brain in my own house.' She stood up abruptly, knocking her shin against the coffee table and snatching up her bag. 'Tony, you need to get some sleep and Nicole needs to leave. I'm going to take our guest here for lunch and quiz him. Then we're going shopping for clothes.' She grabbed Gabriel by the arm and hauled him towards the front door, leaving Tony and Nicole to second guess why she'd left her house without her jacket and in her slippers.

—

Detective Chief Inspector Andrew Prendergast examined the bottom of the bottle of single malt, the concern in his eyes glazed with the effects of its former contents. Snatching a few hours off work to appease his lonely wife, he sat in his home at the desk of his small study, copies of unsolved case notes scattered across the room like fallen leaves after an autumn storm.

In his hands, still trembling from the aftermath of one too many Glenmorangies the previous night, the detective held the forensic report of Suzanne Glover and another from the coroner.

He'd been poring over both all morning. Cause of death: massive blood loss; mechanism of death: incised laceration to the neck; manner of death: murder. Other than what was evident from the state of the corpse, there was little left to go on save that the pattern was similar to that of Dracula's familiar signature: similar, but not exactly the same.

Andy Prendergast let out a deep, heavy breath. A policewoman, one of their own, had joined the increasing pile of bodies and all eyes in the force were now on him to catch this elusive beast and bring him to justice. Only it would've been easier to find that proverbial needle amidst a barn-full of hay bales.

Like the other five murders, the cause of death was a wound to the neck by a sharp blade, possibly a scalpel. The wounds varied in shape and size and forensics believed, in all but one of the cases, that the murderer had attempted to bleed his victims to death by tapping into the subclavian or carotid arteries in the neck with varying degrees of success. The results were always the same, however, and the victim was exsanguinated, probably while still alive. Like the other women, bar one, the policewoman's body had been stripped, drained of blood, soaked in a bath of diluted household bleach and dismembered before being dumped in a spot probably far away from the murder scene.

Officer Glover, however, had put up a fight. This was obvious from the deep cuts to her hands and forearms; the bruising to her knuckles; and the lacerations to her throat. The murderer was careful to remove all of the victim's nails from her hands and feet and, from the gashes on her cheeks and inside and around her mouth, had probably cut out her tongue while she was still screaming.

With no history, no trace evidence and no scene to go by, the diagnostic triangle was difficult, if not impossible, to complete.

He spread out the other five victims' profiles across the desk. They were scant. The women, all aged between twenty-one and fifty-five had gone missing from Balham, Brixton, Forest Hill and Camberwell, with one unknown. Their bodily parts, cleaned of all traces of evidence, had been recovered in wheelie bins, behind bushes and in car parks in various locations far from the areas they had been snatched, all just out of sight of hundreds of CCTV cameras. The women had been Sarah Hill, aged thirty, a legal secretary; Trinity Jimiciw, twenty-one, art student; Dr Susmita Salvarajah, aged fifty-five, general practitioner; thirty-two-year-old Rachael Leverne, a social worker and practising Jewess; and a young blonde woman who, as yet, had not been identified.

All came from different racial, cultural and religious backgrounds, led differing lifestyles and were different shades, shapes and sizes. The only thing they all had in common was their gender, the nature of their deaths and the subsequent disposal of their bodies, apart from one whose body was found on Peckham Rye in close proximity to her head.

Two of the victims were snatched from the streets; one from a train and one from her own home, all during different parts of the day and night. One they had no details of at all. There was no apparent pattern, despite the killer's obvious comfort zone in south east London, and psychologists hoping to piece together an inductive or deductive profile had so far come up with files as blank as their expressions. No witnesses to any of the incidents had ever come forward, despite arduous house to house inquiries; an intensive forensic sweep of the crime scenes; copious appeals for witnesses through posters and the press; and a slot on Crimewatch.

DCI Prendergast didn't enjoy hunting shadows and, the more he appeared to shed some light, the darker the night became.

—

'What the hell do you think you're playing at?' Libby slammed two large glasses of red wine down on the table and hid her scorn behind a fake leather-bound menu that was now, like her arm, covered in fresh splashes of wine. She shoved another in his hand.

She had bundled her charge into the car and sped off, leaving four tyre marks smoking on the tarmac.

They'd endured the hour-long journey in silence: she preoccupied by the storm she'd just averted; while he watched the turbulent urban scenery turning into leafy hedges and peaceful green field from the passenger seat. She stopped at a family-friendly pub, just off the main road to Tonbridge.

Although quintessentially English and relatively busy, no one noticed two more patrons, even though one of them wore a pair of fluffy pink slippers. She hadn't exactly planned it this way, but this was an opportune moment to give Carl a taste of his own medicine. Carl lived nearby in Tonbridge Wells with his dutiful, gullible wife and two spoiled children.

Gabriel's laughter kicked off the conversation. 'You make sport out of gravity in order to direct the finger of blame towards those who do not necessarily deserve it.'

'I don't know what you're talking about.' She pretended to read the menu and gulped at her wine. 'What do you want to eat?'

'Do not change the subject.'

'Then talk to me in a language I'll understand.'

He studied her closely and took a small sip from his glass. 'You choose.'

'What do you like? Carnivore? Veggie?'

He sat back in the ancient wooden bench and let out a deep, heavy breath. 'I eat what I can. If I am prepared to harvest it or kill it myself, then I will eat it.'

Libby turned her eyes up to the oak beamed ceiling. 'So you're a carnivore with a conscience?' He studied her face before shaking his head. 'Vegetarian? Vegan? No, don't tell me, you're one of those fruit-cake-tarians who only eat bruised and worm-ridden things that've fallen off a tree.'

'What do you like to eat, Libby Butler?'

'Steak,' she needed little prompting, 'a thick wedge of juicy red cow flesh, still quivering on the plate, with a generous dab of stilton butter melting over the top of it. Mmmm, yummy!'

'Even though you are well aware of how it is killed and butchered in your vile abattoirs?'

'I don't really give it much thought.' She lied and knew he could see right through her. 'We who work most of the day and evening, don't have time to hunt down and kill our own dinner.'

'Nor worry about its suffering.'

She leaned forward on the table. 'Look, Gabriel, if I'm hungry enough, I don't care where it comes from; what kind of life it has enjoyed; or what kind of death it's suffered. Food is food, whether it bleeds or photosynthesises, and I would kill or chop down the damn thing myself if I was starving.'

'It is just a pity that you carry a similar attitude throughout your wretched, self-indulgent existence.' His black eyes searched her face for defiance, but found only disgrace. He appeared to relent immediately. 'Then you should have your lump of cow ....'

Libby drained her glass. 'Do you like to kill things, Gabriel?'

He smiled, that strange, enigmatic smile she had dreamed about lately. 'Sometimes killing is a necessary evil. Where I come from, one must kill to survive. This world, however, takes life for sport; for power; and for gluttony. You live in a strange place, Libby Butler. You are an anomalous, duplicitous race of man that has somehow buried humanity behind artificial comfort and short-lived prosperity.'

'Wow, that's deep,' she thumped the menu on the table and glared at him, 'and quite insulting.'

'I am attempting to understand you.' He met her glower with mellow eyes.

'Where do you come from Gabriel?'

'A better place than this.'

'You are so weird!'

'Are you ready to order?'

'What?' She'd forgotten where she was as the young waitress loomed at the end of the table with her pen poised over the pad. Libby snatched the menu up again and peered over it. 'Do you want a starter?'

The answer came from a simple shrug.

'We'll have the steak Diane thanks.' She shot him a triumphant sneer. 'Just bring Diane to the table with a gun, a bucket and a load of newspapers to soak up the blood and my friend here will prepare her for the plate himself.'

'Sorry?' The waitress, a mere girl, didn't quite believe she had heard properly. She cast the man at the table a nervous glance before blushing crimson and giggling.

'Just bring us some fish.'

'So you don't want the steak?' She waited for a response but none came. She scribbled out her entry on the pad. 'We have stuffed trout, pan fried Dover sole, monkfish kebabs,' she rolled her eyes to the ceiling as she tried to remember the rest, 'no, sorry, the sole's off. We've got baked or battered cod. Oh, yeah, turbot in tarragon butter is on the specials. I think that's it, or is that one on the dinner menu?'

'That will be fine.'

Libby laughed out loud as the waitress looked once again to her for some logic to the conversation. 'You heard the man, bring it all, but not the cod. It's an endangered species. Is the turbot farmed?'

The girl shrugged.

'No turbot then. Do you serve jellyfish? I think they're the only marine species that don't appear to be endangered. Oh, forget the whole thing and bring me a small selection of everything you have with gills.'

'Chips or boiled potatoes?'

'Neither, I'm on a diet. Can I have another red wine, please?' Libby sat back in her chair for a while and watched him as he examined the low oak rafters of the old building and the small lead-framed windows. She turned her mind back to their first meeting, trying to remember the conversation. She knew so little of him, but he appeared to know much about her. 'How do you do it?'

His penetrating eyes met hers and threatened to shake out her soul. 'It is instinctive.'

'You can read minds for real or are you just good at drawing on observations and making an accurate, educated guess?'

'Yes. Will you take me back to the church after we're finished here?'

'What church?' Libby nodded her thanks to the waitress who brought another drink to the table.

'The one where I first met the policemen?'

'You mean St Paul's?'

He nodded.

'Why?'

'I left something there.'

'I will if you answer my question.'

'Truth for truth?' He laughed at her obstinate nod. 'All right, Miss Butler…'

'Libby.'

'All right, Libby. You have one question.'

'How do you do it?'

'I am either what your psychologists would call telepathic

THE SLEEPING WARRIOR

and psychokinetic or I am simply very intuitive.'

'Wow! Can you also influence the minds of others?'

That non-committal shrug again. 'That is two questions.'

'Your answer was ambiguous.'

'As was your question.'

The young waitress returned to the table with cutlery, neatly folded in a napkin, a basket of bread and a selection of condiment sachets stuffed into a beer mug. She leaned over Gabriel and lingered there for a while, her cheeks aflame.

'Then answer this.' Libby closed her eyes and mentally came up with the first question she could think of. It came and she bit her tongue. There was no way she was going to ask him what colour knickers she was wearing. Was she?

He blinked at her slowly in derision. 'I cannot. There is too much interference in the air.'

'You mean like electro-magnetic charges?'

He nodded. 'Perhaps. Whatever it is called, there is too much noise around me and I cannot concentrate.'

'You can hear electricity?'

'It is like a loud hum. Your mobile phone makes an exceptionally loud noise as did the computers in the police station. I also find, however, that, as these noises disrupt my thought, then so am I able to interrupt their continuity.'

'My God, you can manipulate matter and energy? So it was you who blew the circuits in the police station and in my flat? That's incredible.'

They sat in silence for long moments, she contemplating her next questions, while he looked out of the window, pondering a life far beyond the horizon.

'I have a question.'

'Then I have one answer.' She was beginning to warm to this game.

'Why is an intelligent, witty, beautiful woman like you so angry? What incidences in your past have caused you to become so scornful of life?'

'That's two questions.' She echoed his rules.

'But there is only one answer.'

'Christ! I hope you're starving.' She gasped aloud as the food began to arrive and completely forgot her part of the bargain. Unable to accommodate all the dishes on the small table, the waitress was forced to pull another over and lay the food out on it buffet style. There was barely enough room for their two plates. The mixture of sweet fishy smells flowing from the steaming plates, however, had made her quite hungry.

'This is going to cost a fortune.'

'No doubt.' He watched her with the intensity of a lion focused on its prey as she spooned some of the food onto her plate and unwrapped her knife and fork from the napkin. He mimicked her every movement. 'If I am going to remain here for a while I will need to find employment.'

Libby swallowed her mouthful of monkfish before replying. 'Of course. Money makes the world go round and also puts food on your plate when I'm not going round to pay the bills. What can you do?'

'I can fight.'

'You don't look like a bare knuckle boxer to me.' She had noticed Gabriel was built like a fitness instructor. His forearms, although fairly lean by twenty-first century fast-food-loving standards, rippled with taut muscle and were criss-crossed with thin, silver scars. 'You need to be a British subject to serve in Her Majesty's forces and a national insurance number to work anywhere in this country. I don't believe you hold so much as a library card to prove your identity. Are you a member of some overseas special force?'

'That is close.'

'Then why's your government not paying you for your services?'

He averted his gaze and ate his food in silence, his thoughts buried too deep for her to decipher. She allowed him the privacy, her own mind running away into fantasy as to what he could possibly not be telling her. She decided to change the subject on a question that had been burning on her lips all day. 'This killer you're looking for. Do you know him?'

'Probably.'

'How do you know he's not a she?'

'I am not so young that I cannot tell the difference between male and female.'

'So you do know him.' Her expression couldn't conceal her reservations. 'Why's he killing women?'

Libby had swallowed quite a lot of food already. She was on her third glass of wine and her stomach began to complain by hurling itself against her belt and pushing at it with full force. Her lunch partner, however, had picked at his food and had only taken two sips of his wine. Although she knew he must have been ravenous, he showed remarkable restraint. This was, to her mind, either because he was being overly polite or he didn't care for the chef's culinary talents – or lack of them, as the case may have been.

'I did not say he has killed anyone yet.'

'But he's Dracula.'

'You have obviously misunderstood me. The killer of those women has nothing to do with the relationship between the man that I am looking for and me.'

'Don't you want to at least stop the killer?'

'His criminality is none of my business.'

'Tell that to the ghost of Suzanne Glover. You may've

been the second to last man who saw her the night she was murdered.'

'Who? The female officer at the station? Is she dead?' He was genuinely surprised.

'They found the bits of her yesterday. Tony says it's all over the papers.'

'What, her bits?'

'No, the story, you idiot. Before her, the gory remains of a social worker were found in Streatham.' She felt the hairs on her spine tingling. 'Tony knew her, you know. He said she was a bit of a bitch!' She paused only to empty her wine glass. 'I'm sure she didn't deserve to die such a horrible death though.'

He looked genuinely sorry. 'This Dracula, as you call him, is a coincidental element, thrown into the order of life. His significance will out eventually, it always does.'

'You're talking about the law of total expectation or of probabilities at least?' She believed she was being clever.

'Unlike you, I do not see life's events as a variable in an equation.'

'How do you see life then?'

The shake of his head was barely discernible. 'You are entering into a discussion on a subject you do not understand. I am not interested in why this man kills women but I will bring him to justice when I catch him, if that is your wish.'

'When *you* catch him?' The food and wine sprayed across the table from Libby's mouth. 'I hope you're not thinking of taking justice into your own hands. I, for one, don't wish to be an accomplice to a murder.'

'I will find him first and deal with him accordingly. You need have nothing to do with the outcome.'

'So, what's this bloke got that's so important?'

'Anna Leah was carrying something that must not fall into

the wrong hands. I therefore must find this killer before my enemy does.'

'What was she carrying?'

'Knowledge can be a perilous burden ...' He left his sentence hanging, the danger in his eyes so apparent that the woman in a grey fleece on the next table choked on the chicken nugget she'd pinched from her toddler's plate.

'What?' Libby snapped at the woman while someone, probably the husband, frantically slapped her back. 'What?' She turned to Gabriel.

'You are better off not knowing. Suffice it to say that I cannot let him have it.'

'Gabriel, you have to confide in someone. Sometimes it's prudent to tell the truth.'

She glanced around her to see no one was listening and her eyes instantly fell upon the desk by the door where a family waited to be served. Although dressed in a pair of ill-fitting jeans, dazzling white trainers, white fluffy socks and a blue Barbour jacket, she recognised Carl immediately.

'Oh, no!' she spun back to face Gabriel, her eyes wild with emotion. Enjoying his company, she had quite forgotten why she had dragged him half way across Kent to eat.

'You were saying?'

'Damn!'

'No, I believe you were lecturing me on trust and confidence. Do not look so surprised, Libby. You manipulated this imminent meeting and now your optimism has turned to anxiety over the unpredictability of its outcome.'

'Oh, shut up and stop talking like that. Have they seen me?' She twiddled a strand of hair around her fingers, barely taking in the sense of his words.

'The children are quarrelling and his gaze is diverted towards the young woman in the tight red bodice. I am afraid, however, that the woman has noticed you and is almost upon you.'

'Hello, Liberty isn't it? How are you?'

Libby bared a row of teeth before turning her head to face the voice. 'Hi, Doris.'

'Deidre.'

'Oh God, sorry. I'm terrible with names.'

'Carl, it's Libby.' The woman hailed him over. To Libby's disgrace, Deidre had already cast her dull grey eyes over the tables and the plates of half demolished food. 'My, are you going to finish all that?' She giggled like a little girl. 'Where's Tony?'

Libby knew quite a lot about Carl's wife and wished she was an unpleasant person and not the warm, bubbly woman everyone liked. 'Tony's sleeping at home. He was on night-shift last night.' Libby hoped the woman hadn't noticed her slippers and tucked them beneath the chair. 'Gabriel, this is the senior partner of my firm, Carl, and his wife Deloris. Carl, Daphne, this is Gabriel.'

Deidre lowered her eyes to the floor.

'Gabriel Radley?' Carl stood up tall and, forgetting where he was and who he was with, looked at Libby with what could only be described as pure horror in his expression. 'What's got into you Libby?'

'Your children are misbehaving.'

'What?' Carl was forced to shake his good senses together at the familiar word 'children' – the clanging bell of rationality for any parent.

'Your children are throwing cutlery at each other.'

Carl and the woman whose name began with D, hurried to tell their children off.

'She is a pleasant, harmless woman and you were discourteous to her.'

She didn't like the serious chastisement in his tone. 'What's it got to do with you?' She took an immediate defensive stance and crossed her arms.

'Nothing. I was merely reminding you of your unnecessary bad manners. She is ultimately the injured party after all.'

'Get out of my head, you snooping bastard!'

'I do not need to see beneath the cover of your mind, Libby Butler, for you leave its pages open for all the world to read. Despite your aggressive attempts to scheme and manipulate outwith the knowledge of others, your thoughts and deeds are as transparent as the glass in these windows and far less appealing to look through.'

'You don't like me much, do you?'

'I like you enough but I do not approve of your behaviour. It is churlish and self-indulgent.'

'I can say what I want, to whom I want and when I want, so mind your own damn business,' she waggled one finger at him.

He lunged across the table and grabbed her outstretched wrist before she could snatch it back. 'It does not take a psychiatrist to decipher the reasons for your anxieties, Libby. You are a woman fragmented with shame but you deflect this by your disgraceful behaviour towards others and your irrational fear that life conspires against you. You preserve your bad judgment by wallowing in self-pity in the full belief that you are a natural victim. Do you not see that your irrational fears are a direct manifestation of your own abandon? You must see into yourself to find the reasons behind what in life could possibly have caused you to become so bitter.'

'Oh, just piss off! When I want your opinion, I'll ask for it.' She freed her arm from his grasp with a sharp twist.

'You are being unnecessarily belligerent. I am not your enemy.'

'Then act like a friend and keep your mouth shut.' She drained his glass and looked away from him. 'Unless, of course, you really can read my mind.'

'They are grey?'

'What are?'

'Your undergarments.'

'They're bloody white, you ignoramus!'

'That's not what I see.'

The silence formed a thick wedge between them. She feigned interest in the various paintings and prints dotted around the walls, while he studied her face with an enigmatic smile.

Libby, smarting from his condemnation and embarrassed she hadn't used bleach in her last white wash, refused to feel bad about the incident. Carl, Deidre and badly-behaved children had taken a table on the opposite side of the room.

Of course, Gabriel was absolutely correct once more: she had been expecting to see the Bottomleys at the restaurant. She overheard Sarah make the booking earlier in the week and decided that morning, when she was driving away from Tony, to be half-way through her meal with a gorgeous stranger before Carl arrived.

'I need a pee.'

She didn't have to wait long outside the toilets at the bottom of the narrow stairs before Carl turned up. 'Why are you doing this?' he hissed angrily.

'Having lunch because I was hungry?' She feigned surprise. 'I was here first Carl.'

'Not that. I mean ... I've been trying to get hold of you.' He turned away from her and pretended to study a print of a nineteenth century rural scene on the wall as a woman ambled out of the Ladies rubbing her damp hands together.

'I take it you're not happy about Gabriel.' Her smile was coy.

'He's an interesting lunch companion. Unlike you, he doesn't whine while I dine.'

He grabbed her arm in earnest. 'Libby for God's sake, pull yourself together. What's the matter with you?'

'He's also dazzling, elegant, articulate, beautifully mannered, much smarter and considerably younger than you.' She prized his fingers off her arm. 'Oh, and absolutely gorgeous, too.'

'Those detectives came to the office on Friday night and they told me things, incredible things that even they can't believe. What's going on Libby? There's no mugshot, no CCTV footage nor any other recorded evidence to suggest Radley was ever detained or even exists.'

'What do you mean?'

'He's just not there.'

Libby could have laughed in his face, but chose to look perplexed instead. Gabriel had already told her his presence interferes with energy and so it was not unlikely that digital equipment, such as a CCTV camera, wouldn't record properly. It was a perfectly logical scientific explanation. 'So the officers played out a bogus arrest or are you truly expecting me to believe Gabriel Radley is some kind of spectral being?'

Carl slapped his forehead with his palm: a familiar gesture when he was losing an argument. 'This is too weird.'

'The only monster in this restaurant, Carl, is you and we all know that evidence can become contaminated in incompetent hands and I for one have still to meet a capable copper. What're you trying to say?'

'I don't know Libby, but you have to go to the police. Someone was after you on the Rye that night and it's possible you're being stalked. You may be in terrible danger.' He placed his hands on her shoulders and squeezed.

'Don't be stupid, Carl.' She shook her head at him in

derision. 'God, you are really low, aren't you? Not content with getting off with the loathsome Selina behind my back, you're now trying to mess with my head and my private life. Gabriel is not a ghost, not an alien and certainly not a murderer.'

'How do you know?' He dropped his hands from her shoulders and stood back from her.

At last, she saw jealousy in his eyes and revelled in its presence. Even though she was about to intentionally pervert the course of justice, she couldn't help herself. 'The night Officer Glover disappeared, he was with me.'

'What?' He could hardly contain his misery.

'Until late in the morning.'

'In your bed?'

'In quite a few places, actually.' She folded her arms and leaned against the wall.

'Does Tony know?' His face was one of utter desolation.

'He was on lates that night and, no, he doesn't and you're not going to tell him, are you?' The lie that rolled off her tongue so easily tasted of victory. It was the sweetest of flavours.

'Libby please, Selina was a stupid mistake. I'm so sorry. I really love you. We have to talk. You need help and it may be all my fault. Please forgive me.'

Seeing him in such pain, she wanted to do just that. The urge to fling her arms around him and comfort him was overwhelming as she witnessed an open display of emotion – a gesture purely alien to Carl. She couldn't wipe his secret clinch with Selina out of her memory, however, and gritted her teeth. 'I need to think carefully about all this, Carl. I don't believe we're going anywhere in this relationship. Your wife's difficult enough to cope with, but now I have my work colleague to deal with too. I can't take much more.'

'I told you, Selina is nothing to me. I'll have her transferred to our Kent office if you want.' He clutched her hand tightly.

'Along with your wife?'

He hung his head. 'I can't do that just yet, Libby. It's the kids.'

She snatched her hand from his. 'Then it's over. If I can deal with it, then so can you.'

'Can we at least talk about it?'

'Ask me again in a few months.'

'Don't do this, please.' There were actual tears in his eyes.

'I already have.' She patted his cheek and kicked open the door to the Ladies, the triumph frozen to her smile.

CHAPTER *five*

TRAVELLING ALONG THE NORTHBOUND LANE of Blackfriars Bridge inside a glaring mist of multi-coloured neon, Libby's thoughts turned to Gary Weller and how much she loathed him. She would tell Carl on Monday she no longer felt able to continue on the Saint's personal elite team of super-lawyers and clear some free space in her already over-burdened conscience.

She hit the brake sharply as a police car passed her on the opposite carriageway, the speedometer read forty-two miles per hour and she hoped the patrol officers had been too busy chasing robbers to notice her. Gabriel sat in the front passenger seat, silently taking in the night scene around him. The clock on the dashboard flashed '20.34'.

After her conversation with Carl, she'd finished lunch quickly, dragged Gabriel around the shops in Bromley for clothes and footwear before heading off to St Paul's as she promised.

They argued about dress: she preferring to see him in bikers' leathers and silk; while he preferred Gortex and walking boots. She'd tried to bully him by reminding him that battledress went out of fashion in the mid fourteen hundreds before resorting to the low tactic of who was picking up the tab. He'd simply walked out of the shop and sat in the car.

In the end, she'd been the one to apologise, blaming her churlishness on the childhood trauma of never having owned a

Ken to keep her Barbie doll company. He had no idea what she was talking about.

'Who's Gary Weller?'

Libby's foot involuntarily hit the brake. 'Now, how could you possibly know about him?'

'You have papers in the back of the car. I read some of them.'

'He's a gangland thug and an evil bastard. And you should not be looking at my files, they're confidential.'

'Why are you helping him?'

'It's my job.' She glanced sideways to meet the piercing black eyes. 'He's been a client of the firm for years and is possibly the singular reason why the senior partners of Gore, Matthews and Bottomley enjoy healthy and luxurious lifestyles.'

'Healthy as in spiritually wholesome?' He didn't look convinced.

'No, healthy as in economically sound.' She wanted to talk about it. 'Mr Weller, or the Saint as he's so called, is one of the wealthiest men in the south. He has shares in every crooked deal and a henchman to see his money continues to roll into his bank accounts without impediment, despite the present credit crunch. His corporate interests lie in drugs, money lending, prostitution and human trafficking. His returns are pound notes by the thousands and the misery toll at his hands is the total sum of all his bank accounts plus a few decimal points to the right. His liabilities are his enemies and there is one man who can send him to jail, but he is at present in a safe house under heavy police protection until the trial date, which hasn't been set yet. As you can surmise, Weller is frantic to find him and silence him. He's even offering a cool half million for his head on a spike.'

'What kind of spike?'

She shot him a suspicious side-long glance. 'It's only an expression. Don't get any silly ideas.'

'Who is he?'

'His name is Simon Barry. He was one of Weller's best boys for a while until he found Christianity after visiting an abandoned church near Nunhead, of all places,' she curled her lip at the absurdity of the notion. 'Barry's allegedly been responsible for the murder of sixteen people and the hospitalisation of quite a few more.

He excelled in hurting women and children in particular and took pride in escorting debt-ridden, junkie mothers to the Post Office to snatch their child benefit away from them while kindly offering to push their prams onto a busy road.

Something, however, made him change and he says he's written it all down, the whole truth and nothing but the truth, in his spectacular debut novel entitled 'Saint and Sinner'. The police, as you can imagine, are desperate to get their claws on the manuscript, as are the nationals, and Weller is equally frantic to destroy it along with the author. They say the book is a best-seller and it hasn't even been published yet. If the book exists, there's a lot at stake on both sides.'

'Can the police not help them?' Gabriel looked genuinely annoyed.

'Who? Barry?'

'No, the hapless victims of this criminal organisation.'

'The police have offered Barry a deal: Weller and the manuscript for a seductively reduced sentence. Scotland Yard is also interested in the alleged book as it's supposed to implicate a few high-rankers in the force who're keeping their pensions topped up with the proceeds of criminal activity. As for the poor unfortunates who're gripped by desolation: squealers and their families end up accidentally-on-purpose drowning in their own vomit or floating face down in canals. There's no way out for many vulnerable people, Gabriel, and that's what I can't stand.

In one way, I wish they would bring back the death penalty as I would love to see Weller swinging from a gibbet alongside Simon Barry, but there's also the lawyer in me that wants the challenge of defending the seemingly indefensible. A good outcome would make my career.'

'That is terrible hypocrisy.'

'Is it?'

She stopped the car in front of the cathedral and hauled on the handbrake. The splendid seat of the Bishop of London stood in silence atop the city's highest point. Its magnificent dome, smooth columns and tall towers fashioned from the finest Portland stone, glowed from the darkness like a harvest moon. 'Is this close enough? I'm on a double yellow so you'd better be quick.' She couldn't meet his disapproving gaze again. She had seen it too many times today. Her cheek instinctively moved towards his palm as he turned her head to face him, his touch gentle. 'I suppose you're right, but there's little I can do save wreck my career by badly defending ....'

Libby's sentence finished with a yell of shock as something heavy landed on the roof of the car and blackness fell around her. Her hand spontaneously fumbled for the door lever but she accidentally opened her window instead.

'Stay where you are!' She heard him from somewhere in the distance behind the slamming door and suddenly he was no longer beside her. She banged at the reading light in the ceiling a few times before it came on. She screamed as a painted face appeared at her window and leaned in, the nose almost touching hers.

Cold blue eyes shone from behind sharp features caked in crudely painted red and black stripes and Libby froze with fear. She yelled as another grinning face pressed its mouth against the windscreen and snapped his jaw open and closed. All the teeth had been sharpened to fine points and were blackening around the edges. A hand reached in and grabbed her shoulder, then her breast, squeezing it cruelly, before throwing open the door and dragging her out onto the street by the hair. The cathedral stood in dusk as the sun finally gave up its hold in the sky but there was just enough illumination for her to see what was happening.

Gabriel lay face down on the ground, felled by a heavy baseball bat strike to the back. His assailant, a tall thick-set man wearing loose dark clothing towered above him flicking the bat from one hand to the other with the dexterity of a circus juggler. He placed one boot on Gabriel's head and ground the heel into the side of his face, pressing it into the pavement, before stamping on his back. *'Edo nirrino yo yiande, Torniss Fiorenti, ka ya Vascar, thyrach ya taiche.'*

'Hovir e atile daro?'

She didn't understand the language, but was not surprised Gabriel spoke it. 'Get up, Gabriel.'

The attacker tossed his head to the tawny skies beyond and howled with laughter. 'So, here you are an archangel. It is fitting.' He had a Germanic accent.

'Get up Gabriel, left hand of God, spirit of truth or angel of death?' Dark silhouettes laughed from the shadows. She couldn't count them, but knew instinctively there were many.

Libby fought against the rough hands that held her until a sharp slap to the side of her head sent her brain reeling. The man turned to her, his killer's eyes piercing her soul. 'Is it the end of days, or the beginning of a new revelation?'

'That depends on what religion you follow,' she tried to sound as cordial as possible. Why didn't he get up? 'Please. Leave him alone.'

'Do you know who he is?' The face turned to her now: fanatical eyes blazing from the red and black leer of his face.

THE SLEEPING WARRIOR

He goaded her with a flash of sharpened fangs. 'Do you know what he is?'

He pulled out a handgun from somewhere beneath his robes, the long barrel twinkling in the dim light as he pointed it towards Gabriel's head. 'He can't get up, because I've got my foot on his head. He has no power in this place: the genius loci is trapped behind the cold columns of Christopher Wren's fine architecture. It is I who will decide his fate and yours.'

The laughter echoed around her. 'Why are you doing this?'

'Because I can. Ley lines,' the dark assailant breathed, 'magnets. Differing poles attract and give strength while like poles will push each other apart. He can't draw power from these lines across your good church for they repel him. He's helpless without the right weapon and he doesn't know where that is.'

'What?'

'You believe Christian architects were the first to build great structures of worship and influence?' There was venom in his tone. 'They built them over the top of ancient formations more powerful than their blinded eyes could ever reveal. This cathedral, fashioned by the wealthy, the arrogant and the ambitious to arouse awe and envy in all men, once stood on a great stone circle where the lines of power have collided since time began. The monuments are gone, of course, for stone is only stone and the lives of men are but mere grains of sand in the endless dunes. Are these not your own words En'Iente?' He stamped on Gabriel's head with a studded boot. 'Kill the woman.'

—

'Andy, have you checked the meat?'

DCI Prendergast was snapped from his musings by a yell

from the kitchen. He was astounded to realise it was almost eight o' clock in the evening and he hadn't left his study all day. His mugs lay strewn around the room, all containing various quantities of cold coffee.

He'd put down the files on the victims many hours ago and concentrated all his efforts on the elusive and mysterious Dracula, the Vampire Killer. What does he want? What makes him tick? What are his reasons? Prendergast had taken it upon himself to evaluate the evidence in light of what he'd learned in the force and from books to attempt to put some structure into the killer's identity. He started with the rudiments of the profile.

By the law of averages, there was a high chance the Vampire Killer came from a dysfunctional family background; had sociopathic tendencies; a fixation for fantasy; was white, Caucasian and in his late 20s.

Digging deeper into the scant trail of evidence, it was probable he harboured a profound resentment towards women and had convinced himself he was attacking the basis of his resentment – possibly his mother or a lover who had jilted him. By killing her over and over again, he believed he was satiating a need for power over her that was lacking during his young life.

By stripping his victims naked and dismembering them, was he attempting to dehumanise the outcome of his blood lust or break the source of his hatred apart? By adhering to an obvious signature of draining his victims dry of blood while they were still alive, was he leaving a message? If so, what the hell was he trying to say?

No pattern was associated with the selection of victims and there was no apparent motivation to suggest this man was just a poor, misguided psycho with an Oedipus complex and a reverence for monsters that had got out of hand.

The fact there was no hard evidence on the crime scene

suggested more that this was a calculated, organised killer who took pains to cover his tracks and had no wish to be caught. So what indeed was his motivation? Was he murdering for control, financial gain or purely for sport? Did those women die to satiate an inherent thrill for killing or was he merely trying to make a point?

DCI Prendergast tapped his finger against the thin pile of potential suspects and yawned. 'Bloody shadows!' he spat.

'Andrew, the roast,' his wife Justine popped her head through the door.

'Coming, coming,' he heaved himself from the chair and ambled into the kitchen. He groaned as the irritating, chiming bells ring tone of his mobile sang to him from somewhere inside his pants.

'Prendergast.'

'Sir. Lloyd here. You told me to phone you when something interesting happens.'

'Where're you calling from? The bottom of the Thames?' Prendergast tapped his phone in the hope the buzzing would stop.

'We're parked at a bus stop, just in front of St Paul's. The suspect's sitting in the car. Doesn't look like he's sightseeing.'

'Just keep your distance.' He pulled out the temperature spike from the roast meat resting on the hob. 'Just a bit longer.'

'I've been doing that all day. I could think of better things to do with my Saturdays you know. The cricket for one and I gave up a good game of rugby this afternoon to watch people lunch and shop.'

Prendergast smiled and closed the oven door. 'Detective work can't be interesting all the time. Most of the time, it's a pain in the arse.'

'Huh, so my wife tells me. Bloody hell, the lights have blown.'

'What do you mean?'

'There's been a power cut or something. I can't see a thing. Wait a minute, something's happening. Christ!'

'Lloyd?' Detective Chief Inspector Prendergast was already heading for the door. 'Call for backup and don't do anything stupid,' he yelled down the phone, gripped by the near hysteria in his colleague's voice. 'Sorry love, got to go.'

With one arm in the sleeve of his coat and his mobile wedged between his ear and his neck, he kissed his wife's cheek and snatched up the car keys.

—

Libby shielded her eyes against the glare of flashing blue lights that surrounded her and heard the squealing, distant at first, come to a noisy halt somewhere between her ears. A strong arm helped her to sit up. 'Are you all right, Miss Butler?'

'Am I?' She had no idea what way was up, let alone whether she'd just survived a life-threatening ordeal. She sat on the cold stone pavement amidst a forest of dark blue legs all striding purposefully around her. Her hair, her face, shoulders and back were soaking wet.

'Are you hurt?'

She turned her attention towards the compassionate voice and slowly began to recognise DCI Prendergast kneeling beside her.

'I heard gunshots. Have I been shot?' Dazed and disorientated, Libby felt no emotion and certainly no pain. Remembering the last few moments of consciousness suddenly, she snatched her hand up to her neck. It came away covered in blood. She shrieked and felt her hair. It was soaked in blood also. The smell of iron was sickening.

'The blood isn't yours, love. I've called an ambulance.' There was a quiver in the detective's voice.

'No!' Libby screeched, her senses at last coming together. 'I'm all right, just shaken, that's all. Did you manage to catch anyone?' She wondered where Gabriel had gone and whether in truth he was still alive.

'Anyone? How many were there?'

'There's blood over here, Sir,' one of the many voices barked.

'And here,' yelled another. 'Lots of it. It's got to be arterial.'

'It's all over the place, Sir.'

'Oh, my God, they've killed him.'

'Now, we don't know that for sure.' Prendergast's voice was soothing.

'I want to go home. Please take me home.'

He placed a comforting arm around her shoulder. 'Of course, after you've been given the all-clear by the hospital, I'll get someone to take you home. You've been out cold for a while and you're suffering from shock. You need an ambulance. Is there anyone you want me to call for you?'

She shook her dizzy head before blurting: 'Carl, Carl Bottomley, my boss.' She fumbled for the mobile in her pocket and couldn't remember where she'd put it, 'No, Anthony Ridout, my partner.'

'Would you like me to call both of them, miss?'

DCI Prendergast had suddenly turned into a female officer. She looked tearful.

'No, just Carl, my boss. He's a senior partner in my law firm. No doubt you'll wish to question me.' Her teeth rattled together as a blanket was placed over her shoulders. She noticed the police were now dispersing a large crowd that had gathered around her and she searched the faces in vain for Gabriel. 'They couldn't have killed him,' she whispered in desolation and remembered nothing more.

When Libby awoke again, she lay in a strange bed, in a large, clinical-looking but reasonably well-appointed room. The floral curtains dulled the natural daylight and her blankets were so tight about her body she believed at first she was in a straitjacket. Wriggling free from them, she put her hand up to her temple to rub away the throbbing in her head. She noticed flowers in a vase on the bedside table flanked by a number of get well cards, a copy of the Guardian, an unopened box of chocolates and a hospital welcome pack. She sat up, testing her muscles cautiously. Her throat felt dry.

'All right, I heard you the first time!' A young male nurse in white and blue uniform flapped into the room, his tone and footfall brisk. 'Liberty isn't it?'

'What?'

'Liberty Belle'.

'Yeah, my parents have a sense of humour.'

The nurse turned his eyes up to the ceiling in a playful manner, before lifting her arm up by the wrist. 'You're sitting on the call button.' He gently pulled the handset from under her thigh and shot her a smile of trained tolerance. 'How're you feeling Liberty?'

'Like my pigtails are too tight and I've just swallowed a dead hedgehog. Can I have some water? And it's Libby.'

'Certainly,' he tucked the sheets around her legs. 'What about some food? You must be hungry, you've been asleep for two days now. Poor dear, you've had quite a time of it.' He patted her hand.

She snatched it away with a curl of her lip and wished Carl had organised her stay in an NHS hospital where nurses weren't paid to be patronising. Libby found it difficult to believe she'd been sleeping for such a long time and guessed events of late had exhausted her. 'What's the time?'

'Half two and time for your man to pay his daily visit.'

'He's been here every day?' The news brought a broad smile to her lips.

'Without fail. You must be a very special young woman.' The nurse poured a glass of water from the jug on the table that was hidden behind the vase. He squeezed it into her hand. 'Let's get some light in here for you.' He made towards the curtains.

'No, I've got no make-up on, please leave them shut.'

'As madam wishes,' he made an irreverent bow before winking at her.

She heard him speaking to someone outside the room and Libby sat up straight. Her attempt to comb out the knots in her hair with her fingers was in vain, so she pinched her cheeks and licked her lips instead. She tried her best to maintain the broad smile when the expected Carl turned into the figure of Tony.

'Have you come to take me home?' she could feel the edges of her mouth sagging as he kissed her cheek. There was something different about him she couldn't quite put her finger on.

'Do you want to come home?' It was a strange question.

'Of course, this place must be costing a fortune.'

'Stay as long as you like, he can obviously afford it.' He couldn't look at her.

'Have you seen Gabriel?'

'No, have you?'

Libby bit at her lip. 'No, I think he might be dead.'

'Yeah? Why do you think that then?'

Libby knew Tony well enough to realise he was deeply troubled. 'You are hopeless at hiding things from me, Tony. What's wrong? The bloke had a gun and he fired it. There was blood all over the pavement. Please don't tell me they've found a body.' She tried to swallow the lump in her throat.

'The DNA spilled all over you belonged to some poor bastard ex-medical student who did time for drink driving and knocking over a kid four years ago. They haven't found his body yet and he hasn't turned up at a hospital for treatment, but they say, by the way it was spread around the ground and by its projection, it was probably from the jugular. They think his throat was slit.' He sounded bitter. 'The other victims were a woman in a car who caught a stray bullet in her right eye and two policemen. One was DI Byron, the bloke who came to your office the other day. He took a bullet in his stomach and is fighting for his life in hospital. There was more blood all over the place, the police say it belongs to three or four different people, but they don't know who.'

'What on Earth's going on?' She slumped into the pillows.

'We'll talk about it when you get home and you're better.' There was at least a spike of regret in his angry tone.

'I'm fine, I just need to get out of here.' She waited for a kind response but was answered with silence. She peered down beside the bed to see for herself what was so interesting about his trainers. 'What about a bit of sympathy?'

'You've been getting a lot of that lately, haven't you?' He did look at her this time and she wished he hadn't. His eyes were filled with bitterness and resentment towards her.

'It's not every day someone puts a knife to your throat, you know.'

'Or stabs you in the heart!' He turned away from her, no longer able to meet her gaze.

She froze in panic and for a moment wished someone had slit her throat and relieved her of the unenviable task of facing the inevitable. 'Tony?'

He hissed in anger. 'The police were here last night and so was your boss. They asked us a lot of questions about Gabriel and about you. Carl had to tell them everything.' He spun around to face her. 'Everything.'

'Everything!' she echoed to no one in particular and sank back into her pillows. Faced with a possible charge of perverting the course of justice, Carl had been forced to come clean about their affair. It was out in the open now and he was probably breaking the shattering news to his wife at that moment. Libby should have felt relief had her heart not been so bloated with shame.

'Why, Libby? I thought you loved me.'

'I do.'

'How long has it been going on for?'

'Tony, you don't need to know ....'

'I mean, why all the ruse? The lies? You should've told me about it first, rather than doing it all behind my back. I wouldn't have stopped you. I would've understood.' He didn't allow her to finish her sentence as his thoughts tumbled from his mouth. Although obviously upset, Tony kept a tight rein on his emotions and would not let them drown him before he was finished with what he wanted to say. He stood at the window, his face half-hidden by the curtain, pretending to take in the view below.

'I'm sorry ...'

He hauled the curtain back with such force that it tore from the rail, the hooks pinging across the room. 'So am I. I'm sorry I wasn't good enough to keep you interested; I'm sorry for my faults; and I'm sorry for feeling murderous towards another human being.' He threw the ruined curtain to the carpet. 'All I wish for is that the blood on the pavement does belong to him and someone has blown his bloody brains out!'

Libby was confused. 'You want Gabriel dead?' she mouthed the name carefully.

'He can't hurt me when he's dead.'

'Wait a minute. You believe that Gabriel and I ....?' she felt the familiar panic rising once more.

'You were with him the night that officer disappeared weren't you?'

'No, I was with you.'

'I was on night shift.'

'No you weren't.'

'What?

'You went back to bed after giving me a lift to the station.'

'Bloody hell! So I did.'

'Carl told the police you'd provided the alibi.'

'I lied.'

'So Gabriel and you ....?'

'Of course not, you idiot!'

Tony sat on the comfortable chair beside her bed. She'd never seen a man look so bewildered. He sat in silence for a while, attempting to come to terms with the new twist in his immediate future. She waited uneasily for the next scene to be played out in the farce that was her life. He turned his head towards her, the spark of hope flickering for a moment before being replaced with what could only be described as terrible shame. 'Why have we just had that conversation?' he kept his voice level.

'You jumped to the wrong conclusion. I did tell Carl he was with me because I was sick of his constant questioning.' She suddenly loathed herself and longed to tell him the truth.

'And make me look like a complete sap. Thanks.'

'You can take it,' her smile concealed her profound sadness. 'Why should you care what my stupid boss thinks anyway?' she dared to dig a little further.

'He told the police you said this. Aren't you in trouble for perverting justice or something?'

'That kind of hearsay isn't admissible evidence, Tony. If I tell the police the truth then I can't be perverting the course of justice.'

'Why did you lie to him?'

'Because he's an arrogant bastard as well as a complete control freak. He thinks he knows everything about me – all his staff – but he knows nothing about any of us. I like to keep it that way.' She felt a little better.

Another silence. 'Sorry.'

His angry grey eyes had mellowed and Libby's shame returned unabated. 'Give me a hug and take me home.'

CHAPTER Six

ROSE RED SAT IN A comfortable leather armchair and picked at her wilted salad inside a plastic box. It was Sunday night and the street was quiet. The weekend revellers had settled in for the evening, enjoying the sedate company of friends, families, lovers and casual relations before starting a week of thumping at keyboards, answering phones and putting up with cantankerous clients.

Of course, Rose Red's chosen vocation specialised in difficult customers – only the requirements of the job were vastly dissimilar to those of an office worker: the latter would seek to defuse a tricky situation with a smile, a lie and a show of patience; Rose Red's answer to good public relations was often delivered swiftly from the barrel of a Beretta.

She showered, exchanged her jumper and jeans for a short skirt, sheer black tights, a skimpy red sequined top with matching high heels and snatched a raincoat from the hallstand. Gliding into her car, she disappeared into the London night traffic.

It took her just over an hour to return to Hampstead where hit number thirty-six awaited. Rose Red was not a businesswoman, nor was she prone to attacks of philanthropy in the day to day execution of her work. She kept her distance from a name and face and gave all her victims numbers instead. She preferred to work from a numerical list. That way, she could keep what little conscience she had left clear.

She stood in a street in a quiet residential area. The large front gardens were fringed with trees and tall foliage to deter the prying eyes of curious neighbours. It was a good choice for a safe house, but also a perfect spot for a surprise visit. The two plain clothes officers were easy to spot and easier to kill in the dark, empty street. One in the car died of a single gunshot wound to his head and two through the heart, while the one in the street succumbed to a stiletto blade through his right ear, with an exit wound through his left.

Rose Red wiped the blood from her knife on the man's trouser leg before opening the gate and walking towards the front door where two tall men stood smoking and, after swiftly getting over their surprise, watched her teeter towards them. 'I'm here!' She shouted with a small giggle and stumbled in her four-inch heels.

'That's nice for you, miss. Now you've made it, you can just turn around and piss off back home again. This is private property.' The men laughed together, neither quite knowing whether to reach for their guns or call the drunk woman a taxi.

'But I brought the champagne!' She swiped her hand through her long hair and waggled the bottle of Crystal in her hand. 'I was invited to Sam's party and you are being very bad boys.'

'Isn't it a bit late for a party, miss?' One of them peered into the darkness, looking for his colleagues in the street while the other fumbled with his walkie-talkie.

She laughed. 'You obviously don't know Sam.'

'What's the address?' Although nervous, chivalry was not all dead.

She reached into her bag. 'I have it here.'

'Are you Polish?'

The gun fired twice, the noise dulled to a dim thunk, before the men's faces could even register surprise.

'Polish? How dare you!' She stepped through the front door and threw off her shoes as if she'd been invited to dance. Her sharp senses swept across the hallway. She skipped over the fallen bodies, careful not to step in the blood. Before she even rounded the door, her loyal Beretta fired off another three rounds through the long, black silencer and felled the man and a woman who'd been playing cards in the sitting room. Shifting from room to room like a silent shadow, she made towards the stairs. Changing the magazine with a flick of her hand, she shot a man through the eye as he peered over the balcony. He tumbled over the banisters, taking the wooden railings with him and crashed to the soft carpet below.

Rose Red hesitated at the top of the stairs, listening for movement: throwing her senses into the night to seek out any life that lurked behind the walls.

She heard the hiss of water. She kicked open the bedroom door with her heel and, with legs splayed out, pointed her gun inside the room. A startled woman leaped out from behind a copy of The Sun and fumbled for her gun. Rose Red shook her head and glided into the room, her movement light and elegant. 'I don't think so.' She taunted her victim who carefully placed her hands in the air, a look of bitter resignation on her stern features.

'Where is he?'

'In the shower.' She opened her mouth to speak.

Rose Red recognised that desperate look and pressed one gloved finger against the woman's lips. 'Say one more word and I will put a bullet through your eye. I do not negotiate.' She pulled the gun from the holster at the woman's side and threw it on the bed. 'Open the door.'

She nodded towards the en suite bathroom.

The woman rose carefully and made to turn her back.

Spinning around to deliver a punch to her assailant, she quickly fell foul to the assassin's precision blade and melted to the carpet, clutching at the spray of blood from the assault to her jugular.

Rose Red threw open the bathroom door and hissed in anger. The large wetroom was clad from floor to ceiling in large white Carrara marble tiles, studded with water droplets as if encrusted in thousands of tiny diamonds.

The shower head in the corner spluttered and spat but there was no one underneath it. Through the steam, a wide-eyed man, fully clothed, sat on the ground tied to the toilet bowl with a soap on a rope, his mouth stuffed shut with a sponge gag. He had an ugly bruise on his forehead. Rose Red pointed her gun in his face.

'Where is he?' She hauled the gag from between his teeth.

'Gone!' He spluttered from behind dry lips. 'Someone snatched him about an hour ago. Who are you?'

'Snatched him? Where did he take him?'

'No idea. I asked you a question!'

'You're in no position to be questioning me. Who took him?'

The man laughed, but more out of disorientation than a morbid sense of irony. 'I've no idea. No doubt one of your boss' henchmen.'

'I don't have a boss.' She squeezed the trigger for the last time and permanently wiped the smile from his face.

—

Rose Red was developing a bad headache as she slammed her foot against the brake and moved politely to the side of the road to let the emergency units through. It would take them all night to put out the blaze she'd set. As she sped south across the Thames, she pondered on the possibilities of what had actually taken place before she reached the safe house and what, indeed, she would say to Weller. Barry had been taken, snatched from under the noses of eight armed guards, seven of whom had no idea they'd been protecting an empty house.

She rubbed at her throbbing temples and spat in frustration at having failed to deliver the goods for the first time in her professional career. This was a contract she would not be proud of. She'd searched the house high and low for the manuscript, but it wasn't there – not in a bundle of pages; a removable storage device; or on the hard drive of the only laptop. Rose Red was of the opinion that the manuscript probably never existed in the first place.

The car park at the snooker hall was unusually quiet for a Sunday night and Rose hadn't remembered it to have been so dark. She'd only once met Gary Weller and that was for the briefest of moments. Most of her dealings with him had been conducted through Lars. Weller was a lightweight hoodlum in her eyes. A man with no original thought of his own, he'd adopted all the stereotypical personal and social characteristics of an East End gangster but without the colourful personality.

His Swedish-born minder, Lars, was far more interesting and considerably more intelligent.

The two penguins had been expecting her as they stepped to either side of the glaring 'members only' sign.

'After you, miss.'

Leading her through the corridor, Rose turned her nose up at the garish red carpet, criss-crossed with a loud symmetrical abstract pattern and the lime green paintwork on the wood cladding. The row of fake chandeliers tinkled with synthetic light. The place stank of tackiness. They stopped at two large doors at the end of the corridor: the ornate brass handles polished to a brilliant shine still lacked the lustre of decorative imagination. One of the men knocked lightly. They waited for an answer from within, but none came. He knocked again and peered through the keyhole. When he righted himself, he cast a nervous glance towards his colleague and shook his head.

'It's a bit dark in there.'

After the third knock, they reached in unison inside their jacket pockets and opened the door carefully.

Rose was already armed.

'What the ...'

She smelled the blood before she sidled into the room and pressed her back against the wall. Her two escorts were yelling out in confusion until one of them found the light switch and thumped it on. They both gasped.

Rose Red laughed at what she saw. Gary Weller sat at his desk with a semi automatic in his hand, its muzzle pointed towards the face of another man who sat naked, save for a short towel around his waist, at the other side of the desk. He held a revolver and it was pointed straight at Weller. The outstretched arms of both men shook with the effort to maintain their targets and they both perspired heavily. Neither man took his eyes off the other in his hard-fought silent battle for survival. The bodies of three men lay on the carpet and another lay slumped over a chair. All sported ugly wounds to their heads, with deep puncture marks oozing blood. Rose Red noticed the men were all still breathing.

'Thank Christ,' Weller rasped, still concentrating heavily on his target. 'Kill this bastard.'

'And I'll take you with me!'

The two men standing were at a loss as to what to do. They waggled their guns in the vague direction of Barry. Weller's hand danced in fury as Rose Red moved around the room, examining the scene with the skill of a forensic expert. 'Is someone going to tell me what happened?' She sat at the end of the desk and crossed one slim leg over the other. 'Don't tell me, I can guess. Your new assassin has a sense of humour I see and perhaps even a sense of justice.'

'Finish the job I'm paying you for and kill 'im'. Weller was in no mood for conversation. 'And don't make no sudden moves.'

'Looks like someone's done most of it for you and left you with the dirty bit.' The smile she shot Barry was cold and cruel. 'Give me a good reason why I shouldn't kill you.' She teased the gun against his ear and curled her lip in disgust at the sight of the thick, greying curly hair curtaining his upper torso.

His response came as a chilling surprise. 'Do what you have to, Rose. Either way, you're going to hell.' She wanted to shy back, but her back had frozen. 'I've seen death. I've looked him in the face and he'll be coming for you next.' He turned his eyes towards her. 'You're bad Rose, and him,' he spat on the desk, 'he's bloody evil. You'll both be punished. He'll drag you screaming to hell. Both of you. Do what you want with me but I'm past killing. It's time to repent. I don't want to go where you two're going.'

He turned his attention to Weller for the last time. 'You're gonna go down for this, Gary, in more ways than one, you're going down.' His sudden movement was so violent that Gary Weller's finger instinctively jerked the trigger. The back of Barry's skull burst across the room, taking the soft contents with it and splattering the furniture and carpet.

'Oops!' Rose Red raised her smooth brows. 'That silly move has just bought you a ticket to life in prison.'

'Shut up you stupid Russki bitch,' Weller screamed, well aware of his undeniable implication in a murder. 'Wake those bastards up and get this bloody mess cleaned up!' he bellowed at his confused and worried men.

Barry lay on his back, the huge hole gaping from his ruined skull. 'That is disgusting! Look at the state of his toenails.'

Gary Weller slumped his head on the desk, too exhausted to think.

'What happened here?' She threw the fallen towel over the corpse's exposed parts that offended her most.

'Someone delivered my package, took out my men with 'is bare 'ands and 'elped 'imself to some cash for 'is troubles.' He spat his words through clenched teeth. 'There was a 'undred grand in there.'

'It's no secret you wanted Barry. A hundred grand is cheap for a job done well, I would say.' A shining object on the ground caught her eye. She picked it up and fitted it against her knuckles. 'He took out your big, strong men with this?'

She slipped her hand inside what looked like a knuckle duster, save that it appeared to be made of heavy metal with sharp, diamond-like spikes. She immediately felt a wash of conflicting emotions surge through her body like a swelling wave in an oceanic storm. The raging wind called her name. She let out a small gasp and almost ripped it off her hand and buried it deep into the pocket of her raincoat.

''E took my money and now 'e's fucked me over. I can't see a way out of this one. Where the fuck is Lars?'

'Who did this?'

Weller dragged his head off the desk to shoot her a look of undisguised malevolence. ''ow the fuck should I know? Didn't see 'is bleedin' face.'

Rose Red shrugged her slender shoulders and walked over to the safe. 'He left you some.'

Weller stood up now and hauled at the hem of his white jacket as if the effort would magically pull out the creases. ''ow much?'

'I would say he took half of what was in there.' She turned away from him and began to stuff the money into her bag.

'What do you think ...'

'For my trouble.'

Weller's laughter was a dry, mirthless cackle. 'Consider it advance payment for when you catch the bastard who set me up. This little escapade's gonna get me life.'

'Not necessarily,' Rose Red was already a step in front of him. 'Since you're their number one suspect, the police will already be on their way so you'll have to act quickly. Get the body out of here. Hide it, burn it, do what you want with it but you'll have to torch the place.'

'What? Burn my joint down? This place belonged to the old dear.' His expression was one of utter incredulity.

'And she had disgusting taste in décor. Make it look like a hit. You don't have time for nostalgia.' She patted her bulging bag. 'I'll be in touch.'

'Rose!'

She turned around slowly, her fingers just brushing the door handle.

'How're you gonna find 'im?'

She slid her fingertips against the cold object in her pocket. 'I have a glass slipper. All I need now is to find a few ugly stepsisters that will lead me to the prince. Besides, he's just gunned down a few policemen and burned a business to the ground. I'd say this man has a serious anger problem. I'll just wait for the police to find him and then I'll close in.'

'Rose!'

She didn't bother to turn around this time.

'He's got the manuscript.'

She hesitated for a long moment and clasped the handles of her bag a little tighter. 'Then, when I catch him, I'll just have to ask him nicely to give it back.' She closed the doors softly behind her.

—

Libby sat at her desk beneath a mountain of paperwork ignoring the polite office chatter between Selina and the new boy. She'd spent the morning arguing with the barrister on procedural issues in the Singh case and the eminent QC had stormed out of the office, snorting something about stupid little upstarts. Of course, she knew better than to disagree with those who were being paid an extortionate honorarium for their specialist opinions but, just because he belonged to an elite over-grown boys' club, didn't mean he could bully her into accepting less for her client when she was certain of securing a healthy award for damages.

Her telephone ringing caused her to swear out loud as she scrambled through the mound of briefs, court forms and photo-copied affidavits to reach the handset. 'Yes?' She meant to snap.

'Libby, there's someone in the foyer who wants to see you. He doesn't have an appointment and didn't give his name.'

'Oh no. Please don't tell me it's Sherlock from the Yard. I've had enough of his stupid questions. Tell him I've been fired. If it's another bloody reporter, tell him to go to hell.' Libby slammed the phone down and growled.

Since the incident at St Paul's a month ago, DCI Prendergast had become her shadow as had the national press. She'd answered question after question and then answered them all over again, re-living the events of the evening until she was sick of hearing her own voice. She'd changed her mobile yet again just in case the press had hacked into her new sim. She'd lost her old phone and prayed it hadn't fallen into the wrong hands.

Her picture had been splashed in full colour all over the front pages of every publication with a masthead and it was a particularly terrible one: snapped by a loitering, opportunist photographer as she was putting the rubbish out for the bin men in the morning in her slippers. She was considering suing him, but hadn't got round to reading up on the conflicts between privacy and Article 8 of the Convention.

DI Byron had survived his gunshot wounds and was making a steady recovery – although it was deemed doubtful he would ever walk again. The bullet had come to rest in his backbone and damaged his spinal cord, but at least he had some feeling in his legs and that was a good start.

The press was having a field day. DI Byron was now hailed the 'Hero Cop' and had been all but canonised in the pages. He'd corroborated much that Libby remembered, but no one could explain how the body or bodies had been removed from the crime scene so quickly.

Gabriel's name or presence had not been mentioned once. It was as if he'd never existed and Libby only hoped he'd survived. There was a nagging doubt, however, when she remembered him lying helpless on the ground with a gun to his head, it would've been impossible for him to have escaped. Depressingly, DCI Prendergast concurred with this conclusion and she was forced to harden her heart and get on with life as best she could, but he haunted her.

The phone rang again.

'Why?' she breathed her thoughts out loud.

It appeared that London had become a war zone and the press whipped-up its army of angry protestors into a frenzy. Some papers were using the death of the lady driver who was ruthlessly gunned down outside St Paul's to spearhead a campaign to eliminate gang warfare from the city's streets.

Others were calling for military aid, especially in the aftermath of the killing of eight policemen in a house in north London and the bombing of an East End snooker hall. Some pointed the finger of liability at the Middle East; some claimed illegal immigrants were responsible; while others blamed Jesus.

There was no doubt there was a war going on around her, but Libby rather suspected that both sides were created and manipulated by the toxic imagination of unprincipled newshounds hungry for a crutch to support their crippled circulation figures.

What the tabloids had failed to highlight in their lead pages was the fact that, during the recent bloodbath, Barry and his manuscript had been sprung from police custody, their whereabouts unknown, while Weller was counting his insurance money with a smile on his face after the loss of his precious snooker halls.

But Libby conceded with a small sigh that the trials and tribulations of a couple of southern English hoods didn't sell papers in the same way as a royal wedding, the yo-yo dieting of an ex-member of an untalented 90s' girl band or the bitch battles between two of the country's most important politicians.

'Hello!'

'Sorry, it's Charlotte again. The bloke's still waiting. He says he's not a reporter. I sort of told him you would see him. Sorry.'

'Oh, for God's sake!' Libby slammed down the receiver and sighed. It was almost five o'clock and time to go home. Stomping past the secretarial pool, she wondered if she had the energy or the inclination to take on any new work.

She also hoped this would not be one of Weller's henchmen with some more instructions for her. Nearing the reception, she scanned her eyes across the half empty chairs on the other side of the glass wall and couldn't identify anyone in particular.

'Miss Butler?' A tall man with shoulders the breadth of a garage door held his huge hand out to greet her. He was an exceptionally well-dressed man with a shock of white blond hair tied neatly back in a short pony tail. Libby breathed out slowly through her clenched teeth. 'My name is Lars Andersson and I work for ....'

'I know who you work for Mr Andersson.'

'Oh?'

'The quantity of bling, the flatness of your forehead...'

'Aw, come on, Miss Butler, anyone can wear bling...'

'... that tell-tale break in what's left of your nose and the size of your feet all give it away I'm afraid.'

Lars Andersson's smile was almost coy. 'I hope my charm and personality will make it less obvious then.' He bowed slightly towards her. 'Do you have a few moments? I'll not keep you long.'

'You've just extracted me from a mountain of complicated court forms that should all have been filled in and duly served yesterday,' her stance was defiant. 'You should be more than familiar with complex court procedures,' she waited for a glimmer of annoyance in his eyes, but none came. 'I'm afraid I don't have a moment to spare today. If you ask that nice lady over there, she'll make an appointment for you when I have time to take a breath.'

'Please, Ms Butler, I'll only take ten minutes out of your busy life. That's all I ask.'

Libby didn't know whether it was the wide blue eyes or the Swedish accent that melted her resolve or, indeed, whether she was just a sucker for a big smile: 'Ten minutes.' She spun around to Charlotte. 'Give me an empty room.'

She escorted the man mountain into board room four and sat him at the head of the long table that normally seated thirty people: he almost dwarfed it.

Libby sat on the chair next to him and wedged her hands firmly between her knees. 'What can I do for you Mr Andersson?' she began respectfully.

He sat back on his chair and placed his hands behind his head, seemingly comfortable in the sterile surroundings of the board room. 'It's possible we have a mutual interest.'

Libby feigned a hearty laugh that interrupted him. 'Mr Andersson, I will be frank with you. if I may?'

He nodded politely.

'Let us get things straight at the onset. I am a minor associate of a ruthless lawyer and you are the number one henchman of a merciless criminal. Apart from us both being side-kicks, we'll never have anything in common.'

'We all seek justice in one way or another.'

'The law, however, is on my side, Mr Andersson: our goals may be the same but our methods in exacting justice are completely different. We can never be best friends.'

'I don't need friends, Libby, just information.'

'Will you torture me to get it?'

'If justice necessitates.'

She knew, of course, he was only kidding. At least, she hoped he was. 'What could I possibly know that you would be interested in?' She threw him one of her sweetest smiles.

'We have a mutual friend the boss wants to speak to.'

'But I don't know any murderers!' she maintained the show of teeth.

'His name is Gabriel Radley.'

'I have no idea what you're talking about.' Libby's shriek and shocked expression gave everything away.

'Your ruthless boss has already told us everything about him. I understand he's a client of yours.'

She didn't like his tone. 'He was, but I haven't seen him

in weeks. Clients come and go you know,' Libby made a full recovery. 'What do you want with him?'

'The boss would like to express his gratitude, that's all. We believe he did us a small favour and want to thank him personally.'

'With or without a baseball bat?'

He shot her a wide, innocent grin.

She stood up, unwilling to share the horror of her ordeal with another person. 'Sorry Mr Andersson, but the last time I saw Gabriel Radley, was just before he was killed,' she swallowed the lump in her throat. 'Now if you wouldn't mind, I have some legitimate work to do.'

'How did he become your client?'

'Through my shift as duty solicitor.'

'Who is he?'

She shrugged. 'I never got to know him.'

'I'm asking you, where is he now?'

She slammed her hands down on the table and leaned forward to defeat the irritation in his eyes with anger in her own. 'And I'm telling you he's probably dead.'

They were almost nose to nose by now. 'Probably?'

'That's right, it is a word that means insofar as is reasonably true – but I would not go so far as to say beyond reasonable doubt because I didn't actually witness his death. I'd say, however, that on a balance of probabilities ....'

'You have a bad attitude, Libby.' He also stood up and towered over her, his face leering towards hers as if sniffing at a meal.

'And you have bad breath, Lars. Goodbye.'

'Perhaps you'd find it sweeter with a little persuasion in note form.' He reached into the inside of his jacket and pulled out a bulging wallet.

She wrinkled her nose as if he smelled bad. 'Unlike Carl

Bottomley, Mr Andersson, I only take money I've earned fairly and through climbing to the top of that place they call moral high ground. That place that you will never reach unless, of course, you become a nun and I can't see that happening, can you? I simply can't help you with this.'

'You'll not go far in this world with a manner like that and Mr Weller isn't a patient man. That leaves us with a little problem,' his huge shoulders flexed on the exhale. 'You're a good woman, Libby, but you're not telling me what I want to hear. Perhaps I'll return with something that hits harder than a wallet full of cash.'

Her hand rested on the door handle and the urge to run was overwhelming, yet Libby took a sudden, impractical fit of indignation. 'Is that a threat Mr Andersson?' She had no idea where the bravado had come from, but it surged like a great tide and threatened to drown her. She spun around to face him. 'You may be accustomed to bullying my boss with threats and bribes, but I'm afraid I'm nothing like him.'

'Libby. Libby,' to her surprise Lars Andersson was laughing. 'We have only just met. Why are we falling out with each other? I haven't come here to threaten you. I just want to know where I can find out some information on Radley.'

She dropped her defences. 'Find the bunch of mutants that killed him. They seemed to know all about him.'

'Mutants?'

Libby walked to the table and perched on the end of the desk, hoping her tight skirt would withstand the strain of staying half-seated in one position for any length of time. The safety pin holding the waistband together was already showing signs of strain. She told Lars Andersson an abridged version of how she'd met Gabriel Radley; the incident outside St Paul's; and the strange, cult-like assailants that caused so much mayhem that evening.

Lars listened with the intensity of one who was trying to understand directions to somewhere important.

In the end, he was satisfied she knew nothing else and left without further questions.

Libby sat for a while in the empty boardroom with her head in her hands wondering what on earth that was all about and whether or not she'd given too much away. Lars Andersson seemed cordial enough, but he was a henchman to an underworld monster with a full agenda of criminal activity and Libby couldn't understand why he'd come at all or what his interest was in a dead man. She decided she didn't wish to know. It was a long time before she rose, grabbed her coat and briefcase and left the office with her in-tray vomiting paperwork.

Walking along the tree-lined side of Goose Green from the station, Libby was deep in thought. The Singh case was to be heard on Monday but the team was far from ready. She'd tried to bury the barrister's incessant questioning with a number of procedural issues but the man had seen straight through her. No doubt she would have to take it up with Carl tomorrow morning.

She wondered when the time would come when she no longer needed his guidance. Carl was a high calibre Oxford graduate with a towering IQ and an impressive list of qualifications, honours and publications. She, on the other hand, just scraped a second class LlB Honours at a second rate university – mainly to prove to her school teachers she wasn't as thick as they kept telling her.

That was why Carl enjoyed an expensive life in a mansion house in Kent and she was forced to pull two wages in order to subsist in a two-bedroomed flat in a recently built, three-storey cardboard block with panoramic views of a row of rooftops, a main road and a car park.

'Hello, Sergeant Fry, isn't it?' She was hauled away from her musings by the silent shape lurking at her door. 'Are you working undercover?' He wore his brown cords and Pringle sweater uneasily.

'Just a social visit, Ms Butler,' he spluttered. 'Your neighbour let me in.'

Libby turned the key and ushered him in. She threw her briefcase and coat onto the chair and sifted through the mail. 'Junk, junk, bill, bill and junk!' She tossed them into the plastic waste paper bin. 'What can I do for you, sergeant?'

'Have you heard of the Safer Neighbourhood team or the Safer Southwark Partnership, Ms Butler?' He began with an awkward grimace.

'Do they sell pepper spray and tasers?' She couldn't help the sarcasm as she threw the dirty socks off the sofa and politely offered him a seat. 'Can I get you a cup of tea?'

'That would be lovely, thank you, miss.'

After a few minutes, Libby returned with a mug of tea and found the sergeant studying the colourful painting on her wall. The thought had crossed her mind as to what he'd been doing before that and why he looked so guilty. He wore a nervous expression and began awkwardly: 'The work of Safer Neighbourhood teams is central to our commitment to creating a visible, accessible and responsive policing service with staff that understand and address local crime and safety issues raised by residents and visitors.' He took the tea from her with a gracious smile.

Libby waited for more, but was greeted with a strained silence. 'Did you learn that off by heart, Sarge? I'm impressed.' Of course, Libby wasn't at all impressed with the sergeant's robotic narrative of the leaflet he was trying to plug.

She sat down on the floor behind the low table, lit a cigarette and glanced at the wall clock.

'The Met's produced a leaflet which provides personal safety advice for people like yourself to give them confidence and make them safer when they're out on the streets. It's called Take Care of Yourself.' His eyes darted around the room, sometimes stopping briefly at her chest area, as he carefully delivered his speech. Libby crossed her arms, hoping to God her blouse buttons hadn't popped off.

'That's nice.'

'In view of the, er, latest incidents in Southwark, we're launching a campaign to help prevent, er, further crimes of a similar nature taking place on our streets and to safeguard victims of crime.'

'Do you not mean potential victims?'

He snorted a yes.

'Have you singled me out as the Vampire Killer's next hit?'

'No, no, Ms Butler, we simply believe that information is the key to safety. Your partner works odd hours and you're often left alone and vulnerable. With the right kind of advice ...'

'I'm perfectly capable of looking after myself, thank you, sergeant. Now, I'm very sorry but I've a party to attend tonight and I'm already late. I'll get a telling off for ruining the buffet. Perhaps we could have this little chat another time?'

'What time will you be back? I could come around then.'

Libby didn't like the urgency in his tone. 'Well after you're tucked up in your little bed.'

'Is your partner here?'

'He's at the hostel tonight.' She could've kicked herself for telling a lie, but she wasn't quite sure where the questions were going and certainly didn't want to subject Tony to the sergeant's asinine advice. 'Sorry, Sarge, maybe another time. I'll make an appointment at the station.'

The annoyance in his eyes turned into a flash of danger.

Its flare was sudden and lingered for a brief second before disappearing behind a mild façade once more. Libby shuffled backwards unconsciously as he stood up.

'Of course, your safety can wait. Enjoy your evening.'

'Thanks, Sarge, now you take care of yourself.'

Ten minutes later, she was still sitting on the carpet, the uneasiness turning her spine to ice.

CHAPTER Seven

'DAMN, LOOK AT THE TIME!' The clock registered '20:07'. A quick shower, change of clothes and swipe of make-up later, Libby hurled herself into the car and took off towards London Bridge where she would pick up Tony and head to the city's financial heart for Nicole's party.

Ms Blais lived at the top of a tower building on the Barbican Estate. The capacious apartment had five enormous rooms and one of the most beautiful kitchens Claudio Celiberti had ever crafted.

Nicole's kitchen was more an inspiring work of contemporary art than a utility room. Carefully sculptured from copper, crystal and marble, the décor was an aesthetic blend of fine lines and curves that concealed every conceivable culinary gadget and kitchen device known to man.

There were no scratches on the smooth surfaces, no stains on the shining doors and certainly no signs of food anywhere to be seen. Nicole's immaculate kitchen was a shrine to domestic Athenians.

Libby couldn't help her scepticism as she drove in silence through the rain, the wipers thumping rhythmically against the windscreen. 'She can't cook.'

A bedraggled Tony forced a smile, despite having been obliged to wait for her on the pavement in his party clothes in the pouring rain for over an hour.

'Just because we haven't had the privilege of sampling her cooking, doesn't mean she can't. She's probably been watching Masterchef on the telly and decided she can win next year. You know how competitive she is. Besides, it's a buffet for her dad's birthday; she probably wanted to do something special for him to show she cares.'

Libby curled her lip, impervious to the sentiment. 'I bet she doesn't even eat it. Women who cook don't have skinny waist lines. She'll have called in an expensive caterer and is probably destroying the evidence right now. She's probably eating the bill: that'll be some calories!'

'Just don't start anything tonight, Libby, at least she's trying. And please don't mention anything about dress. You're obsessed with what other women wear.'

'That's because most of them don't wear it well.' Libby swerved into the car park and slammed on the brakes. 'I can think of better things to do on a Friday night. Have you got Maurice's present?'

'Of course, do you think I would leave such a complicated task to you?'

He slipped his hand in hers as they dashed across the car park. After having successfully negotiated an entrance into the building through the tight security, every one of them a former member of the KGB to Libby's mind, they took the lift to the top floor.

'Nicole, you look stunning.' Tony kissed his hostess on the cheek as she opened the door, while Libby's small nod acknowledged her presence. The large flat was filled with smartly-dressed bodies, the aroma of champagne and the noise of polite chatter.

'I like your dress.'

Tony winced.

Nicole had dressed to kill, or at least cause serious injury. Libby took in every minor detail in one glance as she nudged her way through the revellers to the sitting room to greet Maurice and say hello to his new partner for the first time. Nicole's dress, if it could be called that, was a long black number with a V-neckline plunging to her navel. One long slit up the side of the skirt revealed a perfectly waxed, shiny leg and a high-heeled sandal with jewel encrusted ankle strap. Libby's dress, on the other hand, was a knee-length, chiffon flouncy thing in a large floral pattern of greens and pinks. She had loved the dress until tonight.

'How do you keep your tits in?'

Nicole lowered her long lashes to the wedge of smooth skin between the tiny folds of her bodice. 'Tape. What about you?' She eyed Libby's cleavage straining above her ill-fitting bra with a cool indifference.

'Prayer.'

'Happy birthday Maurice.' Tony's cordial call back to reality broke the hostilities. 'You must be Kevin,' he held out his hand in greeting to the man standing at Maurice's shoulder – a tall, skinny man with rodent features and glasses who sipped his champagne gracelessly – not Maurice's type at all.

'Trevor!' was the stilted reply.

'Good start, darling. You should've mentioned his choice of tie, it would've been more diplomatic.'

Libby snatched a glass of champagne from the table with one hand and a canapé with the other and threw herself into the sofa.

The deep cushions melted beneath her unexpectedly and her glass flew from her hand, its contents landing on the expensive upholstery, the carpet, her bodice and the woman sitting next to her. Her legs flailed like a trapped fly as she struggled to sit up against the soft, yielding fabric and pick the tiny balls of Sevruga caviar out of her hair.

'I'll get a cloth.'

'I hope it's a designer one!'

Nicole swaggered off to her kitchen with a derisory click of her tongue.

'I didn't realise Nicole had so many friends.' Libby recovered with another glass of champagne which she downed flat, aware that a few pairs of eyes at least regarded her with disdain. 'In fact, I didn't know she had *any* friends.'

Maurice shrugged his narrow shoulders and offered her his hand. 'Nicole has always been popular; people adore her. You should too, Libby.'

'Is Carl here?' she whispered in his ear while taking a surreptitious glance around the sea of flushed faces.

'Sorry, CHÉRIE, he had another engagement.'

She hid her disappointment. 'You look very distinguished tonight, birthday boy,' she laughed as he hauled her from the sofa. 'I like the tie and tails, they suit you. We should've all gone out tonight to show you off.'

'Nicole was very specific she wanted to celebrate my birthday here. It's not like her.' He whispered in her ear, 'I think there's someone here she wants to show off to.'

Libby's wide-eyed expression over-exaggerated her interest. 'What number husband will this be?' She watched Nicole as she ineptly dabbed at the wet stains on her cushions with a tea towel that was just out of its packaging, her stack of golden bangles chiming against her perfumed wrist – she was obviously unaccustomed to spills. 'Where is he then?'

'Where is who?' Nicole feigned indifference.

'Number six.'

'I'm not sure. He comes and goes.' There was a strange

expression on Nicole's face that Libby didn't believe she was seeing. Nicole had never been a woman to show sentiment when a cold sneer would suffice, but it was there for all her guests to witness. Nicole clutched at the tea towel and wrung it between her fingers.

'I have a confession to make. I met him a month ago. He phoned me from your mobile. He was in trouble. He had a bullet wound in his side and heavy bruising on his back. The gunshot only scratched him, but it needed cleaning. He had nowhere else to go and so I told him he could stay here. He made me promise not to tell you, but I didn't think it was fair on you. Merde, he'll be angry with me.'

Libby stood in confusion as Nicole narrated a rambling, disjointed story in her sultry accent, the words firing from her mouth at random like bullets from a Gatling gun. 'What on earth are you talking about?'

'Qu'avez-vous fait?'

Libby spun around at the angry voice at the doorway.

'Oh, my God!' The tall, dark figure moved towards them, his familiar black eyes hooded with fury. His hair had been cut and his clothes looked neater.

'Well, if it isn't Santa!' Libby felt her own anger rising above the mixed emotions of relief and elation. 'I thought he was dead.' His furious gaze levelled on her briefly before turning once more to the object of his ire.

Nicole took a step back, teetering on her heels. 'This is my house, Gabriel, and it's my father's birthday. You are welcome to join us in celebration.' Her show of strength, although admirable, was unconvincing.

'Can we speak in private?'

'Of course, we can use the bedroom.'

'D'accord.'

Everyone leaped backwards as he threw off his long coat. Realising he had terrified them, he sighed heavily. 'Damn!' he shook his head and followed Nicole into her bedroom.

Maurice had a star-struck look on his face. 'Mon Dieu, she's a lucky bitch.'

'Why do you think he's so cross with her?' Tony craned his neck like the others to peer into the bedroom. 'He's got his hand on her shoulder. Do you think they're lovers?'

'He's reassuring her. Look at the way he's keeping his distance. Ma pauvre Nicole.'

'So much for the dress!' Libby snorted.

'What do you think they're talking about?'

The wagging tongues were stilled as Gabriel shot them a disgusted glower and kicked the door shut with his boot.

It was a long time before the two emerged from the room, by which time Libby was drunk. Nicole dabbed the tears from her mascara and bravely dissolved into the mingling guests while Gabriel snatched up his coat and made for the door.

'Where do you think you're going?' Libby hurled herself at the door, blocking his exit. 'I believe you owe me an explanation,' she slurred her words. 'I thought they'd killed you. You nearly got me killed. Who were those people and how did they know you? I like your haircut, it suits you.' She teased the fringe from his eyes.

'Which question do you wish me to answer first?' His expression mellowed to one of simple affection.

'All of them.'

'I agree that I owe you an explanation and I shall respond in full to your questions when you are sober enough to comprehend the answers.' He twisted his wrist from her grip. 'There is something that I have to do. It will not take long.'

'I'm not pissed, I'm just merry,' her bottom lip quivered.

'Libby, you are drunk,' he placed his hands on her shoulders, the amusement melting the ice in his eyes. 'Lie down and sleep it off. In the morning, we will talk at length.'

'Don't you patronise me you b…..'

Libby didn't think she saw the door open and close, but Gabriel had gone. 'Must be more pissed than I thought!' She staggered towards an open bottle of pinot noir.

She had no idea how long it had been between Gabriel's quick exit and his equally swift return. She had been insulting a male estate agent for a while for single-handedly destroying the housing market by extorting his hefty fees from people who could ill afford them before moving on to demolish the confidence of a woman who sold hand-made soaps in Primrose Hill by insisting there was no such things as animal-friendly cosmetics.

Even through her alcohol-addled mind, she could tell all eyes in the room were gawking at Gabriel in marvel as he quietly made his way to the spare room. Libby leaped on him. 'Come and meet your guests.' She hauled on his arm.

'They are not my guests.'

'But this party is for you, nevertheless, and you shouldn't disappoint your hostess. She's gone to a lot of trouble to impress you and your reticence to join in not only offends her but is also very humiliating.' She dragged him into the party, giggling to herself at his loud, resigned sigh.

Nicole's guests hammered into the buffet. The gathering was noisier now and laughter more raucous: the alcohol providing an antidote to shyness and inhibition.

'Are you not going to introduce us?'

Libby spun around to the silky voice she detested and found Selina eyeing up Gabriel with wanton appreciation. 'Who invited you?'

'As a matter of fact, it was Maurice.' Selina stood to her full height and cast a cool eye over Libby's dress. 'Wow! Like the retro look. Did you make it yourself?' Selina looked stunning in a short white, off the shoulder lace dress that clung to the soft curves of her body like a protective lover. She traced the contour of her slim waist with her hands and wiggled her hips, knowing full well there were many hungry eyes watching her. 'Valentino,' she breathed, enjoying the familiar bitchy banter between them. She shot a radiant smile at Gabriel who returned the sentiment with an amused one of his own.

'Hmmm, must have been one of his early designs. Did you get it in the Pound Shop?'

'Hardly, this cost me over five thousand pounds.' Selina swallowed the bait with her champagne beautifully.

'God, I could buy my own designer for that sort of money. You were obviously robbed. Who'd pay over five grand for a support stocking?'

The problem with the relationship between Libby and Selina was one of unilateral misunderstanding. Selina believed the playful repartee between two work colleagues alleviated the stresses of the day; was a bit of fun; and kept the boredom at bay. Unfortunately for Selina, she had no idea Libby actually meant every insult she made and took to heart each crushing observation of her own imperfections.

'I haven't really had time to speak to you since the incident in Carl's room, Libby. Do you know that the bastard's transferred me to the Kent office? It's just not fair. I don't want to leave London.'

'Find another firm, then. I'm certain a girl with your, er,' she moved her eyes slowly up and down Selina's body, 'assets, shouldn't find it hard to …'

'But I haven't done anything wrong. Carl grabbed me in

his office and thank God you interrupted him. It was really embarrassing, but I suppose he's far too arrogant to take rejection graciously.'

'Rejection? You were all over him.'

'That's not how it was, Libby.'

Libby spun around to Gabriel. 'Is she telling the truth?'

'She has no reason to lie.'

Libby felt the world closing in once more and fought back the wasted tears. 'I'm really sorry, Selina. For everything. It is a beautiful dress and doesn't look anything like a support stocking.'

'Thank you,' Selina smiled brightly.

'It's more like a bandage!'

Gabriel grabbed her by the back of the neck and marched her away.

'Whose dress do you prefer, mine or Nicole's?' She hiccoughed loudly and the band that hauled her unruly hair back from her face pinged across the room, hitting a woman on the back of the head.

'Yours. Nicole's attire is inappropriate in front of her father and friends. Her intention is purely to seduce.'

'And I take it that she hasn't managed that yet?'

'That is none of your business.'

'Oh, go on. You can tell me. We nearly died together, after all. Are you shagging her?' She stumbled on to her knees and looked up at him helplessly through her melting mascara. 'I feel sick.'

He pulled her to her feet. 'She needs to lie down.'

'He likes my dress,' Libby giggled, 'you like my dress, don't you Gabe?' She patted his cheek playfully.

'No.'

Tony spun around at the sound of the concerned voice. 'She'll be fine. She always gets like this. She drinks too much and eats too little. It's a lethal combination. She'll verbally abuse everyone in the room, collapse in a heap somewhere and wake up in the taxi feeling sick.'

Libby swayed on her feet and noticed Nicole had embedded her hooks into Gabriel's arm in an attempt to take him away from the situation by showing him off to her curious guests. He didn't look at all comfortable with the idea and Libby decided to go to his aid in the only way she knew how. 'He doesn't fancy you, do you Gabriel? And he doesn't like what you're wearing either. He thinks ..'

'That's enough.' His expression remained inscrutable.

'... he thinks you're ugly!'

'Do you Gabriel?' Nicole had lost her cool façade of indifference and looked genuinely concerned.

'No.'

Their eyes locked.

'I think I'm going to be sick!' Libby clapped her hand over her mouth and staggered towards the bathroom while Nicole and Gabriel attempted to keep her upright. Fighting back the nausea, she nudged her way rudely through the drunken revellers but it was too late. The contents of Libby's stomach emptied violently and burst through her fingers to spray Nicole and her elite guest list with multi-directional vomit before she landed on the floor in a heap.

—

'Here, take some water?'

Libby awoke slowly. 'That was some party. I think someone kicked sand in my eyes; soldered my tongue to the roof of my mouth; and hit me over the back of the head with a spiked club last night.' She sat up slowly and squeezed her eyes shut. 'Oh

God, I think I must have swallowed my own urine during the night.' She wanted to spit the acrid taste from her mouth, but had no wish to ruin Nicole's expensive silk sheets.

'You have too vivid an imagination. You were simply drunk.' Gabriel laughed.

'Have you been sitting there all night?' Libby could see the London dawn seeping through the curtains.

Gabriel sat beside the bed on a comfortable armchair.

'I fell asleep.'

'What's that horrible vomit smell?'

'You.'

Her eyes widened in horror. 'Oh God, I thought it was just a terrible dream. I can't believe I threw up in front of Nicole's guests. Where's Tony?'

'You threw up *over* Nicole's guests and I am not sure. He went back to your home with Nicole. They should have returned by now.'

'What are you talking about? Why did Nicole go with him?'

'Drink your water.'

She fell back into her pillows and squeezed her eyes shut. 'Why didn't you let me know you were still alive? I thought they'd killed you. Why didn't you contact me and tell me you were all right?'

'You have asked the same question twice.' A small smile creased his lips but his eyes betrayed sinister misgivings.

'So give me an answer.' She folded her arms and waited.

'I was protecting you.'

Libby studied him as he sat in the chair and pulled his hand through his dark hair. He wore plain black jeans with a simple white t-shirt, evidence that Nicole had not managed to seduce him to the dark side of designer wear yet. He looked worried. 'You can barely protect yourself.' She took his fingers in hers.

'What's the matter with you Gabriel?'

'They want something from you. For reasons that elude me, you have become the nucleus to all this mayhem. I am trying my best to understand but it is impossible to predict their next move.'

'Those people at St Paul's?' Her attempts to swallow her fear with the water when he nodded ended in a coughing fit. He shot off the chair and gently tapped her back with the flat of his hand and placed his arm around her shoulder: the gesture purely to reassure her. 'Who are they?'

He shrugged. 'I do not know yet. I have searched for clues for days now, but this city is an eternal maze with no beginning and no end. I hoped for more time but this changes everything. At least now I have a lead.'

'I don't understand any of this. What lead?'

'I caught one of them in this building last night. He followed you here.'

Libby gasped. 'What did you do with him?'

'I put him in the wardrobe.' He indicated with his head to the panelled door of the antique mahogany wardrobe. 'He is in there, behaving himself.'

'What?' Libby couldn't snap her mouth shut. She rose carefully, ignoring her pounding head, and shuffled over to the wardrobe door.

With a trembling hand, she opened it. She leaped back with a scream as a pair of terrified eyes looked up at her through a melting painted mask, the remainder of the face hung in an expression of pained resolve. 'Oh my God! Aren't you going to tie him up?'

'There is no need. He will not run from me.'

'Are his limbs broken or something?'

Gabriel laughed. 'He simply knows what is good for his

health. Survival is man's strongest instinct when there is nothing else left.'

'What is he?'

'A scout.'

The vanquished man in the wardrobe merely hung his head.

'What did you do to him?'

'I merely re-educated him.'

'Has he been in that wardrobe all night?'

'Of course.'

'Ask him if he's gonna kill me,' the man in the wardrobe gibbered, but concentrated his gaze on the inside of his wooden prison.

Libby turned around to Gabriel, confounded as to why the man was so terrified of him. His hands trembled uncontrollably. 'Are you?'

'That depends on him.'

'Gabriel, you're kidding aren't you?' She didn't sound convinced by her own words.'I mean, you're not going to murder him in cold blood are you?' She stammered her words out, suddenly remembering the night at St Paul's and all the blood, especially the blood over her.'Are you capable of murder?' She felt the world closing in on her and regarded Gabriel in a new light. He stood, tall and powerful in his defiance, his expression would have frozen the Thames.'How did you escape that night? How did I? The man had a knife to my neck. I felt the blade against my skin. I thought he'd cut me.' She prodded her neck with the tips of her fingers, the gesture purely to reassure herself there was no scar. 'Did you cause that carnage?' She'd quite forgotten about the man in the wardrobe.

'No, I was not the cause of it.'

The man made to open his mouth but snapped it shut as he met Gabriel's perilous scowl.

Gabriel stood deep in thought for long moments before he sighed and walked casually towards his prisoner. The man shied away from him with a shriek, his shoulders shaking in fear, his hands batting the air as if to fend off a swarm of angry wasps.

Gabriel grabbed his arm and dragged him up to stand before him. 'If I see you again I will kill you without further question. If she comes to any harm, I shall take it as a personal affront and shall hold you responsible. You know what will happen to you when I come for you.' It was not a question.

The man didn't need to wait to give an answer and didn't even bother to slam the doors behind him in his panicked flight from the object of all his fears. Gabriel threw on his coat once more.

'Where are you going?'

'After him. Stay here until I return. Lock the door. Nicole and Tony should be back soon.'

'Wait a minute, Angel Gabriel. You're not flying off anywhere until you tell me what's going on.' She grabbed him by the front of his t-shirt and twisted it in her fist. 'Did you kill those men?'

To her horror, he shrugged. 'They managed to kill each other in their confusion. I merely caused a distraction.'

'What kind of distraction? As I remember it, you had a foot on your back and a gun to your head.'

She didn't release her grip on his clothes.

'He was clumsy and is probably attempting to extract the stock from between his eyes as we speak.'

'What?'

'I jarred the end of the gun into his nose. His finger squeezed the trigger and it fired outwards, killing and injuring some of his men. In the ensuing mayhem, more shots were fired but, by that time, you were safe, the police were there and I was gone.'

'Nicole said you were shot.' She lifted his t-shirt up to

examine the wound, but could find nothing but sleek muscle.

'It was only a graze. I heal quickly.' He answered her silent question.

'You saved me, didn't you? God knows how you managed it, but you stopped him from slitting my throat.'

She knew the answer as if by instinct as she breathed her words out. 'Did you kill him?'

The sound of a gentle knock saved a difficult moment between them. A half-dressed woman waggled a phone in her hand. 'Are you Libby?' She waited for the nod. 'It's for you.' She smiled seductively at Gabriel.

Libby picked up the phone that was hurled on the bed and placed her hand against the mouthpiece. 'It'll be Tony with some stupid excuse as to why he's not back yet. Don't worry, Gabriel, this isn't the first time he's disappeared with the voluptuous Ms Blais. Why do you think I hate her in the first place? Hello? What? No! Oh God! No! No! Of course I'll be there. What time is it? Damn!' She threw the phone onto the bed as if it was burning. 'That was Maurice. Nicole disappeared last night from the car park outside my flat. Tony's at the police station. He was arrested on suspicion. God, what a mess. I have to go to him.'

—

Rose Red held her breath and eased the gun from the holster inside her jacket. Pressing her back against the cold stone, she listened in the still night air for movement inside the cottage. She had followed the blue Alfa Romeo for over two hours as it steered a careful course through south London, and into the Surrey countryside. So as not to arouse suspicion, she'd kept a good distance from her quarry and wondered whether or not she should continue on a mission that was not paying her.

The fact was Rose Red hated men who disrespected women more than she hated policemen. During her latest stake-out at the lawyer's house, she'd stumbled upon the kidnapping of two women and couldn't let the perpetrator get away with it. Rose didn't normally meddle with situations that didn't concern her, but she had heard her name being called softly from somewhere deep within. It was her own name, her birth name, and it had shattered her professional shield of emotional detachment and called upon her to act. The personal sensibilities of Rose's alter-ego were immediately violated when she saw the man grab both of the women, bundle them into a car and transport them to this remote moonlit cottage in the middle of nowhere.

She had no choice but to help.

She heard a male voice and a light sparked into life in the window furthest away from her. She checked the terrain and moved cautiously towards it. The curtains were closed, but Rose Red could just see the terrified woman tied to a chair, her hands bound tightly behind her by the tattered silk of her own dress. She wore a gag; the bodice of her dress hung in ruins around her waist and blood trickled from the gash in her forehead.

The man was speaking to her about tea, cooing his reassurance in a rasping voice and singing a song about crying. Rose could hear the chiming of china and a cupboard opening and closing. The window, although small, was low enough for her to peer into without standing on tip-toe. The woman's eyes widened in horror; a pointed blade teased the contours of her neck; and Rose Red decided she'd seen enough.

She stabbed the barrel of her gun through the window and the glass shattered inwards. She heard a panicked yell and a door slam shut. Rose Red hurled herself towards the back door in the hope of catching the man and putting a bullet through his head, but was forced to kick it in.

She heard the sound of a car engine firing up at the front of the house and the wheels churning the mud up before it sped away into the night. She cursed not wearing the right shoes for the job and made her way through the dark utility room into the door where the orange light oozed between the frame. With her Beretta readied for trouble, she kicked the door open.

'мой бог!'

The woman sat slumped in her chair, the blood cascading across her body and spilling onto the floor, creeping across the tiles to form a wide slick of crimson oil. Rose Red walked carefully around the table to examine the crime scene and the dying woman. Their gazes met for the briefest of moments and in that tiny space of time they exchanged a potent intimacy: a brief understanding of killer and cruelty shining from the vibrant green eyes; and victim and forgiveness from the mellow blue eyes that softly closed forever. Rose Red was not accustomed to feelings of compassion for the dead, but this woman would haunt her for eternity.

She swiped the hair from her face, settled the gun back inside her jacket and wished to бог she'd stayed at home.

CHAPTER Eight

'OH, GOD, CARL, THIS IS not good.' The tea cup clattered against the saucer as Libby tried to sip at it, willing her hands to stop shaking. 'Selina is dead and Nicole's missing. They think Tony did it. The police were crawling all over the flat yesterday. They won't let anyone see him. They've been holding him now for almost twenty-four hours.'

'You look a mess, Libby. Why don't you go for a shower and get some clean clothes on. Did you let the police see you looking like that? Lord knows what they think.' Carl paced the room in his usual way. She felt comforted by his presence even though this was the first time he'd ever visited her flat.

'I think my dress sense is the least thing on their minds. Christ! They think he murdered those women.' She fumbled in her bag for a cigarette packet and was relieved to find a few still in it. 'I'm nearly out of fags.' Carl snatched the lighter away from her trembling hands and lit the end.

'Have they told you when you could see him?'

She shook her head and took a long, deep draw. 'The cops are doing what cops do best. Flouting the rules and delaying his right to a lawyer, hoping probably that he'll say something incriminating. But Tony knows his rights and has probably chucked the Code of Practice in their faces and asked for a pad and pen to take notes. He's lived with me long enough to understand he keeps his mouth shut until his lawyer turns up. I hope you're going to represent him.'

'Have they charged him yet?'

She shrugged. 'The PACE clock is ticking, but it's only a matter of time. They wouldn't stop asking questions. It was horrible. I've sat through interviews so many times and really thought I could hold out under personal examination. I really thought I was too experienced to be taken by surprise, but it's different when it's someone you're close to. I felt I was on trial. They kept asking me what I thought he'd done with Nicole. I didn't sleep at all last night and I feel filthy.'

DCI Prendergast had questioned her about the evening Suzanne Glover disappeared and why she told her boss Tony had been working that night. Despite her protests that Carl's evidence was purely hearsay and he'd not heard her correctly, she couldn't convince the police who'd checked Tony's workplace to discover he'd not been there on the night of PC Glover's disappearance. She couldn't tell them the whole truth about Carl and so her statement remained highly suspicious.

The situation was exacerbated with statements from neighbours who heard her screaming in the middle of the night. The police were particularly interested in what could cause her such severe distress as to wake up the neighbourhood. Her excuse of arachnophobia didn't go down well with the wary detectives. 'I think they believe I'm another Maxine Carr. I suppose I could do with a drastic make-over; a brand new identity; and a healthy new bank account.'

'Don't be silly. Have they found anything substantial, apart from the car and familiarity, that connects Tony to Selina's murder?' Carl placed a placating hand on her shoulder.

'God, I hope not.' Her tears flowed freely down her cheeks with the remnants of yesterday's mascara.

He knelt down in front of her chair and took her hand in

his. 'I'll speak to DCI Prendergast and find out what he's got on Tony. His detention should be up for review again by now. They can't withhold legal representation forever. Let me get this right. Tony says he came back here with Nicole.'

'And Selina.'

'Yes, why was Selina there?'

'She was at the party. He was to give her a lift home to Clapham, but stopped off here first.'

'Why?'

She was not sure how much she should tell him at this stage. 'To get me a change of clothes. I was in a bit of a state that night and Maurice wanted to go for breakfast at the Maze Grill for a treat. He booked it over a year ago.'

'So why did Tony take Nicole with him?'

'She doesn't drink. She was the only one at the party sober enough to drive.'

'So Tony left the party with Nicole and Selina. Stopped off here and then what?'

'He apparently told the police he left Nicole to take Selina home in his car and then he went to bed. He was pretty inebriated.' God, I sound like a copper. It's hot in here.' She swept her hand down her neck and it came away running with sweat.

'They found his car abandoned ...'

'Don't be stupid, Carl, he's a gentle, sweet man and wouldn't swat a fly if it landed on his sandwich. He's a charity worker for goodness' sake.'

'So where is Nicole?'

Libby shook her head again. 'I don't know.'

He stopped to think for a moment before starting his next question in a soft voice. 'Libby, I don't want you to take this the wrong way, but you know the person closest to a murderer is often the last to realise it. Do you think there is even the slightest possibility that Tony could've killed those women?'

'Don't be a bloody fool! Of course not. If he was the Vampire Killer, I would certainly know about it. He's never even read the Twilight saga.'

'What about your sudden fear of the dark, Libby? Perhaps you always knew about it, but your sub-conscious sought to repress it by manifesting itself into an irrational phobia.'

'Oh, that's just great. Now you're a shrink. Tony's not a murderer.'

Carl slapped his palm against his forehead. 'Look, I'm going to see this Prendergast chap, find out what he's got and we'll take it from there. You get yourself washed and changed and I'll speak to you later. You're not going out are you?'

'I'm not sure.' With all that had happened over the past few days, Libby had quite forgotten about Gabriel's warnings. She didn't even know where he was or whether she was safe. She suddenly felt very vulnerable. 'Please don't leave yet.'

She hoped it wasn't a vain request.

'Do you want me to help Tony or not?' She didn't like the clinical clip to his tone.

'Of course I do. What kind of question is that?'

'Well, I'll phone you later.' He bent down to kiss her but she snapped her head to the side. His lips caught her ear. 'We need to talk.' He spat out the strands of her hair.

'Later, Carl.'

'Now's as good a time as any.' He sat down next to her, placing his hands on his knees. She noticed they were now trembling. 'I don't want to lose you. You are all I think about these days.'

'And what about home-loving Dorothy?'

'Deidre.' He laughed at the irony of his situation: a deep-throated chuckle of bitter despair. The days when he had possessed the very best of two blissful worlds were now a lifetime away and he was faced with the misery left by the remnants of both. 'You're right, Libby. I have to make a choice and I will. I just need a little more time to sort things out in my head.' He twisted his neck around to face her and she noticed the wretchedness in his eyes: another unfamiliar expression of recent times.

'Do you love her?' She stubbed the cigarette out in the ashtray.

'I don't know. I don't know anything anymore.'

She placed her hand on his. 'Why don't you go and see Tony and, when you come back here, I'll see if I can help to remind you.'

—

It had been a busy two days for DCI Prendergast and a time that he would never forget in all his career. He'd hoped, no prayed, for a single clue to the solution of the Vampire killings for months and now the evidence was coming in thick and fast.

He had a suspect in custody with some damning circumstantial evidence: a personal connection with at least three of the victims; he was probably the last man to see Suzanne Glover alive; but there was no apparent motive as yet. He hoped that such would come after some careful questioning. Do psychos need a motive?

The force didn't want to allow this one to slip through the mesh of justice by a verdict of insanity. They had a vehicle in the pound waiting for forensics and now a crime scene, thanks to an anonymous tip-off. A message had been left on Crimestoppers from an unregistered mobile giving explicit directions to a lonely cottage in the Surrey countryside where a fresh body was found. The house had belonged to an elderly lady who had died two years ago and attempts to find her relatives had been in vain. It, therefore, lay abandoned, but for the occasional visitation of a killer and his victims.

The bathroom stank of bleach and the outbuilding, a small shed, was stacked with bottles of the stuff. His men crawled all over the grounds and the nearby village but had so far come up with no information: the cottage was too remote to give up its secrets so quickly. They would have to start digging up the garden.

The unfortunate victim was one Selina Fotheringham-Taylor, a twenty-six-year-old lawyer with everything going for her. Her description from the suspect fitted her profile. Her throat had been slit but there was much more. Forensics had only just started their lengthy investigations, but it was looking very much like a similar weapon had been used on all the other victims. The incision suggested he was right-handed and that the victim was assaulted from the front. Her father had visited the morgue and identified the body: his little girl whose life had come to a sudden and violent end at the edge of an icy blade.

The most important outcome from all this, though, was that the killer had been interrupted and couldn't complete his sadistic ritual. The two sets of fresh tyre tracks in the drive had been all but washed out by the rain, but it was likely that one set matched the tread of the suspect's Alfa Brera registered to Anthony John Ridout and another set that were yet to be identified. There was a smashed window and the back door had been broken open from the outside. Furthermore, a set of size nine footprints matched the shoe size of Ridout and another set of footprints in the mud indicated the person was female.

There was possibly a witness out there who could give a

positive ID and DCI Prendergast had to find her.

Yes, everything was falling into place. There were no traces of blood on the suspect's clothing, unless he had time to change before he was arrested, and a sweep of his flat came up with nothing. DCI Prendergast shook the doubts from his head as if they itched.

'Puzzles.' He spat and patted the latest report on his desk. The Surrey crime scene had been compromised last night and the house vandalised, as if someone or some ones had been desperately searching for something. The duty police officers guarding the scene had apparently seen and heard nothing. A body had been found floating in the Thames near Blackfriars. It belonged to a young man with black and red traces of paint on his face and canine teeth had been crudely sharpened to a point. It looked prima facie like suicide but forensics had not finished with him yet.

'Sir! Sir!' He was interrupted from his musings by an excited officer who leaped through the door. 'We've found the Blais woman. She's alive!'

DCI Prendergast didn't have time to open his mouth before the officer gushed out his information. 'One of the boys was examining the suspect's vehicle and heard yelling coming from the boot. She was in there screaming blue murder. She had a nasty knock on her head and she's shaking from shock but she's alive. The ambulance should be here any minute.'

Prendergast cast a glance up to the heavens and knew someone up there was looking out for him. The months of investigation and the public humiliation at coming up with nothing suddenly paled into history. This would be a day he would never forget and he would soon wallow in one of those fine moments of life-defining glory when he closed the Dracula files forever.

All he had to do now was place the fractured pieces of a multi-dimensional jigsaw together to make an intelligible picture and get ready for the onslaught of ravenous reporters.

—

Libby was lost to hysteria. One minute Carl had been on top of her and in the next breath he had been jerked away.

Now he dangled in the air by his arm and leg, completely naked. Carl's screams caused her to join him and she sat up in bed, hurled the covers over her body and yelled as if she was being murdered. It was only when Gabriel threw open the window to her bedroom that she realised, to her horror, what he was about to do.

'No, Gabriel!' she found her senses at last, 'this is the second floor, for Christ's sake, you can't chuck him out from the second floor. You'll kill him.'

'That would be a most constructive outcome!'

Carl was not a small man, but Gabriel had a firm grip of his wrist and ankle and swung him around like a broom.

'Put him down!' Libby felt the relief wash through her body as Gabriel kicked the window shut and marched out of the room carrying a still screaming Carl.

She leaped from the bed, draped the sheet around her and scuttled after them.

Gabriel stood by the door and fumbled with the lock while Carl's face turned purple against the grip of an arm around his neck. The door opened and, before Libby could reach him, Carl was hurled like a sack of rubbish onto the stairwell, landing on his left shoulder with a painful thump. Gabriel slammed the door behind him and crossed his arms, barring her way to Carl's rescue. 'A good man whose love you do not deserve sits in a cold cell awaiting injustice and your response to his cry for help is to continue your salacious affair with another who does not merit your affection.'

Libby heard a woman screaming outside. 'For God's sake, at least give him his clothes and his car keys!'

Gabriel stood firm, his dark brows meeting between his eyes. 'He will leave with nothing!'

'This isn't the bloody Weakest Link, Gabriel. He'll be arrested!'

'Then he will get what he deserves. What is wrong with you?'

She could see in those angry features that a lecture was imminent. Her shoulders dropped with the heavy sigh. 'I love him.'

'Nonsense! You are in love with the concept of sharing his spurious success. Happiness is not dependent upon another, Libby, it comes from within.'

'Oh, that's just rich: suddenly you've become an agony aunt!'

'Your so-called agony is self-inflicted.'

Libby didn't know how to answer that and so she resorted to her familiar contingency plan: the fail-safe method she utilised to maximum effect when she was trailing in an argument or lost for words.

'How dare you!' she started off with a low growl and tightened the sheet around her chest. 'Who the hell do you think you are, coming into my home and meddling with my personal life? You hardly know me, yet you think it's acceptable to sneak into my home when I'm ...' she had to think carefully about the next lines, '...doing personal things and physically assault my guests.' Her voice rose an octave. 'You have no bloody right. GET OUT!'

He merely glowered and the shouting in the street riled her

further as she suffered the distress and humiliation that Carl would be simultaneously facing.

She cursed as his hand caught her wrist before she could deliver the punch to his face. She stood close to him, her mood defiant, her nose almost touching his and their eyes locked: his glowing softly and hers sparking with rage.

Something passed between them that Libby felt she'd missed. He relinquished his grip as if she had just bitten his knuckles.

Libby was left breathless and confused as he turned away from her.

'I see.' He said in a soft voice.

'You see what?' She yelled.

'Nothing. I see nothing.'

'Can I get dressed or do you intend to throw me onto the streets naked too?'

His silence confounded her and she wondered whether he had seen something inside her that troubled him. She shuffled into the bedroom and searched for any sign of Carl from the window. His car was still parked outside, the driver's window had been vandalised, but he was nowhere to be seen. She worried he may have been arrested.

A long shower and a change of clothes later, Libby felt human again. She found Gabriel in the sitting room, lying on the sofa, plugged into Tony's earphones: the faint tinkle of Puccini spilling into the air. He wore an expression of exquisite pleasure.

His eyes were closed, his breathing heavy as the music massaged his senses, causing his body to now and again spasm involuntarily. She smiled despite his previous outrageous behaviour and watched as the melody overpowered him.

Instinctively, he held out his hand to her, his eyes still shut, and she took it, feeling the soft warmth of affection in this extraordinary man. Their fingers entwined and she smiled as she felt the familiar surge of excitement that rattled her body whenever she touched him.

She knelt down beside him and lay her head on his stomach while he stroked her hair. It was an innocent gesture: one that neither commanded a price nor made a promise.

All her worries melted away at every stroke of his fingers: Tony, Nicole and even Carl faded into shadowy insignificance beneath his cleansing touch. She emptied her mind, eavesdropping on the rousing chorus that chimed from the headphones, and she closed her eyes to its alluring embrace. This was one of the most perfect moments that Libby would ever experience and one that would make her smile for the rest of her life.

She jumped at the sharp knock on the door and, seeing Gabriel chose to ignore the intrusion, felt she was not in any danger from answering it.

'I have nothing more to say to the police, detective chief inspector, and your warrant is only good for one visit, which you have already made.' She made to shut the door in his face.

'Please Miss Butler, I just want to speak to you. Off the record if you wish. I do understand what you must be going through and won't take up much of your time,' his soft Yorkshire accent was barely perceptible today

'Not today detective, sorry.' Libby hadn't forgotten Gabriel was still in the flat. 'I've already had the low-down on keeping safe and I really don't think my nerves would take any more bad news today.'

'Then I have some good news. Nicole Blais is safe and well, Miss Butler, I just want to talk that's all.'

Her eyebrows rose. 'Did she tell you what happened? Thank God, now you know that Tony's not your murderer.'

'I didn't say that, Miss Butler.'

'Let the detective in, Libby. It will be all right.'

She took a step backwards and slammed into Gabriel's body. She noticed a strange expression on the detective's face and wondered whether it was curiosity or fear. She held the door open for him and led him into the sitting room in silence.

'Would you mind turning off your mobile please detective, the noise upsets him.' She spun around to Gabriel, 'I know he hasn't got a notebook with him and says he's here unofficially, but don't trust anyone from the CID, they're all corrupt. Say nothing and ....'

'I know what I'm doing, Libby. It will be all right.'

—

'The elusive Mr Radley?' the detective began a cordial exchange of words as he took the seat that was offered and fumbled ineptly with the tiny buttons on his phone. 'You've cost a couple of constabularies a good few pounds in man power and property, not to mention a few pieces of one of our officers.'

Gabriel, falling into the chair opposite, answered him with the faintest of smiles. 'Your officer was clumsy and mutilated himself but I do not believe you have come here to chide or arrest me, Andrew Galbraith Prendergast.'

Prendergast was too well-experienced a police officer to register astonishment that a stranger knew his middle name – a piece of information only his closest relatives were aware of.

'So Nicole turned up alive and well? That's fantastic news. Is she OK?' Libby took up a position on the floor by the low table, mid-way between the two men. Having been taken unawares yesterday morning, Prendergast correctly assumed she was not about to let him get the better of her this time. She sat with her pen poised at her notebook, as if she was about to take down his life story. 'You'll have to release Tony now.'

'I haven't had the opportunity to speak with Miss Blais yet, but one of our female officers did manage to get some information from her. Miss Blais is in a bad state of shock and was taken to King's for treatment.'

'King's is a hospital.' Libby threw the piece of information to Gabriel before he could ask. 'An NHS one.'

'I will speak frankly with you Libby. I'm not here to make accusations ...'

'Or beat out a confession?'

Prendergast laughed uncharacteristically, pretending to share her humour. 'No, at least not in front of a witness. I am just a cop trying to piece together a murder case and hopefully exclude Mr Ridout from our investigations. It appears Ms Blais' assailant hit her over the head with a flat object and bundled her into the boot of the Alfa Brera registered to Mr Ridout. The assailant took her to an address near Ockham in Surrey. Another female travelled in the back seat. I think we have already been over this with you.'

'Yes, yes. The blood and urine stains on the upholstery belonged to Selina. I already know about this, detective. How did she die?'

The detective had been the bearer of bad tidings many times in his career, but somehow he felt the sharing of this information particularly uncomfortable. 'Her throat was slit.'

Libby's hand snatched to her mouth. 'Oh, God!'

'Libby, you are forgetting your manners.' Gabriel's silken voice tore through the heavy atmosphere. 'Perhaps the inspector would care for some tea.'

'And perhaps you would like to go and make it for him. I'm always making tea for coppers.'

'Your manners?'

Libby rose with an air of defiance. 'Pale and milky like your complexion, or black like his heart?'

'Sweet and strong like you, thank you Miss Butler.'

'Patronising git,' she muttered under her breath and stomped off into the kitchen.

The two men sat for long moments in silence: Gabriel examining the contours of the inspector's face while the latter hid his discomfiture behind his curiosity. It was Gabriel who spoke first.

'You have your opportunity. Now ask.'

'I was lucky you were here.'

'Fortune had nothing to do with it. The police have been sitting outside this house for weeks. The only reason you are here now is because I have let you in.'

DCI Prendergast gave a small nod of his head. 'Then I thank you for allowing this meeting.'

'I do not like insincerity.'

Prendergast could only tip his head in apology. 'I know you were at Ms Blais' apartment all night when the murder took place and I know you are not the killer.'

'Do you?'

'You could, however, be an accomplice. How long have you known Tony Ridout?'

Gabriel shrugged. 'A few hours perhaps.'

Prendergast nodded slowly. 'Tell me, Gabriel, if I may call you that? ...'

Another shrug.

'What is your relationship to Miss Butler?'

'We are not related.'

'You know what I mean.'

'She was kind enough to offer me advice and help when I needed it.'

'So it is purely one of client and lawyer?'

The nod was barely perceptible.

'And Nicole Blais?'

'She is a friend.'

'Someone you care about?'

More silence.

'And are you not worried about her?'

'Should I be?'

'She could've been killed.'

He was answered with a stare. Prendergast diverted his gaze to the pictures on the table of Libby and boyfriend Ridout in their swimming costumes somewhere sunny. He noticed her eyes in the picture had been gouged out with what was probably a blue ball-point pen and wondered what kind of quarrel the two must have had to warrant such violent assault to an otherwise happy scene. 'Where were you last night?'

'Looking for someone.'

'In Surrey?'

'I do not know where Surrey is.'

Prendergast shook the demons from his head and tried to clear his mind. Gabriel Radley, although tightly guarded, exuded an air of complete honesty. Either he was an excellent liar or was simply telling the truth. Whatever his game, he played it very well.

'Why would I need to lie?'

'Why indeed?' Prendergast left the question hanging, not having remembered asking it out loud. 'Can you tell me why you and, er, Miss Butler were almost killed outside St Paul's a few weeks ago?'

'I can tell you how but not why.'

'Do you know who your attackers were?'

'No.'

'Do you remember how you got away from them?'

'Yes.'

'Did you have to injure or kill anyone in order to get away?'

'That is a leading question.'

Prendergast set his jaw. 'Do you know why your assailants paint their faces?'

'Are you asking me to hazard a guess?'

'I am asking you to tell me what you know.'

'I believe it is a tribal thing: a symbol of ownership and belonging.'

'Like a cult?'

'Yes, like a cult.'

'So, these people are gullible, vulnerable individuals who have been brainwashed by a leader?'

'Each with the same inherent defects in their temporal lobes? Doubtful.'

DCI Prendergast, taken aback by the informed answer, took a few moments to formulate his next question. 'The body of a man with traces of similar markings on his face to the men Libby described after the St Paul's incident was found floating in the Thames this morning. Do you know anything about that?'

'I would guess that he either fell or was pushed.'

The detective felt his back teeth squealing together. 'This "cult", for want of a better word, took pains to cover their tracks by taking away the bodies after the shootings at St Paul's, yet one of them is left dead for us to find. Do you not think that strange, Mr Radley?'

'I find many things strange in this place. Nothing surprises me anymore.'

'This place? Are you not from around here?'

'No.'

'Then may I ask where?'

'You may ask.'

'Then where?' Prendergast was getting tired of this verbal cat and mouse and became restive with the ensuing silence. He decided to change tack and attack with the law, something he believed they would both understand. 'Look, Mr Radley, I don't know where you're from and I can arrest you simply for that, but I won't because I'm smart and I've a gut feeling you wouldn't remain in custody for long. Secondly, I believe you're the centrepiece of this enormous puzzle and that things aren't what they seem. I hope you're not a murderer; I hope you're not an accomplice to a murderer; and I hope you're not a terrorist. If you're any of these things, I will soon find out and when I do, it will be very bad news for you. Are you a terrorist, Gabriel?'

'That is a question that is difficult to answer, inspector, for all acts of public hostility are neatly folded into the definition of terrorism. That being so, we are all guilty of terrorism of varying degrees – your own police officers are, in particular, prime culprits. Yet I am not here to overthrow a regime, neither would I contemplate the taking of innocent lives as a means by which to draw attention to my cause, if I had one. I know nothing about firearms or explosives and do not care to know either. I am simply here to find something I have lost and, when I find it, I hope to leave without further incident.'

'May I ask what you're looking for? I may be able to help you make a swift departure.'

'I am looking for a stone, about this size.' He held out his palm and drew an oval on it with his index finger. 'The stone looks very much like a ruby and has been carved in the shape of an arrowhead.'

'Is it valuable?'

'Its value is beyond financial measure and, indeed, mortal imagination.'

Prendergast whistled. 'And you say you've lost it?'

'Yes.'

'Where?' He noticed a slight hesitation and suddenly realised Radley was opening to him a little. Was he beginning to trust someone or was this just another game?

'It is possible the Vampire Killer has it.'

'Good God! How could you possibly come to a conclusion like that?' DCI Prendergast didn't realise he was sitting on the edge of his seat.

'Because the Vampire Killer murdered his friend Anna Leah who had the stone first.'

Libby had been listening for a while and made it obvious she didn't understand why Gabriel was putting his trust in a man who could have him locked up for months simply for failing to add his name and address to the force's ever-expanding public database. She put the tray down on the table on top of the stack of last year's magazines.

'Unless she hid the stone before he killed her or one of your boys in blue have stolen it, the Vampire Killer has it.'

'The young blond woman who hasn't been identified yet? She was a friend of yours?'

'An acquaintance.'

'And I take it she'll remain anonymous?'

'Yes.'

'Hmmmm'. DCI Prendergast sat in thought and distractedly sipped at his tea. 'Do you think Tony Ridout is the Vampire Killer?' .

'No. I do not believe Tony Ridout is capable of violent thought or deed. He is a good man.'

'I didn't ask whether you thought he had the intention, just whether he killed those women or not.'

'Once again you are asking for my opinion, detective

inspector.'

'I obviously value it.' He coughed in embarrassment.

'I think you already know the answer to that, in your heart, but he is safer where he is at the moment.'

'Believe me, there's nothing safe about Brixton Prison!' The inspector chuckled, before the smile left him. He leaned forward in his chair. 'What do you mean by safer?'

'Release him and they will kill him.'

'They? Why?'

'Systematic elimination of the enemy, inspector. It is simple. The fewer allies I have, the more chance they have of killing me. Besides, they like to kill and are hoping the deaths of the friends I have made here will somehow rile me into making a mistake.'

'I get it. This cult is after you. You've been their target all along and everyone you become acquainted with is a potential victim? Who the hell are you Radley?'

Prendergast had serious misgivings about allowing his professionalism to slip by following instinct alone. He had absolutely no doubt in his mind that Radley was dangerous.

The way he moved, the way he commanded attention and those eyes … trouble appeared to dog him. Yet, there was something strangely compelling about the personality he couldn't quite put his finger on. Whatever Radley was, DCI Prendergast knew he needed him. 'Are we on the same side Mr Radley?'

'I shall assume that you are asking whether I am good or evil. Do you fight for good Detective Chief Inspector Prendergast?'

The detective took a few seconds to answer. 'I like to consider myself a crime fighter. I believe my life's been committed to doing good.'

'You execute the law which works for and against mankind.'

'That is true, but the law is the law. We have rights to protect'

'And you do so by the violation of the rights of others. Who decides which evil is more necessary than the other?'

Prendergast didn't like the way this conversation was going. As a police officer, he had been forced to justify his motives and his very reason for being to cynics all of his life, but never to a man who seemingly knew his thoughts before he had even spoken them out loud. 'When a person is convicted of a criminal offence, he or she loses his rights as an ordinary citizen ...'

'By the simple assumption that he or she is no longer law-abiding?'

'Yes!' he didn't mean to raise his voice.

'But the law is not perfect. Where is the justice, for example, in prosecuting an elderly woman for petty theft when she is suffering from dementia?'

DCI Prendergast squirmed. That occurred back in his youth.

'Where is the justice in bargaining with the prosecution simply to secure a conviction while the victim of his irrepressible violence lies bruised and broken in a hospital bed? Will any conviction do DCI Prendergast? Is it so very important to get your man?'

'Of course not, but we do our best. The law is a complicated machine.'

'I shall tell you what I think.' Radley leaned forward in his chair, his eyes glowing with censure. 'Most men, at some stage in their lives, perform actions outside society's acceptable boundaries for the benefit of the common good. It is the reason behind the action that matters. Not the deed itself.'

'I'm not sure what you're trying to tell me. I assume you're telling me something.' He waited for a response but was answered only by the raising of one eyebrow. Prendergast nodded slowly to himself and sipped at his tea, allowing the ensuing silence to speak the words he couldn't. He would trust this man's words for

THE SLEEPING WARRIOR

now. He had a hunch that Radley would aid his investigations more than hinder them. He'd worked with hunches before and they hadn't let him down yet. He would, nevertheless, keep Radley close and fall on him hard if he stepped out of line. 'If what you say is true, and you weren't in Ockham last night, then is there any other person who could possibly be looking for this stone?'

'Yes, the leader of this cult you are so obsessed with'. There was a hint of playfulness in his smile.

'So you do know who they are?'

'You are making an assumption, detective, and it is a wrong one. Suffice it to say that I know what is behind them.'

'What? Is that a cause, a man or a woman perhaps?'

'None of those, he is a monster.'

'And he wants this stone too no doubt.'

'He would prefer my head on the end of a stake.'

'Somehow I believe he will have his work cut out in attempting that particular feat.' The detective laughed before the seriousness of the matter returned. 'I would like to speak with this man.'

'As would I.'

'I don't suppose you know where I can find him?'

'If I knew that, I would not be here now but you *will* meet him and, when you do, remember to remain in the light and do not ask his name.'

'The light?'

Gabriel's smile was enigmatic. 'Light, no matter how dim, will illuminate you. Do not believe his lies and, should you decide to hit him, make certain you hit him hard.'

'From what you say, I'm not sure whether I want to meet him at all.'

'He will, nevertheless, reveal himself soon. His killer's instinct consumes him and every moment I am alive erodes the scarce remnants of his sanity. He will summon you and you will answer his call.'

'This man needs to be behind bars!'

'Your bars will not hold him, Detective Chief Inspector, any more than they are able to hold me.'

CHAPTER Nine

'Роза Красная, мы встречаемся наконец'

Rose Red buried her hands deeper inside the pockets of her cardigan and tried to relax the rigidity in her shoulder blades. 'Your Russian is terrible.' She refused to flinch as the searing breath scalded her neck and the squealing nose took a deep, rattling sniff behind her ear.

'We, at least understand each other.'

'That is a question of opinion.' She turned her head slightly to view the intruder, but he pulled his away and placed his hands lightly on her shoulders. She stifled the shudder.

'A matter.'

'You see, accurate communication can be lost through literal translation. You cannot speak Russian, you are only able to translate the words, not the meaning. What are you doing in my home?'

Rose Red smarted against the intrusion and her own negligence in not having sniffed him out as soon as she'd walked through the door. It was a normal weekday night. She'd come home, changed her clothes, made herself something to eat and sat down in the comfortable chair in front of the television. After flicking through the endless list of channels, she'd chosen a documentary on Egypt on the Discovery Channel and settled down to watch it. She had no idea she was being spied on from very close proximity until she heard the voice behind her. She wondered how long he'd been there. She felt violated, but bit back her anger. He was good.

'I have come to collect.' The voice growled in her ear.

She felt him move from behind her chair and kept her senses sharp. 'I have nothing that belongs to you.' She wondered if he had a weapon.

'That, as they say Anzhela Mihailova, is a matter of opinion.'

She watched with cool dispassion as the man moved across the room and threw himself on the opposite chair without invitation. He was a tall man with a powerful physique. He wore an ankle-length coat over long black boots that were polished to an infeasible shine.

The lengthy hanks of black matted hair did little to cover his ruined face though and Rose hesitated to ask how he'd received such horrible deformities. His nose had been broken at the bridge and his left brow smashed into his skull. There was an enormous gash beneath his left eye that extended into his forehead, just missing the eyeball. The swelling and colour around the injuries and beneath his eyes told her the damage was sustained a good few weeks ago, but he'd received no medical treatment for them. She'd seen similar faces in zombie movies.

'You need a doctor.'

'Do you not find me handsome Anzhela?' his laughter was cruel and violent.

'That is not the point. Your skull looks fractured, you need medical treatment.'

'Your concern is touching,' he sneered, 'but I like it this way. I look in the mirror in the mornings and my reflection only strengthens my resolve to hunt down the man who did this. The pain keeps me focused on the task.'

Rose Red knew this man meant every word he said. She

could see the violence in his eyes: the gnawing hatred that guzzled all decency like an aggressive cancer on newborn flesh. She would have to be careful.

'Are you asking me to do something for you?'

The stranger threw his head back and shook with hollow laughter. 'I do not need someone else to do my work Rosa Krasner. It is an honour and a pleasure to take a life. You kill for cash, while I kill for sport. Either way, the pay-off is always satisfactory.'

The man's accent sounded a mix of Hispanic and Germanic and Rose didn't quite know where on the atlas to place him. 'Then tell me what you're here to collect.'

He paused for long moments, regarding her in silence with his one good eye while the sick one, bloodshot and swollen, quivered in its socket.

She felt the disgust welling in her stomach, but kept her gaze as level as she could.

He leaned forward in his chair. 'You were there that night. You took something from me.'

Her expression remained unreadable.

'That thing is mine and I want it back.'

'What did I take?' Rose Red hid her apprehension behind an ice-cool façade and froze the rising panic with years of practice. She knew this wasn't the Vampire Killer. She'd seen the man and could pick him out from a line-up of thousands. Why, therefore, had this intruder been following her or had he been following someone else?

'You know what it is Anzhela.'

'And when did I get to take it from you?'

The shattered face contorted in anger and Rose knew she should change her tactics or suffer a violent demise in her own home. Although the man showed no signs of animosity towards her, he had a killer's instinct – a characteristic she could recognise in others straight away – but he was also out of control. She would be no match for him, even if she had a gun. Behind the ruined features and the indifferent, almost cordial temperament, she knew this soul was as black as sin. He oozed evil and seethed with a malevolence so powerful she could feel it prickling her skin and the air around her became cloying and claustrophobic. She felt filthy just sitting in the same room as him.

'Give it to me and I will go away.'

'I do not have it.'

'You are lying.'

Rose had a sudden thought. Could this be the man she was sent by Weller to bring in? It seemed the hunted stalked the hunter and she now found herself in a very dangerous, if not fatal, position. She dared to ease herself out of the chair, taking care to stand slowly and without any sudden moves, calling on years of training to keep her body under strict control. She kept her hands soft and in plain sight. 'I think I know what you're talking about. It's in that drawer.' His silence allowed her to move slowly towards the pitch pine dresser in the corner. 'May I?' her hand hesitated over the drawer. The humour in his good eye told her she had his permission. She folded her fingers around the cold metal object and pulled it out. 'There!' she threw it in his direction.

He opened his hand and, on examining his catch, began to laugh. At first it sounded like a low rumbling of thunder, before it cracked into a violent peel of forked lightning. He laughed until even his bad eye streamed with water. 'How in this putrid little earth did you come by this?' He tossed the strange metal knuckle into the air and caught it in his other hand, playing with it like a delighted child.

It was only then she noticed his palms were thickly tattooed with strange black symbols. 'This is a typical Vascaran toy,' he twiddled it around his broad fingers, delivering his information like a specialist antiques dealer. 'It is a beautiful piece of craftsmanship, but it has been fashioned purely with vanity in mind. The Vascarans adorn themselves with metal in a rude display of prowess in battle.' He put the knuckle on his head and grinned. 'Look at me! Look how frightening I am decked in pieces of shiny bling.' He made a poor attempt at impersonating a giggling girl before hurling the object to the floor as if it had bitten him. 'I myself prefer a PS90. Where did you get it?'

Rose Red realised her mistake while she watched the crazed scene unfold before her eyes and in her own living room. She didn't know what a Vascaran was and neither did she care.

'Ah! He is the subject matter of a contract!'

The man was insane but sharp as a razor. Rose could only remain silent.

'That's why you were outside the lawyer's house that night.' His chuckle sounded more like he was clearing his throat, forcing the laughter to conceal a more hidden emotion. Did Rose Red see anxiety in that disfigured face? If it was there, it was gone in the next second. 'You were waiting for *him*. It appears, Anzhela, we are after the same quarry. What did he do to annoy your client?'

'He stole money.' She decided, if she was to offer information for nothing, then she would keep it vague.

The man tutted in disdain. 'Now you obviously know nothing about him, for that is definitely not his style. You'll have to start telling me the truth Anzhela or you'll not survive to find him.'

'I'll find him when I'm ready.'

'You'll find him when he allows it. First, you must let him know you are hunting him. The Vascaran is an honourable adversary, he will give you one chance to strike him and consider it a mistake on your part. If you take that second strike, he will consider it rude and will not allow you another. My advice to you is kill him before he sees you coming.'

'You seem to know this man well.'

He smiled, a knowing, charismatic leer that hinted at promise. 'I know what he is.'

'And from the fear in your eyes, you've obviously struck him twice.'

Rose regretted her sentence immediately as the unwelcome stranger leaped from his chair, his disfigured face a mask of fury. The ornaments on the desk shattered as her back slammed hard into the wood and his sharp fingers squeezed the breath from her throat. Just as she felt the consciousness drifting from her temples, the hand released her and she fell to the ground choking.

'Look', she gagged, 'I would love to speak to you more, but I have friends coming over any minute and...'

'People like you don't have friends, Anzhela. You could die in this flat and no one would know.' He sat back down in his chair, the mania in his ruined eye spinning out of control. 'The smell of your bloated, stinking corpse would give it away eventually, but only after your bodily fluids have been dried into the carpet for weeks and your beautiful skin has been withered to an empty, brittle husk. Now tell me what he's done to attract such attention. Amuse me.' He crossed his arms and settled back in the chair.

The despair at the truth of his words shuddered through her spine, leaving it brittle with ice. But Rose Red was a master in killing and the spin-off from this talent was an expertise in survival. She would tell him what he wanted to know and then she would get rid of him.

In all her career, Rose had never come across a man who could not be killed. If they bled, they were able to die and this one had been badly injured by someone who he'd allowed to come too close: someone he obviously admired and clearly feared. It was a tentative start, but it was enough.

Keeping her information as thin as possible and naming no names, pleading client confidentiality, she told him of the frustration of her contract, how she had come across the metal knuckle and what she'd been tasked to do next. 'That is why I was outside the lawyer's house that night.' She finished abruptly, realising her third mistake of the evening.

'The night you stole something from me. You saw the murderer didn't you? You went to the house and interrupted him.'

'I was not fast enough to save her.'

The man laughed again, finding humour in the irony of her inward struggle between practised professionalism and raw sentiment. 'Conscience, Anzhela, you have developed a sense of right and wrong at last. Will it save your soul? I mean, after all those lives you've brutally taken, are you seeking atonement?'

She hated his mocking tone. 'For what? I don't believe in hell or heaven.'

'What about good and evil?'

'Both are inherent in everyone.'

'Even in me?'

She couldn't think of a suitable answer that wouldn't offend him. 'I don't know you.'

'Yet you steal from me. You took something from the murderer's house that night. It is mine and I want it back. Give it to me and I will let you live.'

Rose Red wished she'd followed her own instinct and not stuck her nose into a situation that was none of her business.

How could she have known she was also being stalked that night? She relied on her survival instinct.

'Had you cared to follow me to the house, you would know I had no time to case the place. I interrupted a murderer, but was not quick enough to stop a murder. He fled out the front door and I ran after him. I lost him as soon as I was out of the drive, but I didn't return to the house. I wasn't about to be implicated in a murder investigation. That would ruin my career.

'Whatever you're looking for will probably be in police custody by now or still there.'

'It is not in the house, believe me, I have searched.'

'Then the police must have it.'

'They don't.'

She merely shrugged: he obviously had friends in the right places. 'Then the murderer?'

'You saw him?' there was a cold hunger in his ruined eye.

'   .'

He studied her face for long moments, his good eye frowning in disappointment. 'You frustrate me Anzhela,' he stood up quickly and Rose instinctively leaped backwards, her fingers clawing for the imaginary gun at her side.

His damaged face knotted into a grotesque grin. 'You have one week to hunt down your killer and return the jewel to me, Rosa Krasner,' he flicked what looked like a business card at her and it floated to the carpet.

'Call me when you find him. If I don't hear from you by this time next week, your dancing days will be well and truly over.'

'I can't give you what I don't have.' She watched him intently as he moved towards the door, his wide strides swallowing up the distance. 'Maybe your Vascaran has it.'

'Burial or cremation?'

She blinked as he opened the door.

'I look forward very much to hearing from you. Good luck with your hunt.'

It was a long time before she felt it was safe enough to move again.

—

'Would you please slow down, I can't keep up with you.' Libby shuffled across the hospital car park as fast as a pair of three-inch heels would allow.

'Your shoes were not crafted for walking. Why did you wear them?'

'Walking is not the problem. Had I realised I would be made to sprint everywhere, I would've put on a pair of jogging pants and brought a skateboard.'

She stopped to catch her breath and slammed her fists against her hips. "What's the hurry?' she wheezed.

'Something is not right.'

She rolled her eyes to the skies before flopping to the ground. She sat on the tarmac, crossed her arms and refused to budge, relieved the pressure was at least off her aching feet. 'You've been saying that all morning. Now we're not going a step further until you tell me exactly what you mean by 'not right'. Nicole is coming out of hospital today and all we have to do is collect her and take her to Maurice's house.'

She sighed as she watched him disappearing into the main entrance and was forced to roll out of the way as an ambulance hurried past her with flashing blue lights. She picked herself up and dusted the grit from her skirt, casting a sneaky glance around the car park to see if anyone had witnessed her embarrassing display of floor gymnastics.

'Come on.'

She jumped in fright as he grabbed her arm and hauled her through the entrance. She noticed Gabriel's discomfort as soon as they walked through the doors. Hospitals, with their complete reliance on electricity and digital technology, would be making his ears hurt and sending his brain into a jumble of nonsense.

'I hate hospitals,' she placed a hand on his shoulder as she scurried after him. 'I hate the smell of disinfectant because it's the stench of disease.'

'Are you finished?'

'I've only just started. Do you know how hard it is for an injured party to sue a hospital for clinical negligence?'

'Should I?' He ignored her panting as she scurried after him.

She cast him a surreptitious, side-long glance through a lock of hair that had come loose from her bulldog clip. 'I used to specialise in defending personal injury claims. It's really hard. Medical litigation is an overly-long, expensive process that can take over ten years for a plaintiff to receive damages. It's a frustrating, drawn-out process where only those with money, time and determination succeed.'

She leaped out of the way of a man in a wheelchair.

'The health board does it on purpose, you know. Their staff are fully insured and have some of the best lawyers in the business – like me, of course. They can afford to just sit and wait it out. Hi, Sophie, how are you?'

She sped after Gabriel, leaving her bemused acquaintance mouthing a return greeting to thin air. They took the stairs two at a time.

'Many firms take on clients on a no-win-no-fee basis but it's a scam. If the case is won, then the lawyer takes his cut and, after court fees, there is precious little left for a grieving widow whose husband died as a result of misdiagnosis. My firm is even worse, it defends the health boards.' Libby stopped abruptly to pull off her shoes. She wiggled her toes 'Bloody heels. I think, when I get back to work, I'm going to try to change things a little. I know it'll be a case of the voice of one crying in the wilderness but our legal system is a shambles. It's only available to the very rich or the very poor and court fees are extortionate. Please don't tell the Law Society I said that. They would strike me down with my rolled-up P45.' She suddenly noticed they were standing still, while the hospital staff, patients and visitors, trundled around them like competitors in a trolley dash.

'What?'

Gabriel had forgotten his urgency and was staring at her, an enigmatic smile on his lips.

'What have I said now?'

He shook his head and threw his arm around her shoulder. 'You are an extraordinary woman, Libby Butler,' he squeezed her into him.

'Does that mean you're beginning to like me?'

'I have always liked you, but now I like you even more.'

'Then will you carry my shoes for me?'

'No.'

They stood outside the ward doors and stared at the empty reception area. 'I'll find a nurse.'

'Excuse me, can I help you?'

She was stopped in mid-stride. 'We're here to check out Nicole Blais, I believe she's a patient on this ward.'

'Are you a relative?' The tiny nurse with the unfeasibly narrow waistline and shock of glistening curly brown hair eyed Gabriel with the glowing promise of seduction.

He ignored the unwanted attention.

'Yes, I am her father.'

The nurse snapped her head back towards Libby and blinked

in incomprehension. It took a while for it to sink in that the visitor was actually being cheeky. Feeling humiliated in front of an outrageously handsome man, the nurse narrowed her eyes. 'Sorry Mister Blais, I didn't recognise you. I think your beard has grown since the last time I saw you.'

Libby stood for a while, formulating a suitable retort, but eventually let it drop.

The nurse grinned victoriously. 'Ward visiting hours are from 2pm to 4pm and 7pm to 8pm, you'll have to come back later.'

'We've come to check Ms Blais out of her five-star accommodation. I was told she'd be ready?'

'Wait here please, miss. You, however,' she shot Gabriel a most seductive smile, 'can come with me.'

Libby waited for less than a minute, before putting on her shoes and entering the ward. She knew Nicole would be dressed in a less than seductive hospital gown and look a mess. With no straighteners or lip gloss, the glorious Ms Blais would not be at her pristine best. Meanwhile, Libby had dressed to impress. She had spent two hours on her appearance that morning while Gabriel impatiently paced the flat. She took a deep breath, flung her head back and strode into the ward with a flash of white teeth.

Her smile fled at the sight before her. Nicole and Gabriel were locked in a lovers' clinch. She sat on the bed, while he stood beside it. Her arms were wound around his neck, her bare legs wrapped around his pelvis and her face buried in his chest. He held her softly, protectively. He cooed words of comfort and reassurance in her ear and stroked her hair. It was an intimate scene of two people sharing a mutual affection for each other. Libby's heart felt leaden, her throat dry and the tears welled behind her eyes. What was worse, she'd no idea why she felt so emotional and couldn't understand the overbearing sense of loss that pressed against her ribs and threatened to stop her breathing. She turned around and ran from the ward sobbing.

She sat for a long time in a chair in the foyer of the hospital's main entrance and watched the world go by through swollen eyes. She cried for what seemed like hours and had been forced to decline help from concerned staff and patients who offered kind advice on dealing with grief and a number for bereavement counselling. Now she just felt numb and was too exhausted to work out the reason for her irrational sorrow. So Libby sat in silence with her feet on the chair, hugging her knees to her chest.

She watched the bustle of life without seeing and heard the idle chatter and the clanking noises of the hospital without listening. Her contemplation turned to Selina and regret. She thought of Tony and worried for their future together.

It was Carl's turn next and Libby wondered whether he'd been able to get home and, if so, how, without his clothes and credit cards. She only hoped he wasn't sitting next to Tony in a cold cell.

She pondered on her life and what a mess it was in, but knew she was changing. She was getting more angry with the world and questioning even her own existence. She judged herself more often and reflected on her actions, albeit after the fact. Suddenly everything was beginning to matter and she could barely cope with the responsibility of her own conscience. She saw his dark eyes and she shut her own, willing her mind to relinquish its reliance on him. She rested her chin on her knees. The world darkened around her.

Locked in her trance of misery, her eyes followed a group of youths who crossed the foyer as the emergency lighting flickered on.

They walked with purpose after a tall man whose boots thumped silently against the thin carpet and his long coat billowed behind him like the tattered sail of a ghost ship. His hair, thick as shredded black felt, concealed his face but Libby's heart vaulted in her chest.

He halted, sniffed at the air, turned towards her and grinned. In the panic around her as the hospital's electric lifeline snuffed out and a chorus of high-pitched beepers squealed in chaos, she could see his teeth shining behind the clumps of matted hair and the dark eye burning with recognition. He brought his arm up and pointed straight at her with a long, gnarled finger.

'Hello Libby!' His greeting was tipped with poison.

She didn't know whether to scream for help or run for her life, but she did know why he was here. She had to warn Gabriel.

The group continued on, their laughter echoing around the walls while men and women ran around in a twilight bedlam. Libby seized her resolve, grabbed her bag and her shoes and ran to the reception desk.

'Please, put me through to the Waddington ward,' she hopped from foot to foot.

The receptionist looked as though she was about to throw up: 'The phones aren't working. Nothing's working. There's been a power cut or something.'

'Never mind, it'll be quicker if I run.'

Throwing caution to the wind and having no clue as to what she would do when she got there, Libby hurtled down the corridors, knocking people and trolleys out of her way as she ran through the strobing lights.

Reaching the ward, she leaped through the doors and was immediately shocked by the stillness around her.

Something didn't feel right. She could no longer hear the multiple beep-beep-beeps of life-saving monitors or smell the disinfectant. She peered around the doors, but couldn't see anything apart from a few humps beneath the tight blankets. Nicole's bed had been freshly made, but she was not there and neither was Gabriel. Her attention was drawn to a bed in the far corner by the window where the curtain had been pulled across.

She felt the creeping dread bristling against her skin long before she heard the voice.

'Come in Libby and join the party.'

Libby had no option than to cross the space. Her destination seemed like years away. She kept her eyes level on the still, blue curtains and tried to keep her breathing shallow. She made it across the room on wobbling legs and raised a hand. The material was cold, but soft against her touch. She took a deep breath and hauled the curtains open ...

... to find an empty bed.

The laughter behind her broke the tension and she spun around, shaking with terror or anger, she no longer knew how to feel.

'I'm afraid the Hospicom system is temporarily out of order, but we have plenty alternative entertainment for you.'

All hell broke loose in the ward as the lumps in the bed sprang to life: laughing men leaped from the metal cots and stifling patients whimpered for mercy.

She had a horrible sense of déjà vu when the gnarled lips grinned at her, but the face she remembered in her nightmares had been re-arranged into a grotesque mask of ugliness and pain. Libby felt sick. His henchmen stood behind him, and the nurse she had been rude to stood laughing next to them with crossed arms.

A woman in a long nightdress, obviously once a patient, sported an ugly gash in her chest and the front of her laced bodice was streaked with a broad, wet crimson stain. She dangled from one man's hands like a macabre puppet, her wide eyes staring into oblivion.

Nicole whimpered as the edge of a blade stroked her neck; another nurse struggled for freedom against the tight grip of her assailant; and Gabriel sat slumped in a chair, his glazed eyes rolling in their sockets.

'What have you done to him?' The urge to run to him was overwhelming, but Libby's feet refused to respond.

'I've given him something for his pain,' the voice growled. 'He is going to need it.'

Two men moved slowly towards her, their white fangs glistening in the dim light. Libby had been here before. 'Gabriel?' she called his name like a summons to morning prayer. 'Wake up!'

'He has enough diamorphine hydrochloride running through his veins to put a herd of elephants to sleep. He hears you, but he'll not be able to find you.'

For reasons completely alien to Libby, she felt the bravado surging. 'You loathsome coward! You are just like every school bully I've ever known. You are … what? …' she made a swift mental count, 'seven men and a Silent Hill nurse against one? You need your little chums to protect you from him, don't you? He terrifies you.'

'And so, Libby Butler, still you don't know what he is.'

'No, but I am confident *who* he is and it doesn't take Inspector Morse to work out which one of you is the good guy.'

The man smiled, a cold and ruthless smile that promised an infinity of torture. 'Then let me enlighten you.' He moved over to Gabriel and hauled his head up by the hair, he teased an ugly, serrated blade between the rolling eyes. 'His blood is contaminated with opiates. Only he can cure this. He needs good blood to purify his own. How good is this shrink Libby? She messes with people's minds. She hides behind professional formulae to conceal her own immorality. She has even seduced your partner into adultery.'

Libby froze with indignation. She bit back the frustration as two men grabbed Nicole's arms and yanked her towards Gabriel. A strong arm pressed her shoulders so hard that she sank to her knees and a hand yanked her head to the side, exposing the side of her neck.

'How good is he, Libby?' The man slapped Gabriel hard in the face and grabbed him harshly by the hair. 'Let's find out!' The angry guffaw rattled from his throat. Libby could only watch as a screaming Nicole was roughly pulled nearer to Gabriel.

'Let her go!' Libby snapped, wondering where the courage had come from. 'She may be a bitch but she's done nothing to you, she's not a part of this. Take me instead.'

'Honour? From a lawyer? Now, who would've thought?' The ward erupted in tumultuous laughter.

He threw Nicole to the ground, her head bounced off the wall as she fell and someone grabbed Libby from behind and roughly hauled her towards Gabriel.

Face to face, she widened her eyes in earnest appeal as she thought she saw a fleeting glint of defiance in his. 'You really have to wake up, we are in big trouble,' she hissed.

His eyes dulled, then closed.

Her head was roughly shoved towards his. They were so close now that their chests were pressed together and she could feel his breath on her neck. In the circumstances, it should have been a terrible sensation but Libby felt the trance wash over her and she began to drown in its bitter-sweet embrace. She could hear the laughter, but it felt far away.

She could see Nicole's face, dazed first, then filled with

horror, then awe; she could hear the pounding of his heart and smell his familiar scent: it was bitter but there was an irresistible sweetness to it that compelled her to touch him. The corners of his mouth sparkled. She shivered ... and noticed the sudden silence around her, dragging her from her wonderful dream.

The hands that held her slackened. Not daring to move and concentrating on Gabriel, she cocked her head to the side as if listening for bird song. She heard a familiar voice and dared to turn her head.

Lars Andersson stood behind her, larger than life, one eye staring down the shortened barrel of a shotgun. It was pointed straight at the ugly man's head. A slim, striking woman stole up behind the ugly man with what looked like an open metal ring in her hands. Libby suddenly regained her natural ability to breathe.

'Never thought you much of a knight in shining armour, Mr Andersson.' She didn't dare to move.

The woman slipped the ring around the ugly man's neck before his colleagues could warn him. They stood around him twitching, not knowing what to do. The ring closed with an ominous click.

'Now, I have the remote control for your new necklace in my pocket. Try not to make any sudden moves because the explosive device inside it is very sensitive.' The woman with what sounded like an Eastern bloc accent purred her orders as she moved away from him slowly and placed her hand in the pocket of her jacket. 'I will leave it in reception if you are nice. If any of you make a move against me, I will push the button and save your   the expense of plastic surgery.' The clatter of weapons dropping was deafening. She turned to Libby and kicked an abandoned wheelchair towards her. 'Get him in the chair, now, and get him out of here.'

'He comes with us,' Lars growled.

'Not this time, Lars. He and his precious stone are the only life assurance policies I have at the moment.' She struck like a snake and, before Lars could stop her, he was wheezing against the grip of a metal choker around his own neck. She teased the gun from his hands.

'You're going to regret this Rose,' he rasped.

'Do you want to get out of here or not?' She turned her attention to Libby who sat gawking in confusion. 'I would move away from here if I were you. You wouldn't want to ruin your lovely clothes with bits of flying brain if this gets ugly.'

Libby almost threw Gabriel into the wheelchair, grabbed Nicole by the front of her starched gown and ran from the ward, through the dark, frenzied corridors and out into the car park where a battalion of emergency vehicles and squad cars had just arrived, their loud sirens flashing and screaming in outrage.

Before taking the northbound carriage of the M1, Libby stopped only once to pick up a car and some of Nicole's belongings from her Barbican home. They decided between them, by now, the police and the baddies would be able to trace Libby's licence plate and they needed transport that would not so easily give them away.

Fortunately, Nicole's long list of former husbands and boyfriends had left her with a suitcase full of diamond jewellery; some beautiful antique ornaments; and a four-year-old Bentley Azure convertible, the owner of which left for a job Stateside three years ago and hadn't come back to claim it – a small price to pay, Libby thought, to rid himself of the costly Ms Blais.

The car had been kept in pristine condition inside an expensive lock-up and the boot had been used to keep Gabriel's 'stuff' in, or so Nicole had said.

What she meant by 'stuff', Libby couldn't even guess at. She remembered him in a dark prison cell with not even a pair of socks to his name.

With her own car safely hidden behind the locked garage doors, Libby headed for the motorway in the only direction she knew. North

EVENING HAD JUST TOUCHED THE west as the ferry neared Brodick. The failing sun released its hold on the sky as the fire-tinged wisps of cloud snuffed out another day. In the distance, across a sleepy Firth of Clyde, the familiar dark peaks of the island's distant mountains lay at peace, the light mist caressing their jagged contours with feathery fingers. On the deck, leaning against the rail, Libby and Nicole breathed in the sea air and, with a good few miles of deep salt water between them and land, felt safe for the first time in a while.

'Do you think he will be all right eventually? I mean, do you think what they gave him will have any permanent side-effects?' Libby glanced over to Gabriel who lay sprawled out on the wooden benches beneath the sky, a dark coat draped over him and the hood of his sweatshirt pulled over his head.

'He's stopped vomiting at least, but he's had enough water during the journey, so I'm hoping he's just sleeping it off. It's difficult to tell at this stage, he's very weak. He's breathing better though and his skin feels less clammy. I think he'll be all right.' They turned once more to the western horizon and smiled at nothing in particular. 'It's very beautiful, your Scotland.'

'I used to come here for holidays when I was a little girl. See that.' Libby pointed like an excited child to the angular peaks embossed against the skyline. 'Those mountains are called Beinn Nuis and Beinn Tarsuinn and form a really familiar sight from the Ayrshire coast. In fact, it's one of the most brutal yet most beautiful sights in the world. I've always loved it.' Lost to happier memories, Libby quite forgot how much she disliked her newfound travelling companion. 'See how the contours look like a recumbent man? They call him the Sleeping Warrior.' She turned her head to check on Gabriel and was surprised momentarily by the similarity of the two sights. 'The Sleeping Warrior,' she mouthed the words soundlessly. 'Good God, I wonder who he is!' They stood for a long while, watching both magnificent views before Brodick harbour finally pulled into sight.

Libby gibbered throughout the remainder of the journey, the lies spilling easily from her tongue. She told her passengers that the remote cottage in the hillside near Lochranza belonged to her uncle. She could hardly tell them Carl had bought it two years ago for a secret love nest, used only when they pretended to their respective partners to be attending conferences. She was glad Gabriel was out cold in the back of the car for the remainder of their journey.

'This is your uncle's home?' Nicole's expensive heels tapped against the wooden floorboards as she made her way to the window and peered out. She drew the curtains and leaped back with a yell as her fingers brushed against the dusty cobwebs hanging from the rail.

'There's only wildlife and trees out there for at least two miles, Nicole, there's no need for city anxieties in this place.' Libby stood at the front door, her arms straining against the bags of supermarket provisions they'd picked up on the way. She hoped she'd sounded convincing enough to influence her own fears.

'It's basic, in a quaint sort of way.' Nicole's fine nostrils contracted against the smell of desertion over the winter.

Libby dropped the bags. 'Just because the furniture's not genuine Queen Anne, doesn't mean it's not comfortable or tasteful. Besides, you'd better get used to it because it's going to be our haven for a while.' She hated that disdainful sneer. 'If the accommodation's not up to your fastidious standards, Nicole, there is a really nice cave not far from here that doesn't have curtains.

'This will do just fine.'

'Help me get the food in then.' Libby spun on her heels and stumbled in the dark to the car. She fumbled for the door and, as her hand reached the cold metal, she froze. She peered out into the blackness of the surrounding trees and remembered how much she hated the dark. The light of the cottage was a dim glow behind her, yet in front of her was an infinity of shadow where something sinister and malevolent stirred just outside her vision. The leaves rustled and something screeched. She whimpered and managed to open the passenger door through sheer strength of will. The interior courtesy lights came on at once and Libby was startled from her panic.

A cool hand enveloped hers and caused her body to spasm. 'You are fine.'

His smile chased the horror into the night. He looked tired.

'I should get him to bed.' Nicole rudely shoved her out of the way and hauled Gabriel out of the back of the car. 'We'll take the bedroom at the back, the one with the pitch pine dresser and tacky, cliché tartan curtains. I'll look after Gabriel if you get the rest of the food in.'

'Hey, that's my room!' Libby slammed the car door and shuffled after them, not wishing to be left alone in the dark. She remembered choosing those curtains during a trip to Braehead. 'They weren't bloody cheap!' she protested as she watched Nicole and Gabriel disappearing into her bedroom. 'Snotty, arrogant bitch!' she snorted as the door closed behind them.

Many hours later, sitting by the kitchen table with a cigarette stub in one hand and an empty glass in the other, Libby had never felt so alone in her life as she watched the dawn break through the small sash windows. She'd always loved this place: its calm serenity and its remote anonymity. She could smell the same faint whisper of a sea breeze and the fresh tang of pine forest, but somehow neither felt as familiar as before.

Libby gazed at the drained bottle on the table and wondered how it had all come to this. A few days ago, she had a job, a home, a partner and a life. All she knew had gone and she was left to face an unknown future by herself. She gazed around at the characterless walls, their colours drained by the morning light, and noticed that the tiles, the sink and the cooker were in dire need of a good scrub.

She turned her attention to the closed door beyond the sitting room and sighed. The place that had always been a haven of excitement and expectation had now become a soulless tomb. The chair legs screamed against the wooden boards as she rose and staggered towards the couch. Flopping against the cushions she fell into an uneasy sleep.

—

Maurice Blais staggered out of the taxi and fumbled in his pockets for his wallet. He threw the driver a tenner and waved a plump hand before slamming the door. He watched the black cab disappear into the neon mist, the rain splashing from the tyres above a steaming tarmac. He swayed once or twice before pointing himself in the direction of his front door.

Maurice had just endured possibly the worst day of his life but he had cause to celebrate and believed he deserved to be drunk. The rum and coke swilled in his stomach and waged war with his ulcers, but the discomfort was nothing in comparison with the headache he'd suffered from the barrage of constant questioning.

It seemed to Maurice that everyone expected answers from him: answers that he clearly didn't have but that didn't stop everyone from asking the questions.

First Carl Bottomley hauled him into his office for an interrogation. He wanted to know if he knew where Nicole was; whether he had heard from Libby; if he knew anything about Gabriel Radley; what happened in the hospital and why? Carl appeared very agitated, almost frightened.

When he'd finished with Maurice, the police had asked exactly the same questions in the same order. Then, when Maurice's headache was at its most severe, Lars Andersson had questioned him all over again. Everyone had questions and no one would take 'no idea' for an answer.

He'd kept a piece of vital information to himself and hoped he wouldn't be charged with obstruction once this all blew over. Nicole was safe and well. He received a text from her a few hours after her apparent escape from the hospital which told him she would be lying low for a while until it was safe to return.

What that quite meant, Maurice didn't know. He worried for her safety and wondered, not for the first time, why all this was happening.

The point of the key scratched the paintwork of the door as he attempted to get into his house. His one point two million pound ground and garden maisonette in a Georgian terrace in Primrose Hill had been his pride and joy for over twenty years. It was his sanctuary and provided him the bedrock from where he could recover from the knocks and blows that fleeting disappointment and transient lovers dealt him from time to time.

'Trevor, are you home?'

'In the kitchen, sweetie, it's pasta and pesto again, I'm afraid.'

'A perfect end to a perfect day,' Maurice felt his stomach groaning in complaint. He hated pesto. 'Hope it's not the green stuff ...'

His sentence was cut from his tongue as if a sharp razor had just swept across it. The kitchen walls and surfaces were covered in blood, Trevor's blood. It was as if someone had taken buckets of the stuff and chucked it haphazardly at the walls. The carcase of his now former lover lay in a butchered heap on the slippery tiles and a man with a ruined face sat in Maurice's favourite chair by the range, wiping his knife with kitchen towel.

'I have some questions to ask you.'

—

Libby sighed as she ended the call and placed the mobile down on the kitchen table. Feeling vulnerable and alone, she needed to hear from someone who loved her. Her father was the last comfort she had left and the sound of his concerned voice made her feel like a child again.

She spent the entire day watching a closed door, afraid to leave the cottage, her anger brimming with each passing hour she'd been forced to spend in the company of only herself. She'd broken her crushing silence by phoning Carl and Maurice, but neither was picking up.

Eventually, she found her father who'd helped her work through her fears until the battery ran out of charge. She'd told him everything she knew and made up most of what she didn't. The only thing she failed to tell him was where she was, hoping not knowing her whereabouts would somehow protect him from her.

'What's for dinner, I'm starving!' Nicole shuffled from the bedroom wearing only a sheet. She stank of sweat as she passed Libby towards the kettle.

'I'll just give the concierge a ring and ask him for room service!'

'There's no need for that tone ...' Nicole sighed and ran her fingers through her matted hair. 'I look a fright. This place stinks of cigarettes.'

'That's because I smoke.' Libby couldn't bring herself to ask after Gabriel.

'He is the most extraordinary man I have ever met.' The sentiment came out of the blue. 'He is ...'

'Oh spare me the details.' Libby felt her hackles rising.

'... a most intense and intuitive lover.'

'I think I'm going to be sick.'

'He's in the shower. He wants us to talk.'

'Does he really? What could he possibly want us to talk about?'

Nicole sat at the kitchen table, obviously trying to formulate her words. The effort looked as though it was about to kill her. 'He wants me to go back to London and speak to the police. He says I must get Tony's name cleared.'

'You?' Libby laughed. 'Are you both conspiring to have him sectioned?'

The Divine Ms Blais looked nervous: she twitched with unease as she stared into her empty mug and wrapped her manicured fingers around it. She started awkwardly. 'Tony and I went back to your flat on the night of the party. We made love while Selina sat in the car.' She closed her eyes as if to fend off an invisible blow. 'Lá, ça suffice, I have said it.'

'You did what?'

'The person attacked me as I was coming out of the flat. It couldn't have been Tony, he wouldn't have had enough time to put on his clothes and follow me down the stairs. Besides, I left him sleeping. He was very drunk and passed out.'

Libby looked at Nicole as if she'd just produced a hand grenade from under her sheet and pulled the pin. For once she was lost for words.

'I'm sorry Libby. Tony has been in love with me for years. I never meant this to happen and now I can tell you because it's important. I thought I loved him, but I now know I never did. I'm in love with someone else now and I know the difference. I've been foolish and I need to make amends. I want to make it better.'

Libby heard Nicole's inane rantings as if the words were gurgling from the bottom of a drain. Bewildered and shaken, she didn't even realise her fist had curled into a tight ball until she took the swing. Nicole flew from the chair, her teeth splitting through her lips before she could yell out.

'You bitch!' Libby leaped on her and pummelled at whatever flesh and bone she could come into contact with. Sitting on her chest, she grabbed a handful of fringe and smacked Nicole's head against the tiled floor a couple of times before slapping her face. 'You patronising, lying bitch! I've spilled out my guts to you on your Chippendale couch for all these months and all the time you've been using that knowledge against me to ...' She couldn't bring herself to say it. Instead she raised her fist for the final knock-out and squealed in frustration as a firm hand caught her wrist.

Gabriel lifted her off the ground, her arms and legs flailing wildly. 'Put me down, you bastard! I hate her! I hate her! And I hate you too.'

She kicked for a few moments more until the futility of her efforts and finally exhaustion overwhelmed her. She burst into tears and flopped into the arms that held her. 'You despicable cow!' she managed one final insult before she ran from the room screaming.

—

It was a long time before Gabriel quietly entered her bedroom and sat down beside her on the bed. She shrugged his arm away. 'Fuck off!'

'I have done nothing to offend you, so do not offend me.' She sat up, making to leave. He grabbed her wrist and she struggled against his grip but he held firm and finally managed to haul her into him, hugging her closely. She ceased her protest, softly enfolded in the first comforting gesture in days. She felt the tears returning.

'We must both learn to control our fear if we are to survive this.' He stroked her hair with soothing fingers.

'You don't seem like the kind of bloke who's frightened of anything.' She wiped the dampness from her eyes with a brisk swipe of her sleeve.

'Up until now, I would have agreed with you but I now know what it is like to lose control and I never want that to happen again. Fear is a very dark place for the lost.'

'Welcome to the world of mortals,' she felt him shiver and conceded a cheerless smile. 'You just have to stay off the class A drugs and you'll be fine. All I have to do is get used to the life of a fugitive and keep a bit of distance from a bunch of snarling assassins with guns and sharp teeth.' She let out a deep, heavy sigh. 'I really should've seen that coming, you know. I suppose I've always suspected it, deep down I mean, but was probably too busy living the lies of my own life to realise what was staring me in the face. It appears even that bloke with the ugly face knew before me. Did you know also?'

He nodded.

'Then why didn't you tell me?'

'It was not my tale to tell. Sometimes the truth is too difficult to brave, but it must be faced in the end. Nicole has been courageous enough to reveal her truth and in doing so will spare an innocent man from injustice and you from a future of lies. You will have to bare yours eventually.'

'There's nothing honourable about that bitch.'

'She will do the right thing. You must now speak to her with civility and bury your hypocrisy. You will feel better for it.'

'I already feel better for having smacked her in the mouth.' Libby wriggled free from his arms. 'What about your truth Gabriel? When will you practise what you so eloquently preach? Isn't it about time you came clean and told me who you are? What you are? Why you're really here and what you're here to do? I don't believe for one minute that you've lost your memory or lost your way. You know exactly what's going on and you're deliberately keeping me in the dark. I've lost everything I know because of you and it's about time you told me why. Don't I also deserve the truth?'

'You are not ready for it.'

She hauled his arm from his eyes. 'Now is as good a time as any. Who are you?'

He swung his legs over the side of the bed and leaned back on his hands. His jaw was set to 'resolved'. 'I am a stranger to these lands.'

'No shit! Now tell me what I don't know, like who are those people that are always trying to kill you? In particular, who's the ugly one that's scared of you?'

'He is of no consequence to me. I was sent here to find another and bring him back. I do not have much time left.' His eyes darkened with frustration.

'How long have you got?' Libby was gripped by a sudden jolt of panic. She'd never thought of Gabriel ever leaving and now he was telling her their time together was limited.

'I will know when the time comes.'

'Oh, for God's sake, there you go again with your nonsensical answers.'

'Sorry.'

She waited for a better response but none came. 'OK, then Gabriel or whatever your name is, if we're going to play dirty then now's not the time for my truths either. I'll keep mine for as long as you keep yours and Nicole can go jump in the Clyde.'

His laughter surprised her: it was bitter, yet resigned.

'You're never going to get rid of her now, you know. Nicole Blais has a set of ugly hooks and they leave horrible scars on anyone attempting escape.'

'I have handled difficult women before.'

'No doubt. I hope you've got a good pair of running shoes.' She felt the anger welling once more and knew Tony had little to do with it. Somehow the perfect Gabriel had become soiled: dirtied by the filthy claws of Nicole Blais.

'Nicole and I are consenting adults, Libby, and neither of us has emotional commitment, not even to each other.'

'She's in love with you.'

'Nonsense.'

'She told me she was.'

'When?'

'In the kitchen just before you stopped me from ripping her head off.'

'Love! I have heard that word bandied about so many times

throughout the short duration of my stay in this insane place, but I have never been convinced that anyone actually understands the meaning of the word.'

'That's a really mean thing to say. I saw her face, it was starstruck and Nicole's not a woman to reveal raw emotion so casually – especially to another woman. You're stuck with her I'm afraid.'

He searched her eyes for artifice.

'Damn!' He obviously found none.

'Didn't see that one coming, did you? Now who's the hypocrite?'

'I am.' He threw his arm over his eyes once more. 'I am a very long way from home.'

Libby sat for a while, knowing Nicole would be anxious as to what was happening in the bedroom and smarting from her burst lip, swollen jaw and broken tooth.

At this point in time, Libby didn't care if she sued her for criminal assault. It was worth being arrested for. Her concern, however, turned to Gabriel who appeared uncharacteristically morose.

'You can't afford to be frightened. You have to look after me. You've got me into deep trouble and I don't want to die just for having had the privilege of knowing you. I don't want to spend the rest of my life running from people who want to kill me and I certainly don't want to spend any more effort trying to protect you – aren't you supposed to be the heroic one?'

'Heroes!' He sat up beside her, ran his hand through his hair and laughed at the irony of the situation. 'I have seen so much violence and death, but I find myself fighting this battle at a severe disadvantage. There is too much that I do not understand and too little time to train for it properly. Meanwhile my enemies exploit my weaknesses to their advantage. I fear that the outcome of this will be a bad one for me and everything I know. I must draw him out, but I have lost the means by which to do so.'

Libby suddenly realised the loss of his mind through a near fatal dose of morphine had knocked the stuffing from Gabriel and she wondered whether his long spell in the bedroom with Nicole was really an effort to hide from the outside world and the violence that awaited him.

'You can't afford to lose confidence, Gabriel. Pessimism will only lead to defeat. You must have an advantage of some sort, otherwise you would be dead by now. Twice they've tried to kill you and twice they've failed. Now, all those men with all that impressive hardware couldn't manage that simple little feat and it's not as if they don't have the disposition to murder.' Libby turned to him and picked a tiny white feather from his hair. 'Now I don't know much about killing people, but I would say they're toying with you; trying to break down your confidence.'

He idly traced the contours of the pattern on the bedspread with his finger, apparently deep in thought.

'Maybe they need to keep you alive and are only taunting you or maybe they think you have that stone that you're all so obsessed with.'

There was a very long pause and Libby thought he must have fallen asleep.

'Could it be that simple?'

'What?'

'I believe you may be right. If there is any chance I have the stone, then they know they will have to take it from me. He will have to take it from me.'

'Who the bloke whose face you rearranged?'

'No, the person who I am here to take back – a monster who calls himself Shinar – he will remain in hiding and continue to elude me until the stone is found.'

'Monster?'

His nod was grave.

Libby shuddered. 'And you're talking about this stone as if it was the One Ring.'

He studied her for long moments, trying to understand the connotations of what she just said.

'Would not a professional jewel thief be inexorably drawn to the world's most precious diamond? Would a scientist risk turning his back on a definitive cure for cancer? The stone compels him. He cannot resist its pull.'

'Is he a hobbit?' She stared at him for long moments, half expecting him to say yes. 'What'll happen to him if you manage to get hold of this stone first and catch him?'

'A fate worse than death awaits him.'

Libby could almost hear the clanging of a funeral bell. 'What can be worse than death?'

He turned to her now, his black eyes dangerous, 'Believe me, death can be the sweetest of embraces in comparison with some things.'

She didn't want to know what those 'some things' could be. 'We could set a trap. The police could help and even that Russian woman, whoever she is. I trust she is a friend of yours.' His questioning look was enough to tell her he had no idea what she was talking about.

'A trap it is then.' He kissed the side of her head as if she'd just given him a birthday present.

'Does this stone have special powers?'

'It is only a stone, but Shinar believes it is important: so important that he hides from it.'

'He must be terrified that it'll do something horrible to him. What was Anna Leah doing with this stone?'

'She stole it and was taking it to Shinar before she was intercepted by circumstance. I was sent to retrieve it, and him.'

'So Anna Leah was an enemy of yours also?' Libby, trying hard to understand the complexities of Gabriel's mission, couldn't help but shudder. 'Well, Sleeping Warrior, you've set yourself an impossible mission.' She stood up and stretched her back. She groaned as her vertebrae let out an audible crack. 'First you have to find a killer; then you have to wrestle a stone from him before catching a monster and taking it back in chains to wherever 'back' is. No pressure then?'

—

Rose Red kicked off her high-heeled shoes and ran through the streets as if she was being chased by a horde of demons. She felt her heart pounding in her mouth as every breath became more painful and her lungs threatened to burst, but she couldn't stop.

Too terrified to look behind her and whimpering in fear, Rose truly felt there was nowhere safe in her world any more. Reaching her car at last, she fumbled in her bag for the keys, screaming at her fingers to co-ordinate swiftly. She sped off, sucking in each breath in agonising gasps and trying her best to keep her eyes on the road instead of on the rear view mirror from where she expected any moment to see a twisted face leering at her.

Rose drove for the best part of the night, unwilling to return home for fear of meeting the man whose company she had been subjected to for less than three minutes. Those one hundred and eighty seconds felt like a lifetime and she barely took in his instructions as he told her what he wanted from her. The man called Shinar was, without doubt, the most malevolent creature

Rose Red had ever encountered and she would forever feel tainted and filthy.

CHAPTER Eleven

IN ALL HIS YEARS WITH the Force, DCI Prendergast had never experienced such a violent time.

'*In four hundred yards, at the junction, turn right.*'

There had been yet another murder in the long list of brutal crimes that hounded the enigmatic Radley. This time, the lover of Nicole Blais' father: stabbed to death in his own kitchen. And then there was Monsieur Blais himself, a point blank blast had shattered his skull but hadn't managed to kill him. He'd been left for dead but was lying in intensive care with only half a cranium and under heavy police protection. It would be a long time before he could talk again, if at all.

'*In two hundred yards, at the junction, turn right.*'

It had been difficult to keep the newshounds from ruining the investigations. Baying for blood and a front page splash, they were normally more of a hindrance than a help and their constant thirst for sensationalised half-truths was becoming more than a small annoyance. Occasionally, however, their interference would have its advantages.

With little information to bulk-up their word counts but a series of violent incidents to report and prime suspect Anthony Ridout charged with murder, the case would now be impossible to report until the court hearing when it would return to the public domain. Eager to fill the white space in the front pages with anything they could attach to 'vampire' 'Dracula' and 'killing', the press were now linking the serial murders and all the recent sprees of brutality in London to a member or members of an elusive cult calling themselves The Awakened. The sharpened teeth and red face paint, plus the movie-world's love of monsters, gave the media both the perfect headlines and the perfect suspects.

'*Turn right.*'

'Damn!' He winced at the loud squealing of wheels and the angry horn from an on-coming van.

Fortunately, the press coverage had given the police the first real lead since Ridout was charged. A female caller had left an anonymous message on the Crimestoppers number which said she had seen a man fitting the description of the so-called Vampire cult exiting a former church in south east London and DCI Prendergast was on his way to check it out.

'*You have reached your destination.*'

Andrew Galbraith Prendergast didn't know whether it was the dishevelled building before him that caused his muscles to fail or a sudden, inexplicable panic attack. His fingers gripped the door handle but resisted his attempts to open it. Nausea overwhelmed him. The former house of worship stood alone on the corner between the bleached rows of Victorian terraces with contemporary interiors: a once humble area built for honest workers but which was now home to the credit-hooked nouveau riche of the times.

The church stood like a rotten tooth in a pretty smile. The bleached patches of grass and weeds, withered from their stalks, thrust their parched leaves skywards: fossilised in a final, desperate prayer. The building stooped forlorn and abandoned of all hope; its once delicate glass panels blackened with age and neglect; its heavy doors clinging to squealing hinges. Water wept down the crumbling stone face and dark brooding clouds hung over the ruined steeple, frowning at the ominous absence of the cross. This was a most forsaken place.

'Yeay, though I walk in the valley of the shadow of death,' he heard himself reciting what he remembered of the prayer unconsciously before his fingers twitched against the handle and the car door swung open. He braved his misgivings and righted himself, wishing he'd spent more of his Sundays on his knees in worship than on his feet washing the car.

'Pull yourself together, man,' he chided himself through clenched teeth as he picked his way carefully up the path towards the ruined church doors. He curled his fist into a ball but decided against knocking; fearful the rusted hinges would yield to the impact of his knuckles. 'Anyone home?' he called into the darkness beyond the doors but was answered only with silence.

The inspector stood listening for an answer from the gloom inside. Each passing moment brought a fresh sensation of unease until he could hear his own pulse banging against his temples. A car horn sounded and he leaped in panic. The involuntary action caused his muscles to spasm; he caught his toe on the worn step and lost his balance. With a yell he plunged head-first through the doors and landed hard on his knees. 'Damn it! Damn it!'

'Are you seeking punishment from the divine, inspector?' A rasping voice greeted him from the other end of the nave behind the ruined altar. As DCI Prendergast stood up and dusted down his trousers, he noticed a small figure dressed in a red coat shuffling towards him on the right aisle. He was forced to rub at his eyes. He could've sworn the figure was standing at the vestry door but it was half way across the aisle.

'Sorry about the door, I lost my footing,' he started with a stammered apology, still reeling from the strangeness of his host. 'This place needs to be demolished. I don't think it's safe.' He took a long look about him and could almost feel the holy building's outrage at having been left to fall into ruin. The place stank of damp and rot.

'Would you seek to destroy everything that is unsightly in your eyes, inspector?' the voice growled.

'There are health and safety issues here.' DCI Prendergast felt his tongue soldering slowly to the roof of his mouth and his eyelids lost their impulse to blink. He had seen many things in his career that could have been described as evil, and on more than one occasion, but the man before him took the description to the very top of its limits and re-defined the concept.

The figure was small and twisted with corruption; the wrinkled, leathery complexion brittle with vice. DCI Prendergast had seen more life in the eyes of a corpse. This was a filthy, unholy creature and the experienced detective had trouble resisting the urge to punch the sneer from its contorted features.

'You are perspiring heavily,' the voice cackled. 'I am Shinar.'

'Is that an Arabic name?' The inspector found his voice at last but only by averting his gaze from the deadened eyes that watched him as if he were a gourmet meal. Taking a deep breath, Prendergast smarted against his own fears and tried to pull himself together. Realising the man and his surroundings ticked the descriptions of every house of horrors cliché Hammer ever invented, he managed to claw back his rationality and, with it, some of his failing dignity.

'It is a Biblical one.'

'Of course,' Prendergast was beginning to believe he'd been set up for some elaborate joke. 'And no doubt it has a divine significance.' He scanned the corners of the church with quick, sidelong glances, half expecting his colleagues from the Yard to leap out at him laughing.

'It means the watch of he who sleeps.'

'Like a night nurse?'

The eyes blinked slowly and only once and Prendergast felt his soul recoiling against the imminent assault they promised.

'Why are you here inspector?'

'Just a routine check, Mr Shinar. We've had reports of antisocial behaviour in the neighbourhood and I just wanted to check it out.'

'The force is using the well-paid members of its expensive criminal branch to do the job of a patrol officer? Come now, inspector, I would not want to call you a liar to your face.'

'Of course, not. Forgive me, Mr Shinar, I am ...'

'Oh, I know who you are detective chief inspector,' the interruption was meant to be challenging as the malicious eyes cast a vague glance at the flash of badge.

Prendergast cleared his throat and pondered on the man's age. He eventually decided it was impossible to tell. He could have been fifty or one hundred and fifty. 'I am conducting an extremely complicated ...', he hesitated to wipe the sweat from his brow and coughed into the steaming hanky, '... investigation and I've been given reason to believe that a possible suspect or suspects have been seen in or around these premises. I am merely following a lead. Do you live here alone Mr Shinar?'

The smell of rotten flesh and excrement invaded his senses suddenly and the detective did all he could to prevent himself from choking. The stench cloyed at his nostrils and burrowed deeply into his lungs, causing his breathing to become rapid and shallow.

'Sometimes.'

Prendergast didn't know what to make of the answer and called upon his years of experience to pull himself together.

'Does that mean you have occasional lodgers or an occasional partner?'

The thought of the latter made him want to vomit. He fought back the nausea welling in his stomach but could feel the lump creeping steadily up his gullet, despite his efforts to gulp it down.

'Do you have good reason to be asking me these questions, detective chief inspector?'

'I have good reason to believe that a member or members of a distinctive gang or cult that call themselves The Awakened may be operating in this area and Scotland Yard would like to question them.'

'What have they done?'

DCI Prendergast took a few moments to ponder on how much he should give away. He was loath to scare off his suspects before he'd even caught them. 'We just want to eliminate them from our inquiries.'

The man laughed, a dry, throaty cackle that was devoid of humour but thick with irony. 'Or implicate them?'

'Them?' It was not so much Prendergast heard a noise from the vestry door or whether he just had a strong feeling he was being watched: watched and laughed at. 'The members of this cult, for want of a better word, paint their faces and sharpen their teeth ...'

'Yes, I am familiar with them.'

'Are they a Christian cult?' Prendergast could not conceal his doubt.

'They are a highly religious order.'

'Where are they based?'

'Here, everywhere.' Shinar spread his gnarled fingers out wide.

'Who's their leader?'

Shinar shrugged, but the coldness in his eyes betrayed his insincerity. 'I cannot help you with that'

'Can't or won't?' He waited for an answer but none came. He was hit by another wave of nausea and that rotten smell again, only this time it was so strong, he could taste it in his mouth.

'You do not look very well.'

'Think I'm coming down with something. Damn summer colds.' He swabbed his fevered brow with the wet hanky. 'Mind if I take a look around?' He made to take a step forward, but Shinar barred his way. He was only a small man but projected a presence so powerful he could've been a giant.

'Do you have a warrant?'

'Do I need one?'

Both men stood facing each other, the challenge rising in the backs of their necks. 'You will find nothing in this place, detective chief inspector. Salvation abandoned it years ago. If it is dangerous criminals you seek, then you are looking in the wrong place.'

'Then where should I be looking, Mr Shinar?' DCI Prendergast felt his knees buckling; he had to get out of this place. The urge to run overwhelmed him and he grabbed the back of a splintered pew to steady himself. He fought against the dizziness but felt his stomach heaving.

'This violence will end once the Vascaran is gone. He is the sole cause of this chaos. I understand there is a serial killer on the loose and the force lost some officers in a safe house recently. The member of a notorious gang is dead and his manuscript stolen. Now would you not love to find out who is responsible for the deaths of your own, detective chief inspector, and the reason behind all this destruction?'

'The Vascaran?'

'He is a most accomplished assassin.'

'But why ...?' He coughed out his words as another wave of nausea struck.

'A Vascaran does not require a reason. He kills because he can.'

'What is a Vascaran?' The words now staggered from his mouth and Prendergast could not remember waiting for an answer. He just managed to reach the doors before his stomach heaved the contents of his half-digested breakfast onto the step. Swaying on his feet, he fled down the ruined pathway and hurled himself into the car. DCI Prendergast didn't recall the drive back home but did know the journey felt like the longest one he'd ever made in his life.

—

Libby smiled as the morning sun touched her eyes. It felt good to wake up to the sound of happy birdsong over roaring engines and to take in clean air instead of choking on exhaust fumes. She'd been awake for a while and, snuggled in a warm duvet, enjoyed the benefit of time to ponder on the beautiful things in life. Nicole had been gone for two days now: her farewell had been heated with challenge but Tony would hopefully be in the clear and the police lavishing him with embarrassed apologies about 'just doing a difficult job'. The national press, however, would be far less willing to let a month's worth of sensational front page splashes end a long run of excellent circulation figures and newshounds, whipped into action by frenzied editors, would be sniffing around Tony and everyone he knew.

Tony. Her relationship with him would be over and Libby couldn't help but regret the circumstances that had ended it. After all the craziness that had taken place over the past few months, however, she felt strangely detached from the man she'd lived with for over five years. She was glad the first part of his suffering was over and hoped the mud wouldn't stick to him and ruin his life. Somehow she knew this was only just the beginning of his ordeal and she'd have to help him through it, but not just yet. The water gushing under that particular bridge was a bore. Yet, Libby couldn't help her uncharacteristic urge to forgive: to condemn Tony for his folly would be to condemn herself and there was little point in lengthy deliberations on what could have been.

She hadn't seen Gabriel much, but was content he wouldn't be far away and watching over her. He appeared to spend his time exploring the island on foot; climbing mountains and running around the hillsides. Occasionally, he'd come back to the cottage to eat and last night he came home to sleep and was still in bed. It was, after all, five thirty in the morning: a stunning morning in Arran it seemed from the kiss of sunlight through the curtains, and she would enjoy the calm before the violent storm to come.

It wasn't until the clunk of a car door outside her window made her realise she'd also heard wheels scraping on the drive. She leaped from the bed and peered out into the morning sunlight.

'Oh, my God!' Carl's familiar figure in baggy tracksuit and stark white trainers stood beside his BMW estate as he looked around and stretched. Nicole must've told him she was here.

Libby's elation swiftly turned to anguish, however, when the passenger door swung open and a dishevelled Deidre staggered from the car. 'No!' Libby momentarily froze in horror. She sprang into action. Swiftly making the bed, she gathered up her belongings into the cradle of her nightdress and hurtled into Gabriel's room. She threw her stuff around the room and leaped into bed. 'Just shut up and read my mind,' was all the warning she gave him.

'I will not be a willing participant to this ridiculous farce, Libby.' He made to get up.

She pressed herself into him. 'Please, please, please do this for me, Gabriel. I'm not asking you to lie, just go along with me.'

'You want me to pretend that we are lovers in order to make him jealous and to mislead his poor wife? I am outraged!'

'It's not like that at all.' She threw the duvet over her head at the sound of a closing door. 'Oh God, they're coming inside, look busy.'

'Look busy?' He made to sit up again, but she threw her arms around his neck.

'What are they saying?' Her whisper hissed in his ear.

'They were not expecting anyone to be here. He is confused and she is frightened. Now get up and go and speak to them before he does something stupid.' He peeled her arms from his neck, obviously amused by Libby's anxiety.

'Ssshh, he's heard us!' Libby pulled her nightdress over her head and stuffed it underneath the duvet. 'Don't get any wrong ideas!' she giggled and snuggled into him.

'I suppose there is only one way to do this honourably and without the necessity for subterfuge,' he slid over the top of her and Libby's eyes widened.

His dark eyes glowed softly as he teased the hair from her face and ran his fingers down the side of her neck. She shuddered as a firm hand found the soft flesh at her side and he buried his mouth in her neck. His muscles were taught, his body lithe and powerful. He smelled of passion. 'Gabriel, what are you doing?'

It was too pleasant a sensation to stop him and her words came out as tiny gasps as heavy waves of electric shocks rippled through her body. Her back arched and her pelvis melted into his.

A loud knock on the door broke them apart and Gabriel spun onto his back laughing.

Libby was annoyed he hadn't taken the moment as seriously as she.

'Hello? Is there anyone in there?'

'Hello. I'll be right out!' She shot the triumphant Gabriel a withering glower. 'Ha, ha! You're so funny!' Gliding from the bed on her hands and knees, hoping he wasn't peeking, Libby found the discarded pair of jeans and a t-shirt on the floor and slipped them on.

'Carl, Deidre, what a pleasant surprise!' She tried to sound as unconvincing as possible as she closed the door softly behind her and sidled out from the bedroom. Carl looked devastated to see her.

'Hello Libby, we weren't expecting anyone else to be here. Were we Carl?' Deidre remained as pleasant as ever through her confusion, while Carl couldn't make eye contact. 'It's awfully nice of your uncle to offer us his cottage for the week.'

'Yes, he's a very generous man. I think one of us has got the holiday dates wrong though.' Her sentence was directed straight at Carl but she couldn't help but notice Deidre's twin plaits hanging limply from pink checked ribbons on either side of her head.

'Would you mind if I used the bathroom? It's been a long journey.' Deidre's legs were crossed beneath her pink checked skirt.

'This is your home too, Deidre, you don't have to ask. It's over there.' Libby waited until she heard the bathroom door close. 'What the hell are you doing here?'

'I could ask you the same thing.' There was a madness in Carl's eyes that shocked her. 'I've stuck to our little ruse and told

Deidre this place belongs to your uncle.'

'That's what I said too.'

'We've all been worried sick about you. Have you any idea how much trouble you've got us all into?'

'What are you talking about?'

'Selina is dead; Nicole is missing; and Maurice is in intensive care, fighting for his life. They blew half his head away. It seems that, wherever you go, you leave a huge body count and no one who knows you is safe anymore. I tell you, Tony is better off where he is. If they let him out, he'll be dead before he makes it home.'

'Maurice?' Libby was forced to sit down before she fell. 'Who? How?'

'I'll fill you in with that in a moment. Suffice it to say it looks as though he's going to survive. In the meantime, what are you doing here?'

'It was the only place I could think of that was safe. What about you?'

He turned his eyes to the ground. 'Same. The kids are at my sister's in Guernsey. Thank God you're all right. I half expected you'd be dead, but I received information that you'd escaped that terrible attack on the hospital ward. You know people were killed?'

'I take it Mr Andersson managed to relieve himself of his expensive necklace without suffering a messy make-over.' She could've laughed had the subject matter not been so serious. 'Were you followed?'

'I hope not, otherwise this will be the shortest holiday I've ever taken.' He began to pace the room, the agitation twitching in his cheeks. 'What's going on Libby? How can this be fixed? There are eyes everywhere and they're all pointed at you and everyone you know.'

'Including you, Carl.' The realisation dawned. Carl had come to escape the growing possibility of ending up in a morgue wearing only a toe tag.

'Where is Radley?'

'Sleeping.' His nervous expression turned to one of utter horror. Libby did laugh this time and ignored Deidre's questioning look as she sat down at the kitchen table next to her. 'That's very good, Carl. Trust no one, keep your own counsel and stay out of trouble. It's a jungle out there and everything wants to eat you. Would you like some tea?'

'No thanks.'

'Some midge repellent then?'

'We are leaving.'

'But we have only just got here.'

'Your wife is right, Carl, you have come a long way to find safety. Welcome to a few days of sanctuary. It will not last long, but at least we have time for me to teach you how to stay alive. I offer you peace.'

Carl visibly shrank as Gabriel, dark and commanding, crossed the space between them and held out his hand in cordial greeting. Carl had no option but to shake it. He cringed as the same geniality was offered to Deidre who took the firm hand with a soft smile.

'Offer our guests some refreshments please, Libby.'

'Certainly, Master Karlof, but I'm afraid we're fresh out of virgin's blood. Will the bile of young children suffice?' She was surprised by Carl's horrified gasp. 'I'm kidding Carl!' Her eyes rolled naturally to the ceiling. Instead of reaching for the kettle, Libby poured her guests a large gin and tonic, plus a larger one for herself.

All three were downed flat.

'I've never been to Scotland before. This is a lovely place,'

Deidre began with the pleasantries, hoping to thaw the icy atmosphere. 'Aren't you Scottish, Libby?'

'Born and raised in the outskirts of Stirling, but my parents moved to the south of England when I was eleven. My father went to Edinburgh after my mother died. I stayed in London to finish my degree, but never managed to leave.'

'Do you think you'll ever come back here to live?'

Libby shot a glance to Gabriel who stood at the sink with his arms crossed.

He returned a small smile.

'I suppose I don't really want to return to parochial life where people's minds are as narrow as their arteries.' She let out a little sigh, 'Who knows what the future holds? It may contain nothing.'

'What do you mean by teaching us to stay alive?' Carl couldn't help himself. His anxiety for his own safety and his hatred for Gabriel brimming dangerously, he had to ask.

'Gabriel is going to help you find your backbone.' Libby answered swiftly, still smarting from Carl's despicable cowardice. 'It's not so much your association with me as your knowledge of him that's made it dangerous for you.'

'But I don't know anything about him!'

'On the contrary, Mr Bottomley. You know where he is right now and it's your fault there's so much interest in him. You told your gangland buddies about my association with Gabriel otherwise why else would Lars Andersson be on my case? Why else would he also turn up at the hospital? Why is Weller so interested in Gabriel?'

'He's not the man you think he is Libby. He's a dangerous killer. More dangerous than you can imagine. He kidnapped Simon Barry, stole his manuscript and killed half a dozen policemen in doing so. He then took out Mr Weller's men in front of him; put a bullet in Barry's face; stole Weller's money and blew up his business. That's why Lars Andersson was sent to find him. There's now a contract on his head and it's only a matter of time before the hit is made: he's a dead man, Libby, Weller does not miss.'

'Did you kidnap Simon Barry, Gabriel?'

'I sprung him from police custody and I delivered him alive.'

Libby's mouth dropped open. 'Why?'

'You told me yourself that there was an employment opportunity with a cash incentive and that Weller wanted the man delivered to him.'

'Where is the cash?'

'In a suitcase under the bed.'

'Good God.' She was forced to sit down before she fell. 'You stole his manuscript?'

'He left it lying around.'

'You killed those policemen to get him?'

'No. I did not need to. They were careless watchmen and I took advantage of that.'

'Liar!' Carl's bravado turned to terror in an instant when he found himself slammed against the kitchen door choking against the hand that pinned him by the neck. The roaring in his ears drowned out the yells from the women in the room.

'Let us get this straight between us,' Gabriel began with a low growl as Carl's face turned an unhealthy red, 'I do not lie and, until this moment, have had no necessity to kill civilians, but you are fast forcing me to change my mind.'

'That isn't the truth and you know it.' Despite Carl's precarious position, his temper had consumed him. 'You may have tricked gullible Libby into your confidence with your silver tongue, Radley, but you can't fool me. I know too much about you now. Are you going to kill me like you murdered all the others?' The hand squeezed his neck harder and his face began to turn purple. 'Did you silence them like you're trying to silence me?'

'What are you talking about, Carl?'

Libby could only stand helpless while Carl spluttered his accusations out as if spitting out a bad taste.

'He killed the woman in the park. You were there that night, Libby. Perhaps it was you he was stalking all along. Tell her what you are Gabriel Radley.'

'Please, Gabriel, put him down.' Deidre's desperate pleas fell on deaf ears as Carl began to choke and his eyes began to roll.

'He's a monster.'

'SILENCE!' Gabriel roared. It was a terrifying sound and turned Libby's backbone to ice and caused Deidre to run whimpering for cover. It was a command that would have stopped an advancing army in its tracks and sent grown men screaming into the hills. The grip on Carl released and he fell choking to the floor.

'Monster!' Carl spluttered. 'Murderer!'

Although Gabriel stood with his back to her, Libby noticed something passed between Carl and him that she could not see. What she did see was Carl's face turning ashen: to say he was stricken by abject terror would be to grossly understate the apparent. He sat flopped against the wall with his mouth agape, his eyes welling with the fear. 'Fiend!' he gasped.

Libby looked to Carl and then to Gabriel, wondering if she'd suddenly gone mad.

The door banged open and Gabriel was gone, with no one having seen him leave.

'**DON'T BE STUPID, CARL, THERE** are no such things as monsters, vampires, zombies or creatures from the Black Lagoon.'

Libby sipped at her tea and watched the ferry shifting slowly over the calm water towards the harbour. The morning mist had retreated from the sun with the pledge of another fine day on Arran with blue skies and a warm, but brisk sea breeze. Libby understood Scottish weather well enough to know the sky rarely kept its promises.

'Even the Vampire Killer is not a real Transylvanian monster. I mean, he just thinks he is.'

As Libby gazed out over the Firth of Clyde, the mainland was just about visible. She smiled at nothing in particular and felt her irritation dissipating into the blue horizon. Libby loved the Isle of Arran, mainly for its seclusion from the rest of the busy world just across a strip of sea.

Brodick was unusually quiet as Libby and the Bottomleys sat at a familiar table looking out to sea. For the past three days they'd visited the same wooden table at the same café in the town for breakfast where they'd remain for a few hours, feeling less vulnerable in the company of strangers. Each new day brought fresh anxieties: Carl's for his safety; Deidre for the children she'd been separated from; and Libby's for the man whose absence left a large hole in her heart.

Deidre had also been quieter than normal. Over the days she

seemed to have withdrawn into herself and barely spoke at all. She sat next to Carl with her eyes downcast, pushing her cold eggs around the plate with her knife.

'Gabriel walks in the daylight without getting fried. He doesn't have fangs...'

'... Doesn't he?'

' ...And he doesn't drink the blood of maidens. Furthermore, I've seen him eat whole cloves of garlic and he sleeps in a bed, not a coffin. For God's sake, you're an intelligent adult who's enjoyed a privileged education. Dracula was invented by Bram Stoker and adopted by Hammer Horror to elevate Christopher Lee into the Lairdship of Summerisle. Next you'll be telling us you're Van Helsing and Deidre's an orc!'

'I don't care whether he's a real vampire or Frankenstein's monster, what matters is what *he* thinks he is. If he thinks he's a vampire, then he's probably the one responsible for killing all those women. He's delusional, Libby. Delusional and dangerous.'

'He's not a killer.'

'No? What about Tony. Is he a serial killer?'

'You seemed to think so.' Libby sat back in her wooden chair and crossed her arms: a gesture that barred Carl from taking the subject further. They fell into silence again.

Libby would never have believed she'd be sitting in such close proximity to her lover and his wife, holding idle conversation and sharing intimate space.

It was an unusual situation to find herself in, yet the bizarre events taking place around them bound them by circumstance and, even odder to Libby, it didn't feel uncomfortable or difficult to live side by side with the Bottomleys as a couple. She wondered what Deidre was thinking.

Gazing at her from across the narrow table, Carl's normally well-groomed wife appeared dishevelled and morose. Her grey eyes focused on the plate in front of her and she either failed or was not in the mood to make eye contact with either of her companions.

'Where do you think he's gone?' Obviously aware she was being scrutinised, Deidre placed her knife and fork neatly on her plate.

'I don't know.'

'Who cares?' Carl growled.

'I do.'

Carl turned his head around slowly towards his wife, the bewilderment hanging from his jaw. 'Why?'

'Because he's alone and possibly very upset. You did insult him terribly after all.'

'Insult him?' Carl was genuinely taken aback.

'You called him a liar and then a monster. You don't even know the man and you hurt his feelings. You're very good at that, aren't you Carl?'

Libby wondered whether there was a deeper import to Deidre's sudden outburst.

'He could've hurt you, you know,' the glee shone from her eyes momentarily. 'He could've hurt you quite badly, but he didn't. He decided to leave instead. Is that the stroke of a delusional murderer? Now we don't know where he is or what he's doing apart from he's by himself with no friends and no one to support him.'

'Deidre?'

Carl turned that whining voice on and Libby rolled her eyes to the ceiling.

'I think he's seen and been through a lot.'

'Oh, yeah, how do you make that out then?' Libby was quite amused at the thought of a smitten Deidre. Perhaps she was taking her revenge.

'He's just got that look about him. He's such a handsome man but there's a terrible sadness to him also. I wish I could've got to know him better but that's not going to happen now, thanks to Carl.'

'Deidre!'

'I'm going for a walk. I'll leave you two to bicker about what is or could've been. Thanks for breakfast ... again.'

Libby's walk took a little longer than expected. Her idea of following the shoreline along the beach turned out to be a fairly difficult feat. The rain had come on suddenly in a deluge, despite the promise of a beautiful day only an hour ago. She'd been forced to thrash through bracken, clamber over slippery rocks and even get her feet and legs wet a few times before she eventually made it back to the café where the frantic Bottomleys were just about to scramble the police, the coastguard and the mountain rescue team.

A furious Carl chastised her for her short disappearance, believing she'd encountered the worst kind of trouble and perhaps been killed.

She'd taken her usual defensive stance and they'd argued all the way to the car on either side of a sullen Deidre. The three made the journey back to the cottage near Lochranza in silence. As they passed the mountains to their left, the Sleeping Warrior lay shrouded in mist between the mountain peaks and roiling clouds and Libby's heart sank into a renewed despair. By the time they reached the cottage, she was almost in tears.

'Good morning, Carl.'

Carl had barely pulled the key from the front door when a voice greeted him from the inside. He stopped still in his tracks and Libby ploughed into his back. 'For God's sake!' she hissed before the shock registered on her own face. 'If it isn't the great Geat, Mr Andersson.'

'Aw, Libby, you're insulting me again. I'm from the north of Sweden, Beowulf was from the south.'

'Can I ask what you're doing here?' Libby crossed the threshold swatting at the opportunist midges that had taken advantage of the grey skies to come out of their shady hiding places and feast on her. Lars Andersson sat on a stool in her kitchen, his hand dwarfing a large mug of coffee.

Two equally proportioned men, their shifty eyes scanning the room, stood behind him, one of them tucking into something he'd found in the fridge. He had a nasty scar embroidered into the top of his head.

'Don't bother to answer that question. I'm glad you've made yourself at home.' She turned to Carl. 'This is your doing, isn't it?'

'Mr Andersson's come for his own reasons, Libby, and I must admit I'm quite relieved to have him here.'

'Here?' Libby's eyebrows arched into her hairline, 'there's no way those over-dressed baboons are staying here with ...'

'Rude little cow, this little lackey of yours, Carl. You gonna let a bitch talk to you like that?'

Libby swallowed the brimming outrage along with her bravado when Gary Weller emerged from the bathroom zipping up his flies. She cast Carl a questioning but furious glower.

'Gary,' Carl gushed as he pushed past her and held his hand out in greeting, crossing the kitchen floor, 'this is a pleasant surprise.' The hand was shaken firmly. 'You've met my wife, Deidre?'

'That your wife?' Weller eyed Deidre with undisguised distaste. 'No wonder you've got a mistress!'

After a brief but tense pause, Carl guffawed but the audibleness of his laughter revealed only his nervousness.

'No doubt you're wondering why I've come all the way to this God-forsaken, gnat-ridden 'ovel?'

Libby thought Lars Andersson looked uneasy. Although his posture was casual, his shoulders were so tense they could've been chiselled from granite and his fingers were wound a little too tightly around his cup.

'Seems like, if a job's worth doin', may as well do it meself. Where is 'e?'

'Gone.' Carl whimpered the word and sat down next to Lars before his knees buckled and caused him a painful and embarrassing fall.

Weller leaned over the kitchen table, his fingertips digging into the wood, his gold rings winking from his manicured fingers. He brought his face up a shallow breath away from Carl's. 'Gone where?'

Libby noticed the two standing men behind Carl began to slip closer, one still chewing on the cold sausage, but she was too frightened to cry out the warning.

'I ... I ... I'm not sure.'

'You're not sure?' His grin could've frozen the sun in seconds. 'Could I ask you to 'azard a fuckin' guess?'

'I only saw him briefly. We argued and he left.'

'I thought I asked you to keep 'im in your sight till Lars got 'ere.' The bellies of Weller's pair of minders pressed against Carl's back. Weller was accustomed to getting his own way all of the time.

'He's too dangerous. I have women to protect.'

'You 'ave women to protect?' the echo jeered.

Weller had shifted into one of those moods that would be impossible to snap out of without hurting or maiming something. Libby realised Carl's position had now become extremely precarious. One part of her believed this should serve him right. She knew he'd told Weller the whereabouts of Gabriel and afforded himself some protection in the process.

He'd been waiting anxiously for Lars to turn up for three days, scanning the harbour for the morning boat from the vantage point of the Brodick café window. He hadn't expected Weller to be with him.

She could see the beads of sweat seeping from the fretful furrows on Carl's forehead and she couldn't help but fear for him. Weller had a nasty temper and was more than capable of ordering Carl's murder.

Two large pairs of hands grasped his shoulder and Libby opened her mouth ...

'Gabriel left three days ago. We haven't seen him since.' To everyone's surprise, it was Deidre who spoke. She busied herself by casually emptying the contents of her shopping bag on to the kitchen table. 'No doubt he's returned to London. I don't think he'll be coming back.'

'No? And why do you say that?' Weller looked more stunned than intrigued. The hands slid off Carl's shoulders.

'He took all his stuff and left.'

'Had a lot of stuff did 'e?' Libby noticed the surreptitious glances between Lars and Weller.

'A couple of bags,' she shrugged.

'Any idea what was in those bags?'

Deidre twisted the lid off a new jar of coffee and stabbed a teaspoon into the paper seal. 'I'm not in the habit of rifling through other people's belongings, Mr Weller.'

'Did 'e leave anythin' 'ere?'

She shook her head and flicked the switch on the kettle. 'No, I believe he took it all. I vacuumed quite thoroughly this morning. Coffee anyone?'

Libby was impressed. She certainly hadn't seen that coming. Deidre's attempts to diffuse a volatile situation appeared to be working. Weller's violent mood had quelled as curiosity replaced anger. Carl's long-suffering wife could possibly have saved him from painful injury or worse.

'You're quite close to this Radley bloke. Maybe you know where 'e went.'

It took Libby a few seconds to realise Weller's attention had turned exclusively on her. She didn't like being under the spotlight and visibly flinched. 'I'm sorry, Mr Weller, but I can't help you. Gabriel left the house like Diedre said and ...'

'I think she's lying. She's a lying little bitch, isn't she, Carl?'

'I don't think Libby's done anything to deserve your rudeness, Mr Weller.'

Deidre was silenced by a hard slap to the face that knocked her to the floor and left her spitting blood onto the tiles. 'Shut up you stupid cow!'

Libby aimed her shocked eyes towards Lars who continued to sip at his coffee, his expression unreadable. The shrill whistle of the kettle and the loud click as it switched itself off caused her to jump.

Her next move astounded even her. She had no idea where it came from and certainly didn't intend it to happen. Outraged by the cowardly assault on Deidre and Carl's failure to protect his wife, Libby hurled the shuddering kettle at Weller. His quick duck in advance of the impact caused it to hit the doorframe behind him, but not before a stream of scalding water slapped the left side of his face. She stood staring at her outstretched hand as if it had just betrayed her.

'You know that a person can still live after 'is belly's been slit open?' Weller struck up a casual conversation with the air as he ambled towards the work surface by the range and picked up a roll of clingfilm. His eye was half closed and his cheek was streaked an unhealthy purple. 'I've seen it 'appen a few times. The skin parts and the guts come tumblin' out. Guts stink, you know, and they make a sickening, squelching noise when they spill.' He unravelled the roll slowly, stretching out the transparent sheet to the width of his ample stomach. 'If you don't nick the gut when you're stabbin' it and you wind this stuff round the wet bits', he demonstrated by pretending to bandage his girth with the clingfilm, 'then you can get to the 'ospital and get stitched up and, apart from a nasty scar, you'll live to remember all the gory details. You got your knife on you Stevie?'

Libby took a step backwards into Carl. Her features, contorted in disgust, changed to blind panic when she noticed Weller was directing his information straight at her. 'You wouldn't dare!'

The chair legs made a deafening shriek against the tiles as Lars Andersson stood up, 'I need to take a piss,' and ambled from the room.

Stevie stepped towards her with a sharp blade glinting in his hand.

'Just a shallow cut now Stevie. One gutless legal brief's more than enough for me, eh Carl?' Weller grabbed her arm as Stevie lumbered towards her.

—

Rose Red had been listening to the conversation outside the window of the small cottage and felt history repeating itself with depressing regularity. She could not get that voice out of her head: the one that called her name with such urgency that she needed to break the door down.

She followed Gary Weller and his henchmen from London, knowing they would lead her to the elusive Vascaran, whatever that was, but once more she was faced with a palpable predicament. Her last intervention cost her a lot of trouble: it heralded the end of a once lucrative career, her anonymity and possibly her ultimate health. The Vascaran was the only lifeline she had left. She needed that manuscript as an insurance policy against Weller's retribution for the double-cross at the hospital and she needed that precious stone as a bargaining tool for her life.

Choosing sides was not something Rose Red had often been faced with, since she'd always worked alone. Now she found herself staring down the barrels of twin guns and two equal evils twitched against the triggers.

When this was over, she promised herself she'd take her cash, leave her guns behind, buy a vineyard in the South of France and live out a cliché European millionaire's existence. That's if she lived long enough.

She let out a long, deep sigh, shook the soft voice from between her ears and made her career move.

—

Carl yelled as the front door burst open and a single shot felled the man with the knife. The noise made a dull thunk and Stevie's eyes appeared to cross before he teetered backwards like a falling oak and thudded to the floor, his hand still clutching the handle of the long blade. The hole in his forehead oozed sticky blood and the wall behind him displayed a Rorschach blot of bone and brain.

'Oh, my God, he's dead!' Carl shrieked, choking on his own disbelief. 'You've killed him!'

'Yep, that's Rose for you.' Gary Weller chuckled loudly as Rose Red aimed her sight at him. 'Now what did Stevie Myers ever do to you?' If he was shocked or annoyed at the violent intrusion, he didn't show it. 'E only got out of 'ospital a couple of weeks ago. Now look at 'im.'

'Should I put a bullet in your fat stomach, Weller, and see how well that clingfilm works in keeping your stinking guts in?' She turned to the two women who could only gawp in incredulity at the dead man on the ground. 'You two, get over here!' The end of the gun twitched and Deidre took less than a second to choose a side. She scrambled behind Rose, followed closely by Libby.

'What about me?'

'Please, miss, he's my husband.' Deidre's appeal was from the heart.

'Your husband?' Rose could hardly contain her disgust. 'Some husband.'

'And what about me, miss? I don't have children but I do have a gun.'

Rose Red felt the cold metal against the side of her head, closed her eyes and smiled as she lowered her weapons. 'Hello Lars. Never thought you one to oversee the torture of innocent women.'

'Never thought you'd be one to save them. We're all full of surprises, Rose.'

'You stupid bitch, Rose, what the fuck were you expecting to gain from that little scene?' Weller snatched the Berettas from her hands and threw them into the sink beside him. 'This is comical, this is. What the fuck are we all doing 'ere?' He hurled his hands in the air to over-dramatise the predicament. 'Take 'er outside and shoot 'er. She's no fuckin' use to us now.' He spun around to Rose Red: 'Consider our contract terminated. You!' he yelled at Libby, 'get back over 'ere. We've got some unfinished business.' He marched across to the dead man and wrestled the knife from the cooling fingers before offering it to his other minder who already had his gun drawn. Weller hurled his eyes to the ceiling as Libby hesitated. 'Don't make me 'ave to

shoot you too. I 'ate guns. Now get over 'ere! And Carl, fuck off
back to the Smoke. I'm gonna need to speak to you on Monday
morning.'

'We're going nowhere without Libby,' Deidre shook off the
hand that attempted to haul her out the door.

'What did you say?'

'I said we aren't leaving without Libby. If you make me, I'll
go straight to the police.'

'Deidre, shut up!'

'I mean it, Carl.'

'Don't bother, I'll strangle the bitch with me own bare 'ands!'
Weller lumbered towards Deidre.

'You're not capable of doing your own dirty work, you little
coward!' Libby added more anarchy to the situation and Weller
whirled around as if caught in the eye of a tornado.

'Come on Libby, let's go.'

Weller spun again as Deidre continued to defy him. 'Will
someone give me a fuckin' shooter.' he screamed.

'The gun is such an arbitrary weapon.'

A coolly-composed Gabriel sat at the end of the table in
padded trousers, a black t-shirt and a broad leather strap pulled
diagonally across his chest. His forearms were clad in the leather
vambraces he'd been wearing when Libby first met him. He had
a calm look about him: elegant and composed.

He twisted Lars' gun around in one hand and the elaborate
hilt of a long, heavy sword rested in the other. The blade lay
against his leg. There was blood on its otherwise pristine surface.
The sharp edges were as thin as razors and blinked in the light
with the promise of instant death.

'Vascaran, assassin, chaos? What the hell was that all about?' DCI Prendergast sat in his office somewhere inside the multi-storied block of concrete and glass made famous by the place-name on a large revolving sign. He had enjoyed many career firsts from the same desk over the years but all faded into inconsequentiality in comparison with this. The detective inspector, who had what could be called a successful career to date, could've made a fatal error in judgment and thoughts of the consequences kept him awake at nights.

He had just returned from a long walk along Victoria Street, through Buckingham Gate and back to the Yard via Petty France. Coming from rural Yorkshire, DCI Prendergast had come to London twenty-two years ago as a fresh-faced bobby where the biggest action he'd encountered was replacing the chain of his bicycle. London had widened his horizons as well as his eyes then and he still reeled from the culture shock to his system.

England's capital city was the loneliest place in the world. Despite the droves of people who swarmed the pavements and buildings, to work, to shop and to visit, all of them in a determined rush, not one face was memorable; not one character notable. En masse, London's vast population lacked individual significance: a city full of nameless faces all wearing the same fixed expressions; all of them on a mission to somewhere.

Yet, out of the incessant throng, there were two that left an indelible imprint on the soul of DCI Prendergast: the man he'd met in the church yesterday and the one that was called The Vascaran. And, somehow, Andrew Prendergast knew in his gut just who the Vascaran was. His instinct told him the former was capable of the foulest of deeds, including murder. But it was the latter that troubled him most. From what Shinar had surreptitiously divulged, Gabriel Radley was a murderer and a cop killer and it didn't take a detective with the acumen of

Einstein to reasonably deduce he could also be the elusive serial killer.

If this was true, then DCI Prendergast had made the biggest mistake of his career. Could he have been wrong to trust him? He remembered Radley's words during the only conversation he'd had with him: 'It is the reason behind the action that matters. Not the deed itself.' Was he somehow justifying mass murder with some form of proper motive? If so, then it didn't matter where Radley was from, what he was doing here, or why: he was breaking the law and he would be caught, tried and punished accordingly. Catching him, however, was going to prove difficult, for the man did not exist.

—

Libby's brain felt as if it had taken a violent jolt as the scene before her appeared to jump forward. Before the last blink, she was staring at Gary Weller's outstretched arm as he made to take the gun from his minder. Deidre stood by the Russian woman with her hands on her hips while Carl tried in vain to haul her through the open door. Lars Andersson held a gun to Rose's head.

After the blink, both Gary Weller and his suited henchman were doubled over clutching at their sleeves screaming. There were splashes of blood everywhere. A gun, a knife and severed fingers lay scattered over the tiles.

A dazed Lars Andersson searched his pockets and jacket for something while Rose Red, Carl and Deidre stood frozen in time, their mouths gaping wide.

'A sword is far more discriminate,' Gabriel continued as if delivering a lecture in weaponry to children. 'Learn to use it properly and you will not miss. Neither will you kill by accident.'

He turned to Libby and smiled. 'We have to leave now.' He leaped from the table and threw the gun across the room, far enough away for no one to be able to reach it before he could strike. Gary Weller cried out in shock at the sudden, infeasible, movement towards him.

Libby didn't hesitate to ask why. She trusted him. 'We'll have to bring Deidre along with us and Carl I suppose.' She exchanged a small smile with Deidre.

Gabriel merely nodded and, with an outstretched arm, brought the tip of his blade up to rest lightly against Weller's jugular. 'So you are The Saint? I regret that the last time we met, I was in too much of a hurry to make your acquaintance properly.'

'That's what they call me. And you are?'

'I am the one who does not venerate you.'

'What's in a name anyway? Weller cackled. 'You're the bloke that brought me Barry. What did you do to 'im?'

'I merely reminded him of the consequences of his actions, something that you sorely need to come to terms with.'

'You're nothin' but a fuckin' thief!' Weller rasped.

Gabriel's eyes narrowed dangerously. 'Now, you were talking about gutting a person. I am not certain whether your methods will work in preserving life but am more than willing to try them out on you.'

He teased the tip of the blade down the centre of Weller's chest, hovering over his heart for a brief moment before slicing the buckle from his leather belt with a perfectly-placed incision.

Gary Weller had lived too long in crime to be afraid of losing the physical contents of his stomach. He was, however, not accustomed to pain from a personal perspective and the stinging from the loss of his fingers and the burn to his face made him reluctant to discuss the merits of his hallmark system of torture.

Despite Weller's outward bravado and his defiant eye contact with his stronger adversary, Libby did notice the pools of sweat beneath the armpits of his jacket and the moistness of his over-tanned brow that made the strands of hair stick to his forehead like wet grass. 'Where's the manuscript?' He didn't mean to whimper.

'In a safe place.'

'You see.' Carl made a sudden move and regretted it immediately. He slowly lowered his pointing finger at the behest of Gabriel's dark scowl. 'I told you he was a murderer, Libby. All those policemen, what did they do to him? He's not the man you think he is. He's not even a man. He's a …. Tell them Gary.'

'Yes, tell them Gary.'

Libby smiled. Those black eyes, those eyes that violated the soul and hauled it out shrieking for all the world to judge, had a devastating effect on Weller. Calm now, Weller turned his attention to Carl. ''E didn't kill them coppers. She did. Rose don't like coppers, do you Rose?'

Rose Red simply smiled.

''E didn't kill Simon neither. I blew an 'ole in 'is 'ead. Didn't 'ave much choice cos 'e 'ad a loaded gun pointed at me face. It was 'is idea.' He nodded towards Gabriel. 'You're right Rose, 'e's either got a bleedin' good sense of justice or a lovely sense of 'umour!' He paused, seemingly lost to despair. 'Judgment!' he let out a bitter chuckle. 'You weighed 'im; 'e come up short, didn't 'e? 'E wanted to die. 'E was ready. You can't cheat the executioner.'

No one but Gabriel had any idea what Weller was talking about. To Libby, it looked as though Gary Weller knew fear for the first time in his life and it didn't sit comfortably on his padded silk shoulders. She almost pitied him.

Yet, looking closer and listening to his garbled words and disjointed reasoning, it was more as if he was making his last confession. Gary Weller truly believed Gabriel had come for him.

'Put the sword down, Gabriel, he's not worth serving a life sentence for.'

'You wish me to spare his life, why? Was it not you, Libby, who hoped you would see him swinging from a gibbet?'

'Nice!' Weller hissed.

'Yes, it was. But that was only a figure of speech. I'd rather see him castigated lawfully than allow you to take the punishment for teaching him a lesson in life and death. He's useless without his henchmen. God ...', she spun around to Weller, 'you can't even do your own dirty work.'

With a flick of his arm, Gabriel sheathed the sword in the ornamental scabbard slung at his back.

'Neither of you will bleed to death.'

'You're gonna pay for this, you...' Weller's words trailed. 'I've lost three of me fuckin' fingers.'

'You still have your thumb and small finger and you will learn to grip with them. You will, however, never be able to hold a gun again in a hand that matters. Miss Butler's words are true: your hand is worth the same as your head and both equate to nothing. Both are destitute of purposeful significance and this world is better off without either of them. I should remove your head for the evil you have inflicted upon others in the name of greed and power, but my quarrel is not with you for now and so, against my better judgment, I am going to spare you. The woman you were so set on gutting has just saved your life. You should thank her.' It was not a request.

Gary Weller growled his thanks through a set of tightly clenched teeth.

'That's better. Now I want you to write something down for me.' Gabriel pulled a piece of notepaper from the pad on the table and threw it at Weller. It landed at his feet.

Weller snatched it up with a puzzled expression. He looked at Gabriel and something passed silently between them. He began to laugh. 'Now what the fuck would I want to do that for?' He cast a suspicious glance over to Lars who returned it with a perplexed one of his own.

'Insurance. No man can divine his own future with any great certainty. Is there anyone else who is more capable of safeguarding your assets?'

Another glance at Lars. 'S'pose not. You 'ave to call me an ambulance then. I need them fuckin' fingers.'

'Write and I give you my word that an ambulance will appear for you very soon after we are gone, which is now.'

Reluctantly, Weller scribbled something on the paper with his left hand, scrunched it in his fist and hurled it back at Gabriel.

Libby watched the scene unfold before her as if in a trance. Her mind took a step back from the grim reality in the room and she felt a surging emotion wash over her like a tropical tide.

Gabriel had not only come to save her but, such was the power of his presence, even the burly and confident Lars Andersson felt futile and impotent against him. She had no idea how he had done it, but Gabriel managed to disarm Lars and accurately chop the three inner fingers off the right hands of Weller and his man before anyone even realised he was there. He then castigated a gangland thug for his bad behaviour, offered to spare his life and forced him to divulge private information in writing by the use of gentle persuasion.

Despite his outward beauty, an inner magnificence shone

from within Gabriel like a blazing fire on a dark mid-winter's night. Gabriel Radley didn't need a weapon to cow his enemies and hold them spell-bound in awe, his entire countenance commanded respect and he received it wordlessly with immediate effect.

He was ruthless yet forgiving; terrible yet gentle: it was this perfect balance of conflicting qualities that made him so captivating to his friends and bewildering to his enemies.

At this crazy moment in time, where all the world felt surreal and abstract, where the kitchen tiles were strewn with blood, fingers, weapons and even a dead body, Libby believed in superheroes.

'So, the Sleeping Warrior has finally woken up?' She moved across the space as if there was no one else in the room, stroked the hair from his face with a soft hand and kissed his cheek. 'Where have you been?'

She jumped as he spun around angrily to the Russian woman who had sidled her way to the sink. His sword shrieked from the scabbard. 'Touch those guns and I shall remove both your hands. Those things are not toys, woman, they could kill someone!'

Rose Red's face was a mask of outrage, but she buried it swiftly and breathed out the calm. The effort almost killed her. She eventually held both hands up in supplication and took a broad step backwards. Lars Andersson lay on the ground, coughing unspent bullets carefully from his mouth. A gun lay at his side, the chamber open and empty. He had a haunted look about him.

'Thank you Gabriel. Can you get us out of here now please? I don't like the company Carl keeps. Are you well?'

Carl could hardly believe what Deidre was saying.

Gabriel's features softened. He turned to Deidre with pure

affection in his eyes. 'Yes, thank you Deidre, I am very well and your concern is touching', there was no hint of sarcasm in his tone. 'We need to go.'

CHAPTER thirteen

'**HOW ARE YOU LLOYD?**' DCI Prendergast took a deep breath before shuffling into the room where his colleague sat in a wheelchair by the window.

The once strong muscles of Lloyd Byron's limbs lay wasted on the metal rests and his feet, stuffed into black leather trainers, turned curiously inwards.

'As well as can be expected in the circumstances, so I'm told.' The response was stilted, even morose as his head pivoted between the broad shoulders to face his guest. 'I can't move my legs or feel a thing from the waist down, apart from excruciating pain. Funny that. At least they let me home so's I can work. Don't know how long I would've lasted in that hospital with nothing to do.'

'I've been told you're making an excellent recovery. You'll be out of that chair in no time.' Prendergast awkwardly laid the box of chocolates by the bedside table, knowing full well his friend didn't believe a word of his lies. 'Don't over-do it though, or you may find hospital's the best place for you, until you recover I mean.'

'I don't enjoy being treated like a child.'

'Any idea when you can return to work, properly that is? Can't wait to see you walk into the department.' Prendergast could've kicked himself for the unfortunate choice of phrase.

'Sorry ...'

Lloyd put a supplicating hand in the air. 'It's OK, Prendy. I'll take a bit of getting used to.' He gestured for his nervous guest to sit before he stumbled. 'I suppose you want to know about my conversation with Nicole Blais.'

'Yes, indeed, when did she visit you?' Prendergast was relieved his colleague had no intention of speaking about the weather or the latest score in the county test match. No doubt, he wanted to say his piece then get rid of his guest as quickly as possible.

'Two days ago. She told me that Ridout was innocent and should be released.'

'Oh yes, so how does she come to that conclusion then?'

'She left him in his flat sleeping. He was drunk and passed out. There isn't enough time lapse between when she left the flat and when she got knocked on the head.

'A good defence would run rings around us with that one. Besides, she was having an affair with him.'

'So she could be shielding him?'

'I thought of that. There's nothing to say she's not an accomplice and didn't lock herself in the boot of his car.'

'Do you think that's why she came to you and not me? Why didn't she come straight to the police?' Prendergast for the second time regretted his social insensitivities when he saw the hurt in his colleague's face. He had worked with Lloyd Byron for over 10 years and they'd cracked many difficult cases together. 'Sorry, Lloyd, I've got a stupid mouth. You know what I mean.'

'It's lucky for you I've put up with your idiocy for so long,' Lloyd conceded a smile. 'Don't think she trusts you, Prendy, and I'm hardly in a position to run after her if she made a bid to get away. I've been thinking about this a lot. I've looked up this Awakened cult but there's nothing on them, not even on the internet. The blood samples on the ground at St Paul's matched a few ex-cons, all did time in various prisons, but there's no link between any of them that I can see and, believe me, I've had three teams on it'.

'There's no doubt we're missing something.'

'Ms Blais believes they're after her. She's terrified that she'll be the next to end up in the morgue.'

'Did she ask for protection?'

Lloyd shook his head. 'She doesn't trust police protection.'

'Can't say I blame her after the Simon Barry shambles.'

'Yes, that's a strange one. He's just disappeared. No doubt he's sunning himself on a beach in South America or his corpse will turn up in the Thames at some stage. Where did the Blais woman disappear to after the hospital attack?'

Lloyd's wide yawn reminded him to move the visit along swiftly.

'She was too frightened to tell me. She said she's running for her life and wants to stay out of London for a while. I did try the threat of perverting the course of justice, but she seemed willing to take the chance. She visited Ridout, her dad and then me and no doubt she's left the city again. She's a very frightened woman.'

'Did she say anything about the Butler woman and Gabriel Radley?'

Lloyd shook his head. 'Only that they're safe.'

'Oh, I don't doubt that for a second'.

'Why do you say that?'

Prendergast took a deep breath. He wanted to talk about it. 'Gary Weller's dead. His body, along with those of his two henchmen, was found in a cottage on the Isle of Arran. Weller died from a single shot to the head at almost point blank range. Someone got very close.'

'Ironic end to that bastard to go out with a bullet in the brain!'

'Strathclyde Police say they found his trigger finger, as well as two other digits of his right hand on the kitchen tiles. They'd been sliced off before he died.'

'What do you mean sliced off?'

'Cut clean off with a sharp weapon.'

'The three middle fingers on the right hand?'

'Yes, has someone already filled you in?

'Sounds familiar, doesn't it? Something similar happened to one of the city boys when he was making an arrest not too long ago.'

Prendergast froze to his seat. 'Radley?'

'Who else?'

The long silence was taken up with both men looking through the patio doors to very different horizons.

'You know Lloyd, in all my career as a cop, I've never come across anything I couldn't explain. I understand killers, I can get into their heads and I see what they see. I've got a good record in crime detection, that's why they put me on this case in the first place, but nothing adds up. There's a pattern here somewhere that I keep missing. Things have gone too deep.'

Lloyd Byron, noticing the anxiety in his colleague by the beads of sweat on his brow, the disjointed argument and wildness in his eyes, began to worry that Prendergast was perhaps burning out. 'What do you mean by deep?'

Prendergast spun around so fast that his friend spasmed in his chair. 'This has become more than a chase for a simple serial killer. This is a case about life and death, the rudimentary argument of whether good or evil will prevail. This Radley chap's at the centre of it. I've no doubt that he's got blood on his hands, but the Vampire Killer, the Barry-Weller saga, The Awakened, they're all linked in some way to the Butler woman.'

'She's a nutcase.'

'Maybe, but I've got a sneaking suspicion there's going to be a lot more deaths before this little act plays out.'

'Arrest her then.'

'For what? For being a catalyst to all this mayhem? What can we prove?'

'Radley's left his signature in that house on Arran.'

'Mutilation of a hand hardly amounts to murder, Lloyd. Besides, I don't believe firearms are his thing and we haven't got a shred of proof. Weller and his men were assassinated but the blood results from the loss of his fingers showed they were cut off before he was killed.'

'Good job too!'

Prendergast nodded distractedly. 'There's something else. I met a man the other day who calls himself Shinar. I bumped into him when following up a lead to this Awakened cult. I've got a strong feeling he may be their leader.' He handed Lloyd a brown envelope from his jacket pocket and noticed his own hands were shaking. 'That's all I know about him.'

'Do you want me to do a bit of research on him?'

'NO!' Lloyd twitched in his chair at the sudden, emotional outburst. Prendergast clawed back some semblance of composure. 'No, just find me the Vampire Killer. Have another look at the profile of all the victims and get back to me.'

'Blimey, Prendy, you're sweating. God, you're as white as a sheet. You coming down with something or drank too much whisky last night?'

DCI Prendergast swallowed the nausea with a difficult gulp. 'Remember that conversation I had with Radley in Miss Butler's flat a few weeks back?'

'I think so.'

'Radley warned me about the leader of this cult.'

'Didn't he call him a monster?'

Prendergast nodded. 'There's another thing too. Shinar said a notorious gangland boss was dead. Could he have been speaking about Weller?'

'Sounds pretty suspicious to me. Maybe he was trying to warn you of what was going to happen or perhaps he was just saying the Saint's death was a fait accompli.'

'Whatever he meant, he's either a prophet or had something to do with Weller's death. I rather suspect it's the latter.' The inspector almost gagged as Shinar's disfigured features invaded his memory. 'He's the one after Radley and that stone of his. I just know it. Radley said he was a monster and, after having met the creep, I'd tend to agree. I've never met anyone like him and I hope I never will again. Do you believe a person can be completely evil, Lloyd? I don't mean a man who just commits evil things but one who breathes and sweats it too. Every time I think of him, I get this sick feeling inside me, like something's wriggling in my guts and then there's the pain ...' He swatted his seeping brow. 'Do you think that a man can do that to someone in just one meeting?'

'Not unless he's drugged your single malt.' Lloyd laughed again and Prendergast smiled back at the familiar twinkle in his friend's eyes: something he thought he would never see again.

'Good to have you back, Lloyd, I've missed you.'

'Thanks Prendy', he tapped the envelope against the side of his head. 'It's good to feel useful again.'

—

'Have you seen the bloody papers? Look! Just look!' Carl's high-pitched shrieking caused Libby to burn her hand on the frying pan. He threw the paper down on the worn oak table and stabbed his finger at the picture that spanned the breadth of the cover.

Libby craned her neck to see what he was shouting about.

'That's a picture of ME! ME! I'm plastered all over the front pages of the tabloids. Weller's dead! DEAD! They say he was shot dead in the kitchen of a cottage on Arran two days ago.'

'Well, we sure as hell didn't kill him. He was alive the shouting when we left.'

'I think it was probably that dreadful trigger-happy Russian woman who shot him, although they say they don't know who did it or why. They've traced the owner of the cottage to my company, Libby, and now everyone – the police, the papers and probably Weller's successors – is looking for me. What am I going to do?'

'You're going to calm down, Carl, and stop shouting. Do you want a bacon roll?'

'She'll know we've been lying, Libby. She'll find out about us.'

'I think she already knows, Carl.' Libby pulled out a plaster from the depth of her bag and picked the tobacco and grit from the tatty paper before administering her treatment to the burned hand with fingers and teeth.

'What do you mean by that?'

'Trust me. I'm a woman and know these things. You're going to have to talk to her and get it over with. I'm past worrying about it. We've got far more important things to fret about.'

'There's nothing more important to me than my family, Libby.' Carl slumped down on the bench and wrung his hands together.

'You should've thought about that before you took your trousers off the first time all those years ago. Didn't you strike up an affair with Sarah just after your honeymoon?'

'Stop it.'

'No, Carl. Deal with it!' She jabbed the pan of sizzling bacon at him as if it was an accusatory finger. 'You're the type of bloke who's never content with what you've got because you're incapable of realising real worth when you see it. Money and people have always come easily to you so you believe everyone and everything's been put on this earth to serve or entertain you.'

She thumped the pan down on the stove and eyed him critically. She saw a lost and powerless middle-aged man. Stripped of all confidence and the hard shell of pretence he'd carried though his life like a shield, he had that look about him which said it was everyone else's fault. She wondered what she'd ever seen in him.

'It's taken a life-threatening situation to lay you bare, Carl. You don't have your toys or any of your playmates to fall back on any more. I'm glad Weller's gone. Maybe his death will make an honest man of you yet but, before that time, you're going to have to do the right thing and tell Deidre before she reads the papers.'

'Where is Deidre?' Carl, having overlooked the possibility of eavesdroppers, suddenly lowered his voice to a whisper.

'She went for lobsters with the others just after you left.'

'Lobster? There aren't any shops around here for thirty-eight miles.'

'They're diving for them'. She slapped some burned bacon into a roll and slammed it on top of his picture.

'Deidre can't swim!' Carl shrieked again. 'How could you leave my wife alone with those people? Their lives have known only violence. They're murderers and cut-throats!'

'Her name is Rose and she did try to save our lives and Gabe will look after Deidre. I thought you and Lars were good friends.'

'We are business acquaintances, Libby, there's a big difference.' As Carl laughed, his face bore the expression of a tortured animal. 'God, this is surreal. I should be in my office reading law reports and case notes, sitting in meetings and drinking coffee. Instead, I'm holed-up in a strange house in a part of my own country I didn't even know existed, miles away from anywhere, with my wife, lover and a few professional assassins as company, eating a burned bacon roll. You couldn't make this kind of thing up if you tried.'

'You're on the beautiful coast of Wester Ross with your wife, *former* lover, and three of the only people on this earth who can protect you ... and the bacon's not burned, it's crispy. I would say you're fairly lucky to be here at all. No one will ever find us here because no one's looking for Rose, who rented this house, remember? Coffee?'

'This is not fair, Libby. This is all your doing.' He chewed slowly, too preoccupied with his own misfortune to taste what he was eating. 'There's no way we can send Deidre to Guernsey now. She'd never get through customs without being identified and that would put the kids' lives at risk as well as my sister's and her family. God, this gets messier by the second. Do you think whoever killed Weller is looking for us? How did they know we were here?'

'It's either they tailed Weller; Rose is a double-crosser; or you unwittingly led them here.'

'I wouldn't put it past Rose Red. She frightens the living daylights out of me. Can't understand why Deidre's so fond of her.'

'I'd be careful what I say, if I were you, Carl. Rose doesn't like you and she keeps those guns very close to her. I'd watch my back if I were you.'

'That's all I need...'

'Shut up! They're back.'

Carl sprang up and, as if dodging the bullets of an automatic rifle, ran around the kitchen with the newspaper in his hand, searching desperately for somewhere to hide it. He finally opted for a door in the cast iron range, cursing when he realised there were no flames burning in the oven.

'It's oil fired, you dope!'

Libby watched from the farmhouse window as Lars Andersson's huge Range Rover rumbled across the stone chippings.

She smiled as she saw Deidre laughing while she waggled her prize at Libby: an oil cloth bag, obviously with a few large crustacea inside it. As he jumped from the car, Lars instinctively scanned his raptorial eyes across the garden and then the mountains before looking out to sea. His right hand rested just inside his jacket.

'Once a thug ...' Libby mused to no one in particular. 'Where's Gabriel?'

'He went for a swim,' Deidre said. 'He said he'll be back later.'

'And what about Rose?'

'We let her off at the bottom of the track. She said she wanted to go for a walk. I saw her walking back to the beach.'

'Did she have her guns with her?'

'Hope so,' Carl said. 'She can do us all a favour and put a couple of bullets in his head. Then we could all go home and get our lives back.'

Scrubbing her wet hair with a towel, Deidre sat down on the bench opposite Carl. 'I don't think she'll do that, somehow. I think she's quite taken with our handsome Mr Radley. You should've seen the look on her face when he stripped down to his underwear and waded into the water. The waves weren't the only things rippling on that beach!'

'Deidre!' Carl didn't like the star-struck expression on his wife's face.

'Amazing man, that Gabriel.' Lars added his thoughts to the conversation and winked at Deidre. 'I think he's part fish. He can hold his breath for a very long time under water. I almost got the bends following him. That water's freezing and deep.'

'This is Scotland, Lars. We don't do luke-warm and shallow here. I'm glad you're getting along well with him. You wouldn't want to be in his bad books. Has he spoken to you?'

'He hasn't said a word to either Rose or me since we got here. I don't think we'll ever be best friends.'

'You'll have to earn his trust first.'

'You'll have to put in a good word for us, Libby.'

She didn't know whether Lars was being serious or sarcastic. She guessed it was the latter. Notwithstanding Lars' warped sense of humour, Libby felt proud to be the one closest to the man whose qualities all other men should be measured against. She fed on the confidence that gave her and used it as a weapon against the world. With Gabriel by her side, Libby felt invincible and nothing that had taken place in her former lifetime would ever seriously matter again. She would even tolerate living under the same roof as two murdering thugs because Gabriel had allowed it. For what reason, only he would know.

'Maybe you and I should go for a walk, Lars.' Libby hoped her wide-eyed expression would speak the words she couldn't.

'But I've been swimming all morning and I'm starving.' He eyed the frazzled bacon in a pan of congealed fat with longing appreciation.

'Still, more exercise will help to burn off those violent tendencies of yours. You never know, you may even turn into a nice, kind person after a few miles.'

'Aw Libby, and I was just beginning to like you again.'

Rose Red wrote her initials in the sand with a long finger, wiggled her toes and looked out to sea. A rare glimpse of sunshine had just enough warmth in it to soothe her troubled thoughts. Somewhere beneath the cool blue waters of the Northern Atlantic, her quarry glided as if he'd been born with fins.

Now and again she would see his dark head breaching the surface like a seal before it disappeared again to emerge many minutes later on the other side of the cove. She hadn't seen any signs of him for over an hour and wondered if he'd swum across to one of the Summer Isles or another part of the ragged coastline fringing the north west Highlands.

Most of his clothes lay in a neat heap on the beach so she knew he would eventually return to them. She just hoped it would be sooner rather than later for time was the only thing Rose Red couldn't afford to kill.

While she waited, she mulled over events of the last few days and how circumstances had led her to following and finding the elusive man who was called Gabriel Radley. He made an enigma look like a children's puzzle. He could move faster than the eye could blink and had the ability to haul the thoughts out of people's heads. She envied his power and his seemingly supernatural abilities and wondered whether he was born with them or acquired them through intensive life-long secret military training.

The call of the seabirds above her head pulled her away from her musings. Rose liked this part of the world with its rugged mountains and raging waters. It was a place she could relate to. The Highlands had a wild, unfettered heart beneath its angry skies.

'Its beauty is perilous. доброе утро!'

Rose smiled to herself and it was only then she noticed the footprints in the sand leading towards her. She turned her eyes into the sun and blinked at his silhouette.

'You speak Russian?'

'Что Вы думаете?'

'я впечатлен.'

'You should be.' His smile lit up the skies.

'Yes, a perilous beauty, that's what makes it so alluring.'

'Tell me what you know.'

'What makes you think I know anything?'

He pulled on his jeans and sat down beside her. She felt her body spasm and her mind reel as his cold arm brushed against hers for a brief moment. The power of the sensation left her twitching. He laughed and held out his hand.

'You want me to cross your palm with silver?' He answered her with a smile. She pulled the metal knuckle from the back pocket of her jeans and slammed it into his hand. 'You have some very impressive skills but you don't like to kill.'

'That's right Anzhela, I do not kill for sport or money.' He lay back in the sand and closed his eyes while the sun dried the beads of water from his skin.

'What would you kill for, Mr Radley?'

'Survival and necessity.'

'What about pay-back?'

'I do not hold a grudge for long. Retribution is not my style.'

'Then you're very lucky to still be alive, for I know of a few people who most definitely hold a grudge against you.' She shuddered in remembrance of her ordeal in the church and bit back the nausea.

'So you have met him and have led him to me.' He didn't appear in the least perturbed.

'It's nothing personal, Mr Radley, I'm one of life's survivors but I'm not unreasonable. You have something he wants and if you give it up, then we may all come out of this smiling and rich'.

To her annoyance Gabriel laughed at her. He sat up and brushed the sand from his hair before hauling on his t-shirt. 'You obviously know nothing about the man you are working for nor the connotations of your contract. When he has finished with you, he will discard you like a gnawed bone but not before splintering your body and infecting your soul.'

'You're not exaggerating, are you? Who is he?'

'I find little practical necessity in overstatement. You will not survive this contract, Anzhela. Shinar is death. To speak his name or even think about him sickens and weakens your life. He has marked you and it is only a matter of time before you die. All that is left for you to worry about is the manner in which he chooses to kill you.'

Rose Red's blood froze in her veins. She knew instinctively Gabriel meant every word of what he said. She suddenly hated him for being so honest with her.

'Would you rather I lied to you?'

'Yes. It would've been kinder.'

He twisted his torso to face her, his dark eyes sparking with irritation.

She was taken aback by his sudden change of mood that made her recoil from him.

'What kindness do you show the people whose lives you take from them in cold blood? How do you know that any of your victims would have wished to have known the time of their own deaths and given them the opportunity to prepare themselves for it? How do you know that your hapless targets would not have wished for even a few brief moments to say goodbye to their friends, their families, their wives, their lovers? I have given you a gift that you do not deserve but, by the very woman you have become, will be unable to enjoy, for you have no one to bid farewell to, Anzhela. I am not the first one to tell you this, but it is true that you shall die alone, unmourned and irrelevant.'

She swallowed her despair and refused to allow him to manipulate her sentiments or her fears.

'Then it looks as though we're both in a lot of trouble. You've obviously met him too, which means your life will also come to a sudden and violent halt at this man's whim.' She shot him a self-satisfied smile.

'I am not like you, Anzhela. He cannot infect me with his dark tricks. I am the only one who can stop him and I intend to bring him to justice. That is why I am here.'

'So you are special?'

'Very.'

'He says you are a Vascaran.'

'He is right.' He folded his arms.

She folded hers, waiting for the explanation that was not forthcoming. 'Are you going to tell me what a Vascaran is?'

He looked amused at her obvious irritation. 'It is a person from Vascar.'

'Which is where?'

'A long way from here.'

'And do all Vascarans have the same powers as you?'

'Similar, but I am very special.'

'I don't doubt that at all,' she conceded the faintest smile that forgave him for his obstinacy. 'You're going to kill him?'

'No, his life is not mine to take. I intend to take him home in chains.'

'You're going to arrest him all by yourself?' She couldn't

help but laugh. 'This шеф has an army of trained killers at his disposal and he knows your weaknesses. He aims to use your compassion to draw you to him. If I were you, I would watch my loved ones very closely.' She knew he read her silent message by the angry narrowing of his eyes. 'Sentiment will kill you. That's why I prefer to live alone.'

'Empathy is not a vice but, you are right, it does have its drawbacks when danger is close.'

'None of your companions are worth risking your life or your cause for, Mr Radley. They are all fractured individuals who only care about themselves.'

'You are wrong.'

She accurately read the concern in his exquisite features: 'Ah, yes, the wonderful Libby Butler, the English legal system's golden girl. She's a good defence lawyer, you know. So good, in fact, she's made quite a name for herself in successfully defending personal injury claims.'

'Where exactly is this going?'

'What's wrong, Gabriel, have you suddenly lost the ability to read my mind or do you just not like what you see there? Why are you so protective of her?'

He grabbed his boots and thrust his feet into them.

'I'm very thorough in my research of people. You say I deserve to die without mercy and without being mourned because I'm a killer. Cold blood requires a lack of sympathy for the victim. Your precious lawyer was so good at her job she denied many innocent people the justice they deserved.'

'Stop it!'

He made to walk away but she snatched his arm. Ignoring the shocking sensation from that touch, she spun him around to face her, determined to return his cruelty. 'A young woman who lost her baby to a hospital's blatant negligence, also lost her case, thanks to Carl Bottomley and his team of hot-shot solicitors, led by the ambitious and frozen-hearted Miss Butler. The girl slit her wrists a week later. Her father found her bloodless body in a cold bath and has been killing women ever since.'

'What did you say?' He grabbed her by the shoulders sending shock waves into her arms and chest. He searched her eyes with a fevered intensity until he had yanked her soul from her heart and stuffed it back in pieces. His expression was one of utter surprise. 'You have found the killer.'

'Yes, I know who he is and why he is killing women. I even know why he has picked those women and who's probably next. He thinks he's got away with it for now because they've arrested Ridout for his crimes. However, he hasn't finished, there are more still to kill and he won't be able to stop himself. When this is all over, I intend for him to be my final hit before I retire. This is one man who doesn't deserve to live.'

'Since when did you convince yourself that you had the power over life and death?'

'Since I held my first gun.' They reached her car and she hesitated before opening the door. 'Why is this stone so important?'

'It has certain qualities that will help bring Shinar down'.

'So he fears it?'

'He should.'

'And how come the serial killer has it now?'

'I no longer believe he has, but it is convenient for others to think so.'

The information surprised Rose. 'Then who?'

'Libby does, she just does not know it yet.'

'What?' Rose's shock manifested itself into a loud yell.

'She has buried it.'

'So it's in her garden somewhere?'

'No, it is locked inside her head and cannot get out.'

'**WE SHOULD STAY TOGETHER.** We're safer in numbers and I can't stay here any longer. I have children.'

'The three of you are lambs in the midst of a gathering of lone wolves. You'll be gobbled up by one of us eventually.' Lars wiped the tears from Deidre's eyes with the end of her silk scarf. 'Besides, we haven't quite made up our minds yet.'

Libby watched the interaction between her housemates from her seat on the patio. Lars had shocked them all this morning by his announcement. 'What does Gabriel think?'

Lars' shoulders touched his ears. 'He's still thinking.'

'So, let me get this right. You're thinking that you, Rose and Gabriel are all going back to London to recover the stone from a serial killer and snatch this bloke Shinar from under the noses of his private army with snapping teeth? The Bottomleys and I will stay here until you say it's safe to come out of hiding or until we've strangled one another, whichever is the sooner?'

'Sounds like a plan to me.' Lars' customary good humour didn't manage to quell the disquiet in her stomach.

'Well, it doesn't to me.' She waited for Carl and Deidre to begin their bickering before she patted the cold seat of the ornate cast iron patio chair. Weller's trusted former bodyguard ignored the chips of flaking paint and sat.

'Who are you working for Lars? Weller is dead so you don't have a boss any more. And Rose, why has she agreed to help

Gabriel? He doesn't have the kind of money she would be interested in and he doesn't own a gun. What's in it for you?'

'There's some emergency offshore accounts from Weller's fortune. Carl has a plan as to how we can get our hands on them, provided we help your Mr Radley. You see, if we can assist him to take this man down, the sooner he will be out of our lives and we can enjoy the spoils of this little personal war.'

'You're not going to double-cross him are you?'

Lars' normally wicked grin was transformed into one of amusement. 'And how do you think I would end up if I betray a man like that? I might be big and tough, Libby, but I'm certainly not stupid.'

'Do you know who killed Weller?'

'Of course. I took the advice of someone who knows better than to defend a lost cause. In any case, it was Weller's time.'

'I can't see you settling for a life as a tax exile on the profits from a few off-shore accounts.'

'I'm to become a millionaire. That piece of paper Radley made Weller write on contains the code to his safe which has some very expensive bling. And you know how I love my bling, Libby. There's a fortune in diamonds inside that lead box and it now belongs to me. He may not have said two words to me since we left Arran, but I'm beginning to love that man.'

'*Clever!*' Libby kept that thought to herself. Gabriel used the promise of a fortune to manipulate the loyalty of Weller's favourite bodyguard. That was a sly and subtle move and one that required much forethought and certainty of outcome. Lars' motives were purely based on economics: he was entirely unsentimental and could never be trusted.

'Rose didn't kill Weller, did she?' She already knew the answer.

'Like I said, Libby, it was his time. Besides, those diamonds would never be mine so long as he was alive. He wrote down that code very quickly, knowing he'd never keep to his end of the bargain. Otherwise, my little legal beagle, it was nothing personal.'

'I can see that one on your headstone,' she scoffed, 'here lies Lars Andersson, it was nothing personal!'

Libby took a moment to review how she'd just reacted to the news that the man standing beside her, speaking to her as a friend, actually murdered his employer with such cold indifference.

Instead of sidling away from him and rushing for the emergency line, however, she simply felt nothing. She wondered whether her chilled heart could be put down to her wish for Weller's demise in the first place or whether she'd become desensitised to death and all its associated horrors.

'We shall see how far your new love extends when you meet Shinar.' Rose had been standing at the door taking advantage of the short burst of sunshine between shifting banks of heavy rain clouds drifting in from the sea.

'Now how did you find out about him?'

'It's a long story and one I can tell you about on the way back to London.'

'We're thinking Libby shouldn't go back to London. Not just yet anyway.'

'Sorry Lars, but she's important. We're all going home. The Bottomleys need to speak to the police and Gabriel's time's running out. Pack up all of you, we've wasted enough of our lives here.'

'I don't believe our time together has been wasted at all,' Deidre joined the conversation. The chair legs squealed against the patio flags before she sat down. 'I believe we're all here together for a reason and that reason has been to find the truths in our lives. Who we really are and not just who we think we are.'

Libby suddenly found her own hands very interesting.

'None of us are nice people: two are killers; two are adulterers and I must also be a bad person because I'm also here for some reason. This is our judgment.'

'You're not a bad person, Deidre. In fact, you're probably the nicest person that anyone will ever meet.' Libby felt the treacherous tears welling and could do nothing to stop them. 'You're kind, sensitive, empathic and considerate. You're also fiercely loyal and a really brave woman. Carl is very lucky to have you,' her voice cracked, 'I'm so sorry.'

Lars and Rose took this as a signal to sidle away from the patio while Deidre sat quietly watching her cry.

'It's funny, you know,' Libby dabbed at her eyes with the sleeve of her cardigan, 'when you're doing something that's obviously wrong, you never think of the consequences on others, nor the long-term effects it'll have on their lives or yours. You just live for the day, as if that day will never end.'

'But it does end. Everyone has to face their own reality at some point in their lives. I'm equally guilty of ignoring the truth. I have been for years because it was more convenient for me to do so and far less painful.' It was Deidre's turn to cry. 'I'm so stupid. The pain doesn't go away, it just collects inside and slowly boils. Only, mine never boils over. It just simmers inside.'

'It's OK, Deidre. You can take it all out on me: all your anger, all your hatred. I won't blame you and I won't retaliate. I deserve it all.' Libby's remorse was sincere and heartfelt. She wanted Deidre's condemnation; she needed it.

'There's no point,' Deidre sniffed. 'I can't hate you. I'm not capable of hating anyone, not even Carl. I know I'm the complete opposite of what he's looking for in a woman, but he still keeps coming back. I suppose it's the opposite bit that attracts.' She twiddled the huge diamond on the third finger of her left hand. 'I could never confront him. I've always been a bit of a sap when it comes to quarrelling, so it's my own fault I didn't address this problem sooner. The past few days have taught me there are more important things in life to consider: like staying alive for one. Fear is a real leveller.'

'Yes, and a very dark place to the lost,' she echoed his words.

'He's a very unusual man you know.'

'Who? Carl?' Her lip curled into her cheek.

'No, not him. Gabriel. Haven't you realised he's an archetype in the company of stereotypes? We are all clichés of the anti-hero: Weller, the cockney mobster, infected with little man syndrome and contaminated by all the vices that have made him rich; Carl, the public schoolboy businessman, motivated by money and corrupted by ambition; Lars, the muscle-bound Nordic thug, loyal only to the chap who pays him the most; Rose, the Nakita, the femme fatale with a Russian accent...'

' ... and the fire power of the collective Soviet land forces.'

They giggled together.

'And me, the down-trodden wife whose true identity is rotting in the attic along with all the photographs from her past, her padded shoulders and her Rick Astley LPs.'

'And me?'

'You know what you are Libby. You don't need me to analyse you.' She left the sentence hanging. 'There's something about Gabriel that makes you come to terms with yourself. He doesn't judge you for your stupidity or condemn you for your wrongs, he just looks at you with those gorgeous black eyes and you know he accepts you despite your faults. It spurs you on to do better, for him. Carl irritates him but, even though he's said and done some terrible things, Gabriel doesn't seem to think it matters. He's taught me a good lesson in what's really important in life and what's not. If he can forgive Carl, then why shouldn't I? Gabriel's helped me to see all this and I really wish I had a quiet time to thank him for it. He's a very great man, your Gabriel.'

'My Gabriel.' Libby rested her chin in her hand, her thoughts wistful. 'I'm going to come back to Scotland, I think. I've always hated London. Life's a lot simpler up here.'

'What about Tony?'

'I don't want to be the person I was a few weeks ago any more. I've come too far now and I can't go back. I am sick of my own hypocrisy and I'm sick of hurting people who don't deserve to be hurt. I choose to repel my former self and, you're right about Gabriel, he's purging all of us.'

'He's getting rid of all the evil around him. Barry, The Saint, they're all gone and only good will come out of their deaths. He even appears to be making decent human beings out of Lars and Rose. Carl, however, is proving to be his most difficult conquest.' Deidre giggled.

Libby fell into a sudden silence, watching Deidre's diamond ring sparkling in the sunshine. 'Opposite poles attract', she whispered. 'Like poles repel,' she said a bit more loudly. 'What did he mean?'

'Who?'

'The lines repel him. Differing poles attract and give strength while like poles will push apart; he's helpless without the right weapon.'

'What on Earth are you talking about Libby?'

'It's got to be something to do with the stone. Maybe Shinar has similar powers to him and that's why he can't get close: like poles push apart. Perhaps this stone may somehow reverse the polarity of the person who possesses it. Without the stone,

Gabriel will never find Shinar or vice versa and, for some reason, whoever has it, has the advantage over the other. We must find it before Shinar does and that means we have to hunt down the Vampire Killer.'

'Well, well, well. A smart lawyer. That's got to be a first.' Rose Red's leather soles tapped against the wooden deck as she glided towards them in that elegant gait of hers with her back held straight and toes and legs turned out in opposite directions. 'I have a plan to catch a killer and it involves you.'

'Me?' Libby didn't like the flint in the woman's tone.

'Yes, you.' She put up her hand to stem questioning shrieks, 'I'll explain everything on our way back to London.'

—

'Come on, sir, it could've been a lot worse. At least no one's calling for your resignation.'

'Yet.' DCI Prendergast glanced up at the young inspector and raised an eyebrow before carefully laying the paper down on his desk, sports side up.

He never did like the tabloid press, but now he liked them even less as they splashed his failures across their front pages with a strong emphasis on what he hadn't done as opposed to what he had. 'They should try being bloody police officers,' he muttered behind gritted teeth. 'Those young journos wouldn't know a good story if it landed in their coffee and bit them on the tongue. The tabloids like to pick on coppers: it helps take the heat away from their phone hacking misdemeanours.'

The officer slinked away, coughing out a poor excuse about work he had to do.

There'd been another murder with Dracula's signature all

over it and communal anger was being fed and watered by voracious newshounds.

Tony Ridout had been exonerated and was leaving prison to a hero's salute complete with a sea of 'Justice for Tony' banners; angry remonstrations behind loud hailers against the apparent lack of integrity of Scotland Yard's murder investigation teams; and a couple of students in raster plaits chaining themselves to the railings outside Brixton prison.

As senior officer on his particular murder investigation team, DCI Prendergast was forced to shoulder all the blame. It was time to get that well-used chestnut out of its box and get it working: desperate measures for a desperate man. He had to pay another visit to the church of his nightmares.

His undercovers reported movement of cult members in and out of the building and this time he had a warrant. He would scramble a team together, pay a surprise visit and search the premises thoroughly.

He only hoped, and was more than ashamed to admit, the beast that called himself Shinar would not be at home.

—

Rose Red disliked many things in life. People's company had always been one of them, until now. As she watched the members of the party scrambling to get their worldly belongings into the car, she smiled as Carl barked orders to his wife and the haughty Ms Butler threw a few insults at a muscle-bound giant who could squash her like a soft bug. Standing half way up the cliff, in a miniature forest of wild gorse, Rose cast her eyes seaward and allowed the brisk breeze to carry her thoughts away from the present and into the past.

Unfortunately for Rose, her past was as bitter an ordeal as

her imminent future. Her father had been taken as a political prisoner when she was a small child and she had never heard from him again. Her mother was a brutal, unsympathetic woman who would have sold her children into sex slavery had such a lucrative business opportunity arisen. Rose had learned from a very early age to trust no one and that friendship was merely a burden.

Lately, however, she found herself enjoying the company of strangers and the humorous banter over a driftwood fire on the beach while waiting for the freshly-picked mussels in sea water to come to the boil in the camping pot.

That alien emotion of sentiment was beginning to affect her judgment and Rose had found her professional career melting into incompetence over the warmth of human relationships. It was time she put a stop to it or lose herself to its sweet embrace.

'Why are we here?' She gazed wistfully southwards where the multiple peninsulas of Scotland's west coast tapered into the horizon.

'We are healing.'

She felt his body behind her and the rise and fall of his chest. 'We are wasting time.'

'No, we are using time to our advantage.'

'I have better things to do than sit around waiting for something to happen.'

'Something has happened, Anzhela, and it has happened to you. You simply needed this space to find it.'

'I'm the same woman I've always been.'

'Yes, and you have finally found yourself.'

'Beside the mountains of a barren wasteland?'

'Inside you.'

Her eyes widened in shock as she felt moistness in them and

she bit her quivering lip until she could taste blood. 'It's too late for me, Gabriel. I'm beyond redemption.'

'You fear for your future?'

'Is it written in stone?'

'Destiny is a series of options. Your decisions in life and sympathy towards others will either make you or break you. Life's choices are forever open, it is the ones you take that will define your outcome.'

'So you're saying destiny is in our own hands?'

'Why not?'

'Can God forgive a person like me, Gabriel?'

'Forgiveness is a human instinct based on trust, it is not solely a privilege of the Gods.'

'But I do not have a heart. Can you trust me?'

'Can you trust yourself?'

'Yes.'

'Then trust your natural instincts and do what you believe to be right. There is no more margin for error so choose your side carefully. I will call you again when I need you.'

He took her hand and slipped the ornate metal weapon she had found in Weller's office onto her knuckles. She heard the gentle voice inside her head and immediately knew who had been calling her.

'You!' She spun around to face him, her normally smooth features frowning in wonder. 'You've been manipulating me all along.'

'You chose to answer my call.' His smile was more radiant than the sun over the mountains.

'I had no real choice. You forced me to save that lawyer's hide on a number of occasions and against my better judgment.'

'Libby must be protected at all costs. Thank you for your alliance. You did what was right.'

'For who?' Rose should have felt her anger rising, but it wasn't there. Instead she laughed and felt her heart lighten. 'How did you know my name?' She turned around to face the house once more, no longer able to meet his dark eyes.

'I read it in your heart.'

She felt his presence retreating. Rose Red took a deep breath and a tentative step down from the hillside as Anzhela Mihailova, a woman she hadn't seen in years.

She didn't know what caused the strange and sudden sense of impending doom that stopped her in her tracks.

Something was wrong and it didn't take years of watching her back or a supernatural voice in her head to know when trouble was at large.

From her high vantage point, she could see Carl heaving the last of the suitcases across the gravel. His face looked flushed as he slammed the boot shut. Lars was making a call on his mobile. He stood with his back pressed against the side of the house, now and then braving a peek around the corner.

Rose narrowed her eyes. 'What's he up to?'

There was only one way out of the property to the road and that was via a narrow gravelled track with fencing on either side.

Lars was off the phone now and whispered something to Carl. Rose made to duck behind the gorse as the big Swede's keen eyes scanned the hillside for her, but he spotted her. He gave a little wave as she stood up to face him. Laughing, she made the shape of a gun with her thumb and index finger and pointed it straight at him as the party got into the car, hurried-up by a frantic Carl.

Lars saluted once, his familiar grin straining his cheek muscles, before thumping into the driver's seat.

Rose watched as the Range Rover sped off down the track, its screaming tyres throwing up dust and stone chips into the air.

It wasn't long before she heard the blades of a helicopter and the sirens of police cars hurtling towards the house.

Lars had chosen his side and an unknown female assassin would take the blame for the Arran killings and go down as a mere cog in the continuing problem of underworld violence.

'Nice.' She breathed away her despair and replaced it instead with anger.

If she got out of this, Anzhela Mihailova would have to wait, for Rose Red had yet another score to settle and this time it was a personal number on her list.

Fifteen

'OH, NO, NOT AGAIN!' Libby wriggled inside the starched sheets that bonded her tightly to the bed. She squinted against the strong shaft of sunlight glaring from the window framed by those tasteless floral curtains. The room stank of regulated hygiene.

She was in the hospital again with no idea why. She reached for the buzzer and kept her finger down on it until the door opened. She was shocked to see Nicole.

'So, the NHS, has finally come to its senses and demoted you to emptying bed pans?' She hid her bewilderment behind feigned animosity.

'No, Libby. I'm your doctor.' Nicole stood at the end of the bed and studied the loose pages on a clipboard. She looked as though she meant business.

Wearing a formal grey trouser suit, Libby would've mistaken her for any other NHS official were it not for the intricate latticed pattern that pulled her hair back from her ears.

'That must've taken a while to create. Did your hairdresser use a pair of knitting needles?'

Nicole hung the clipboard back on the bed's metal rail. 'Does my hairstyle offend you, Libby?'

Libby rolled her eyes to the ceiling, she was accustomed to Ms Blais' psychological traps. 'No, but the amount of money you spend on your vanity when the country's in economic declivity does.'

'Then, by the same token, you should also be pleased I'm putting my wages back into the local economy. It's people like me who keep small businesses from folding.'

'Is this a personal visit or are you here to lecture me on public fiscal policy?'

'You started it.' The smile was strained.

'So why are you here?'

Nicole sat down on the hygienic armchair beside the bed and crossed her legs. 'I'm here to talk about the past few weeks, Libby. You've not been yourself,' she hesitated long enough for Libby to understand the menacing portent behind her words. 'Do you know what I'm talking about?'

Believing this was another psycho-analytical snare, Libby sat up in the bed, wriggled against her pillows, folded her arms tightly across her chest and narrowed her eyes.

'You tell me.' She noticed Nicole's broken tooth had been repaired.

'Have you ever heard of disassociated identity disorder?'

'Yes, it's a designer disease isn't it? Why, do you suffer from it?'

'No, but I believe you do.'

Libby laughed out loud. 'You think I'm a schizo?' Her laughter trailed when she saw the concern in Nicole's dark eyes. 'What I've been through recently would turn any reasonable person into a raving nutter.'

'I didn't say you were a nutter, Libby. I believe you've lost contact with the real world and I'm going to try and bring you back to reality. We can do this together, but only if you're willing.'

'What the bloody hell are you talking about?' Libby felt fear for the first time in a while. She felt the room getting smaller and the floral curtains strangling her. 'This is a private hospital, you've got no authority here.'

'This is a mental health hospital, Libby. It has been since it was built.'

Libby felt like a cornered animal. 'Where's Gabriel?'

'I don't know, Libby, where is he?'

There was something about the way Nicole asked the question that rattled her. 'I don't know. He comes and goes.'

'Is he here now?'

Libby suddenly knew where this was going and leaped from the bed as if fired from it. She pressed her back against the opposite wall in an effort to put as much space between herself and her perceived enemy as possible. 'Just wait a minute. You know Gabriel, you had a bloody relationship with him!'

'Did I?'

Her spine squeezed against the cold wall and she could feel the beads of sweat tickling her sternum. 'Nicole, what are you trying to do to me? Are you trying to get me sectioned in order to get your own back? Tony met him and so did Carl. Lars and Deidre and that Russian assassin, they all spent time with him. That chief inspector interviewed him for God's sake.'

'They spent time with *you* Libby and, I've spoken to DCI Prendergast who will confirm what I'm just about to tell you. Sit down and I'll explain.'

Libby felt her back sliding down the wall and she landed on her rump with her legs splayed out in front of her, her jaws slack with shock.

As if speaking about the weather, Nicole began in her condescending drone. 'The trauma you suffered in the park has triggered a response deep down in your psyche. What started as a fear of the dark, distorted views of your own body, and all those little warning signs, have manifested into something much more serious. You've blurred the lines between fantasy and reality and can no longer tell the difference between what's imaginary and what's real. Your response to that high level of stress has been flight or fight and you've decided to take on your fears by manifesting a definitive hero to champion you. Gabriel is you, Libby. He is the Sleeping Warrior inside you, to coin your phrase, he only exists in your mind.'

'If that's so, why didn't you tell me before?'

'We decided to go along with it. All of us. From the first time you invented Gabriel, we believed we were doing the right thing in helping you through this. I even accompanied you to Scotland in the hope it would be sufficiently far away for you to leave behind your altered state of mind. The human brain is a very complicated organ and cases like yours are very difficult to treat...'

'Who's we?'

'Tony, the policeman, Carl ... all of us. I believed if you were allowed to play this out, you would eventually see the holes in your own reasoning. You're a smart woman, Libby.'

'Oh, please, spare me the insincerity.' Libby stood up and paced the room in her nightdress. 'So you're telling me it was me who threw Carl out of my flat?'

'That was the emotional side of your personality trying to do the right thing.'

'And this emotional side of me spoke to the detective when he came to my home?'

'Yes, it must've been very difficult for him. DCI Prendergast is a very straight-forward man.'

'But I was standing at the door and Gabriel was sitting down. I made tea while they were conversing.'

'That was your perception of the event. That's not how it happened in reality.'

Libby felt the world closing in on her. 'The time in the hospital. That thug was trying to tell me something?'

'It was your own reflection he was showing you. He held you up in front of a mirror and called you a Vascaran.'

'What does that mean?'

Nicole shrugged. 'Probably a word invented by the cult, who knows. What matters is you adopted it to give Gabriel an identity of place and other-worldliness. Can't you see it now?'

'So it was me who attacked Carl and me who threatened Gary Weller with a sword?'

'It was a kitchen knife that you believed to be a sword, but yes, it was you and that's why we had to put a stop to all this. You were becoming progressively violent, even dangerous, and, contrary to the laws of medical science, actually adopted the strength and powers of your alter ego.'

'So who sprung Simon Barry from custody and delivered him to Weller? No, don't tell me, that was me too.'

'The same man who attacked you in St Paul's and the hospital.' Nicole stood by the window, gazing out into the failing daylight. 'He calls himself The Messenger, that's all we know about him.'

'A messenger to whom?'

Nicole remained silent.

Libby wracked her memory for incidents that would convince Nicole that Gabriel was not just a figment of her warped imagination, but everything she recalled left niggling doubts in the back of her mind. Did he really have the ability to read her mind, or was she reading her own?

'Carl hated Gabriel but Deidre loved him.'

'They were humouring you and then it developed into a

personal battle between them. When you became violent with me, I thought Carl might be able to help. It was me who told him where you were staying and, because Carl needed to distance himself from whoever was killing all your friends, both of them played along with the ruse. I used them in the hope that, faced with a real predicament of coping with your lover and his wife, you would eventually come to your senses. I think, however, the two became too embroiled in their own personal charade and managed to convince you further that Gabriel was real.'

After a short hesitation, Libby managed to laugh in confidence this time. 'Why are you doing this Nicole? I want a witness in here now.'

'Your condition – merde, I hate that word – is often associated with bouts of memory loss. You've been through a few very violent ordeals and have blotted much from your mind, replacing it with imaginary scenarios. It's common in cases of delusional disorders.' She spun around to face her. 'It's time to try and reason with that other side of you – the apparently normal part of your personality – the one I'm speaking to now.'

'OK, then what about the police station where I first met him?'

'That's where you invented him in the first place. There was a man in custody that night. The duty sergeant said you spoke to him briefly but couldn't get an answer so went home. In your mind, for some reason, you merged that reality into the fantasy of Gabriel.'

'No, that's not right. That female officer saw him.'

'Which female officer was that, Libby?'

'The one who was murdered the next day.' Her words trailed to a whisper. 'But Rose Red told me she spoke to him on the beach.'

'She lied.'

'Why would she?'

'She is a killer, Libby. She'd have her reasons. There's another part to your story you should also know and I don't want you to be frightened or take this the wrong way. For some reason, you are the nucleus of all the violence that's been taking place lately: the south London murders, the cult, Weller. The police think they're all linked and that's the main reason they agreed to pretend Gabriel was real. They believe, somewhere locked away in the back of your mind, you know who the serial killer is and will be able to tell them who could possibly be his next victim. He has to be caught. All we have to do is unlock the door to your memory. It's time to put the warrior back to sleep where he belongs.'

'That's my line.' Libby, although shaken, was not convinced. She felt perfectly sane. 'I want to speak to Deidre.'

'She's in Guernsey with her children and under police protection. You may compromise her safety if you try to contact her.'

'Tony then.'

'He's also gone into hiding. He doesn't want to be the cult's next victim.'

'How very convenient for all of you.'

Nicole sighed. 'You still don't believe me, do you?'

'No I don't. I think you've got good reason to hurt me. Perhaps this is a perverted way of getting your own back on me for loosening your tooth. It's a very good repair, you know. It must've cost you a fortune.'

'Why would I want to hurt you? Can't you see that's your irrational paranoia talking? Maybe someone else can persuade you. I'll be here after he's gone if you need me.'

No sooner had Nicole left than Carl replaced her as if conjured by a stage magician. He looked extremely uncomfortable as the door was locked behind him.

'Come to stare at the lunatic?' Libby sat on the end of the bed and wrung her hands together.

'So, Nicole's told you everything? I did try to warn you.'

'Why are you doing this, Carl? I know you're trying to stitch the shaggy remnants of your marriage back together, but there's no need to stitch me up along with it. This is a horrible conspiracy and I don't understand any of it. I feel ... I feel so persecuted.'

'That's part of your illness, Libby.' His tone was gentle, for Carl.

'Tell me this is all a bad dream, Carl,' she grabbed the front of his shirt and twisted it. 'Tell me I'm not schizophrenic and Gabriel is real and not part of some bonkers behaviour on my part.'

'I can't do that Libby. I would love to, but I can't. The sooner you realise Gabriel Radley was just an alter ego you made up as a defence mechanism, the sooner you can return to your normal life.' He gently prized her fists from his shirt before he lost a few buttons.

She wished Carl was not so truthful. 'I don't have a normal life anymore!' Her shriek caused him to leap with fright and his eyes scanned the room for something to hide behind. 'According to the rest of the world, I'm a freak. My marbles are rolling all over the place and there's no way I'll ever be able to find all of them ever again. God, this is terrible. I can't believe you think I think I'm two people. Get me out of this place now.' She crumpled to her knees. 'I want to go home.'

Carl knelt down to her level and, in an uncustomary display of sympathy, placed his arm gently around her shoulder.

'You are a talented, intelligent, beautiful woman. You recently suffered a terrible emotional trauma but you found a way to cope with it and have come out the other end, I think, a much better person,' he swept a lock of hair from her forehead, 'not completely unscathed, but everything's going to be fine. After a rest for a couple of months, we'll talk about your future and the possibilities of promotion, but we don't want to worry about all that yet. We want you to get better first.'

'If what everyone believes is true then I have every cause to be really embarrassed. Oh God! I'll never be able to look that detective in the eye ever again.'

Libby took a deep, resigned breath and decided she'd never find out what was going on from the comfort of a locked room in a psychiatric unit.

'You're going to have to, Libby, because he needs to speak to you, but only when you feel fit enough.'

'I feel fine, Carl. Gabriel Radley may have been a figment of my imagination but he's gone now and I'm never going to see him again. I mean, he's just gone. Now help me find my clothes, I want to go home.' She tried to sound as convincing as she could.

'Can't do that Libby.' There was genuine regret in his eyes. 'You've been sectioned for treatment and assessment.'

'I'm not staying in this place for 28 days. I want to appeal.'

'You don't want to do that Libby. Just play along with them. It's for your own good. Besides, you're safer here than at home. There's still a killer on the loose and there's a strong reason to suspect you're on his list of victims. Sit tight for a while. This is a good hospital and they'll take care of you. Just keep your head down and your mouth shut and you'll be out in no time.'

'A hospital won't protect me, Carl. Look what happened at King's.'

'If those people wanted to kill you they would've done it then. They're not after your life Libby; they're after what you know but perhaps can't remember.'

'But I don't know anything.'

'Then maybe a good rest will help along with a course of hypnotherapy.'

—

'He's in there, sir.'

Detective Chief Inspector Prendergast threw his coat at the stand as he stormed past the duty sergeant.

Giving himself a few seconds to collect his wits, his hand hesitated at the door handle to the interview room. 'This better be bloody good', he growled to no one in particular.

The search of the Nunhead church had come up with nothing. There was evidence of multiple occupancy at some time but the inhabitants had long since gone: dispersed into the city ether; dissolving into the disorganised ranks of nameless faces forever. There'd been no reported sightings of The Awakened for weeks now and, once again, all trails had gone stone cold.

Until today, when two men walked into Scotland Yard with the promise of information.

'Good afternoon, I'm DCI Prendergast, I believe you've got some information for me.' He began the pleasantries and held back the shudder at the sorry state before him.

Inside the sparsely furnished room, a young man sat behind the empty table in filthy, tattered clothing. He looked as though he'd been born on the street. His hair was so dirty that it was difficult to make out what colour it was and his complexion bore the same consistency as warm lard. His face and hands were covered in red and brown scaly patches and there was no spark of life evident in those hopeless eyes. Another man sat beside him, he wore a brown monk's cassock and his skin was as dark and sleek as polished ebony.

'My name is Brother Raymond,' he began. 'I'm a Franciscan friar from the Stratford Priory. We've known this boy for some time. He's gravely ill, but has some information that may help with your current investigations.'

'So sorry to hear that, what's your name, son?'

'I've got many names,' the boy rasped, 'but you can call me Thomas'.

'All right, Thomas, where do you live?'

'Thomas is homeless, inspector.'

'The streets of London can be a harsh place for a youngster. Where're you from, originally I mean?'

'Liverpool, but that was some years back. I haven't been home for a long time.'

The kid was barely older than Prendergast's youngest son. 'When was the last time you ate something?'

He was answered with a shrug.

From the nervous glances the boy was casting to the friar and the corners of the room, DCI Prendergast decided to get straight to the point. 'I'll tell you what. I'll get someone to get you a hot meal and some clean clothes. I'll then phone around to see if I can get you a bed for a couple of nights in a hostel. In the meantime, what did you come here to tell me?'

The boy's expression changed from despair to fear. Gently goaded by a reassuring hand on his back, he nodded to Brother Raymond.

'Thomas ran away from home at the age of fifteen.' The friar began. 'Since his first days on the streets of London he's suffered terrible abuse at the hands of evil predators. A few years ago, he met a man who calls himself The Messenger. He's one of the main figures behind that cult you're looking for, The Awakened. Thomas was a member for three years. They took him in, looked after him and lately he ran away. Since then, he's been sick. He has advanced skin cancer which has spread to his liver and lungs. His prognosis is poor and he has nowhere to turn apart from to the Lord for mercy.'

DCI Prendergast, although filled with pity for the boy's ordeal, contained his excitement with a gruff cough. He could've leaped over the table and kissed both the friar and his dishevelled charge for this fortunate turn of events. The boy, however, was terrified. He would have to step softly.

'Where did you stay when you were with the cult, Thomas?'

'They have a few places around the country. They move around a lot. They're a really secret order and tend to stay indoors most of the time. Shinar likes it that way. He keeps his soldiers very close.'

The name turned his spine to ice. 'Shinar is the cult's leader?'

'He is the founding father of The Awakened.'

Shaking off the nausea, Prendergast noticed the boy's teeth, or what was left of them, were unnaturally pointed and blackened with decay. 'Why did you do that to your teeth?'

'We sharpen them with wood files to make them pointed. It's part of our identity as a brotherhood.'

Prendergast winced at the thought. 'And what does this brotherhood do with itself all day?'

'We watch and, for a long time, all we did was watch. Something happened recently though that brought the army to London.'

'Something?'

The boy nodded so vigorously that Prendergast half imagined his head would snap off his scrawny neck. 'The lady lawyer in the papers. She has something that belongs to Shinar. He wants it back and he's sent out his soldiers to retrieve it. I was one of them until recently.'

'And what is this something the lady lawyer is allegedly said to have?'

'It's a scrying stone or something. That's all I know.'

'A scrying stone? What, one that's used to divine the future? Is Shinar some kind of witch?'

'He has power over life and death.' The boy became increasingly uncomfortable and squirmed in his seat as if his pants itched.

'We all have that, son. It's the circumstances in which we choose to use that power that decides whether or not we're criminals.' For a brief moment, Prendergast wondered where that had come from.

'No, you don't understand,' he leaned over the table, the spittle dribbling from the side of his mouth, 'Shinar can kill with his mind. He knows everything and his eyes are everywhere. He gave me this cancer as a punishment for running away. Most runners, as they're called, top themselves because they're too scared of what Shinar'll do to them when he catches them. And he always does, catch them I mean.'

'And you? Are you not scared, Thomas?'

'Thomas has made his peace with God, inspector, evil may have taken his flesh, but it will not claim his soul.'

Prendergast turned his attention to the friar. 'His soul?'

'There are many forms of evil on this world, Inspector.'

Only his years of professionalism and self-discipline prevented DCI Prendergast's terror from consuming him. Could a man cause a terminal illness by suggestion or will-power alone or were there other forces at play?

'Why does Shinar want this stone so badly?'

'He doesn't. He wants to destroy it. It terrifies him for some reason. That's why The Messenger's looking for it and not Shinar. I think it might be able to kill him in some way.'

'And what makes you think the lady lawyer has it?' Prendergast had been feeling progressively ill since the first mention of Shinar. He felt the hot sweat pooling at the top of his head before pouring down his temples.'

'He's marked you too, hasn't he?'

'What do you mean by that?' Prendergast felt the acid welling up into his throat and his stomach spasming.

'I'd get to a doctor quick, if I were you, or find this stone really fast. You won't survive it if you don't'

The boy stood up from his seat and tried to straighten himself as best he could. 'I'm knackered and starving. Can I get some food now and then maybe we'll talk a bit more. I'll tell you anything you want to know.'

The very mention of food caused Prendergast's innards to churn. He could only nod as he fled the room with his hand held tightly across his mouth.

It was a long time before he eventually staggered from the gents, his mind reeling with a barrage of questions, but the boy had left with his monastic friend and Prendergast was left alone with his thoughts and a vicious ache in his guts.

CHAPTER Sixteen

'**MISS BUTLER, DO YOU THINK** you could be the Vampire Killer's next victim?'

'Miss Butler, Miss Butler, where is Tony Ridout now? Is he going to sue for wrongful arrest?'

'Libby, will you go back to criminal law after all this blows over?'

'Miss Butler, over here, Libby, do you think they let you out the asylum too early?'

'Libby, Libby, what can you tell us about your kidnap ordeal in Scotland?'

Libby shouldered her way through a wave of reporters and flashing cameras flooding the car park outside her home. It was late afternoon and the tarmac steamed with the unusual heat of the day. Having just come back from her first trip to the supermarket in ages, she was confronted with a tsunami of earnest faces, all rolling over each other, hoping to catch her attention and a morning scoop. Most of them looked as though they were about to melt and some showed the physical evidence of standing in the heat too long.

'Wow, that's going to sting!' She patted the throbbing red cheek of a tall photographer who'd obviously left his sunhat at home.

She turned to the youngest reporter closest to her. 'Be a love and grab some of these bags for me would you? I'll tell you everything, but just you.' Libby carefully picked a few light bags to carry and turned to the expectant faces with the sweetest of smiles. 'I have no comment at this time so get lost the lot of you or I'll personally make a complaint to the Press Complaints Commission for violating my rights of privacy as well as trespassing on private property.'

The young woman put her pen behind her ear, her notebook between her teeth and snatched up as many bags from Libby's boot as she could carry without giving herself a hernia. With the sunlight glancing off her white enamels and mirrored sunglasses, she shot her peers a triumphant sneer before staggering up to the second floor behind her quarry as fast as her clicking heels would take her.

Libby stopped at the door and dumped her bags just inside the threshold. 'Oh God, I left my handbag in the car. Be a love and fetch it for me would you before those hounds get hold of all my personal contacts.'

With the image of the award in her hands, plus a contact book worth more than the title deeds to a goldmine, the young woman sped off, delighted she'd won the right to the exclusive that would fire her career into orbit.

Libby slammed the door and slapped the chain on. 'Sucker!'

She reached into her handbag for a cigarette and laughed.

It had been exactly twenty eight days since she first found herself in the hospital and Libby felt like cooking something nice.

She'd never felt the urge to don the mantle of domestic Goddess at any time during her adulthood but her newfound freedom and a month of hospital food had brought on the notion to create something special in her own kitchen.

'Come to mamma!' She pulled the bottle of Veuve Clicquot brut from the bag and cooed with pleasure. It wasn't her favourite, but it was on special at the supermarket. It would do for an evening alone with her thoughts and the dish she'd fantasised about making while her stomach did its best to digest the bowls of treacle pudding and lumpy custard from the hospital kitchens.

She ignored the frantic knocking on the door and waited for the young journalist to come to terms with the fact she'd been had by a woman with more experience and far more cynicism than she.

'Steak Diane tonight.' She imagined Gabriel frowning at her and quickly shook the image from her head, but it was so clear.

Despite the therapies, the tests, the psychoanalyses, the interviews, talks and commitments, Libby was still not convinced Gabriel had simply been a mere hallucination. She'd obviously persuaded her captors she was sane enough to go home and Nicole even signed the discharge papers, but the ghost of Gabriel Radley haunted her relentlessly and she was not prepared to exorcise him just yet.

Her spell at the hospital hadn't been completely futile, however, and it had been established that her psyche was hiding something. There was a part of her memory that remained closed, even from herself, and Libby knew it was important to everyone that she remembered. Moreover, it was vital to her recovery that she unlock her own subconscious to find out what caused this mortally embarrassing psychosis in the first place.

DCI Prendergast had been a darling. He merely spluttered a few well-meaning words after her earnest apology for behaving bonkers. Coppers, however, were not good at hiding their feelings when faced with a situation outside their professional remit and he'd turned cherry-red with discomfiture at the very mention of Gabriel's name.

Hypnotherapy was a bit of a laugh. Libby remembered going into the room and then she remembered walking out. By the look on Nicole's face, though, the sessions hadn't gone to plan and the pouting lips, smothered in the latest Chanel shades, were a tell-tale sign the Divine Ms Blais hadn't got the answers she'd been hoping for.

After a shower, a brief tidy-up and a good hour or so familiarising herself with the home she'd shared with Tony for over five years, Libby set about the task in hand.

'Filet mignon in pan fried juices. God that's so eighties, maybe I should have beans with that.' She pondered on the criminality of her suggestion. She held the heavy meat tenderiser above the red steak. 'OK, Diane, consider this your last moo because I'm bloody starving.'

Realising she was speaking to a piece of mutilated animal, Libby glanced around behind her in case anyone was listening. The silence returned to mock her.

She made to smash the tenderiser down on the meat and cursed as the head parted from the handle, flew across the kitchen and landed on the draining board, smashing a couple of glasses. 'Bloody cheap shit. It's not even solid metal.' She sighed and thought it could've been worse.

She jumped as the phone rang.

'Hi, Carl. I was just speaking to the dormouse in the teapot. Hang on a minute, I think he has some news for you.' She put her index finger over the small receiver and waited a few seconds. 'He says, Twinkle twinkle little bat, how I wonder what you're at. Got that?' She pressed the red button and waited.

As if summoned by a powerful spell, Carl's figure appeared at the door within an hour.

'Bloody hell, Libby, are you feeling all right?'

'Have the press given up their siege of my car park?'

'I think they're all at my house. Hey, you look good in those shorts. You've lost a bit of weight. It suits you.'

'Thanks, I always hoped if I kept hold of them long enough, I'd shrink back into them. I've still got a way to go, but at least there's less backside hanging out from them than before. I'm home and I'm happy for once. As well as your compliments, I need your help.'

For many days Libby had been plotting ways to jog her memory, but she didn't want to do it alone. With most of her friends and allies dead or imagined, she'd few left to turn to for aid, apart from Carl. He wasn't the best of her friends, but she was certain she could manipulate his sentiments, especially with his wife and children absent.

'I need to find out what I'm hiding and have to retrace my steps. Will you come with me tonight for a walk across the Rye?'

'Are you sure that's a good idea, Libby?'

'I've been thinking about this and I'm certain it'll help. From what I understand, I hold a key piece to this puzzle – the serial killings, the cult, and ... well, you know the rest – so I have to find out what happened to me.'

'Shouldn't you leave this up to a police re-enactment or something?' Carl looked genuinely concerned. He noticed the empty bottle of champagne on the low table and sighed. 'Maybe you should sleep on it first.'

Libby melted into the familiar sofa. 'No, I've spent the past month setting this up.' She lit another cigarette and curled her legs beneath her. 'The night I was at Juliette's, I had steak Diane and a bottle of champagne. We were celebrating her new job. At twelve thirty-ish, I'm going to take a walk and you're going to stay close behind me in case someone tries to mug me or worse. Do you think you could find the gelatine in your spine to do that, Carl? I'm not asking for backbone, just enough courage to keep me from harm. You can keep your mobile set to 999 if you want and you could always run away.'

'Please, Libby.'

She relented only because she needed him.

They watched television for a while and chatted now and then about their time in Scotland and the dangers they'd shared. He spoke fondly of Deidre and the kids and convinced her he missed his family enough to worry about them. During those few hours, Libby noticed a subtle change in Carl. He was more humble, more eager to please and far less arrogant than he'd been a month ago. Perhaps he'd learned humility, Libby didn't know, but, although she would never consider continuing a sexual relationship with him, she decided to keep him as a constant in her life.

'Did anyone find out what happened to Rose?'

'The police are still hunting her.' Carl greedily mauled a bowl of crisps as if he hadn't eaten in days.

'She didn't kill Gary Weller and his men, you know. It was Lars, he set her up.'

'And we all went along with it.'

Libby grabbed the bowl from his hands and hugged it protectively into her chest. 'What do you mean by we? Lars told us Rose was driving her own car home. He failed to mention the police were on their way with the sole purpose of arresting her for the Arran murders and kidnapping us in that house near ACHILTIBUIE. The police won't believe my statement that Rose was a member of our party because they all think I'm mentally incapacitated. Are you telling me Rose thinks we're all co-conspirators?'

'It doesn't matter what she thinks. She's on the run and they believe she's probably left the country by now with one of her many different IDs. They know who she is and they're working with Interpol and a few other agencies to find her and bring her to justice. SCO19 have also been put on alert, just in case she sticks her head above the parapet.'

'It's going to take more than a nine millimetre Heckler and Koch to take down Rose Red, Carl, and I personally hope they don't catch her.'

'She's a bloody killer, Libby, she deserves the cell that's waiting for her for the remainder of her miserable life. It doesn't matter whether she killed Weller or not, the police believe she's been responsible for ninety killings around the world and they've matched the bullets of her Berettas to those of the poor cops she shot dead with malice aforethought at the Barry safe house. God, she doesn't look old enough to be a seasoned hit-woman. Just goes to show looks can definitely be deceptive.'

'How do you know what circumstances in her life turned her into a killer? Of course, you don't. How could you? You live in a completely different world to anyone else.' She thrust the bowl back in his hand and, pushing her back deep into the sofa, crossed her arms. 'Lars killed Weller and he's set her up by using her guns to do the job. I've got a feeling she's close and she's waiting for her chance to get revenge. I don't think Rose Red likes unfinished business. It's a matter of principle for her.'

'So, now you're a criminal psychologist?'

'No, but I've been through enough personal journeys recently to recognise pain or sympathy in others. She's going to get him, Carl, and that means she's also coming for you. Let's just hope she's smart enough to realise Deidre and I had nothing to do with the set-up.'

—

Midnight came and went and the pair drove to the other side of the park with a fair amount of trepidation. The night was hot, so hot that Carl was forced to remove his jacket and carry it.

Libby stepped out of the car and, mechanically placing one foot in front of the other, made her way home across the common.

A few minutes passed and Libby felt good. She could hear the light thump of Carl's feet behind her and imagined she could even hear his breath.

She took a right off Strakers Road and used the short-cut to the car park, cutting off the bend. She felt her pulse beginning to pick up speed and didn't know whether it was the exertion from the brisk walk or something more ominous.

'Shit, damn irresponsible dog owners.'

'Shut up, Carl, you're ruining my concentration.'

'Well, I've just ruined my bloody work shoes on dog excrement. Oh God, it's got nuts in it!'

The street lights became dimmer behind her as she neared the car park and the row of recycling bins where a woman's body, or most of it at least, had been found.

She stopped to squint at the scene, her eyes and breath probing the darkness for a random thought. She could hear her own breathing and the soft thud of her heart inside her chest but she felt nothing.

Moving on, along the tree-lined path leading to the main road through the centre of the common, she realised the darkness no longer frightened her. She tried to imagine something or someone behind the trees and willed the panic to rise, but it didn't come. As she reached the spill of light around the fringes of the park and could see the main road, she felt only bitter disappointment.

'Anything?'

They stood on the pavement, he searching her face for answers while she scanned the darkness beyond the trees. He mopped his sweating brow with a pristine hanky.

'Nothing,' she breathed eventually. 'Absolutely nothing.'

'Then let's get back. I have to go home and get some sleep. I've got work tomorrow.'

'Take me back to the car.'

'Of course.'

'No, I mean take me back, Carl. I want to try again.'

'Look, Peckham Common's not the safest of areas to go for a stroll in the middle of the night, Libby. We can't do this all night. We'd just be courting trouble.'

'Just once more. Please.'

They walked back through the park as briskly as the heat of the night would allow and reached the car.

'Take the car around the park, Carl, and meet me on the other side. I have to do this alone.'

'Don't be ridiculous, Libby, it's too dangerous. Supposing the Vampire Killer's waiting for you there?'

'Then I'll have to take my chances. Look out for me.'

She left without another word and a frantic Carl could only watch as she disappeared into the night.

She took a right off Strakers Road and used the short-cut to the car park cutting off the bend. She felt her pulse beginning to pick up speed and didn't know whether it was the exertion from the brisk walk or something more ominous.

Was that the sound of footsteps behind her?

The street lights became distant as she neared the car park and the row of recycling bins where a woman's body, or most of it at least, had been found.

Footsteps stopped some distance behind her. She was being followed.

She stopped to squint at the scene, her eyes and breath probing the darkness for a random thought. There was something there. A tall dark figure leaning over something on the ground.

Her pulse boomed in her temples and her heart thudded

beneath her ribs as she crossed the tarmac to rejoin the path where a line of trees stood like menacing sentinels lining the road to hell. A few more steps and this is where it happened: between the trees and the low buildings, this is where she witnessed the aftermath of a murder. The darkness closed in and Libby heard her throat squealing, as if a wailing banshee was trapped inside her neck.

She saw a woman on the ground. Her long blonde hair splayed out like rippling waves on either side of her head.

'What the hell... are you all right?' Libby ran towards the stricken woman but didn't know what to do. It was dark, but there was enough light to make out the woman, a pretty woman, was bleeding from the neck. She took the warm hand and realised the victim lay paralysed, her wide eyes transfixed on a tiny point in the vast universe above her.

A rustle from the trees and Libby's throat finally freed itself from its tangled knots. She screamed in panic. 'Help me! He's going to kill me too!'

She heard the booted feet thumping in perfect synchronicity to hers and she felt his breath on her neck. She wailed and whimpered and screamed as if it was her last dying effort. She felt her lungs trying to explode from her chest as she ran with the heat of hell burning her heels. She ran until her feet hit the main road. 'God, please, someone help me!'

'Libby, Libby, you're safe. You're fine. Shit, why did I allow this to happen?'

Libby couldn't catch her breath as she threw her arms around Carl with her fists tightly clenched. 'He was there, Carl. He was there. I saw him. I saw him!'

'You saw his face?'

'No, but I saw him. Please, we need to finish this. I have to go home.'

By the time Libby and Carl returned to the flat, their lungs were on fire and they were sure the heat had melted away a large fraction of their body mass. Carl hadn't intended to be performing a thousand metre sprint along a main road in his work shoes and looked as though he'd never recover from the exertion. He ran to the sink and drank a few tall glasses of water before ducking under the stream. Libby, however, stood in the centre of the living room staring at the bathroom door, her body shaking with shock.

As if in a trance, her gaze locked on her trembling palm which she opened slowly.

'What are you doing?'

Carl could only watch as Libby moved into the bathroom, her teeth clattering together inside her jaw like a pneumatic drill. She knelt down beside the toilet.

'That's a girl. Let it all out, Libby. You'll feel better after you've been sick.'

Instead of sticking her head into the bowl, Libby picked up a packet of night-time sanitary towels and ripped the plastic cover open with her teeth. Snatching a handful of the neatly-wrapped parcels, she squeezed each one carefully.

'No way!'

She unfolded one of the towels and pulled out a shining object that had been hidden inside it. 'She pushed it into my hand. She wasn't dead, Carl, she was alive. She just couldn't move that's all. She was alive and someone came back for her or found her immobilised and killed her in a horrible way.'

'And you came home afterwards?'

'I came home and hid the stone here.'

She unfurled her fingers to reveal a sparkling red stone. Shorter and slimmer than her palm. Its edges were sharp as razor blades and sliced fine lines through her flesh, yet the light danced off its multiple facets casting a spectacular show of dazzling rainbows across the bathroom tiles.

'Why on God's earth did you hide it there?'

Libby shrugged, too enthralled by the spinning lights that whirled and eddied like a miniature aurora borealis around her. 'No one found it, did they? And it's not from a lack of searching. I think everyone and his wife must've been in this flat at some point looking for this gem. I suppose a packet of oversized sanitary towels is the last place anyone would think of looking for a precious stone, and look at it Carl, it's amazing. I've never seen or heard of anything like it. It must be worth an absolute fortune.'

'We're going to have to hand it over to the police.' Carl passed Libby a large glass of spirits he found in her cupboard. He hadn't even bothered to read the label. He poured a larger one for himself and momentarily worried about the prospects of being hospitalised after drinking paint stripper before shrugging and downing it flat.

'Why, what would they do with it? I can't trust the coppers with this. I'm going to hide it again until the time comes to bargain with it.'

'So now you want to extort cash for ransom. Come on, Libby, that's surely not your style.'

'I don't want money, Carl, I just want to do the right thing. There are a lot of people after this stone. A woman died for it and I just want to make sure the proper owner gets his or her hands on it first. There's no way I'm going to hand it over to that Shinar or the police. I just need a bit of time to think, that's all.'

'Libby,' Carl looked genuinely concerned, 'you're not thinking of keeping it for Gabriel Radley are you?'

She sighed and shook her head in feigned despair. 'Gabriel who?'

'Thank you Miss, er, Filpo.. Filiopo... Filopoo ...'

'Filipowicz.'

'Ah, yes, so sorry, Ms Flipovick. Is there anything else I can do for you?'

Anzhela smiled as widely as her patience with the spluttering female bank teller would allow. 'No thank you. Goodbye.'

'Er, miss ...'

She carefully placed the money in her bag, alongside the contents of the deposit box, snapped it shut and slowly sat back down.

'... I note you haven't had a review of your account for at least three years. Would you like me to make you an appointment with a financial adviser?'

'If I wanted advice, I would ask for it. I know what to do with my money, thanks.'

'It would only take about twenty minutes. Your account is very healthy but not paying you enough interest. I'm certain that .....'

'And I'm certain you can suck in more gullible customers to buy your useless products. I don't want any advice, I don't want any more accounts, I don't want insurance and I don't want an appointment.'

With her index finger, she pulled her glasses down to the tip of her nose and glared at the girl through a pair of striking blue contact lenses. Anzhela resisted the urge to reach for the weapons in her bag.

'Is that clear?'

'Thanks a lot.' The girl mumbled.

'Is there anything else I can do for you?'

'No thank you.'

Walking towards the wall of smoked glass panels, Anzhela caught a glimpse of her reflection here and there and decided she could barely recognise herself.

She'd swapped the red tresses and natural look for a sleek short bob with a severe fringe, dark red lipstick and thin-framed glasses. In her tight black suit, she felt like a city stockbroker and had to admit to herself she'd made a really good job of changing her looks so effectively that not even her own mother would recognise her.

She stepped out into the city's morning light and her lenses reacted immediately, dimming the glare of the sun by turning black.

Standing between the glorious architectural lines of London's Georgian era and contemporary offices fashioned from ugly lumps of concrete, she decided to walk for a while and get to know the city a bit more before taking a taxi to London Bridge Station and embarking on the last mission of what was to be her former career.

—

'This is nice.'

Libby sat upright in her chair and sipped at her glass of iced soda water.

'Thought it might rekindle a dying flame somewhere inside you. I quite miss the old us.'

She sighed. 'You don't get it, do you, Carl? After all that's happened there can be no more 'us'. Deidre's a really good woman and you've never deserved that level of loyalty.'

'There's always two sides to a story, Libby.'

'And I've heard and seen the other side.'

'Are you ready to order?'

Libby smiled at the familiar face of the girl who'd served her the last time she'd lunched at the Tonbridge pub. She suddenly remembered believing she was not alone then and hid her face in the menu, hoping either the girl wouldn't recognise her or the fire alarm would go off.

'Give us a few moments, please.' Carl came to the rescue. 'Would you prefer to go somewhere else?'

'No, it's OK. I'll have to face the world as I knew it at some stage. This is as good a start as any.'

'How's Maurice?'

'Miserable. His jaw's wired shut and his head's an odd shape but Nicole says he'll be getting a titanium plate to replace the lost skull bits and his jaw will eventually heal well enough for him to continue with his tales. He's going to have to do some explaining the next time he goes through an airport metal detector though.'

'At least he's on the mend.' Carl paused to think, the furrows on his brow almost meeting his nose. Libby knew that look. She narrowed her eyes. He leaned over the table and whispered to her. 'Have you decided what you're going to do with the stone?'

In feigned earnestness, she leaned across the table to place her face very close to his. 'Not yet. It's in a safe place though where no one will find it.' Her eyes looked left and then right before meeting Carl's once more. 'Not even me.'

'You're playing a very dangerous game, my girl.' He sat back and gulped a mouthful of real ale.

'I don't know what it's like to play safe any more. I don't trust anyone and I'm constantly watching my back for assailants with sharp teeth and painted faces or even a flash of red hair. It's an odd way to live and I'm sure the coppers are following me. I trust they'll bungle my rescue and I'll end up again on the front pages of the tabloids lying in a pool of my own blood with my skirt over my head.'

'Give the stone to the police, Libby. They're better equipped to deal with things like this. The longer you have it, the more you're placing your life and everyone else's in danger. Hand it over, please.'

'You know, Carl, that's almost exactly, word for word, what Nicole advised me to do over the phone this morning and she doesn't even know I've got the stone. Unless, of course, you've told her.'

'I swear, Libby, on my children's lives, I haven't breathed a word to anyone. Not even Deidre. You never know who's listening in to conversations these days. They may be listening in now.'

'Who's they?'

'The police; the press; The Awakened; Lars; or even that bloody Nakita.'

Libby giggled. 'Well, you'd better be nice behind her back just in case she is listening and doesn't like your tone. Oh no, here comes that waitress again. Tell her I'll have the steak and ale pie with chips.'

Carl ordered while Libby ducked under the table, pretending to pick up something she'd dropped.

'You can come out now, she's gone.'

'Thank God for that. I could feel the blood rushing to my head.'

'She probably wouldn't recognise you anyway. She deals with hundreds of customers every week and she doesn't exactly look as though she's a member of Mensa.'

'I'm sure she'd remember the wacky woman who spoke to her imaginary friend and ordered enough fish to feed a pod of dolphins for a year.'

'I don't understand why you're keeping hold of it.'

'Drop it, Carl.'

'I can't. You won't be able to get back to an ordinary life while all eyes are looking at you. They know you've got it.'

'They?' Libby was beginning to suspect Carl knew more than he was prepared to tell. 'What aren't you telling me?'

She accurately read the discomfiture in his body language as he crossed and uncrossed his arms before taking another gulp of ale. 'It doesn't take an idiot to work that one out, Libby. A lot of bad people want that stone for whatever reason. It's only a matter of time before it's taken from you. There are only so many sanitary towels you can hide behind.'

'You never asked me who the man in the park was.'

She watched him squirm as he crossed his arms tightly against his torso once more. 'I didn't want to put you through any more. You were already freaked out by your little midnight walk.'

'Why didn't you ask me who I saw there? Don't you want to catch him?'

'Ah, the food. That's great.' Carl rubbed his hands together. 'I didn't know how hungry I was until now.'

'Carl? What's going on?'

'Eat up, Libby, it'll go cold.' He pushed his food around his plate. 'Damn! I'm trying to protect you.' She jumped as he slammed his knife and fork down on the table. 'They promised to leave you alone once they had the stone. God, I've really done it now. Why are you always so good at getting me to say things I don't want to? Now we're both for it.'

'They who?'

'You don't want to know.'

'Yes, I do.'

'Is everything OK?'

Libby looked up at the waitress and tried her best to smile. 'Yes, thanks, everything's fine.'

'Thought you'd order the fish today, seeing you like fish.' The girl giggled.

'I ate too much of it the last time. I wanted something different today. You know, to test the culinary talents of your chef.'

'Thank you, miss, that'll be all.'

Libby turned her head slowly towards Carl and shot him a curious glance. 'That's a bit rude, she's just being polite. Sorry about him.'

'That's OK, miss.' She hesitated for a moment, her nose twitching. 'By the way, will that bloke you brought in last time ever come here again?'

'Which one?' Libby felt her spine tingling.

'Oh, m' God,' the girl placed her hand on her chest to accentuate her wonderment, 'the really fit one with the dark eyes and the soft voice. We all went mad when he came here for lunch. We haven't stopped talking about him since. Tell him he's welcome here any time, won't you? We'd all sooooo love to see him again.'

Libby turned to Carl with her mouth wide open and watched him choke on his ale.

Seventeen

'HOW'S OUR GUEST?'

Lars Andersson removed his booted feet from the desk and shrugged. 'Quiet as always.' He watched the man moving across the room, leaving muddy footprints on the cream carpet. 'Have you come alone?'

'The Awakened are never alone.'

'Well, they should be.' He muttered under his breath. 'You really should get that seen to, you know.'

'What?' The Messenger spun around, one side of his mutilated face quivering inside the sagging skin like a bag of live worms. The very sight of it made the big Swede feel queasy.

'Your face. You should get it seen to before it stays like that for good.'

'Maybe one day, when this is over. In the meantime, has he been giving you any trouble?'

'No, he's a lovely little lamb. Once you get to know him, he's quite an amiable young fellow. Hard to believe you're all so terrified of him.'

The Messenger turned around to sneer at his associate. 'You obviously haven't seen what he's capable of when he puts his mind to it.'

Lars' deep chuckle caused his expansive shoulders to spasm. 'Believe me, I've seen him at work and admit he's very impressive. But he doesn't like to kill and that's good enough for me. I'm very safety conscious you know. I did a course in managing safely. Got a merit.'

'Is he still behind bars?'

'I regularly risk assess the situation and decided that bars were probably still a good idea. He hasn't attempted to escape yet, if that was your next question. If he does, I'll send for you immediately. I don't want to be alone to face his anger.'

'I want to see him.' The strange Messenger put his hands up in the air, revealing the intricate latticed ink-work on his palms.

'Don't worry, I've already been frisked. He's not mine to kill. Shinar wants this one.'

'So your boss has finally allowed you to see him. Why the change of heart? Doesn't he trust I'm looking after him properly?'

Lars didn't like doing business inside his own home, especially with this particular kind of criminal, but there were few places left for him to hide. Fortunately, no one knew his personal address on Wimbledon's west side so he was able to remain under the radar of the nosey press and the police, provided he stayed indoors.

He met his weekly visits from The Messenger with a fair amount of disrelish. He hated the man. Sometimes, like today, he appeared almost sensible. His conversation was occasionally interesting, he seemed well schooled in social sciences and had a wide knowledge of the world.

Most of the time, however, the cracks would appear across the surface of his sanity, revealing the demented and tortured soul writhing beneath. Lars didn't know what to make of him but the very thought of being in the same room made him uneasy. His boss was even worse. Lars shuddered at the thought of having to face Shinar one day. He'd never met the man but had heard enough accounts of him to know when to stay well clear.

'Why would one man need seven bedrooms?'

'I like a choice,' was all Lars offered as he led his guest to the commodious basement which contained a games room, indoor pool, wet room, sauna and a single holding cell for people he didn't trust to keep their mouths shut.

He placed his hand against the panel beside the metal door between two moulded plaster of paris doric columns and it slid open with a hiss. The prisoner sat in a comfortable room behind strong steel bars. He lay on a sofa with his nose in a book. He ignored the intrusion and turned the page.

'He looks pale. Have you been feeding him properly?'

'For the past month I've been meals on heels. He gets three meals a day and I make sure he eats them. What do you mean he looks pale?'

Lars peered into the cell and admitted to himself that, over time, his prisoner was appearing more gaunt.

'I don't think he likes being locked up, but he does like his books,' Lars suffixed his sentence with a quiet rumble of laughter. 'He finished one on Radical Enlightenment in a morning after his exercise – which, by the way, he seems to do a lot of. I've run out of intellectual material for him, so he's reading The Name of the Rose by Umberto Eco. What do you think of it, Gabe?'

He was answered with silence.

'I quite liked it. I especially liked the bit about the poisoned pages. Sneaky little murdering bastards, those medieval friars!'

'Every story tells a story that has never been told.'

Gabriel turned his head slowly towards The Messenger, the censure in those eyes would have killed him instantly had they had a mechanical firing mechanism behind them. 'And a symbolic figure can be so rich in meanings that by now it hardly has any meaning left'.

'We will see how much meaning the stone has when Shinar

kills you with it En'Iente.' Despite the brave talk, Lars detected fear and perhaps uncertainty in The Messenger's eyes.

'Stat rosa pristina nomine, nomina nuda tenemus.'

'Did the author not replace Roma with rosa?'

'It makes little difference to the meaning. Besides, I cannot believe that semiotics is one of your fortes. Just stick to the intention of the author and you will understand what he was trying to say.'

The Messenger set his jaw in anger at Gabriel's blatant disrespect.

'Sorry, boys, you've lost me.' Lars' voice tore the atmosphere like the ripping of a heavy velvet curtain.

'I've come to let you know, En'Iente, that the stone has been found. It's only a matter of hours before your execution and your ultimate disgrace.'

The Messenger turned to Lars. 'Shinar rewards the loyal well. He wants to see the Vascaran.'

'Then take him away. I'm tired of babysitting him anyway.'

'Shinar wants to see the Vascaran now.'

'Fine by me. I'll just unlock this door ....'

'He is waiting outside.'

Lars felt the cold fingers of dread scraping at his spine. 'He wants to come in? Now? Shinar?'

The Messenger nodded slowly, the black omen shining from his eyes. 'Now.'

—

'What's the urgency Lloyd?'

Walking through the front door, DCI Prendergast kissed the cheek of Muriel, Lloyd's wife, and ruffled the hair of his seven-year-old son. 'Hell, it's hot today.'

'You're not going to believe this, Prendy, but I think I'm one step away from finding our Vampire Killer.'

Prendergast looked for a seat to collapse on. 'What do you mean?'

'Look at this, Prendy.' He wheeled himself across the floor to a computer in the corner of the room. 'Someone put a message through my door. It wasn't signed but the writing's beautiful. The paper smells of expensive perfume, but what a lead ...'

'Well?'

'Sorry, sir.' He handed the notepaper to Prendergast.

'Looking for Dracula?', he read, 'You'll find him stalking the jurors and defence team in NHS Surrey v Swann.'

'What's that supposed to mean?'

Lloyd laughed and puffed his chest out. 'Sarah Hill, aged thirty, legal secretary; Trinity Jimiciw, twenty-one, art student; Dr Susmita Salvarajah, fifty-five, GP; Rachael Leverne, thiry-two, social worker; a young blonde woman whose first name we know to be Anna Leah; Selina Fotheringham-Taylor, twenty-six, lawyer; and recently Patricia Frost, forty-six, housewife. What could they all have in common?'

Prendergast squinted at the list before reaching into his top pocket for his glasses. 'What indeed?'

'I'll tell you.' Lloyd's excitement had already caused his voice to rise an octave. 'Sarah Hill was a juror in a personal injury case a couple of years ago. Amy Swann, the plaintiff, lost a baby and was suing the Surrey health board for negligence. She lost and committed suicide a few weeks after the verdict was announced.'

'Poor girl, but what's she got to do with the Vampire Killings?'

'Wait, that's not the best bit. The defence team was headed up by no other than our special needs lawyer, Libby Butler.'

'I'm listening.' DCI Prendergast felt the excitement surging.

'Trinity Jamiciw, was an art student, but her father Thomas

was a member of that jury; as was Dr Susmita Salvarajah's husband. Rachael Laverne was the wife of Howard Laverne ...'

'A member of the jury?'

'Precisely! Patricia Frost was the head juror and Selina Fotheringham-Taylor was part of the legal hit team.'

DCI Prendergast flopped down into the computer chair and almost toppled over. 'The woman Anna Leah doesn't fit.'

'I think the killer was after the Butler woman that night but came across Anna Leah during the hunt. I think the poor girl just got caught in the cross-fire, which was good news for Libby Butler, but bad news for her.'

'What about Suzanne Glover?'

'She doesn't fit either. All I can argue is she made contact with Radley and Miss Butler that night in the cell. She could've been given some incriminating information. It's a long-shot, but that's all I've come up with so far on her. I'm still working on it.'

'Gabriel Radley.' DCI Prendergast felt the sting of contrition in his heart. He wondered what would happen to Radley once the stone was found. It had been very difficult for him, a down-to-earth Yorkshireman, to lie so blatantly, but there was too much at stake, or so he had forced himself to believe. The trouble was that Andrew Galbraith Prendergast had been exposed as a coward in his own eyes and that didn't rest well against the badges of his office or his own sense of honour.

'So who's the killer?'

'Someone with an axe to grind.'

'How did the victim die?'

'She slit her wrists in the bathtub.'

'Hmm, that would explain the killer's obsession with bleeding his victims dry. He no doubt chopped them up in a bid to either dehumanise them ...'

'.... or tear apart the reason for his hatred.'

'Did the victim have a brother, a husband or a father perhaps?'

'Don't rule out the possibility the killer might be another woman.'

'I'll get the team on to it straight away.' Prendergast checked his excitement with a long pause. 'How do you fancy coming back to the yard and helping out? You've almost cracked this case, it would be inappropriate for someone else to take the glory. We'll rearrange the place to accommodate that chariot of yours.'

Lloyd answered him with a smile wider than his face: 'Thought you'd never ask!'

—

'You bastard! You despicable, lying bastard!' Libby stormed across the car park with Carl chasing after her.

'Libby stop and hear me out, please.'

They'd spent the entire car journey from the pub with her screaming at him. Carl's ears still rang. This was the first opportunity he'd had to get a word in and he was going to make sure he took it. She slammed the security door in his face, but he just managed to wedge his foot in the gap.

He yelled in pain when she stamped her heel into his toe, but his shoe stayed firm.

'You made me believe I was completely insane. You, Nicole and that bloody copper. Grrr, I knew I should never trust a bloody cop. They're all corrupt. Every last bloody one of them.' She took the stairs three at a time. 'Get away from me. I hate you.'

Carl just managed to smash his fist against the door before she broke his nose with it. 'Get lost, Carl. I never want to see you again.'

'Libby please.' Inside her flat, he closed the door behind him and his eyes widened with shock. 'Good grief!'

The entire apartment had been ransacked. The chairs, sofas and soft furnishings had been ripped apart and shaken out, their fluffy contents lying across the floors and surfaces alongside pieces of broken china and shattered glass. The carpets had been torn up and there was not an ornament left intact. All the pictures had been hurled to the ground and smashed and the contents of drawers and cupboards lay strewn about like leaves in a forest after a violent storm.

'So, you didn't tell anyone, on your children's lives, I'd found the stone? Nice one, Carl.' She walked into the kitchen. 'What a mess! Looks like someone's chucked a hand grenade through the window.'

'We'll get it cleared-up. I'll get you new furniture. It's only material stuff.'

'This was my home. I feel violated.' Appearing strangely calm, she began to pick up the kitchen utensils and place them inside the shattered drawer.

'Is the stone missing?'

She spun around and slapped his face with a fish slice. 'Is that all you care about? Why is everyone so obsessed with it? It's only a bloody stone!'

He grabbed her shoulders and shook the temper from her. 'Yes, it's only a stone, but it's very important to certain people. To some, it's a matter of life and death, and that some includes me. Have they taken it? Have they got it? Tell me.'

Carl's words were accompanied by a torrent of tears.

'No, they haven't.'

His arms flopped to his sides and, as his legs gave way, he sat on the floor as if felled by a heavy hammer blow. 'This has all got to stop, Libby. It must end now.'

'The stone belongs to Gabriel. That's what he came here for and I'll only give it to him.'

Carl shook his head and howled with demented laughter as if he'd just been delivered a death sentence. 'They won't let you do that. Don't you see? All this death; all this pain, is all because of you. The stone was locked away inside your head and everything you've been through has been planned from the start. Shinar got to Nicole, he got to Prendergast and recently he paid a visit to me. He's going to kill us all, Libby, unless you hand the stone over to him. I tried to protect you. I told them you'd found it and hidden it again. I took you away today to give them a chance to find it, but they've gone home empty handed and now they'll be coming for me.'

'Where's Gabriel?'

'In a safe place. He's alive. Where's the stone?'

'In a safe place, it's also alive, but I'm surprised you'd think I was stupid enough, with all the people after it, to keep it here.'

'So where is it?'

'They're going to kill him, Carl. Once the stone is in Shinar's hands, Gabriel will die. I'm not going to let that happen. I want to give him the advantage.'

'For God's sake, Libby, you hardly know the chap. Too many people have died in the cross-fire of this little personal war and I don't want to be one of them. This has to end here and now. Please!'

'The stone for Gabriel.' She closed her eyes and breathed out her courage. 'Tell them that's the deal. They, and I assume 'they' includes Detective Chief Inspector Prendergast, will deliver Gabriel to me, alive and unharmed, and I'll give that bent copper the stone. Let him run to Shinar with it and see how far he gets on his way home without growing horns. If I see any sign of a painted face and sharp black teeth, the deal's off. They can kill me, but they'll never find out where the stone is. I'll deal only with Prendergast. You scurry along like a good little dog and tell them that.' She began to push him out the door. 'Oh yes, and I can't stay here any more. Book me an indefinite stay in a nice, comfortable five-star hotel close to St Paul's, starting from tonight.'

'Why there?' Carl almost fell out the door.

'I like that part of the city and public places will work to my advantage. Now do as I say or no deal.'

She watched him staggering down the hallway. 'I want a nice suite overlooking the cathedral. In fact, I want it to be so close to the cathedral that I can reach out from my window and touch the dome with my hand.'

'That's not going to be possible, Libby.'

'I'm exaggerating, you oaf. Get me as close as possible.'

'I'll try.'

She hesitated before closing the door after his shuffling feet. 'And don't think for one minute that I'm not going to sue the bloody lot of you … starting with that bitch Nicole!'

The walls shuddered as she slammed the door.

—

Lars Andersson was an intelligent, resourceful man who had an uncanny aptitude for avoiding danger. He called it his 'strong nose for trouble', that had kept him alive throughout his career in a highly capricious business and had never let him down until now.

It wasn't so much Lars didn't want to receive Shinar as a guest in his house, but more that he hadn't prepared for this eventuality. He knew he would one day have to meet him before this business was concluded, he just wasn't expecting that day to have come so soon. This left the big Swede in a quandary.

He looked over to Gabriel behind the heavy bars and searched his face for an answer. The young man appeared unfazed by the news and simply continued to read. Lars wondered if he had even heard the conversation.

'What do you think, Gabe? Are you up to receiving a guest?'

Gabriel shot him a smile of cold indifference and, not for the first time, Lars marvelled at the man's unwavering ability, despite his impossible odds of survival, to control his emotions. He turned his attention to The Messenger.

'Has Shinar come to kill him or just to gloat? If he's come to kill him, then he's not doing it here. This is a nice, friendly neighbourhood and the residents scare easily.'

'That's for Shinar to decide. I don't speak for him.'

'So you just do his dirty work?'

The Messenger laughed and his bad eye quivered in its slack socket. 'Am I detecting a note of censure in the work I do from one who has committed his entire lifetime to the same field of employment, and for money?'

'We're not the same, you and I. For one, I have a proper name. Secondly, I don't run around killing people for shiny stones.'

'No?'

Lars was forced to laugh. 'OK, but I still have a proper name.'

'Names are empty vessels used solely for the purpose of identification. I know who I am, I don't need a name.'

The Messenger shuddered and suddenly snapped his head around to Gabriel whose expression gave nothing away. Lars knew from that look of wide-eyed enlightenment that Shinar's favourite lieutenant had realised something very important. Unfortunately for Lars, he was not about to share it. A strange expression crossed The Messenger's face. Was it uncertainty or was it awe? Whatever it was, the man continued to stare at Gabriel as if he'd just seen God in a cloud.

'Er, I hate to break up the bromance boys, but, from my experience of bosses, I wouldn't keep a man like Mr Shinar waiting.'

'I'll tell Mr Shinar the En'Iente refuses to see him.'

'What's that supposed to mean? He's behind bars and why do you call him that?'

'It is what he is.'

Lars heard the breath of respect in The Messenger's words but knew he would get nowhere with further questioning. 'Will he be mad?'

The Messenger made a sniggering, guttural sound that Lars eventually realised was laughter. 'He already is.'

'Let him in. He will not harm me.'

Both men eyed the prisoner before The Messenger obediently left the room, the thumping of his boots echoing across the marble floor.

Lars wasn't sure what he'd witnessed or whether he'd indeed witnessed anything. All he knew was he was very confused. Gabriel, although cordial, was confoundedly taciturn. He kept all thought as well as all emotion secured behind his dark eyes and left everything to supposition. Even at the eve of his impending death, he seemed peculiarly complacent.

'Aren't you scared? Of what they're going to do to you, I mean?'

Gabriel put his book down and stood up slowly, testing his limbs with a small stretch. 'Do you care?'

'Not really.'

'Then do not ask.'

'You must be afraid of something.'

'Many things, but my basic survival mechanism has always been to dash towards danger, to meet it eye to eye, in the stead of running from it.'

'There's a name for that. Ah, yes, I believe it's called stupidity!'

'Attack, I have found, is always the best form of defence. Release me from these bars and I will show you how it is done.'

'Sorry, Gabe, but I'm not paid to do that. Plus, I'm your gaoler. I don't think for one minute you won't take a month's worth of incarceration and boredom out on me. You've had too long to dwell on it.'

'I bear you no ill will, Lars Andersson. I do not kill men for committing acts of folly. I will allow you to learn from it. Besides, this is only your first strike against me. You will not make another.'

'Says the one behind the bars!' Lars' laughter trailed as he felt rather than witnessed the approach of the one who called himself Shinar. His spine tingled before it became rigid and he turned around to the soundless footsteps softly padding towards him. He took a few wide steps to the side as if the small man in the red cloak had physically moved him out of the way. His nostrils made an involuntary spasm against the terrible odour that invaded them and he felt the sudden urge to plunge into a hot bath and scrub himself for days.

Fortunately for Lars, Shinar shuffled forwards with his dead eyes locked on Gabriel, seemingly oblivious to anything or anyone else in the room.

'Why is the Vascaran not in chains?' Shinar's outrage cracked across the room.

'He's got bars. Chains would be over-kill.'

He snapped his twisted gaze on Lars, the spittle flying from his lips. 'I want him chained,' he roared and Lars, shaken by the sudden violent outburst, put his hands out in appeasement. Shinar turned his attention back to Gabriel. 'So, Vascar, this is where it ends.'

Lars didn't realise he was holding his breath as Gabriel moved up to the bars. He did note, however, Shinar kept a safe distance from his adversary's reach.

'Your ordeal, Shinar, has not yet begun.'

'Can you really be as perfect as your legend advocates?'

'Can you smell worse than does yours?'

Lars checked himself for chuckling as he watched the scene unfold from the stage of his own basement. The air cracked around his ears and his hair bristled with static.

Unprovoked by the prisoner's jibes, Shinar continued his optical inspection. 'This is what they have sent after me? I see a mere boy.'

'Even children have the ability to slay monsters.' The dark eyes narrowed.

'A monster to slay a monster, or a boy who bears his insufferable losses behind a rigid shield of over-confidence?'

He hit a nerve, for Lars saw a barely perceptible line of pain twist Gabriel's smooth features.

'Yes, my beautiful boy, over-confidence and sentiment have ever been your downfall. The fatal flaws in an otherwise perfect being. I feel your loss and I feel your agony and they tear out my heart. Ah, such sweet but such terrible torment. You have been sent to take me back in chains, but you have failed. I will see you in those chains before you die and I will revel in your regret.'

Gabriel closed his eyes and sank to his knees, his hands sliding slowly down the bars.

Lars felt an unprecedented pang of contrition as he watched his prisoner reeling in uncertainty and the terrible power the little man in the red cloak had over a seemingly indomitable spirit.

'You're not going to take that from Rumpelstiltskin are you, Gabe?' He spoke before thinking.

'I would doubt whether your heart could be found beneath

the folds of your twisted trunk, for evil has been your master for far too long.' As if answering a rallying call, Gabriel's voice was soft, yet rebellious. 'You cannot infect me by mental ambush, Shinar, for I have already come to terms with my failures and I do not dwell on them. Failure merely gives me the opportunity to strive harder. You have come to a crossroads in your schemes, for, although it appears you have me, you neither know what to do with me nor how to get close enough to do it.'

He rose from the floor, glorious.

Shinar shrank back from him.

'You are weakening, Vascar. You have lingered too long here and you become weaker by the day. By the time this is over, I doubt whether you will have the strength to repel me, let alone arrest me. Time is something that I have on my side and I am in no hurry to see your end. The longer you remain alive, the more time I have to relish your death.'

'You will not defeat me without the stone, so let us settle this now between us. Come closer and we will end this siege for good, or run until you feel strong enough to face me alone.'

The unfettered rage rattled Shinar's body beneath his cloak. His ugly leer transformed to murderous fury that caused a tremor of terror to rip through the heart of even the fearless Lars.

'CHAIN HIM!' Shinar's command was like a rumble of angry thunder as he marched across the room, putting as much distance as possible between him and the object of his ire.

Lars was left shivering as the ice thawed in his spine.

'I think he's in love with you,' he managed to find his voice at last. 'I think Mr Shinar's got more problems with his own sexuality than he has with good versus evil.'

'I will agree that I impassion him, but I do not believe his responses to me are erotic. Hatred can be a very powerful passion.'

'Sorry, Gabe, I'm the kind of man who sees it like it is. I don't do love and hate, I prefer to always stay on the fence of wild emotion. Shinar has some poorly repressed homoerotic adoration for you that, because you don't return it, has manifested into anger. He doesn't need a stone; he just needs you to give him a damn good shag with a bit of perversion thrown in.'

Gabriel shot him such a violent scowl that Lars took comfort in the bars between them.

'It's OK, I know that won't happen in your lifetime.'

'You are a master of understatement.' Gabriel conceded one of his wry smiles, although Lars noted his hands were shaking.

'Well, I'm glad you think I'm good at something.'

'Thank you.'

'You're welcome but what did I do?'

'You broke his concentration and spared me a psychological lashing. He is very powerful and even I find it difficult to lock him out. I owe you a favour.'

Lars grinned before feigning seriousness once more. 'Sorry, Gabe, my friend, but I've got a bit of a problem.'

He was answered by the raising of one amused eyebrow.

'First, I've got to find some nice chains for you to wear and, second, I have to work out how I'm going to put them on. Oh yes, you owe me a favour, don't you?'

 Eighteen

WITH A TREMBLING HAND, DETECTIVE Chief Inspector Prendergast reached for the latch of the battered door of the Nunhead church. He cursed himself for his weakness in allowing terror to take hold of him and wring out the professional part of his character. The place was bad enough during the day, he thought, but nothing could prepare him for the crushing sensations of foreboding and horror that now faced him in the night.

Alone with only irrepressible trepidation, the inspector felt as if all his childhood fears had returned to terrorise him; the horrors of life surrounded him and squeezed the air from his lungs. The hinges yielded with screams for mercy and the door swung open to reveal the repressive darkness of the church's belly. He felt as though he was at the threshold of hell itself.

'Come in, Andrew.'

'Mr Shinar.' He heard the summons and felt the sickness return to claim him; constricting his throat and sapping the energy from his stomach. This was one appointment he was compelled to honour; a possible finality to all the chaos that had gone before. It was time to act and finish this and put his repulsion and reluctance aside. He took a few deep breaths and stepped inside.

'Oh God!' he choked out the contents of his guts, unable to control the queasiness churning inside him. Shinar stood in front of him in long red robes, his twisted features made more repulsive by the light of a single candle that wavered and spat as if repelled by the man who held it. His eyes glinted like sharp blades.

'I understand the stone has been found.'

Prendergast made an attempt to stand upright and fight back the nausea, but it consumed him. 'Your intelligence is correct,' he managed to utter through watering eyes

'Then you will hand it over to my messenger, as was agreed?'

'There is a price.'

'Ah!' Shinar took a step towards him, his eyes ravenous. 'There is always a price. Name it.'

'Miss Butler is prepared to exchange the stone for the Vascaran.'

The leer dissolved into the deep crevices of his skin and was replaced by an anger so violent that Prendergast gasped.

'I do not believe you fully understand the importance of your task, Detective Chief Inspector. You are a leading light in this country's most powerful law enforcement unit and you cannot compel a civilian to give up something that does not belong to her?'

'Miss Butler has been through some terrible ordeals, Mr Shinar. I am not at liberty to compel her to do anything she doesn't want to do. She's not committed any crime I know of and, so far as I'm aware, the stone belongs to her. Possession is, after all, nine tenths of the law.'

'Crime?' Shinar's furious bellow caused the fragile rafters to shake and Prendergast to fall backwards. Decades of dust and splintered wood rained down on them as if the heavens were caught in a violent battle. 'Is sin not a crime?'

A brittle window shattered somewhere in the darkness. Shinar teetered forwards and Prendergast, finding his feet once more, snatched the candle from his hand before it was dropped.

Seeking strength in the light, he held the spluttering flame before him like a dagger.

'We are all of us sinners, Mr Shinar. Some more so than most.' He was unable to prevent his body from shaking as black shadows slithered across the walls and ceiling of the forsaken chapel, just beyond the candle's juddering beam. He swallowed his terror as he felt a multitude of eyes with unnatural vision upon him. He held the flame higher. 'But the law doesn't seek to punish sinners, we let the church contend with that. I'm here to prevent a crime and hunt down criminals, that's my job. This has all gone far enough. Too much blood's been shed already and I'll not tolerate any more spilled on my watch. Miss Butler will give you the stone in exchange for Gabriel Radley and I insist he's delivered both alive and unharmed to me.'

To his surprise, Shinar let out a dry cackle. 'You insist?'

'Yes,' Prendergast almost choked, 'I insist. If Radley shows so much as a bruise on him, I will arrest you.'

'And what if Radley is already dead?'

'Then you will never get to touch your precious stone and I'll make sure you spend a large part of your miserable future behind bars.'

'I see.'

'I'm glad we're finally understanding each other.' Prendergast took a few moments to realise the nausea had vanished while he stood with the candle thrust before him like a crucifix to a vampire. He marvelled at his own bravado and how the shadows appeared to flee from it. Mind tricks. That was all he could put it down to. 'The game's over Shinar. It's time to end all of this. The Vascaran for the stone. Deliver him to me, unharmed and alive, and I'll make the exchange.'

'And you believe I can trust you to deliver the stone?'

'You have my word.'

'Your word means nothing to me.'

'Well, I offer you nothing else.'

'Then perhaps I should show you just how far I'm prepared to go to ensure your word is indeed your bond.' Shinar's eyes narrowed in challenge.

'Are you threatening me, Mr Shinar?'

'I'm merely protecting my interests, Detective Chief Inspector.'

—

'No, no, no, no, no!' DI Byron spat a few choice oaths after slamming the phone down and denting the smooth surface of his desk.

'Lloyd, are you sure you're strong enough to go back to work?'

He ignored the concern from his wife and cursed again. 'We were so close.' He breathed out his disappointment with a hiss.

'What's happened now?'

Lloyd sank into his wheelchair. 'She was adopted and the biological father is marked as 'unknown' on her birth certificate. What a mess.'

'You're talking about the girl who lost her baby and killed herself?'

He could only nod.

'Is there any other way of finding out who the father was?'

'Nope. We've hit another dead end. Damn this bloody elusive beast!'

'Then perhaps it was a brother, uncle, grandfather ... What about her adopted father?'

'He died three years ago and the mother suffers from advanced stages of MS. She's hardly capable of holding a fork to her mouth, let alone a knife to someone's throat. There's no brother, no sister and one uncle who has a solid alibi. He lives in Canada.'

Muriel sighed and put her arm about his shoulders. 'You'll get him. Don't worry. He's bound to make a mistake some time.'

'But how many lives will he take before he makes that mistake?'

'You said yourself everyone on the list is under police protection and they're being closely watched. Even if this case has swallowed up some expensive police resources, it will be worth it in the end. When he comes to kill again, you'll be ready for him.'

'I wish ... I just wish I could find him first. What's the bloody point in a homicide and crime command when everyone's paid to chase their tails?'

'That's the door.'

As his wife left to answer the sharp knock, Lloyd idly sifted through the mountain of paperwork on his desk and rued the day he joined the force. Months of work had once again come to nothing and the team had spent more time running up dead ends than coming up with answers.

'Damned elusive beast!' he hissed again. 'Sorry, didn't see you there. What can I do for you? Don't tell me, you've got information for me on the Vampire Killer.'

'Yes, I know who his next victim is going to be.'

His curiosity turned to terror as the stranger moved across the room towards him, the sharp blade winking in his hand.

—

'Damn, stupid hotel key cards!'

Libby snatched the card from the lock and vigorously

rubbed the magnetic strip against her sleeve. She pushed it into the narrow slot again and let out an audible curse when the lights shone red.

'Whatever happened to the humble key?'

She tried again and was not surprised when the door clicked open all by itself. She picked up her shopping and kicked her way into the room before the door slammed shut in her face.

Her jaw dropped with her bags of shopping.

'Can I help you?'

A woman stood with her back to her, staring out the tall window. She had short black hair and a wiry frame wrapped in a knee-length, figure-hugging navy blue dress. It wasn't until she turned around smiling that Libby recognised her.

'I would recognise that sneer from anywhere. God, Rose, you look so different.'

'That's the idea.' Rose Red moved from the window and flopped down on the sofa in front of it. 'Nice view.'

'Yes, I've always preferred a view onto a solid brick wall. It makes me feel protected. I'm not going to ask how you found me because you'll probably need to kill me after giving away one of your best kept secrets. May I ask, therefore, what you're doing in my hotel room?'

'Have you been shopping?' Rose eyed the labelled bags that Libby dumped on the carpet.

'Just a few bits and pieces. I shop when I'm stressed. I suppose it's better than eating myself to death.'

'And are you stressed Libby?'

She didn't like the way Rose was looking at her.

'If you've come here for some sort of revenge killing, then let me explain ...'

'I haven't come for you. Relax. I know you had nothing to do with the incident in Scotland. I've got Lars to thank for that, but I'll deal with him later. I've come for the stone.'

Libby let out a heavy sigh. 'Not you as well. It appears that's all everyone wants these days. I can't give it to you.' She decided honesty was the best policy where Rose Red was concerned. 'Gabriel needs it and I'll give it only to him. If you kill me, you'll never find it.'

'I'll do you a good deal.'

Libby flopped down on the bed, buried her face in her hands and tapped her toes together.

'Yeah, don't tell me. You won't kill me if I give it to you.'

'Yes, that's a good deal, but I have a better one. I'll give you Gabriel for the stone.'

Libby sat up. 'You know where he is?'

'I know much more than that.'

'Have you spoken to him? Is he safe? Is he with friends?' This was the first she'd heard of Gabriel for well over a month.

'No, no and no. Lars has him and his house is built like a fortress. Gabriel is by no means safe, but he's alive for now.'

'Oh, thank God.'

'You are aware Gabriel's not going to survive this?'

Libby's nod was solemn. 'He won't if I don't help him and I've got a plan. DCI Prendergast is going to act as middleman. He's going to deliver up Gabriel to me in the hotel lobby in the middle of a big conference tomorrow at three o' clock and I'll then give him the stone to do what he wants with. If he decides to give it to Shinar, that's up to him. Once Gabriel's here and safe, we'll find a way to send him home. I think the secret to his return is locked somewhere inside St Paul's.'

'He lives in St Paul's?' Rose's expression was daubed with doubt.

'No, well I don't know really. Suffice it to say I believe the cathedral is the safest place for him. Don't ask me why, it's just a hunch.'

'And you're willing to gamble a man's life on a hunch? You'll have to give me more than that.'

'Sometimes we just have to trust our instincts.'

'Do me a favour and never take one of those survival courses. You wouldn't survive more than an hour on instinct alone.' Rose conceded a small smile.

'Why do you want the stone, Rose? Is it money you're after? Do you hope to be able to retire on the proceeds of its sale?'

Rose reached into the mini-bar under the desk. 'Drink?'

'Why not?' Libby prepared the glasses by wiping the rims on the end of her sleeve and handed them to Rose who filled them with some of the contents of the well-stocked mini-bar, courtesy of Carl's tab.

'What would you like?'

'Oh, just anything, surprise me.' Libby sat on the side of the bed.

'I am going to surprise you.' She reached over, slipped a glass into Libby's hand and raised her own. 'I'm finished with killing strangers for money. I've enough to keep me comfortable for the rest of my life. I need to get close to Shinar and I can't do that without the stone. When I'm close enough to him, I want to put a bullet into that brat with the ruined face and then into each of Shinar's eyes. Then I want to take a knife and cut his heart out ...'

' ... and eat it?'

Rose Red sprayed the drink from her mouth. 'Of course not! What do you think I am?'

'Sorry,' Libby wiped the dampness from her face and hands, 'I got carried away. You do know Gabriel wants him alive?'

'If that devil is allowed to remain alive, we're all dead. Gabriel can't have him.'

'Well, you'll have to argue your point with him once he's safely here. Do you have a plan?'

'I always have a plan.' She gave Libby a surreptitious wink and, despite the azure blue contact lenses, Libby could still see the cold green shining through.

'Go on.'

'Do you trust the cop?'

'Absolutely not. He's a lying bastard!'

'Do you know if he's acting alone or will he have the armed forces camped outside your hotel room during the exchange?'

'I have no idea.'

Rose thought for a moment. 'Do you think he'll manage to deliver Gabriel as planned?'

'I was hoping so.'

'Hope's not exactly affirmative action, but we'll have to go with it.'

'You do realise you can't gun down a copper in a public place, don't you?'

Rose just gave her one of those looks that commanded silence.

'Why are you doing this, Rose? I can't pay you for your services and it's doubtful whether DCI Prendergast will hand the stone over to you with his best wishes. I've given him my word and I'm bound to honour that because he's the only chance I have of getting Gabriel out of all this safely. You'll have to take it from him if you want it.'

'I can arrange that.'

'So why?'

Rose reclined deeper into the cushions of the sofa and sipped at her drink. 'I owe Gabriel a favour.'

'He's got to you too, hasn't he?'

'Maybe. I just want to make his odds a bit more even. He's a good man and doesn't deserve to die.'

'And the favour?'

Rose let out a wistful sigh. 'That's between me and him.'

Libby had no idea whether or not she could, or even should, trust an assassin who called herself Rose Red, but she felt she had little choice in the matter. Rose was a survivor and Libby felt the invisible, yet comforting, arms of a strong ally enfold her, dissipating her fear and bringing her solitude to an end.

'Does this mean we're friends?'

Rose raised her glass and smiled.

—

'One of his kids was found wandering the streets, completely traumatised, poor little thing. A neighbour phoned the police. I'm, I mean we, are all so sorry, Prendy.'

DCI Prendergast took a deep inhale and let his sorrow out slowly. He would remain strong in front of his team and especially in front of his boss. He waved a hand at his spluttering chief and didn't watch him creep away and close the door behind him.

His colleague and long-time friend had been ruthlessly killed and Muriel was missing. The killer had taken advantage of his victim's vulnerability and slit his throat. Prendergast had heard the tale a thousand times today, bits of information snatched here and there from whispering colleagues, and he had just been given a sanitised account from his boss.

The entire task force was on the case in a race to find the killer before he claimed his next victim and made two young children orphans. There was, however, the depressing possibility Muriel was already dead and it was just a matter of time before her body was found, bloodless and carved into pieces.

Unless, of course, this was the work of Shinar and killing Lloyd was his way of proving how far he was prepared to go.

DCI Prendergast knew he was already in trouble. By keeping the investigation of Shinar to himself and not involving his team, he would have a lot of explaining to do. He knew this would be enough to have him hauled over the hot coals of the disciplinary board and could cost him his badge, but there were forces at work here that not even the police could control and that could be excuse enough.

Or could it? With Lloyd gone, DCI Prendergast felt suddenly alone and out of his depth. The case of Gabriel Radley had devoured all his reserves and there was nothing left to fight with.

'Enough is enough!' He yelled and made his decision. No matter what the outcome for him personally, he had to involve the team. Libby Butler was playing a dangerous game and he, working alone, could not guarantee her safety. Whatever it took out of police resources, he no longer cared. It was time to do what he should have done a long time ago and bury Shinar under his crumbling church.

Prendergast sprang from his desk as if fired from a bow. He felt like a man who had just awoken from a coma filled with nightmares as he strode out of his office. 'Get the team together,' he yelled, 'We're going after Shinar.'

CHAPTER Nineteen

'OH, MY GOODNESS, TONY?' LIBBY hauled him into her hotel room by the neck of his t-shirt and took a few glances down the corridors to see if anyone was watching. 'What are you doing here?'

'I'm delighted to see you too, dear.'

'That's not what I meant. I mean, what the hell are you doing here? It's two o' clock and I've got something very important to do in an hour's time.'

'Well, I'll just go then.'

She grabbed his arm to prevent him from leaving. 'It's just a bad time, that's all. How are you?'

Tony looked well, despite his recent ordeal. 'Good, thanks. And you?' He also looked uncomfortable.

'How did you find me?'

'Carl told me. He also moaned about how much your little retreat is costing him. We need to talk, Libby.'

'Yes, we do, but now's not a good time. I have a really important engagement I can't miss and you have to go.'

'I know that look. What are you up to?'

Libby wished Tony didn't know her so well. 'I'm making an exchange. Gabriel's in trouble and I've got to help him.'

'Bloody Gabriel again. Hasn't he caused you enough trouble already?' He sat down on the bed and wrung his hands together, just like Carl did when he was lost for words.

'Don't do that.' She placed her hands gently over his.

Taking the gesture to be one of affection, he threw his arms around her waist and buried his head in her stomach. 'I've missed you so much, Libby. This world is a much duller place without you. Can't we just bury the hatchet and start again? I want to come home ... with you.'

'We'll talk about it, but, in the meantime, you have to go. I'm nervous enough already.'

'Five minutes. We haven't seen each other for ages. Let's just talk for five minutes. You can spare me that.'

'OK, five minutes.' She glanced nervously at her watch and noticed her hands were shaking.

'Carl's filled me in with everything that's gone on since I was arrested. Can I help in some way?'

'Sorry, Tony, but it's too dangerous.'

'What've you got yourself into Libby?' His eyes were filled with genuine concern.

'Nothing I can't handle.'

'You're lying.'

'Where're you living at the moment?'

'With mum.'

'How's Leicester?'

'Boring, as usual. Let me help you.'

'You can't.' She hung her head. 'You'll just get in the way.'

'I can make the exchange for you. Gabriel for the stone. That's the deal, isn't it? Where is it?'

'What?'

'The bloody stone.'

Libby felt the hair bristling on her rising hackles. 'Did Carl also send you to retrieve it? Did he think I would give it up to you so easily? Is he that desperate?'

'He wants to stay alive, Libby.'

'As do we all and that's what I'm trying to achieve. You'd better go!'

'Give it to me, Libby. I'll make the exchange with the inspector.'

'Get out!'

'Don't be stupid. You're risking your life for a stranger.'

'My life is worth the risk. While all this has taught you, Nicole, Carl, and even that policeman, nothing, I've been learning one bitter lesson after another. I now live by my wits, trust my hunches and can tell you my instinct has been honed to the sharpness of a new razor. Prendergast is a copper, he's duty-bound to protect me and I'll be fine once Gabriel is back in my custody.'

'*Your* custody? The man's a dangerous wild animal.'

'Then I'll make sure I keep my hands well away from his teeth. Now, if you don't mind, I want to go. Your interference will only get us all killed.'

'I don't want you to die.'

'I'll try my best not to.' She hugged him quickly before bundling him out the door. 'I'll call you when this is all over.'

Libby flung herself into the chair, her confidence lost. Tony always had that kind of effect on her. She now wondered if Rose would keep her promise; whether Prendergast would keep his; and whether Shinar and his messenger would be waiting for her in the lobby amid a pile of dead delegates. Moreover, she wondered whether they would bring Gabriel to the hotel or simply tell her where they were keeping him and lead her on some wild goose chase that would eventually end in her murder.

'I can just see the headlines!'

The minute hand of her watch slowly ticked as Libby felt her bravado failing with every three hundred and sixty degree turn.

It had been a good plan, but she'd failed to think it through. There were too many scenarios she hadn't accounted for and she'd run headlong into danger regardless.

As the five-minute warning came, she stood up and examined her reflection in the mirror. 'Courage, Libby Butler. You can do this.' She hauled at her blouse and smoothed out the creases before checking inside her handbag once more. Satisfied she had everything she needed, she stepped into the corridor and walked towards the lift.

—

DCI Prendergast admitted to himself he was nervous. Despite being watched by a few score of eyes and an armed response unit on stand-by, he couldn't help but worry something would go wrong and the day would end in a blood-bath of innocent staff, delegates and even a few officers. He could only hope his plan would work and minimise loss.

Squinting between the milling delegates who were on a break from their business conference, Prendergast spied Libby Butler walking towards him. She looked afraid as she sat down beside him in a high-backed chair.

'Hello, chief. This is all a bit awkward, isn't it?'

'Yes, Miss Butler. This is a nice hotel. I'll bet it's costing your boss a fortune for you to stay here.'

'Too much glass panelling for me. The place looks like a cathedral for large marine species.'

'Indeed it does.'

'I'm a bit nervous.'

'Everything will be all right, Libby. Do you have the stone?'

'Do you have Gabriel?'

'Someone's bringing him.'

'Then we'll wait.'

'As you wish.'

A long, uncomfortable silence ensued as the clock ticked towards three o' clock.

'I thought you'd be pleased to know that a warrant's been issued for the arrest of Shinar.'

'What's he done?'

'We believe he may have had something to do with the murder of one of my colleagues and the abduction of his wife. We're taking him in for questioning.'

'For as long as the PACE clock allows. So, he hasn't been arrested yet.'

'Not yet. But we know where he lives and there should be a unit knocking on his door by now.'

'Does he have a lawyer?'

'Why, are you offering your services?'

'Not this time. I've gone off criminal law.'

The inspector laughed. 'I don't blame you.'

'It's three o'clock and no sign of Gabriel.' Libby resisted the urge to wring her hands. 'He's not coming, is he?'

'I certainly hope so.'

Another long silence.

'Please forgive me for lying to you about Radley. There was no other way to find out where the stone was hidden.'

'It worked, didn't it?'

'Yes, but I hope it hasn't undermined your confidence in the police.'

'I didn't have any in the first place. Your actions just reinforced that. Don't worry, chief,' she patted his hand, 'I'm not going to make a complaint against you. Are you going to give the stone to Shinar?'

'Yes, I gave him my word I would. It'll be waiting for him,

along with the remainder of his personal effects, once he gets out of jail and, judging by the age of him, that could be well after he's died in his cell.'

'That's if the jury decides he's guilty. Did you know the copper he allegedly killed?'

Prendergast swallowed his misery. 'It was Lloyd Byron. His throat was slit while he watched. He couldn't defend himself and the bastard's got his wife.'

'Oh God, chief, I'm so sorry.'

'That's OK. Once Shinar and his gang of murderers are behind bars, Lloyd's death will be vindicated.'

'Then let's all pray for a guilty verdict.'

'While we're here, Libby, there's something I want to ask you.'

'Fire away.' She swung her feet and glanced again at her watch.

'Do you remember a case you defended for the Surrey health board? The victim's name was Amy Swann?'

'That was a while ago in the days when I was a bitch. I'm not that person any more and I'm really sorry she killed herself. If I could turn back the clock, believe me, I would've defended her and won. Her lawyers were all over the place.'

'I'm not judging you, Libby. I just want you to cast your mind back to the trial and tell me if you remember anyone she was with. Did she have anyone to support her? Family? Friends?'

'She had family with her. Her mum was in a wheelchair, I think.'

'Any male family members?'

'Not that I can remember. Have you asked her lawyer?'

'No, that's our next move. If you do remember anyone else, would you give me a ring?'

'Of course. What's this all about anyway?'

Before Prendergast could answer, a shrill shriek rang out from the high corners of the lobby.

The groans from the delegates were evidence they didn't relish the prospect of spending their break-time outside on the pavement during another eventless fire drill.

'That's the fire alarm.' Panicked from the noise and her shattered nerves, she made to get up.

'Stay where you are, Libby.' He placed his hand on her arm. 'We need to get these people out. It's for their own safety.'

'But I need them.'

'I'm sorry Libby, but I'm not prepared to risk any more innocent lives. My men are in position if there are weapons involved.'

'You didn't come alone?'

Her shriek caused him to wince. 'This is police business. Just sit tight and wait for Gabriel.'

'It's ten past three, I don't think he's coming. That alarm would've put them off and they'll be able to sniff out your boys a mile away.'

'Just wait a little longer. They're testing our mettle.'

Libby could only watch as the lobby was cleared of life. 'Don't let me down, chief.'

'I'm trying my hardest not to. There he is.'

Libby's heart leaped in her chest as Gabriel walked into the lobby, surrounded by a large group of men, headed-up by the ugly Messenger.

'Please remain seated, Libby, and give me the stone.' Prendergast rose from his seat.

'Get rid of those men and the stone's yours.' She stood up next to him. 'He's chained! They've chained his hands and feet. Tell them to release him immediately.' Her voice rose an octave. 'Back off, all of you, or the deal's off.'

Walking swiftly towards her, his black cloak billowing behind him, The Messenger snatched the gun at his side and pointed it straight at her head, then darkness fell. Libby screamed and pandemonium broke loose in the lobby.

'Drop your weapon!'

'Drop the gun!'

She heard shouting and dark figures poured into the lobby.

Prendergast leaped at her, his body thudding heavily over the top of her, and the handbag flew from her grasp.

Her cheek pressed against the floor, she tried to peer into the darkness and jumped as one or two bullets left their chambers. Glass shattered above her head and rained down like a storm of diamonds over the top of them, each one bouncing off the floor like glittering hail. She tried to wriggle free but the policeman used his own body as a personal shield, pinning her to the ground.

She was forced to hold her hands against her ears as the volume of screaming, shouting and exploding glass became deafening.

And then it was all over.

The weight lifted, light poured into her vision and a firm hand hauled her to her feet.

Libby stood amidst yet another scene of chaos but felt strangely detached from it. Uniformed men ran around the lobby shouting orders, the sea of shattered glass crunching under their feet. A large panel was missing from the side of the wall to the street and a soft summer breeze blew through it, teasing the hair from her face. There were no signs of The Awakened nor Gabriel.

'That's ruined the air con. Was anyone hurt?'

'One dead. Looks like a bullet was fired directly into his forehead point blank. His brains are lying all over the street.

Must've been one of theirs. Stupid bastards!' The officer in the bullet proof vest suddenly realised he was speaking to a civilian and ambled off, coughing uncomfortably.

'How horrible.'

'It was mainly covering fire to effect an escape route and there've been one or two arrests, but the rest got away through the hole in the window.' Prendergast stood behind her, one ear pressed against his mobile.

'Didn't you have the place surrounded?'

'Yes and no. The team responded first to the threat to lives. The assailants dispersed into the panicked crowd and fled on foot.'

'My handbag's gone!' Libby felt the panic rising as she threw herself on her hands and knees searching for her bag. 'They've taken it. We'll never get him back now.'

Her hands flew up to her face and she cursed the heavens.

—

Rose Red watched the scene unfold from the road as she stood amongst the whining delegates, every one of them complaining bitterly about the poor timing of a hotel fire alarm.

She spied the team of police and their accompanying ARV parked in the nearby alley and decided it best to merge into the crowd and observe from a distance. It wasn't long before The Awakened turned up with Gabriel who was heavily manacled, but the shootings had started too soon and she was unable to get close as the same whingeing conference delegates stampeded in terror around her. The lobby went dark, glass shattered outwards and a wall of policemen pushed her backwards down the narrow street.

More panic ensued as armed members of The Awakened

leaped out of a hole in the glass panel and into the screaming crowd. It was fortunate for Rose that the one dragging Gabriel behind him ran into the barrel of her gun. The silencer did its job beneath the thundering chaos and she grabbed Gabriel by the arm and hauled him away as swiftly as his chains would allow.

Gabriel sat beside her in silence as her car sped south over Blackfriars Bridge. She watched from the corner of her eye as he hauled off his manacles and dropped the chains into the footwell.

'So escapology can be added to your long list of talents?' She sounded amused.

'They were not locked.'

'Oh?'

'Lars Andersson owed me a favour.'

'Well, that's going to be the last good deed he does, because I owe him a bullet.'

'He is on our side, Rose. He just does not know it yet. I hope we are not going far. You would not want to be stopped by the police looking like you do.' A small smile creased his lips.

Rose took a quick look at herself in the mirror above her windscreen and noticed her face was covered in blood. As was her right hand, arm and chest. 'Killing people is a messy job.'

'Where are we going?'

'Where do you want to go?'

'I have to speak to Libby. Then, tomorrow night, I want you to pick me up from the hotel and take me to Shinar.'

A car horn sounded angrily behind her as Rose hit the brakes and pulled swiftly over to the cycle lane. She twisted her body to face him. 'You do realise The Awakened have the stone now?'

'I know.'

'And that a visit to Shinar would be a suicide mission?'

'Perhaps, but I have to try.'

'You can't go back to that hotel. It will be crawling with police for days.'

'I will find a way.'

Rose let out a deep sigh of exasperation and sat back in her seat, banging her head against the rest. 'Look, Gabriel, that woman's trouble. She bungles everything she touches and she'll no doubt get you killed. I never thought I would find myself saying this, but maybe the police will prove better allies. They're more equipped for the task and your odds of survival would be better with them at your side.'

'You would find it provident to keep driving.' A police car sped past them in the opposite direction and Rose slammed the gears into first. 'They would take Shinar into custody and I would lose him. I cannot afford that to happen. I must take him back with me.'

After a long silence, Rose did a quick U-turn and ignored the angry remonstrations from disgruntled drivers who were forced to stand on their brakes. 'What is more important than your life, Gabriel? Is it failure you're frightened of? Many people have died in the name of Shinar and his precious stone. What is it about the stone that's so powerful?'

Gabriel shrugged. 'To some it is more important than life itself. To others it is merely a rock.'

'And what's it to you?

'It is a means by which to achieve a goal.'

—

'What do you mean, we can't arrest him?' DCI Prendergast stormed into the office and slammed his hands on the desk.

The detective leaped in fright and the pages of the case notes he was studying flew into the air. 'Sorry, sir, he's filed a complaint against you for harassment. The Super says not to touch him unless we can come up with something more concrete than suspicion. He doesn't want you taking any more unscheduled visits to Nunhead either, unless you've got a warrant.'

'This is bloody ridiculous! Have you questioned the detainees?'

'They're in the interrogation room, sitting between their lawyers.'

'Who allowed them lawyers?'

'The Super did, sir.'

'Have forensics come back with their report yet?'

'Not yet, Sir, and neither have ballistics.'

'Then hurry them up. We need to find out whether that dead boy was shot by one of us. God knows, we could do without that kind of publicity.'

Prendergast shook his head in disgust. 'Have the detainees told us anything we don't already know?'

'They're just laughing at us.'

'All right, if Shinar wants to play games, I can play!'

'Sorry, Sir?'

'Oh, never mind. If anyone wants me, I'll be with the Super.'

—

Libby sat in the bathtub with the hot tap running slowly and could not see the walls for steam. Exhausted with misery, she had nothing left to do but go home and tidy up the scattered remnants of her life. She decided to return to Dulwich in the morning and prepare for an empty future. She would give up her job, leave London and perhaps go back to Scotland, where she would have time to think and to heal the wounds of her lonely existence. Despite all she had been through and all the changes that had been forced upon her, she still felt the same gnawing solitude that left her feeling hungry and hollow inside.

'What, in the name of goodness, did you think you were doing?'

Libby let out a piercing shriek as a dark figure melted into the steam. The voice was spiked with anger.

She grabbed for something that would hide her modesty but only managed to snatch a face towel. Still squealing, she couldn't decide which part of her to cover. She threw it over her face and hoped for the best.

A hand grabbed the towel and hurled it away and Libby was forced to come nose to nose with the snarling face of Gabriel.

'Get out!' Was all she could muster, before she felt the relief wash over her. 'I take it you managed to escape your chains?'

'And exactly how did you plan to liberate me all by yourself?' He leaned over her and turned off the bath tap. Libby shrank from him, squirming in embarrassment.

'I had no choice, Gabriel. Everyone wanted the stone and it was only a matter of time before someone came and took it. I had to think fast and act even faster. You may not have liked my plan but it was the best I could come up with at short notice.'

'You could have easily been killed.'

'It's my life and a risk I was prepared to take for you.'

'For me?'

Libby suddenly remembered she was naked and hurled her arms around her chest. 'Yes, for you.'

His stern features melted with his laughter. 'It was a good, but perilous, plan. Thank you for trying, but you will not do anything like that ever again.'

'Pass me a towel. That big one on the rail.'

He politely turned his back while Libby stepped out of the bath and wrapped the towel around herself.

'Why don't we have a whisky out of Bottomley's bottomless bar?'

His silence was acquiescence enough.

'It's not a single malt, but then what do you expect from an English hotel? Malt is something the English put in their milky drinks at bedtime.' She handed him the glass and chinked hers against it. 'Slainte Mhath.'

She was answered with an alluring smile.

'So what's with the moleskins and combat shirt?' She eyed his attire critically, unable suddenly to meet his eyes.

'Why are women so obsessed with dress?'

'I don't know. I think it simply feeds a deep psychosis for looking one's best when one's feeling one's worst.' She shrugged. 'I'll bet Lars Andersson had everything to do with choosing your day-wear.' She tugged the comb through her wet hair.

'You heard?'

He stood by the window, his wistful gaze fixed on the cathedral dome.

'Rose Red told me. Do you know she's trying to help you?'

'She aided my escape yesterday.'

'So you've seen her?' Libby put the comb down.

'She brought me here.'

'And where were you last night?'

'You sound like my wife.'

'Do you have a wife?'

'Mercifully, no.' He shot her a questioning look.

'Does Rose know if Shinar's got the stone?' Libby pulled herself together.

'That is an obvious conclusion.'

'Damn, Gabriel, that means the worst has happened.'

'No, it means the worst is yet to come.'

She watched him from her stool by the dressing table as he scanned the view from the window, his thoughts much further away than the dome of St Paul's. She wondered what he was really thinking.

She knew he would never let her in. She noticed the sleek blackness of his hair and his long, lithe limbs and envied his moleskin trousers for their proximity.

'Let's have sex.'

'What?'

'I said ...'

'Yes, I heard what you said. Why?'

'Because I can't think of anything else I'd rather do when I'm sitting almost naked in a London hotel room with the most attractive man in the universe.'

'Libby, that is not a good idea, considering....' He sounded almost fatherly.

'There's nothing to consider. Either we have sex or we don't. Does your reticence mean you don't want to or you'd rather not?'

'Is that not the same thing?'

'No, there's a subtle difference.' She waited for his response and was beginning to regret asking him and facing the terrible possibility of rejection.

'Intimacy will alter the dimensions of our relationship. Are you prepared for that?'

'I don't know. Are you?'

'No, I do not believe I am.'

'It's only sex, Gabriel, it's not as if I'm asking you to be the father of my children.' She could feel her anger rising.

'I know. I am just not sure.'

'Oh, forget it. Sorry I asked. I didn't realise you were so

childish about a little thing like two people getting together for mutual ...'

'It is not that simple.'

'Nothing is ever simple in your life because you complicate it by hiding your emotions from everyone. What are you hiding from Gabriel? Yourself? Grow up!'

She stood at the vanity table with her hands on her hips, the challenge skewing her face.

He downed his drink and slammed his glass on the window sill.

'If that is what you want, I will give you sex.'

He marched towards her, hauling off his shirt.

'I'm not in the mood anymore.' She took a step back.

He tugged at his belt, his dark eyes sparking with irritation, the muscles rippling against his rib cage.

'Go away!' She threw off her towel and chucked it at him.

It landed on his face.

He grabbed it and hurled it to the carpet.

Both naked, their bodies almost touching, he stood for a while staring at her. It wasn't a critical examination, rather an exploration of his own inner emotions. She watched his expression turn softly from anger to amusement and then to passion. He silently caressed the contours of her shoulders with the tips of his fingers. She fell into the dark eyes and was lost. She was barely aware of her back pressing against the soft mattress as their mouths met.

It wasn't until Libby sat up, damp with sweat and gasping for breath, that she realised the extent of her obsession with him. It had consumed her.

'Wow, that was sex all right. What time is it?'

'Much later than it was before.'

He held out his hand for her and she nestled her head in the crook of his arm.

'Well, do you feel altered in any way?'

'Yes.'

She turned around on her stomach and stroked the taut muscles lining his abdomen. 'Me too. I now have visions of you and me spending our dotage in a wee cottage by the side of a sea loch with mountains behind us and the Western Isles spreading out into the horizon. You hunt for Bambie and bunnies for the pot, while I dig for tatties, wash our rags in the burn and darn our his-and-her socks. There are stags roaring in the forest and eagles sweeping the glens and, of course, it's raining buckets and we're getting eaten alive by midges.'

'But there's a bottle of single malt by the fireside and some salve to put on the itching welts!' He laughed.

She sung a verse from Wild Mountain Thyme about building a bower by a fountain. It was one of her favourite folk songs.

'That's beautiful.'

'Yes, it's a lovely song about Scotland. They use it on all the tourist information adverts on the telly to entice holidaymakers to come up to the Highlands and get their suntans washed off. I don't sing it very well, but it's in my head at the moment and I can't get it out.'

'It is simply a transitory dream, Libby, it will pass like all events in life.'

She already missed him. 'What's your dream?'

'I do not have them. That way, I can never be disappointed.'

'Oh, come on, Gabriel. You must dream sometimes. Everyone has a dream of some description. It's a thing you hope for.'

'In that case, I hope to bring Shinar to justice.'

She slapped him on the side playfully.

'I dream to be at peace with myself.'

'That's not a bad thing to hope for. I'm going to dream the same thing and perhaps someone in my not-too-distant future will help make it come true.'

'You do not need to rely on someone else to realise your dreams, Libby. You are in charge of your own destiny.'

'To a point, but life doesn't always allow people to follow their heart's desire.'

'Then you must focus that desire on what is available. There is no point in attempting to reach the unattainable. You have to be realistic.'

She hid her disappointment well. Libby realised what he was telling her in the most gentle way possible, but she still couldn't help but feel the pain of his loss. Very soon, he would die or walk out of her life for good. Either way, she was going to lose him and she would have to prepare herself for this event and a future without him. With only two possible outcomes to their relationship, she would dream for the latter option but she didn't believe she had the strength or the courage to actually let him go.

'Where are you going now?'

'It is time. Anzhela will be waiting for me.'

She watched him slip out of the bed and begin to dress. She couldn't hide her trepidation.

'Where's she taking you?'

He stopped to look at her, the shirt poised over his head. 'You are better off not knowing. You cannot follow me. If I return tonight, it will be with Shinar in chains. You may help me further then, but I need you to stay here. Promise me?'

She sat up and, biting back her tears, studied the earnest expression. 'I promise, but tell me what's with your apparent fixation with bondage gear?'

'Shinar spent most of his youth in chains. He despises them. He fears them. I intend to lock him into them for good.' He pulled on his boots and worked the laces.

'I do believe you have a very nasty streak, Mr Gabriel Radley.'

'My name is Torniss.'

'Torniss? What kind of a name is that?'

'It is my name.' He leaned over the bed and kissed her on the forehead: the simple gesture said only goodbye.

'I'll wait for you, Gabriel. You'd better come back or I swear I will buy that cottage!'

He smiled for the final time before closing the door softly behind him.

CHAPTER Twenty

GABRIEL STEPPED OUT OF THE car and watched the sun slowly slip into the western horizon. Narrow wisps of cloud with blazing edges lined the skyline above the desolate chapel, followed by dark banks of thunderclouds looming close behind.

'Looks ominous!' He mused to no one in particular.

'What was that?' Rose stuck her head out of the driver's seat window.

'This is a Godless place.'

'Do you believe in God?'

'No.'

'Then you'll wish you had as soon as you've stepped inside that door. I'll keep watch but, if there's any sign of police, you're on your own.' Her foot punched the accelerator and she sped off with a squeal of tyres.

Gabriel adjusted the buckle to his vambrace, tested his arms with a quick flex and cracked his knuckles before taking a deep breath. He emptied his head of all thought and sought tranquillity from deep inside his chest. He heard the slow, steady thump of his beating heart. He was ready.

Moving towards the church doors he felt the malevolent eyes upon him: like ranks of bowmen waiting behind a rampart of darkness before the signal came to release a rain of arrows. He was the sole target. This was not the first time he would face capricious odds and it probably would not be the last.

When he reached the door, he made his charge.

—

Lars Andersson sat on a ruined pew, listening to the conversation between the Blais woman and Carl Bottomley. Libby's ex, Tony, had also joined the party. Neither Lars nor the others had any idea what they were doing in a condemned building in south east London, but understood they'd been summoned for a reason. Lars only hoped that reason would not be to his personal detriment. He moved his arm against the reassuring bulge of the gun in its holster just beneath his jacket and sat quietly waiting.

The church was empty. Lars had taken it upon himself to take a mini reconnaissance and had only found a few decomposing animals, some mouldy furniture, a broken cross, piles of greasy filth and a deep baptismal font filled to the brim with stinking black slime.

He only realised the door had burst open when he felt the trigger against his finger. He pushed the gun back into the holster with a deep sigh of relief.

'You could've knocked and spared us the heart attack!'

Standing at the ruined door in studded leather armour, Gabriel looked like a painting of an ancient warrior ready to do battle and slay his enemies. His sharp sword was readied in his hands. He looked confused. 'Where is Shinar?'

'I thought he was with you.'

'Get out of here. Now!' The warrior barked and Carl leaped from his pew.

Laughter echoed from the rafters and The Awakened descended one by one from the creaking balcony with heavy thumps that sent the old plaster into spasms. It cracked from the walls in great chunks and fell, with a few yelling bodies, into ruined heaps of choking dust.

The wooden columns gave up their protest and yielded to the weight. The balustrade creaked and groaned before tumbling from the wall, causing Gabriel to leap out of the way before he was buried under a mass of splintered wood.

The Messenger picked himself up from the ground where he had fallen and dusted the dirt from his shoulders and the barrel of his pump-action shotgun. 'Thank you for coming ladies and gentlemen,' he began in his rusty baritone voice.

He ignored the moans from a few of his men on the ground who'd broken limbs in the fall. 'That wasn't exactly the entrance I'd planned but you'll agree it was dramatic.'

'Where is Shinar?' Gabriel hissed and took a step forward.

'Careful, Vascaran. You may be able to dodge a few bullets but you won't avoid all the shot in these cartridges at this range. You wouldn't want me to ruin your pretty face by tearing it into chunks now, would you?' He pointed to his bad eye for full effect.

'What do you want with these people?'

The Messenger sat on the edge of a wobbly pew and crossed one long leg over the other, the shotgun pointed directly at Gabriel. 'Mr Shinar sends his greetings and says he'll be along in a moment, but first he wants one of you to give the stone up to him.'

Lars smiled to himself. So it was still missing. He made a guess there were about fifteen armed men, who, by the sloppy way they were holding their weapons, probably hadn't had much target practice since being issued with them. If the situation became ugly, he would be able to do some damage with his gun but could he rely on Gabriel with only a sword?

He knew, or at least thought he knew, what the warrior

was capable of, but the pragmatic Lars didn't want to rely on a man with seemingly supernatural powers to protect him. He pondered over the possibilities of how he would get out of the mess.

The Messenger's hand snapped up to silence the barrage of protests and denials from the three who found themselves in a hostage situation. 'Someone knows where it is but someone's not telling. Now why is that?'

'The stone was in Libby's handbag.' To Lars' amusement, Tony Ridout spoke up. 'She told me that herself.'

'We've ripped that bag apart. The stone's not in it. All that was in it was a purse and a meat tenderiser. No doubt she was hoping to bludgeon someone to death if she was forced to fight for her life. She's a feisty little thing, your Libby Butler.'

'Perhaps one of you may have stolen it.' Carl managed to find his tongue but not his courage as the words fell from his mouth in a desperate whimper.

'I'm afraid that's not possible, Mr Bottomley. We are The Awakened. We do not keep secrets from each other and do not fight for personal gain. But I'm tired of this already.' He turned to Gabriel. 'Shinar wants you to behave before he greets his guests.'

'Shinar is a vile coward.'

'Is the human will to survive before anything else so cowardly to a Vascaran?' he sneered.

'It is right to know when to run from battle and live to fight another day if the odds of winning are slim. But faced with an equal foe, should that man fail to stand his ground to aid others or defend himself or his territories then, yes, he is a coward.'

'Ha! You sound like Ghandi.' Lars, enjoying the conversation, interjected.

'I shall take that as a compliment.'

'Have you ever run from a battle En'Iente?' The Messenger kept all his attention on his target.

He was answered with silence.

'No, I don't believe you ever have. Then let me test your bravery.' He signalled to his men with the smallest of nods and they grabbed the three hostages. Lars was relieved he hadn't been included as a fourth.

'Shinar is ready to meet you, but first you will choose which one of these three people is going to die. If you make a move against him, the other two will head-dive into their graves behind the first.'

'These people mean nothing to me. You are wasting your time.'

'Tut! Tut! En'Iente, your lies debase your integrity,' he made a low but flurried bow. 'Which one do you think is unworthy of your greatness? I'm giving you a choice.'

'I believe the word is dilemma.'

The Messenger's ruined face turned from amused to furious in a fraction of a second. Raking a shaking hand through his matted locks, he turned to Lars, his voice clipped with the effort to contain his anger. 'Since the En'Iente has failed to make a decision, kindly stick a knife into the heart of Mr Ridout, please. We don't want to wake the neighbours with gun fire.'

Lars didn't hide his surprise. 'What, here? In front of all your guests?'

'Take him outside and put him out of his misery then. You're paid by the hour and make sure you twist it when you've buried it deep enough.'

'Wait!'

Ignoring Gabriel's plea, Lars shrugged his huge shoulders, grabbed the gibbering Tony by the arm and led him to the back of the church. 'You should've stayed at home with mum.'

Libby paced the pavement and breathed a heavy sigh of relief when the car pulled up beside her.

'I think they're all in there.'

DCI Prendergast tumbled from his car seat and slammed the door behind him. 'Shinar as well?'

'He must be. I took a peek inside. They've got Nicole, Carl and Tony too. What's going on?'

'Stay here, Libby, I'm going in.'

'What about back-up?'

'Sorry, Libby, there's only me this time. The Super wouldn't give me a team. I'll explain later. Let's just hope your Gabriel is as good as he looks, or this is going to be the worst decision of my career.'

She grabbed his arm. 'Please be careful.'

He smiled at the display of concern. 'Thank you, Libby, I will.'

—

Lars returned to the aisles wiping the blood from his hands with a pristine white handkerchief. 'Knives are such messy weapons,' he grunted and sat down, avoiding Gabriel's stern glare.

'I have seen enough!' Before Lars had a chance to blink, Gabriel stood above The Messenger, his sword sheathed in the sling at his back, one boot on his captor's forehead and the tip of the shotgun barrel wedged deeply into his throat.

The Messenger could only gag as his colleagues dared not move towards him. 'I am leaving. You can tell your master that I refuse to play his games any longer. Should he wish to face me in person, then he will know where to find me, in the meantime ....'

'Vascar. Vascar. Vascar.' Gabriel spun his head around to the voice of Shinar as his short frame shifted into the light. He held a long, serrated blade to the throat of Libby Butler, the tip pointing upwards into the centre of her jaw. They glided down the aisle like a father taking a bride to her groom in a macabre wedding ceremony for the damned. 'The Messenger is a loyal, faithful servant. He doesn't deserve to be treated with such wanton disrespect.'

With a loud but undecipherable oath, Gabriel hauled the gun from The Messenger's mouth and, sliding the shells from the magazine one at a time by pumping the forearm repeatedly, emptied the shotgun of its cartridges. He threw the empty weapon to the ground, just missing The Messenger's good eye.

'It is time, I'm afraid, for all this to end. Miss Butler will tell us where she has hidden the stone or she will die. She will then have the option to leave, or she may stay and watch your execution, it is up to her.'

'I'll tell you where the stone is only if Gabriel is released. Let him walk out of here and I'll give it to you freely.'

Libby was cautious not to make any sudden move and chose her inflections carefully as she felt the knife's teeth pressing into her flesh, ready to take the fatal bite.

'Aw, such devotion in one so tainted with cynicism. It must be love.' He handed her over to Lars. 'Keep the knife to her throat and don't hesitate to thrust it into her flesh until it finds bone if the Vascaran makes so much as a twitch against me.'

He slid towards Gabriel, his red cape flowing behind him like ripples on a sea at sunset. He dared to move a gnarled, misshapen hand from the folds of his cloak to touch him. The fingers flexed slowly, tentatively, like fragile antennae probing the air for danger.

'Even I will profoundly regret extinguishing the flame of

one who shines so brightly, but you have chosen to become my enemy and, although I deeply respect you, I also loathe you. You are a most divine creature.'

He turned to his audience, his body quivering with excitement. 'Do you know that his bite is deadly? Vascarans are a highly evolved race of man and this one is perfect in every way a man can be.'

His crooked fingers hit Gabriel's armour.

'You deprive me of the warm flesh beneath your staunch defences.' He punched the breastplate in anger. 'Perfection comes with its own demons,' he hissed, 'and you must be purged of yours.'

Lars wished he was at home watching television rather than taking part in what, to him, had become a sorry display of amateur dramatics. He didn't understand Shinar. He respected Gabriel; he loathed him; he called him perfect; yet he wanted to kill him. Two of life's most potent, yet conflicting, passions at war with each other inside a twisted mind.

It was all too much for the down-to-earth man from northern Sweden who believed he'd seen and heard enough.

'Come, my dearest child. Come and be purged. Release your pain. Release your sins. Unburden your loss.' He led a staggering Gabriel up the aisle towards the font.

'Please Gabriel,' Libby ignored the bite of the knife at her throat. 'Don't do this for me.'

Gabriel, seemingly lost to a dark enchantment, failed to turn around or hear her.

Lars realised what was happening too late. Shinar plunged Gabriel's head into the black, oozing slime of the font and held it there while he gibbered praise of the warrior's bravery and promises of his salvation into the ruined rafters.

—

'NO!' Libby screamed and wriggled herself free from Lars' grip. She ignored the blood oozing from the accidental nick to her throat. 'Let him go. Don't kill him. The stone was in my bag. You must have it.'

She watched in horror as the tiny bubbles of Gabriel's last breath winked at the surface of the black water before it became still.

Shinar hauled his head from the font and Gabriel's body slid lifeless to the ground.

'No.' She sank to her knees.

'It's not there, Libby, you must try harder.' Shinar's words were soft and reassuring, although he appeared shaken and bemused.

'It's in the head of the meat tenderiser.'

'But the head is fused to the handle,' Lars added.

'That's what I hoped you would think. It's an illusion. It's fused only with a bit of blu-tack and silver metal spray.'

'Well, blow me … !'

She knelt down beside Gabriel's body and inhaled her sobs. 'Take your stone. We no longer need it. He no longer needs it.' She wiped the black gunge from his beautiful face that had found peace at last. His dark eyebrows were no longer furrowed in consternation and his mouth was creased very slightly into a wry smile of amusement, so characteristic of him. 'Oh, Gabriel, why did you let him do this to you? I'm not worth it. I never was.' She allowed the tears to flow freely as she placed her head against his heart.

—

'Brother Raymond! Lad!' Prendergast nodded to the pair of imposters who'd come to his office as a friar and a dishevelled boy with a fatal illness, their sole purpose to terrorise him. They stood now with guns in their hands looking every bit the kind of criminal that left home in a sweat box.

'Mr Shinar, I have been asked by the DIO to bring you in on suspicion that ... er, you have entered this country illegally. Might I say at this moment, you are not under arrest, but are obliged to come with me for questioning.'

Immigration law was not one of DCI Prendergast's specialist subjects and he had trouble remembering what Libby had briefed him on over a short but frantic call on her mobile. He looked over to Libby for support but she barely nodded, so he was forced to make it up as he went along, hoping Shinar would have as much knowledge as he.

'You can add murder to his charge sheet, Detective chief Inspector.' Carl had found his bravado at last.

'Please tell me that Gabriel Radley's not dead.'

'He drowned him in this font. We witnessed it all.'

'Then, Mr Shinar, I am arresting you on the charge of murder of one, Gabriel Radley. You have the right to remain silent...'

'The stone, Messenger, give me the stone.' Shinar swung his fist and Prendergast flew through the air and crashed into the far wall, causing the remainder of the plasterwork to shatter around him.

The Messenger held a shining object in his hand and thrust it into the air like an Olympic torch. 'For what it's worth.'

He hurled the stone at Shinar and the dark priest was forced to leap into the air to catch it. He screamed in pain as the sharp edges ripped through his flesh and the tip of the stone buried itself in his palm. He yanked it out and threw it to the ground.

'A name can be so rich in meaning that it has no meaning at all.' The Messenger echoed.

'The stone is a powerful weapon.' Shinar roared.

'Perhaps to those who believe it. But I regret to tell you

your weapon of destruction is a stone in name only to everyone else.'

'Well, I'll be damned!' Lars joined the conversation. 'Does that mean it's also worth nothing?'

'It's worth is relative to whoever wants it the most. It is still a ruby and possibly the largest one in the world.'

'That's good enough for me. If you don't want it, I'll take it off your hands.' Lars had his gun out now and pointed it towards anyone who twitched. He slowly moved towards the fallen stone.

'He led me to believe the stone had power; that it had meaning, but you are telling me it has no significance at all?' Shinar now shook with rage.

'He led you to believe it was important to your success. How else would he have been able to find you inside this urban maze of bricks and people? He was too clever for you.'

'The Vascaran has infected you too, boy.' Shinar's roar caused the woodwork to groan above their heads and what was left of the stained-glass panels to shatter inwards. Sharp shards found flesh and blood sprayed from the wounds of the terrified cult members. 'Now I must kill you all.'

—

Libby heard the conversation from the ground but was more interested in the thumping of Gabriel's heart as she pressed her ear against it. She felt him squeeze her hand. She should've remembered the extraordinary length of time he could hold his breath.

'Get up, he's going to kill us all.' The Awakened were simultaneously releasing the safety clips from their guns. 'Get up, Gabriel, we need you.'

Gabriel rose slowly from the ground and shook the black slime from his hair.

A blast; a bullet fizzed between them; and Libby's head spun. She sat in the corner of the church, bewildered. She had no idea how or when she'd got there.

In the next second, Carl, Nicole and Lars were sitting next to her vomiting, dumped in the corner like sacks of mouldy grain.

Shinar shrank into the shadows of the ruined altar, cradling his injured hand. Although his eyes remained cold and dead, he bore the expression of a child at the funfair for the very first time: filled with wonderment and expectation of the delights to come.

Three men charged howling at Gabriel and hesitated only briefly as the sword hissed from the scabbard. They stood with dazed expressions, examining the palms of their hands where their guns had been only a breath ago. More bullets were fired, one accidentally finding the shoulder of an attacker who went down screaming in pain. The other two were knocked senseless by the dark warrior's flying fists.

Chaos rained across the aisles as The Awakened discharged the ammunition from their guns, killing each other and demolishing the building in an attempt to hit an impossible target.

The Messenger busied himself on his hands and knees scrambling for the fallen cartridges while the sword sung above his head, its flat smashing the face of one attacker while a booted foot sent another flying into the rafters.

Libby placed her hands over her ears as the deafening sound of bangs and thuds thundered around her. Wood splintered, glass exploded and plaster thumped from the walls as missiles flew indiscriminately around the crumbling church.

One by one, The Awakened found themselves disarmed by an unseen force. Some dropped their weapons and fled the building in terror, while others attempted to stand their ground, only to fall unconscious and bleeding to the hard wooden floor for no apparent reason.

The Messenger rose from the ground, the pump-action shotgun in his hand, spinning around on his heel in the hope of catching a glimpse of the invisible shadow in the night. His men lay around his boots, groaning in pain and coughing blood.

'Show yourself, En'Iente. Let's finish this, man to man.'

Libby heard a flutter from what was left of the balcony and squinted into the gloom to see the dark figure standing there, his sword glowing in the dim light. She gasped as Gabriel leaped from his lofty perch and with, two or three elegant turns in the air, landed on his feet to come face to face with The Messenger. He didn't so much as appear out of breath.

'You are pointing a gun at me again, Messenger. Have you learned nothing from the last time?'

'Sheath your sword and I will put the gun down.'

'As you wish.' With a swift and elegant movement of his arm, the sword slid into the scabbard.

'Now, you die.'

Before Libby could cry out, The Messenger pulled the trigger and pumped his forearm for another shot.

But it didn't come. Gabriel stood over the fallen Messenger, his boot on his throat, crushing the breath from his windpipe.

'Give me a reason why I should not kill you?'

With a scream of metal, the point of the sword kissed The Messenger's breast.

The Messenger wheezed: 'My name is David ... David Phillips.'

Libby held her breath while Gabriel hauled the innermost

thoughts from the man on the ground. She saw those dark eyes soften slightly as anger turned to pity and she breathed a sigh of relief as the blade retracted.

'You should find yourself a master more worthy of your unwavering devotion. Leave now before I change my mind and kill you.'

—

'I'd give him ten out of ten for artistic interpretation but, to be honest, I think he lost points on difficulty value. Those boys were all over the place.' Lars, patting himself down to check for bullet wounds, used humour to understate his complete stupefaction. 'Did anyone see him move?'

There was a haunted look in his eyes once more. The danger averted, he carefully picked up the ruby, wrapped his blood-stained handkerchief around it and placed it into his jacket pocket.

'Mr Shinar, I arrest you on attempt to murder.....' Prendergast had come alive and staggered down the aisle.

Lars heard a sharp whistle behind him and something noisy flew across the room.

Gabriel's hand struck like a bolt of lightning as he grabbed the chains.

'Some ally you are, Rose!' Lars yelled across the space.

Rose Red smiled that cold, calculated grin that Lars knew meant trouble. 'If he needed help, I would've lent him my gun.' She turned around and walked into the moonlight.

'Was that who I think it was?' Prendergast was tossed into a dilemma: which one to arrest first.

'She is a friend,' was all Gabriel offered.

'For now, my friend, for now. Mr Shinar, I ....'

Before Prendergast could finish his sentence Gabriel smashed his fist into the priest's face with such velocity that the crunch of bone echoed around the chapel. Shinar fell to the ground snorting.

'If you are going to hit him, make sure you hit him hard.' Gabriel winked and hauled the senseless priest to his feet by the back of his cloak.

'I can't let you have him, Gabriel.' DCI Prendergast crossed the space between them, choking on dust. 'Justice must be served.'

Uniformed officers poured through the doorway, their barrels shifting between The Awakened and the hostages, seeking out friend from foe.

'Justice is being served, trust me. Your gaols could never hold him. Should you take him into custody, he would be free before the sun rises and you would never find him again in your lifetime.'

'You will take him away and we'll never see him again?'

'You have my word.'

'Or you?'

'I have no wish to cross this path twice.'

'Pity, I was just beginning to like you. Have you ever thought of a career in the force?'

He was answered with an inscrutable smile.

'And I also have your word he will be tried in a court of law?'

'And found guilty. You may also rest assured that he will remain behind bars that are strong enough to hold him in a place he will never escape from.'

'That's good enough for me.' DCI Prendergast held out his hand in cordial respect. 'Good luck, Gabriel Radley, or whatever your name is. I'm sure you'll need it wherever you come from.'

'Thank you, Andrew, forgive me for the body count.'

'You've been away from home for far too long, lad, you're even beginning to speak like one of us!' Prendergast chuckled before his face became grave once more. 'Tell me, Gabriel, will I survive? Does he really have the power over life and death?'

'Only if you believe so. Shinar relies on man's most feared enemy to control them.'

'Which is?'

'Death and every form that may take. Your world is obsessed with death and, in particular, the horror of dying. Incurable disease appears to be the most common of these terrors for those who live their lives without fear and so he exploits this. I told you not to ask him his name.'

'Hypnosis?'

'Call it what you wish. He is a clever man. Clever and intuitive, yet he uses his gifts to do harm to others. This is why I have to take him back and this is the reason he will remain fettered like a beast until he dies, for he fears chains more than he fears death. Ironic, is it not, that a man who so readily removes the freedom of others is so terrified at the prospect of losing his own?'

'Do unto others?'

Gabriel smiled. 'Precisely.'

—

Libby took comfort in the fact she was holding Gabriel's hand as the car sped in silence once more across Blackfriars Bridge. This was one goodbye she wished would not happen.

Shinar sat behind the driver's seat, his heavy chains chiming now and again in recognition of who had won the battle.

All the windows in the car were down and the air conditioning blowing at maximum in an effort to get rid of the terrible smell emanating from the vanquished prisoner. He smelled much worse in a confined space.

Rose Red's green eyes shone sporadically from the mirror above the windscreen. She no longer wore her blue contact lenses but the frigidity in that look couldn't be ignored.

'Do you need anything?' She knew it was a stupid question.

'He probably needs a drink,' Lars Andersson answered from the front passenger seat.

'I have everything I need, thank you.'

The shining dome of St Paul's came into view and Libby felt she could no longer contain her misery.

'We're here.' Even Lars sounded desolate.

Gabriel hauled his prisoner from the back seat and turned towards the friends he had made in his short time in London. 'Words!' he laughed. 'I have none that could come close to expressing my deep gratitude to all of you.'

Rose Red stood at the driver's side of her car. 'Think twice before you kill again, Anzhela. Only take a life out of necessity and hope that such a situation never comes your way again.'

'Can I keep this?' The ornate knuckle duster sat in her palm.

He laughed and pressed her fingers around it. 'You never know, I may find it necessary to call you again.'

'Don't bother. You're too much trouble.' Her smile was coy. 'Here's something to remind you of me'. She kissed him. It was a soft passionate kiss and he responded by winding his arms around her in a tender embrace.

She pulled away panting.

'Now I'll know what I'm missing.' She gasped.

Gabriel opened his hand to reveal a single unspent bullet.

'That will also remind you of me!'

'Well, my friend. You have made me a rich man. I have diamonds, cash and a manuscript that, of course, I have carefully edited, which I am taking to a mainstream publisher tomorrow morning. I believe they'll give me a very healthy advance once I mention the word 'auction'. So are you going to tell us who you are? What is a Vascaran? How you read minds and how you do all those neat moves so quickly?'

Gabriel shook Lars' big hand with a knowing smile.

He turned to Libby and pulled her into his body. Gently wiping the tears from her eyes, he said: 'You are a magnificent woman, Libby Butler, your strength and your fortitude are unparalleled amongst your peers. Seek out a life with meaning and never doubt yourself again.'

'Goodbye Gabriel. I will never forget you.' She could say nothing else.

'Why don't you kill?'

Everyone leaped back as The Messenger landed with a thundering crash on the bonnet of Rose's expensive car, his heavy boots making deep dents in the metal.

'Why would I wish to kill a few misguided souls who are simply obeying the orders of their master?'

'You had the power, you had the motive, why didn't you kill them? Why didn't you kill me? Why did you use the flat of your sword?'

'I did not want to gouge the edges. Do you know how long it takes to sharpen the dents out of blades?'

The Messenger stood on the bonnet of the car.

'Take me with you.'

'Why would I do that?'

'I can serve you. I am loyal. Take me with you.'

'The man belongs in prison.' Lars chuckled.

'I do not need a servant and I do not need another killer.'

'Now wait a minute ...' The big Swede made to protest.

'I will only kill out of necessity, I promise. Please, En'Iente, take me with you. I am a soldier, like you. This place has driven me insane. Take me with you and bring back meaning to my life.'

'Hang on.' Libby didn't trust The Messenger. 'What about all this stuff about the genius loci and repelling poles?'

'Names, Libby. Have you learned nothing?' The Messenger growled.

'Do you understand where you are going?' Gabriel appeared in a hurry as he put a foot on the cathedral's first stone step.

The Messenger nodded.

'You will never be able to return here.'

'That's my dream.'

'Another dreamer!' Gabriel laughed. He looked over to Libby and the silent conversation passed between them.

'Come on then, but I can promise you only nightmares.'

Libby Butler could only watch while the man of her dreams walked out of her life, dragging his prisoner in chains behind him, accompanied by a desolate soul with a ruined face.

She had no idea where he was going or even how he was going to get there, but Libby trusted her instinct and knew he would get home.

She would never find out what a Vascaran was nor what that meant where he came from and she would never understand the causal chain of events that would lead to a marked change in her character.

She also knew in her heart she loved him and that meant she would never be the same person ever again.

CHAPTER Twenty one

'OK, HERE WE GO.' Libby turned the volume up to maximum as Black Eyed Peas sang out 'Where Is the Love' from Tony's expensive music system. The track was a bit vintage for her, but there was a feel-good factor to the words and rhythm that she loved.

The phone rang.

'Pardon? Where is what?'

'Hi, Carl.'

'Are you OK, Libby?'

'I'm fine, thanks. I only got through the door five minutes ago. I'm sitting on a few boxes containing all the contents of my little life, sifting through some old paperwork and waiting for Tony to say cheerio.'

'How's his arm?'

'Lars didn't cut it too deeply, just deep enough to extract a little blood, but he'll live.'

'That's good. Will you see each other again?'

'Oh, no doubt. He's already booked time off in a few weeks' time to come and visit me. We'll probably take it from there.'

'Don't suppose you've heard from Radley?' She knew he was trying to keep his tone as casual as possible.

'No, Carl. I won't be pulling rolling around in the heather with him in the foreseeable future, or at all to that matter. I expect he's home and none of us will ever see him again.' She hoped he didn't notice the tremor in her voice. 'It's funny you know, I'm sitting in the same flat I've lived in for over five years, amidst a few packed boxes and rolls of binder twine, and, even without furniture, it doesn't feel as empty as it did before I met him. I'm not even scared of the dark any more. Isn't that odd?'

'Not odd, Libby. Unusual, considering what you've been through, but maybe you've come to terms with life.'

'Or found myself at last. It's a good feeling.'

'Uhm, Deidre and I want to know, well actually, it was Deidre's idea, if you want to go out to dinner tonight. I know it's your last night, but we could go somewhere nostalgic for your last evening in London. Maybe somewhere near the courts, just to remind you what you're missing?'

'That sounds nice. Will you pick me up?'

'Be ready for seven thirty.'

'OK, that gives me a bit of time. See you later.'

Libby took a quick glance at the paperwork in her hand and decided, since it was all work related, she'd box it up and leave it for Carl to sift through.

'What's that doing here?' She hesitated at the summons at the top of the pile and read out loud: '*In the High Court of Justice, Queen's Bench Division, Swann v NHS Surrey Health Board.*'

She sighed and wished she'd never agreed to defend that case. She felt like a murderer. She cast her mind back to the scene of the girl sitting in court like a lost kitten in the middle of her team of bungling lawyers; how her side had looked so disappointed with the verdict; and how the girl had wept. She also remembered a man's stricken face as he watched helplessly from the empty public benches.

'Oh my God!' She knew that face. 'He's the Vampire Killer.'

She grabbed her mobile and her fingers trembled over

the screen as she searched through her contact list for DCI Prendergast's number.

'You don't remember me do you, Miss Butler?'

Libby screamed as the man stepped out of the spare bedroom and her mobile phone flew across the room.

'Yes, yes, of course I do. You were her father?'

'Her natural father. I agreed with her whore of a mother to have nothing to do with my own child.'

Libby scanned the room for something to hit him with as he moved towards her, his fingers clenching in and out of his palms.

'I'm so sorry for your loss, Sergeant Fry, but Amy's death couldn't be predicted.'

She stepped slowly backwards.

'You of all people should know you must take your victims as you find them, Miss Butler.' He closed his eyes against the pain of the invisible torturer. 'Do you know what it feels like to be denied the love of your own child?'

'I don't have children, Sarge.' She slowly backed towards the kitchen.

'I'd just got to know her and you took her away from me. You, that jury and your team of super-lawyers, you all killed her and she won't rest ... I can't ... until you're all dead.'

'Murdering women won't bring her back, Sergeant Fry.' Libby wished she could gather her courage together but this had knocked the sense from her. Her words came out of her mouth squeaking.

'Do you know how easy it is to make a person disappear if you're a policeman? How easy it is to walk the streets unnoticed between the CCTV cameras and prying eyes? Most people trust the police. Most people trust that law enforcers are on this earth to do them good. You, Miss Butler, are not one of those good people. You disrespect our efforts and you ...'

'Wait a minute, Sarge, your actions right now are proving I'm right. Policemen don't normally go around mutilating women and I do like some of them. I really like DCI Prendergast, he's a good honest man.' She hoped that dropping in a name from the CID would help him to realise the consequences of his actions, but he was too far lost to his grief.

'If it wasn't for that interfering bastard in the park, you would already be dead. I took his woman instead. Do you know she was alive when I sawed her head off?'

Libby cringed.

'I thought of you when I was doing it. That's all I think of these days. Hurting you. Killing you. Making you beg for mercy like my Amy begged for mercy, but you're a very difficult woman to kill, Miss Butler. You know, I didn't recognise him at the station at first. It was only when he'd gone I realised he was the one who'd stopped me. It had me worried for a while, but he wasn't here for me, was he? He protected you. He was always protecting you. And now your personal angel's not here to protect you any more.'

Libby made a quick decision she would try and talk him down. She'd seen it on the television: the victim keeps the killer talking and eventually he realises what he's doing. It was a long shot, but worth a try.

'Why did you kill your colleague, Suzanne Glover, Sergeant Fry?'

'Officer Glover?' He stood for a moment, lost in thought, as if desperately trying to rake through his memories for an answer to the question. He shook his head and the beads of sweat popped like soda bubbles across his forehead.

'I don't know. It was meant to be you. Did I kill Officer Glover?' The alarm on his face was a genuine reaction to the sudden confession of reality. 'Suzanne? Was that true? ....'

'Yes, Sergeant, and Suzanne was one of yours. A policewoman.'

'... Like that detective, Byron, yes, Byron. He got too close. Asked stupid questions. Wanted information.'

Prendergast's words rang in her ears: Byron's wife was missing. 'What did you do with his wife, Sarge?'

'Did he have a wife?'

'Yes, Sarge, he had a wife. You took her away from her home and her children. Did you kill her too?'

'Did I?'

'Well?'

'Mercy... no mercy. I don't know how to ease her pain.' Sergeant Jonathan Fry stood ranting like a madman as if Libby wasn't there. She wondered if she would survive the fall if she leaped out the window. Unfortunately, it wasn't open. She edged very slowly towards the door, her movements tiny and barely perceptible.

'Pain, so much pain,' he gibbered.

Libby decided to make a break for freedom while he deliberated with himself on the varying degrees of agony.

'Kill her. Kill her. Kill her!' He screamed and flew after her.

Libby whimpered as she saw the glint of the blade and grabbed for the lock.

He lunged.

She put her hands out to defend herself as her attacker flew towards her.

She waited for the imminent blow but it didn't come. Instead she heard a crunch and a yell followed by a dull thud and a hot spray of liquid covered her hands.

When she opened her eyes, Rose Red stood in front of her in black leather like a character out of Star Trek. She smiled and kissed the blood-stained weapon swathing her knuckles.

'He left you this'

'What?'

'The Vascaran. He left you the money in this bag.' She threw the familiar bag at Libby and it landed at her feet. 'I've put a bit more in it too. Just cash I found lying around in Lars' house when he was out. That should be enough to buy you a haunted castle in Scotland and land that's able to sustain a few wind farm developments.'

Libby couldn't take it all in. 'Why are you doing this, Rose?'

'I owed Gabriel a favour. I promised to protect you and I've been waiting a long time for this killer to strike. I almost gave up.'

'Is he dead?'

Rose kicked the body onto its back. 'Not quite. He'll probably lose that ear and have a bit of concussion. I didn't hit him that hard so, if his skull's fractured, it'll only be a hairline one. He'll have to get used to that new pattern on his face though.'

Libby shuffled round the boxes to stand a safe distance. 'How did you know?'

'I followed him to that cottage where he killed your colleague. I was too late for her and took it personally. I don't like his sort of killer.'

'Why didn't you tell someone? It would've prevented a lot of trouble for some of us. Tony for a start.'

Rose threw her one of those looks that said 'Stupid question and don't ask another.'

'I'll phone DCI Prendergast and. ..'

'I think we should finish him off.'

'Now, wait a minute. Not in my flat, you're not. I've got a buyer for it and dead bodies are not on the particulars. Let the due process of law handle this, Rose.'

'He's a cop. He knows how to play the game. He'll deny

everything; go down for it for a few years; get the best psychiatric treatment available; and then he'll get out on good behaviour to finish what he started after his probation's expired. He needs to go, otherwise you'll be watching your back for the rest of his life.'

'I'll take my chances. I don't want to be implicated in the murder of a cop, even if he is a serial killer, and I don't want any more blood on my hands. If I've learned anything over this summer, it's that life – any life – is precious and none of us has the right to take it. It's also possible Lloyd Byron's wife is still alive. If we kill him, we'll have her blood on our hands also. And, more importantly, I've only just got rid of the bloody press!'

'Hmm,' Rose Red mused. 'I've also learned something and that's never ask a man his name.'

'Meaning?'

'Life's only precious if it's not on my numerical list.'

'Names also give us a sense of belonging. Isn't your name Anzhela?'

'Don't push your luck, Miss Butler. I still have time and inclination to mark you down as a number in my little book.'

Libby would've continued laughing if the man on the carpet hadn't groaned. 'He's waking up!'

'We'll have to tie him up because I don't want to be here when the cops arrive.'

'I've only got binder twine.'

'That'll do.'

Libby reached for her mobile.

She hesitated before pressing DCI Prendergast's number. 'Have you forgiven Lars yet?'

'You mean number thirty-eight-A?'

'Oh, come on Rose, he came good in the end.'

'OK, I'll do him a deal. I've always fancied a ruby necklace!'

Rose paused before tying up and gagging her prize. 'I can't be there to protect you all the time.'

'That's OK, Rose, I don't need protection all the time. Do you want my number so we can keep in touch? I would like that.'

Rose Red smiled, that cold, calculated smile that caused her green eyes to sparkle with mischief.

'On second thoughts, maybe I'll let you just find me the next time I'm causing trouble.'

THE END

FREELANCE JOURNALIST AND PRESS OFFICER for a number of arts organisations in south west Scotland, London-born Sara Bain is a former newspaper journalist and editor of professional text books. She writes fantasy and paranormal fiction in a unique and individual style with an emphasis on complex plots and strong characterisation.